PRAIS

"Enchanting! With a fabulous blend of memory, myth, and
mystery, of melancholy, comedy, and irony, Anna Porter
conjures up moments of magic. The past comes alive in the
only way it should, as suggestion rather than as truth."
— MODRIS EKSTEINS, author of
Walking Since Daybreak on *The Storyteller*

"This is a gutsy book, passionately written and brilliantly
researched. It is a historical knock-out, a real tour-de-force."
— IRVING ABELLA, Shiff Professor of Canadian Jewish History
at York and co-author of *None Is Too Many* on *Kasztner's Train*

"A tale of breathtaking chutzpa, the gravest personal risk, dark
intrigue, human frailty and devastating clashes of personality."
— MICHAEL R. MARRUS, CHANCELLOR ROSE, and RAY WOLFE,
Professor Emeritus of Holocaust Studies, University of Toronto
on *Kasztner's Train*

"*Kasztner's Train* is *Schindler's List*-plus. Brilliant read.
Brilliant history. Brilliant Porter."
— GEORGE JONAS

"Crisply written, ingeniously plotted . . . an impressive debut."
— *GLOBE AND MAIL* on *Hidden Agenda*

"Superior fiction. Crisp prose, inventive plot,
convincing characters . . . A major new talent."
— *SAN DIEGO UNION* on *Hidden Agenda*

"Lively . . . mysterious deaths and plenty of
insider publishing stuff along the way."
— *NEW YORK TIMES* on *Hidden Agenda*

"*The Storyteller* represents a much higher level of literary
accomplishment, a worthy addition to the growing
literature of displacement, and a poignant reminder that
the best history is not always written by the winners."
— *TORONTO STAR*

"Porter manages a difficult feat — she conveys the
heartbreaking innocence of childhood with an overlay of
the knowledge and humour of the person she is today."
— *GLOBE AND MAIL* on *The Storyteller*

"*The Storyteller* shows that great storytellers are both born
and made. Like grandfather, like granddaughter."
— *CHATELAINE*

"This is a tightly plotted, well-written, and richly atmospheric novel."
— *BOOKLIST* on *Mortal Sins*

THE APPRAISAL

THE APPRAISAL

ANNA PORTER

Published by ECW Press
665 Gerrard Street East
Toronto, Ontario, Canada, M4M 1Y2
416-694-3348 / info@ecwpress.com

Editor for the press: Susan Renouf
Cover design: Michel Vrana
Cover images: chain bridge, Budapest © Pyrosky/
iStockPhoto; painting, Titian's *Woman with
a Mirror*, c. 1515, in the public domain
Author photo: Charles Scott

This is a work of fiction. Names, characters,
places, and incidents either are the product of
the author's imagination or are used fictitiously,
and any resemblance to actual persons, living or
dead, business establishments, events, or locales
is entirely coincidental.

LIBRARY AND ARCHIVES CANADA
CATALOGUING IN PUBLICATION

Porter, Anna, author
The appraisal / Anna Porter.

ISSUED IN PRINT AND ELECTRONIC FORMATS.
ISBN 978-1-77041-410-5 (softcover)
ALSO ISSUED AS: 978-1-77305-115-4 (PDF)
978-1-77305-116-1 (ePUB)

I. TITLE.

PS8581.O7553A66 2017   C813'.54
C2017-902412-4   C2017-902991-6

The publication of *The Appraisal* has been generously supported by the Canada Council for the Arts,
which last year invested $153 million to bring the arts to Canadians throughout the country, and by the
Government of Canada through the Canada Book Fund. *Nous remercions le Conseil des arts du Canada de son
soutien. L'an dernier, le Conseil a investi 153 millions de dollars pour mettre de l'art dans la vie des Canadiennes et
des Canadiens de tout le pays. Ce livre est financé en partie par le gouvernement du Canada.* We also acknowledge
the support of the Ontario Arts Council (OAC), an agency of the Government of Ontario, which last year
funded 1,737 individual artists and 1,095 organizations in 223 communities across Ontario for a total of $52.1
million, and the contribution of the Government of Ontario through the Ontario Book Publishing Tax
Credit and the Ontario Media Development Corporation.

Ontario
Ontario Media Development
Corporation

ONTARIO ARTS COUNCIL
CONSEIL DES ARTS DE L'ONTARIO
an Ontario government agency
un organisme du gouvernement de l'Ontario

MIX
Paper from
responsible sources
FSC
www.fsc.org   FSC® C103560

Canada Council
for the Arts

Conseil des Arts
du Canada

Canadä

PRINTED AND BOUND IN CANADA   PRINTING: NORECOB   5   4   3   2   1

For Julian, the art-lover

 He had been coming to the Gerbeaud for thirty years, but he never tired of it. During the summer he liked to sit under its wide, grey umbrellas on Vörösmarty Square, enjoying snippets of conversation at adjoining tables and watching life go by. It was a cozy respite from the nastiness of work. He didn't much care whether the service was slow, the chrome tabletop wiped clean, or his espresso lukewarm, he loved the tangy black coffee oozing across his tongue and the reassuring normalcy of unfolding the daily paper on its wooden holder. He savoured the familiarity.

Although pretty much everything in Hungary had changed since the advent of the "market economy," the Gerbeaud's sole concession to the winds of capitalism had been a steady increase in prices. The new owners had left the rest of it alone. He could still sit here as long as he wished, nursing the single espresso that cost him a quarter of a good day's wages, and the waitresses never pushed him to reorder.

There had been a time when the manager, sleek as a young trout in her fitted black dress, had refilled his delicate china cup and hadn't charged for it, but she had long gone to greater fortunes in the States. Her name was Klari, now probably changed to Claire, or maybe Clara to preserve a touch of the Continent. She would have discovered by now that it cost a damned sight more than an occasional refill of coffee to buy a policeman in the so-called home of the free. Even in Budapest, bribery was no longer a bargain.

At the table beside his, a young man wearing Gucci wrap-around sunglasses, a gold Tissot watch, a collarless white shirt, and beige calf-leather pants was reading the *Wall Street Journal.* He was sucking on a split of champagne, surreptitiously checking his watch. Someone was keeping him waiting. He didn't like it, but he wasn't going to betray any anxiety. A man in Gucci wrap-around glasses couldn't admit to being kept waiting. He seemed familiar. A long-ago police lineup? Judging from his attire, his career had blossomed since then.

It didn't matter. The real target of Attila's interest was near the first wide window, her back to the pastries counter and across from a frothy-haired man who also looked vaguely familiar. Her elbows were on the table and her long blond hair was dangling over an open blue file folder placed between them. Sheets of paper dropped so fast from her fingers, he presumed she was speed-reading until she came to the last sheet, which she stared at for several minutes. She closed the folder, pushed it toward her companion, and leaned forward as she talked. He listened, then produced something from his breast pocket. A picture? A passport? It was small, dark, and oblong. She palmed it so quickly that had Attila not been watching he would have missed the movement.

He scanned the room, pretending to pay equal attention to all the customers. He was pleased that neither the woman nor her companion had once looked at him.

The waitress, a country girl with short henna-red hair, was asking the *Wall Street Journal* man if she could take his spare chair. A group of German tourists was next in line for a table with not enough chairs. She asked in Hungarian, her hand on the chair, her meaning fairly clear, but he pretended not to understand. Playing for time, Attila thought, time to decide whether to reveal he had been waiting for someone. Without relinquishing her hold on the chair, the waitress — he must find out her name — asked, "Okay?" For emphasis, she jiggled the back of the chair, clattering its metal legs on the asphalt.

The fellow nodded without enthusiasm, swivelling his head toward the group of tourists. One of them waved and shouted "Vielen Dank." The Habsburg Empire had self-destructed some ninety years ago, but German speakers still viewed Budapest as an anachronistic piece of Austrian territory.

At the table behind Attila's, three elderly Hungarian women were debating the relative merits of the chestnut purée — sweet, traditional, brandy-basted — and the kugel loaf — historically more interesting, but less tasty. In the centre of the square, under the seated bronze statue of Mihály Vörösmarty, Hungary's beloved poet, three young men in faded blue jeans were making a small drug deal. Vörösmarty was looking down as if observing the activities of the young men. The vendor pulled a plastic bag from his pocket and offered a taste. Hardly worth the effort, it was no more than ten ounces. "Be faithful to your land for-ever, oh Hungarian . . ." The great poet's words ran around the pedestal, where a bronze phalanx of fellow Hungarians formed Vörösmarty's adoring public. The buyer finger-tasted the coke and nodded to his companion, who would be carrying the cash. Street value of maybe a couple of thousand dollars. Small-time dealer. Attila assumed he worked the hotels on the Pest side and some of the classy apartments along the tramline. A couple of years ago Attila would have been bearing down on them. But back then they'd have already spotted him for a cop and moved the trade somewhere else. What was it about him that had changed so much in only two years?

Attila had been hunched over his table, a broad-shouldered, greying man, balding on top, overweight, ham-fisted, thick-necked, his shirt collar and jacket both too tight. He straightened his back when the young dealer glanced at him, mildly suspicious, but then the dealer palmed the money and handed over the merchandise without a second look at Attila.

The man with the *Wall Street Journal* examined his bill, counted some forints into the tray, and stood up to leave. His pants, caught in the wedge of his ass, stuck to his thighs. He must have gained weight since he bought them, Attila thought with some satisfaction. Anyway, it was too warm for leather pants.

His attention was caught by a young woman, her red hair flying, her light-blue summer dress swinging, and her slender white heels flying over the paving stones as she ran toward the Gerbeaud. She lifted her long legs over the silk rope barrier, straddling it for a second, her cotton skirt billowing around her, offering a glimpse of her white cotton panties, then she was wrapping her arms around the sweaty young man with the calf skin caught between his buttocks. "Jancsi," she called him, her voice soft as the inside of her thighs.

"Where the hell have you been?" he demanded. Obviously, although the days of swooning over Westerners were long gone, he still thought it stylish to sound foreign.

The woman by the window glanced at the gilt-framed mirror above her companion's head. She adjusted her silk scarf, flicked her hair over her shoulder, then made that little moue that some women make when they are checking their makeup. She stood up with her weight on her palms flat against the table. Attila figured she was probably still exhausted from her flight and the long drive from Vienna, but she recovered quickly and walked out fast, her dress clinging to her legs, a leather handbag dangling from her arm. She was pretty, although a little older than pretty warranted, and her bare arms and long legs showed the kind of muscle earned by regular workouts. Her erstwhile companion stayed at the table, sipping coffee and digging into the large serving of chestnut purée that had sat there ignored for the past twenty minutes. He was no longer only vaguely familiar. The narrow forehead under the froth of hair. He ran a posh art shop on Váci Street. Attila had paid him a visit about ten years ago. The man had been caught with some stolen primitive art. Indian. He couldn't remember what the outcome was, except that this man had somehow got away with it.

Attila laid his change on the tray and followed her across the square, past Vörösmarty's statue, the McCafé, the Hard Rock Café, the exorbitantly expensive clothing stores, down to the Danube, where his quarry was marching past the souvenir vendors with only an occasional glance at the river. Although she did pause for a moment to survey Gellért Hill in all its spring glory, she was not behaving like a tourist. A tourist would have stopped at the Shakespeare statue outside the Marriot Hotel and read the words on the brass plaque.

He kept at a distance as she crossed to Buda over the Szabadság Bridge and walked around the periphery of a small square (why the hell was it under construction again?) to the Gellért Hotel.

She had chosen the Gellért less for its old-world charm than for its several entrances. She preferred the small rooms at the back. They didn't offer the view of the Danube for which the hotel was known, but they were adequate. A single bed, a narrow desk, a phone, two shelves, a hanger for clothes, and a safe. She preferred no fuss and not too much cleaning. Maids came only early in the morning for light cleaning and bed making. The view was of the side of Gellért Hill where, late at night, noise makers cavorted and played music and lovers had open-air sex.

Helena had been here before but with different hair, a different name, and a man she had liked more than she wanted to. He had booked a suite at the front of the hotel, ordered flowers, and they had danced to lackadaisical gypsy music in the dining room. She didn't like dancing to gypsy music, but that was not the reason they broke up. She had not been ready for a long-term relationship. She was struggling with too much unresolved anger and a couple of persistent ghosts. The ghosts still refused to go quietly, but she had almost managed to master her rage. But Robert was no longer waiting.

She opened her black canvas holdall and arranged her clothes over the bedcover: black pants, a grey woollen sweater, black T-shirt, a black hoodie, faded black Nike running shoes, thin skin-coloured pantyhose, a short white cardigan, a small-brimmed foldable hat, five cell phones, black leather gloves, dark-rimmed glasses, a long pearl-grey linen jacket with a high collar, a raincoat, a cross-strapped navy bathing suit, four passports, a clear plastic bag containing a black wig with a fringe and a light-brown one, a small Revlon makeup case, a vial of face cream, the photograph Kis had given her, a foldable flashlight, wire cutters, a pocketbook, a Nikon Coolpix 16MP, a suede sheath containing a long-handled straight knife with a thin blade, a snub-nosed SwissMiniGun with six bullets.

She put the wigs and passports into the safe.

She slipped out of her dress, untied the blue silk scarf, placed the slingback shoes next to the door, and pulled on the black pants, the T-shirt, and the hoodie. She removed her blond wig and laid it, its tendrils trailing, on one pillow and pushed the second pillow lengthwise under the covers. From a short distance, it looked like a figure lying knees up, face to the wall.

Her own hair was light brown with a few grey streaks, cut short and soft on the sides, bristly on top. She used a dollop of gel to make it lie flat. Standing in front of the mirror, she removed the blue eyeshadow and thick lashes and peeled off the thin plastic strip over her upper lip. She selected a dark purple lipstick from her collection of makeup pencils and dabbed it on her lips. Her reflection showed an almost middle-aged woman who didn't much care about her appearance. She packed the flashlight, the handgun, the wire cutters, and the camera into her backpack and pulled on the pair of frayed running shoes.

She picked up the slingbacks and left the room, dropping the shoes at the last moment as she pulled the door closed so they would be just inside the door. She hung the "Do Not Disturb" sign on the door handle.

She took the back stairs next to the wrought-iron elevator that ferried guests down to the hotel's famous Turkish baths. She showed her plastic key-card to the attendant, went through the baths' exit between the two stone Grecian figures, and walked down toward the river.

The tall heavy-set man she'd noticed in the Gerbeaud was standing at the tram stop, leaning against the ticket machine, frequently glancing into a paperback book while observing the Gellért's main entrance. He looked at her for only a fraction of a second as she stepped over the tram tracks. She was sure he had not recognized her. He didn't seem very committed to his task. Perhaps he was a retired policeman. She had seen dozens of them all over Prague, Bratislava, and Berlin, even in Warsaw, although not so many there. Most of the old Polish police and security men had long gone to villages where they would be harder to identify. She had tracked one of them a few years ago. It had not been easy. He was now farming potatoes near Częstochowa. Back in the 1980s, he had been high up in the Ministry of Public Works. He had taken a ten-by-twelve-cm Leonardo da Vinci drawing as payment for keeping an informer out of jail. Her job had been to recover it.

The Poles were less forgiving than the Czechs, Slovaks, and the Hungarians. In Budapest, beneficiaries of the Communist era didn't need to hide. That made it easy to find people. Unless they were dead.

Géza Márton had left here in 1956 after the failed Hungarian Revolution. Had he returned recently, he would know whom the system still protected and who could still do him harm. But then he wouldn't need her services.

She ran along the river, taking long strides, pumping her arms, and slowly settling into her usual energetic jog. Although the sun had almost set, it was light enough to see the street signs, and the air was warm. In Toronto, there had still been snow on the ground, it was getting dark at 7:30 p.m., and the few early birds perched in the desolate trees in the Mártons' garden had seemed stunned. The house was on a low hill, with the garden sloping down to more trees and bushes in the valley below. Géza was proud of his Georgian red-brick house with its tall bay windows, its white pillars flanking the entrance, and delighted with his young white oaks, his sugar maples, his spectacularly green rhododendrons, and his long sloping lawn — still brownish in April — that ended at the ravine.

He had been pleased to show off his paintings, the nine quasi-Impressionists, a couple of almost Picassos, a possible Max Ernst, and a Watteau. Over the wide wooden staircase to the second floor, there had been a Rubens drawing of a nude, a Cellini, a Degas, and there were more paintings in the study, although Géza had saved the best for the master bedroom: an early Van Gogh, which he may have bought from her father, Simon. At their initial meeting, he had insisted she see it.

Géza Márton had made most of his money in Vaughan, a town just north of Toronto, but he didn't want to live there.

Rosedale was a sedate, leafy, midtown neighbourhood, a long way from the subdivisions of Vaughan, where immigrant families lived cheek by jowl with their fellows and could hear every altercation, every lovemaking, child's cry, and dog bark on either side of their new homes.

He said this place reminded him of his family's old home in the Buda Hills and that walking through the front door made him feel that he was entering his own small country. Helena had wondered whether his English wife had added her own touches to the décor or just allowed him to recreate a childhood dream.

At Bem József Square, she turned up Fekete Sas Street and started to climb Rózsadomb. She was relieved to find that there were few cameras on the hydro poles on this street, the surveillance that was so ubiquitous on the Pest side seemed lax in the Buda neighbourhoods. She walked on, savouring the smell of the early acacia blossoms, the broad chestnut trees with their candle-like flowers, the shaded garden homes of the wealthy burghers and politicians who had managed to make money and keep it.

She found the house easily. It was set back from the street; a low stone wall enclosed the front garden. Roses climbed over its wrought-iron gate. The single camera on the nearest utility pole was angled to survey the other side of the street. A tall stone fountain stood in a pond at the centre of a grassy knoll to the left of the driveway, and four white-painted, wrought-iron chairs and a table were arranged near it. The house was dark except for one bevelled window with wooden foldout shutters near the front door. Two tall ceramic pots flanked the oak door. To the side, the garage door was open, and inside was a turquoise 2014 S-Class Mercedes Benz sedan with white wheel rims and grey-tinted windows. Its body shone. A camera positioned under the roof overhang was aimed at the garage entrance. Easy to avoid if you were not interested in the Benz.

From where she stood, she could see the electrical box on the inside wall of the garage, next to a door to the house.

Pretending to look for street numbers, she waited for a noisy couple to pass. They were competing with each other to finish a story that made them both hiccup with laughter. When was the last time she had laughed like that?

The stone wall was easy to step over. Keeping low to the grass, she crossed the yard and stopped behind the fountain to look into the lighted room. Even from this distance, she could see tall bookcases, a wide desk facing the garden, a straight-backed, unpadded chair. As she crept closer, she saw a thick rug running the length of the room and a man with his back to her, talking to someone through an inner door.

He had a strong voice. Through the open window, she could hear his tone, if not the words themselves. Imperious. Annoyed. Demanding.

He turned to a bookcase, picked up a book, and stood it upright with the others. He half-turned to the window. He was tall, broad-shouldered, erect, with short white hair, a long neck, a protruding chin, and a high forehead. All he seemed to have in common with the man in the photograph Géza Márton had shown her was his bearing. The rest must have changed with age. Márton had guessed that the man would be in his late eighties, and he could have lost much of his brawn and his bull neck. Certainly his hair would have turned white. Or this was not the right man. Yet Géza had been so certain.

A woman entered the room, carrying a round tray with an open decanter and one glass. She could be a servant, but that was unlikely because she was dressed in a well-cut blue suit with large golden buttons, a frilled blouse showing at the neck. He must have married again in the years since Gertrude had left. Perhaps it had not occurred to the Mártons that such a man would marry twice. Still, they do. And the women seem not to mind that their men are monsters. Even Lavrentiy Beria had a wife. The infamous head of Stalin's secret police was not only a murderer, he was also a sexual sadist, yet his Nina stayed faithful. She enjoyed the material rewards he offered: the Georgian silver, the antique jewels, the purloined Rembrandts and huge Tintoretto that had graced their living room. She had been reluctant to part with any of it.

The man poured from the decanter as he riffled through papers on his desk, casually, distracted, as if he was making sure something was there but was not interested in reading it. He played with the point of a silver letter opener, then replaced it exactly where it had been, an inch to the right of his leather-bound diary. His hands were thin with long fingers, not the massive meat-hooks Géza had mentioned.

The phone rang, a clear metallic tone. He pressed a button on the receiver and listened. His lips did not seem to move, and she did not hear what he said.

It was 7 p.m. They would be gone in less than an hour.

She stepped back over the wall and continued up Fekete Sas Street, past a block of flats and other sizable houses, to a tiny park. There were a couple of benches, a sandbox, and some downtrodden grass. She sat on a bench and watched the small children playing with their mothers, the dogs cavorting on the grass near the one-way entrance, then took out her well-thumbed copy of the *Aeneid*.

The Benz rounded the corner a little too fast, tires whining as it turned onto Margit Boulevard, on its way to the Margit Bridge and on to Pest and the Hungarian State Opera House.

She waited another five minutes, glancing up from the book at cars passing, in case they had forgotten something and returned. At 8 p.m., she pulled the hood over her head, covered her mouth with the scarf, and returned to the house. The shutters were closed. She scanned the wall with her flashlight, once, then edged her way to the garage, keeping to the side closest to the house. Just outside the camera's range, she unlocked the garage door with a twist of the knife, then cut the four electrical cables with the wire cutters and pried the connecting door open with her knife. It was too easy. Inside, she disconnected the alarm just as it began its loud whine.

She had calculated that it would take a car fifteen minutes to get here from the Pest police station. She would hear the siren. She had to be fast.

She examined the windows for separate alarms and found none. She wedged open the door to his office and surveyed the tidy desk, the letter opener, the orderly bookcases, the round tray still there on the round side table, his crystal tumbler with a trace of his evening drink. His study opened onto a hallway lined with sepia photographs of men and women in formal dress, the women wearing gloves and cradling bouquets. There was a framed portrait of the man in a dark suit, hat sitting low on his head, the rim shading his forehead, dark glasses, hands folded in front, still the long, thin neck and long fingers.

There were a few small paintings: an early Poussin, a Raphael with angels and a blue Madonna, something that looked like an Arshile Gorky — a sad-eyed women with scarf — a large, early Monet of boats in shimmering water, and an early Picasso drawing. A dark Velázquez of two overdressed, expressionless children in a chocolate-coloured frame hung above the bar in the dining room. On either side of the door, there were four small paintings by Lajos Kassák that she recognized only because she had seen a collection of his forgettable abstracts at a recent Museum of Modern Art exhibition of Hungarian artists banned during the Communist years.

The painting Géza Márton had described was in the living room, hanging over a long, florid sofa. It was six feet long and four feet high. She felt its presence even before her flashlight found Christ's face. It was the sheer size of the gilded frame and the figures blending into the dark resin background. The small grey donkey in the centre left seemed to have been out-lined with a brush handle or a sharp palette knife. There were dabs of white and yellow on the faces of the figures looking up at the man on the donkey. The paint was laid on thick and heavy, the artist having used both a palette knife and his fingers where the figures blended into the sombre background. It was a very physical painting, with its big figures, his style freed from his times' constraint of mirroring every detail. Palma il Giovane had talked of Titian's vigorous underpainting, the reds, blacks, and yellows, and of his predilection for using a palette knife.

Thin shafts of blue and white emanating from a magenta cloud lit up the back of Christ's head. His face was just a sug-gestion of browns and ochres and his eyes were deep holes. His muddy, sandalled feet were scraping the ground. There were splashes of red on his neck and ankles, as if to prefigure the

Crucifixion. In contrast to Christ's purple robe, the ones worn by the men following him were dirty white. Some were holding their arms aloft, their faces shiny with sweat and anticipation. Two women were laying palm fronds on the uneven path in front of the donkey. Mary Magdalene, walking ahead in her signature green gown, looked out of the painting. Her bright eyes and pink-and-white face made her seem at once beatific and accusatory. Another upturned face and a dash of blue by the donkey's flank depicted the Virgin Mary. Incongruously, two small spaniels in the bottom right-hand corner gazed upward, as if expecting treats. The artist had taken great care in detailing their fur.

It could be a late work, perhaps as late as 1570, when Titian was well into his eighties. There was a hurried, sketchy quality to some of the figures. It was reminiscent of *The Death of Actaeon*, but the stormy sky may have been finished by one of his workshop students, perhaps Polidoro da Lanciano, although she doubted Polidoro would have completed any of the late works. Titian hadn't finished putting on the varnish, but in his final years he often left the varnish off parts of his paintings.

Alternatively, it could be a study for an early work, a mere sketch, something intended for Philip II, who liked both religious paintings and detailed nudes posing as naiads or some other mythological women who cavort about naked.

There was no signature.

Without the right equipment, it was hard for her to tell whether it was a Titian or a good forgery. She had used chromatography and a spectrometer to analyze the paint of a Rubens in St. Petersburg and had determined that it was a late copy. Another time, she had established that a beautifully executed Raphael at the Borghese was an exquisite reinterpretation by the Dutch master-forger, Han van Meegeren. That man could redefine genius. He could imitate the style of any artist, and it would take years of technical examination to identify which paintings were his. She had studied Titian and read all extant documents about his work. There was no mention of this particular painting.

She took photos from all angles, then close-ups of details, shining her flashlight on each part of the painting.

When she was done, she knocked over the bottle of whisky and the glasses on the sideboard, tucked the silver cigar box under her arm, broke the window by the front door, pulled the hood over her face, and left.

It had taken her eleven minutes.

No serious police officer would be convinced by her efforts to stage a break-in, but the smashed window and missing box would offer an easy diagnosis, and experience told her that one should never overestimate the police.

She walked back to the little park, dropped the cigar box in the garbage bin next to a man sleeping on a bench, listened to the sirens of police cars climbing the hill from the river, did a few stretches against the other bench, then loped back to the hotel.

 Attila waved casually at the over-dressed doorman, entered the Gellért Hotel by the revolving door, and walked across the marble lobby with the purposeful steps of a guest. No one even looked at him. The stairway led up to the third floor. A "Do Not Disturb" sign hung from the brass handle of the door to Helena Marsh's room. It took him a full minute to open the electronic lock; less time than an old-fashioned keyed lock would have taken. She hadn't used the chain. It was dark inside the room. The few lights flickering outside the window illuminated her long blond hair spread out on the pillow. Obviously, she had decided to have a nap. Whatever she was up to, it couldn't have been much — or

she had astonishing sang-froid. Why hadn't she put the chain across the door?

He went back down and sat in the bar, which gave him a clear view of both the elevators and the marble stairway. He ordered a Vilmos brandy with a beer chaser.

He hadn't intended to wait till nearly 11, but the barman had been telling him a long, episodic story fitted between serving other guests, and Attila's drinks after the first two had been free. The barman had once been a junior lawyer in the justice department, mostly petty crime but there had been one case of a journalist who had written for a Western paper and was caught, prosecuted, and jailed. He was lucky even to have had a trial. Now, after the advent of democracy, the journalist was a member of parliament and the lawyer was serving Attila Czech beer.

At 10:45 p.m. he took the tram home to Rákóczi Avenue. The street had been spared some of the 1990s' construction boom, and, while many old apartment blocks had been destroyed and replaced by condominiums, Attila's hundred-year-old building, with its small wrought-iron elevator that rarely moved, had remained in its pre-war state. It featured peeling paint, crumbling brick, and uneven floors and was just the way he liked it. His apartment's tall windows, high ceilings, and balcony made up for the street noise. Most of the year, except in the depth of winter, he could leave the balcony door open for Gustav, about the only thing his ex had allowed him to keep from their marriage. A miniature long-haired dachshund mix, Gustav had an uneven temperament but a keen nose for quality food, and, unlike the ex, he was always pleased to see Attila.

After a short walk around the block, they shared a couple of salami sandwiches and settled in to watch the latest episode of an American series about a teacher who turns into a drug dealer. Another advantage of democracy was the plethora of utterly mindless television options. This was better than most. There were times he felt nostalgic for the heavy-handed Soviet propaganda films of the 1970s and the occasional cheap Hungarian tragedies of that time, with their disguised messages of protest or exasperation with the system.

The phone rang at around 1 a.m.

"What the fuck happened to you?"

"Huh?"

"Remember you had a job? You didn't do it. Fell asleep at the bar? Went to a movie? What the hell?" The voice was rough, spittingly breathy, as if he was holding the phone too close to his mouth.

"István?"

"Captain dammit, Detective Tóth to you, never mind the István, and where the hell were you?"

"Waiting," Attila said. "She never came out of her room."

"Bloody funny, that," Tóth shouted. "She was in a house on Fekete Sas Street at eight thirty, walking about like she owned the place. She knew the real owners would be out all evening. She knew the opera schedule. No hurry at all. Took her time. The client is not happy."

"Impossible. I checked her room and she was lying in bed. Sleeping. I watched the elevators and the staircase till 11 p.m. She never came down."

"So, it must have been her ghost." Tóth harrumphed into his cell phone.

"Were there no alarms?"

"She cut the wires."

"How do you know it was her?"

Tóth laughed too loudly. "It was a woman in a black hoodie. About her height and shape."

"It could have been another woman."

"Don't be an ass."

"Cameras?"

"One, hidden, by a big painting in the living room. She didn't try to steal the painting, but that may be because it would be hard to hustle a thing that's about two metres long with a thick gilt frame out of a house in a residential area."

"Did the camera pick up her face?"

"No. Like I said, she was wearing a hoodie."

"Do they have anything else worth stealing?"

"He may have a couple of other paintings. And he has a safe, but it was not disturbed. He's retired and thought they had nothing to worry about. Or didn't. Till now."

"Oh." Even if the guy had nothing to hide, why not install some outside security cameras, just in case a couple of neighbourhood kids decided to relieve him of a few household items? There were more cameras throughout this city than parking meters.

"No valuables?" Attila asked, nonplussed. Everyone had valuables, even if it was only bits of rock from a holiday. Anyone living on Rózsadomb would have valuables; it was an elite part of the city. Their address defined them. That so many former Communists and their fellow travellers had held onto their homes here was, he thought, an indication of capitalism's victory over memory.

"Anything missing?" he asked.

"Only a cigar box. Silver. And they do have security," Tóth said. "Us."

"Last night?"

"You were on the job, last night," Tóth yelled. "Your job was to check if she went anywhere. You were hired to follow her." He must have lighted a cigarette, Attila heard the match scrape the phone, then Tóth let out a long breath, as if exhaling smoke. "Tomorrow morning at eight," he said and disconnected.

"Son of a bitch," Attila murmured after he put the phone down. Eight a.m. was just four hours away, and his mouth felt like a pigsty. What did those Czechs put in their beer? It used to taste better in the 1980s, but that might be his age.

The dog lay on his back at the end of the bed, paws in the air, farting. Salami might not be the best thing to eat just before going to sleep. Too much red pepper.

If the woman had left the hotel, it must have been through the baths' exit. He couldn't see it from the bar, but he had stood on the tram island till after 9 p.m. and had not seen her. What about her blond head lying on the pillow? Was it a set-up? How the hell could she have been on Fekete Sas Street at 8:30?

He made himself an espresso. The machine had been a gift from a grateful store owner on Váci Street after Attila had ended a two-year protection racket that had each of the high-end stores paying into a "beautify the city" fund that existed only in the imagination of the Albanian gang that had failed to pay its own dues to the local police. The gang had learned its lesson and was now happily beautifying Vienna.

He lay down on the sofa — not nearly as comfortable as the squishy corduroy one that had exited with the wife — and tried to read an old Jack Reacher novel, waiting for the machine to heat up. The ex had decided to leave his collection of detective fiction but took most of the quality stuff, along with the book-cases. His remaining books were still in cardboard boxes piled high next to the kitchen. He was too tired to read. Too tired to make coffee, but he persevered till 7 a.m., when Gustav insisted on his morning crap. It was barely daylight, and there was just enough rain to dissuade the dog from going outside. He hunkered down in the long passageway between the elevator and the entrance. Attila kicked the tidy cigarillo of dog turd into the darkest part of the passageway and led the disconsolate Gustav back to the apartment.

At 8 a.m., Attila was at the Police Palace (which is what everyone called the police headquarters after the government added the tall tower), showing his ID to the fat woman who had been on security long enough to know him even in the dark. As usual, she made a big production of examining his photo, looking at him, examining the photo again. Then she waved him through the X-ray machine, minus his holster and wallet. The building had become even more of a mindless fortress since he left.

Naturally, Tóth was not yet in his office, and the young uniform who guarded the second floor didn't know enough to let Attila wait in one of the empty interrogation rooms, so he sat on the bench for petty criminals awaiting questioning. A couple of young offenders wearing American pants with crotches at their knees made room for him. They were discussing why they had been picked up and, coming up empty, focused on a girl they had both tried to take home the night before. He could have told them the reason they had been hauled in was their pants, but decided it was pointless. Most of the policemen (and sole policewoman) looked like they were at the end of a night shift, rather than starting the day. They were slow-moving, damp, bleary-eyed, and smelly.

Tóth arrived close to 9 a.m. He was eating some kind of sugary pastry that left white powder on his thin mustache — the only thin part of the man — and down his ample front.

His shirt barely fit across his belly. One button had already popped, and the day had barely begun. On the other hand, his dung-coloured jacket was just-out-of-the-box new. But why, Attila wondered, had he chosen that shade of brown?

Tóth grunted when he saw Attila and motioned with his chin toward his corner office. Since Attila's last visit, the small fringed rug and the colour photo of the smiling woman at the edge of the desk — the same desk Attila had used when this had been his office — had both disappeared. Tóth finished the pastry before he looked at his former boss and, even then, he seemed reluctant to start the conversation.

"So," he said, at last. He sat with knees wide apart, hands clasped. "She has been on the phone all morning. We have a man with binoculars on the path up Gellért Hill and he has a perfect view of her room. She is using her own phone, not the hotel's. We can't get a fix on the number. She must have one of those cheap disposables you can pick up anywhere. She has a rental car, due back in Vienna in three days. The Ukrainians want her gone before then."

Attila shook his head. "The Ukrainians? What do they have to do with her?"

"Don't know. But they are anxious to have her out of the country. As is Mr. Krestin, the guy whose house she broke into, and he has some influence with the government. The government runs the police, in case you've forgotten." He rubbed his palms together, looked at them, wiped them on his knees. "Your job is to not lose sight of her again."

Attila sighed.

"Is that simple enough?" Tóth asked.

"Krestin?" Attila refused to be baited.

"János Krestin."

"Guy who used to own a studio making utterly dreadful movies?"

"Him."

"And he owned the Lipótváros football team?"

"His house is not in Lipótváros, and it's his house that she couldn't have been in because she was asleep in her bed."

"If he owned Lipótváros, he has some valuables. Did you say nothing was missing?" Attila didn't know a whole lot about János Krestin, but he did know that the man had accumulated a fortune, and some of it might have come from the bribes he collected before 1989. Rumour had it that if you were accused of petty crimes against the state, Krestin could get the state to forget about them. Or he could ensure fewer years in jail.

Most former functionaries had fitted seamlessly into the new system. Many of them had the advantages of knowing other languages, and most had done well since 1989. Back then, ordinary people were still too busy trying to repair their lives to pay much attention to the successes of others. That didn't last.

"I said nothing was stolen except the cigar case."

"So, what was she doing there?"

Tóth shrugged.

"Perhaps she was looking for something but didn't find it?"

Tóth shrugged again.

"And she cut the security system. So, she is a professional?"

"Not exactly," Tóth said, chewing on his thumbnail.

"Do you have some information about her that you are not sharing?" Attila asked. "Something that explains her connection to Krestin? You told me this Helena Marsh hasn't been here for seven years, and, even then, no one knew what she was looking for until after she left. You remember the Bauers and their Rembrandts?"

"Vaguely. Two pictures their neighbours had appropriated during the war. She had nothing to do with that."

"In the end, the Bauers got their Rembrandts back, and the Szilágyis decided not to prefer charges, although they told me at first that their paintings had been stolen."

Tóth shook his head. "Irrelevant."

"It's not irrelevant if that's what she does. She spent time in Germany and Holland, tracking art stolen from Jews during the war. She is some kind of expert. Is that why she is here?"

"This is not about stolen art," Tóth said. "And Krestin was never a Nazi. He was a card-carrying party member. At least for a while."

"A while?"

"There were no card-carrying Communists after '90."

Some guys, Attila thought, could easily have been both Nazi and Communist, or Nazi and then Communist. A willingness to dole out physical violence would have been an advantage after the war. A man could go a long way with those credentials. Not that Krestin had ever been accused of that publicly, but one could never be sure with men of a certain age.

"But she is, as you put it, some kind of expert on art. And if you could encourage her to leave the country, I would be very grateful," Tóth said.

"As would the Ukrainians?"

Tóth didn't answer.

They sat in silence for a while, Attila trying to estimate just how grateful everybody — especially the Ukrainians — would be and how much extra he could charge if he persuaded the woman to go home. Then he got to his feet, buttoned his jacket, and left. Simple enough.

He was halfway across the Szabadság Bridge when he saw

her. She was wearing the same dress as yesterday but she had added a summery cotton hat and a tight-waisted white cardigan. The blue scarf was tied into a knot at her neck. She was heading to the Pest side. Striding fast, her skirt fanning out in the wind off the river, she looked like a tourism commercial: cheerful, carefree, her blond hair swept back. She glanced at him without much interest when they came face to face, but he caught the hint of a smile at the corner of her mouth. Close up, she seemed older than yesterday and older than the photo in his breast pocket. But the blond hair, the slim hips, the confident way she carried herself all added up to fortyish and foreign. Women in Hungary hadn't walked like that for years, not since the economy tanked.

He waited for her to reach the baroque church in Ferenciek Square before he began to follow her. It was ridiculous to imagine she would not notice or that she wouldn't remember swinging past him on the bridge, but he had agreed not to lose sight of her, and he was not about to let her disappear again.

She turned onto Dob Street and stopped outside a dull little café. Attila knew it; sometimes he dropped in for a cream scone. The black-clad Garda louts who had been strolling this neighbourhood for the past few months were across the street, smoking and glaring. Atilla had seen them patrolling this street and had heard that they occasionally tripped some elderly Jew on his way to the grocery shop or, better still, on his way back. Then he would be likely to drop his eggs and milk on the sidewalk. The louts would chortle and would declare that had people been more vigilant in '44, there wouldn't be a "Jew problem" now.

The trouble with allowing free speech, Attila thought, was that this sort of thing could go on unchecked. But then, according to the government, there was no problem. And, according to the government, the Garda had been banned. But here they were, as usual, although only half a dozen of them, unlike the past Sunday when they held a rally on Hösök Square. In the past, when Attila had arrested members of the Garda, they would be out in an hour or less. Hardly worth the effort. Tóth said the Jews and the gypsies could take care of themselves. It wasn't entirely true, but it did save a lot of time and trouble with lawyers and foreign reporters who wanted to know why the Garda was still marching. (Local journalists knew better than to cover Garda events; the government's media council could yank their licences.) The Garda had changed their uniforms, but they were still black, their flags were even more in-your-face patriotic, and they carried on.

Helena stayed at the café take-out window for a moment, examining the aging pastries in the glass case and checking her phone. She ordered an espresso in a Styrofoam cup, looked up and down the street (no doubt spotting him on the other side, talking to himself on his cell phone), and strolled on to number twenty-two. The lads made piggy noises but didn't bother to cross the street.

She pressed the bell to one of the apartments. The door was opened immediately by an elderly man with thin, bent shoulders. He must have been waiting for her. It was murky inside, the only light a flash of sunshine far beyond the door. Attila took a photo with his phone but expected that it would show only the shadows.

The man let her inside and shut the door.

 Gábor Nagy was a small, fragile man dressed in a grey cardigan that sagged over his hips and grey flannel pants that seemed too big for him. His glasses dangled from a silver chain around his neck. His hand was dry and cold, but his grip was surprisingly strong. He held her hand for a moment longer than she had expected.

Géza had told her he was eighty-five years old.

"I may not be able to tell you very much," he said in English as he led her up worn stone steps to an ornate wooden door on the first floor. There was a mezuzah to the right of the door. He touched it as he entered. Looking down to the courtyard, she saw a garden with a wild array of pink and red flowers, tall bushes in bud, and a stone pond with a green metal figure in the centre.

"We try to make it fine for those who still choose to live here," he said, following her gaze. "This is not an easy city to live in, and houses like this are worth more demolished than not. Still," he shrugged, "we persist."

He ushered her into the living room, all bright and cheerful pinks and light blues, cane furniture, a plethora of cushions, as if he had been recreating a nineteenth-century spa. "I have some coffee made," he said. "Or would you prefer a taste of Tokaji?" He spoke quickly with a soft Hungarian accent.

She shook her head. "Nothing. Thank you."

"I have sometimes wondered what happened to him," he said. "Although all that was so long ago that it would be natural for him to have died. Most of us did, you know. Died. And now, your call, after all these years . . ." He waved his hand. "I apologize if I was slow to remember his name. Your pronunciation made it sound American. Those names I do remember, you know. It is important to remember names. Other people I have met more recently, well, it's hard as we get older, but those names and those faces . . . I do not usually forget." He padded into the next room and returned with a small glass of wine. "Are you sure?" he asked, lifting the rim to his lips. "It's very good, late harvest, picked in the '60s. Surprisingly, I have a few bottles left. I may even have picked the grapes myself. Back then, the good stuff wasn't exported before it had time to mature. The Russians didn't much care for sweet wine. Now it's Americans who buy it, and they can't tell the difference between great and merely passable."

She accepted the renewed offer but insisted on just enough to taste, since it was rare to be offered the real thing, she said.

She knew how much it would cost now for that small bottle with five stars.

"Five puttonyos," he told her. She sipped it to make him think she appreciated it. Her own taste was more in line with the Russians'.

"You met Géza on the train," she prompted after he sat down in one of the cane chairs across from her. "He wants me to ask you what you remember."

Gábor leaned in toward her and turned his head to one side, chin down. He was a bit deaf, she surmised. But as she started to repeat the question he raised his hand. "I heard you," he said. "We met long before then.

"We were collected on the same afternoon: February 15, 1945. It was fearfully cold. My family, unlike the Mártons, had been in the ghetto, except for my uncles, who had been rounded up for labour service. Neither of them survived. We were in the cellars because of the bombardments. We had been there for weeks, sitting on concrete floors. There was no food and no heat and nowhere to bury the dead. My aunt died in early January, but her body was still there in Klauzál Square, stacked up with all the others. Frozen, of course. We couldn't bury her. We were walled in, you know."

Helena said she knew. She had met others who had been in the ghetto. Many had died. Gábor said they had subsisted on rotten potatoes. Some of those in the cellar applauded every time a bomb landed. They wanted the Russians to come and save them.

"We melted ice for water. My sister's baby died. The noise was horrific, the ground shook day and night during the bombardment. The building collapsed over us. I don't remember how we got out of there, but I do remember that we were glad to see the Russians. The joy of walking out the ghetto gate and not being stopped. The gendarmes were gone. Good to feel the air on my face. It was very cold air. No colder outside than in the cellar, but it felt clean. I could breathe. You cannot imagine the hell we had endured. Now, here they were: our liberators. That's how it seemed to us Jews at the time. Later, we were not so enthusiastic. Géza was not enthusiastic even from the beginning."

"You met Géza on the fifteenth?"

"Yes, I met him when we were picked up by the Russians near the Iranyi Street bakery. It had been bombed, but there was a lineup outside the ruins. They pointed machine guns at everyone and moved us along to the river where they had open trucks waiting. The only person they left behind was a woman with a baby. I showed them my yellow star (I hadn't had the courage to tear it off yet) and my Jewish identity card from the ghetto, but they weren't interested."

"You said you knew Géza before the war?" Géza had not told her that.

"We were at school together, back before the Jewish laws. After that, I could no longer go to school. He recognized me, though. Did he tell you he saw me once in the summer of 1944 and pretended he didn't know me? I was wearing that yellow star. Did he tell you?"

"He was only sixteen," Helena said apologetically on Géza's behalf.

"Yes. So was I."

They were quiet for a moment.

"It was shocking to see the city. In ruins," Gábor said. "The buildings along the Danube were on fire. So much rubble. So many dead bodies and body parts. Most places had been robbed many times. Our Bajcsy-Zsilinszky Street apartment building had been bombed and lost its outer walls. I remember one floor was tilting downward and a piano had somehow remained stuck to the back wall. A Russian was trying to pry it loose with a gun. I don't know how he thought he would take it home. I think the people who took over our apartment when we were forced to move into the ghetto were all killed."

Gábor was smiling, probably at the thought of those people being killed, Helena thought.

"Old men were cutting up dead horses on the street. It was hard work. Most of the horses were frozen. The Germans left hundreds of them behind, and they had starved like us. The women and children stayed underground. You know about the women?"

She nodded. Thousands raped. Hundreds of thousands. Many killed. "The soldiers picked you up at the bakery . . ."

"They took all of us. Everyone who was lined up, except that one young woman."

"How did they get you out of the city?"

"Trucks to Gödöllő. There were a lot of prisoners: Germans, Hungarians, soldiers, civilians. Some were children, some grandmothers. We just had the clothes we were wearing when they took us. Some soldiers still had their military great-coats, but not for long. I wore my father's winter jacket over a sweater and a shirt. He was in a labour camp. Géza had a loden coat. Three-quarter length, I think. They took our watches and everything else they liked, but they left me my clothes. My coat was filthy, even dirtier than their own clothes. We hadn't washed in months."

"They took you to . . . ?"

"Cattle cars from Gödöllő to Debrecen. No food. We were

part of a shipment of loot from Budapest. Paintings, chande-liers, boxes of wine, children's toys, a white convertible sportscar, whole cases full of sheets and towels, curtains with curtain rods, and watches, of course. They did love watches. We were in the old Debrecen Armory for some days. Maybe a week. There was some kind of trial. A military judge, a man in uniform, and a young interpreter who didn't speak our language but seemed to be talking on our behalf. I still don't know what the charges were. They beat Géza, but they left me alone. I thought at the time that it was because they realized I was a Jew, and they planned to send me home. But that wasn't it. It was because Géza was a big boy and I was not. He'd been on the football team of our school. Maybe he looked like trouble. That's when he lost his hearing in one ear, but it was dangerous not to hear well. Has it been fixed?"

"He uses a hearing aid."

"We all use them now," he said, smiling again. "Géza and I were on the same train afterward. Cattle cars with a hole in the middle and a bucket of water that froze. We slept on shelves with no blankets. Some people froze to death before we got there."

"You remember any of the guards?"

"On the train? No. But most of them were Soviets. A lot of Mongols. Maybe Tajiks. Short, powerful men."

"No one spoke Hungarian?"

"Not until we arrived."

"The mine?"

He nodded. "Vorkuta Gulag. Siberia. A coal mine. We worked sixteen hours a day underground. For four years we barely saw the sun. Didn't Géza tell you?"

"He did."

"Then why do you ask?" He looked past her through the window.

"Sometimes he can't trust his own memory."

"And why is that important? I don't trust mine either, but it doesn't matter."

"Géza wants to find out about the men in charge at the camp," she said.

He looked down at his entwined fingers. "I try not to remember everything," he said almost apologetically.

"Géza had trouble with that, too," she said. "He had willed himself to forget. Now, he wants to remember."

"Why?" Gábor leaned closer to Helena. "What good does it do him to remember?"

"There was someone in Vorkuta he wants to find."

"One of the prisoners?"

"He may have been both a prisoner and a guard."

"Hmmm, one of those," Gábor said.

"What was their job? To make sure no one escaped?"

Gábor laughed. "Escape was not a problem. Some of the men tried during the summer. A few of them were shot. Others disappeared. Either they froze to death or the hunger took them. I used to know all their names. In the first months we all had names. Later, only numbers. In the winter, it was like it used to be in the ghetto. We stacked the bodies behind the toilet ditch, six or seven deep. Had to wait for spring for the ground to thaw before we could dig down to bury them. They had us bury the bodies in the spring because they didn't like the smell. But me, I hardly noticed it. I was used to it from the ghetto."

"Géza asked about the Hungarian guards."

"Yes," Gábor said. "The Hungarians. They were prisoners like us, but they volunteered for extra duty. They got better treatment for working in the system. They took our food rations, our clothes, and beat us if we didn't do exactly what they ordered. They wanted the Russians to treat them better. I shouldn't call them Russians — most of them weren't Russians, you know. They were Ukrainians, Kazakhs, Mongols. A lot of Ukrainians. They wanted preference, favours, but all they got was what they stole from the rest of us. The Soviets had no use for them, and they had no use for us. When we died, they got replacements. More Hungarians, Slovaks, Székelys, Germans, Czechs. It was simple. All they had to do was wait for the next cattle cars."

"The Hungarian guards," she said. "Géza remembered some of the Hungarians. He said they had been criminals before the war. Do you remember them?"

"Some. But they were packed into the trains with the rest of us. When the prison doors opened, it was easy for them, the Arrow Cross, to blend in with their victims. All of them. They took off their uniforms, those who didn't leave with the Germans. The Russians didn't care who you were. They had a quota for how many to pick up every day. It was an Arrow Cross man who broke my fingers. He was our guard in the Gulag." He lifted his right hand to show her. The last two bones of his forefinger were missing, and the middle finger was bent into the space where the forefinger used to be. "I was trying to write to my mother. We thought for a time that we could send letters. But they were never mailed."

"What was his name?"

He shook his head. "I'm not sure . . . now." He made a small choking sound between the last two words. Nervous. Anxious. Or afraid.

"Do you know what happened to them?" she asked after a while.

"The guards? They were among the survivors. Most of them learned to speak some Russian. They ate better and got more rest than we did. Some of the prisoners were so hungry they ate the dead. Have you read Solzhenitsyn?"

She nodded. She had read about Stalin's Gulag before she took this job. There were not many Hungarian stories.

He stood with some effort. "Would you prefer tea?" he asked, looking at her unfinished wine.

Pouring tea would give him time to recover. She nodded, and while he was out of the room, she examined the small collection of black-and-white photographs on the rolltop writing desk. One of them was of a young dark-haired woman with two small children. Another was of a group of duffle-coated figures sitting on a park bench, with the Fisherman's Bastion in the background. There was an artfully posed sepia photo of an elderly woman with a child on her lap and a shaggy dog gazing up at her. "You're a photographer?"

He shook his head. "Sugar?" he asked.

The tea was very dark, the leaves had been brewing too long while they talked. It tasted bitter.

"I saw one of them in '65. It was the middle of the Kadar era. He was wearing a Party pin in his lapel. He was with another man I recognized. We were in the same bar. It was dark, but I would have known this man anywhere. In the camp, they called him Bika but that was not his real name. He was big, with a thick neck, flat nose, low forehead. Looked just like a bull." János Krestin, she knew, was thin with receding hair and a high forehead, but time changed people. "He ordered some of the prisoners to beat Géza again. He said he didn't like the way Géza looked at him. Is Géza trying to find him? Why?"

"It's just an unfinished chapter," Helena said carefully. She could hardly blame Gábor for asking, but she was not going to risk telling him anything she wouldn't say to Géza's enemies. If Géza's assumption was correct, the foes he had when he left Hungary may still be influential. And Gábor may have given in at some point. He could have been blackmailed or threatened. Prisoners sometimes assume the colouration of their guards, if only as a survival strategy. Gábor had lived here for a long time after Géza left.

"Do you have any idea what this Bika's real name was?"

"No."

"Or where he lives? Or what he did after he came home from the Gulag?"

Gábor shook his head. "But I think he was in the state police service."

"The ÁVO?"

"Yes. In the ÁVO," Gábor said, lowering his voice to a whisper.

"Why do you think he was in the ÁVO?"

He shrugged. "You hear things . . ."

"And after 90? Did you ever see him again?"

"Never."

"Have you any idea what happened to him?"

"No." He was looking at the photos on the desk. "And it doesn't matter now."

"Have you seen some of the other men from Vorkuta?"

"A few of us had drinks in '90, toasting that the Soviets had left. A celebration. But after that we made no effort to see each other." Gábor leaned closer to Helena and studied her face. "Have you ever been in a prison?"

"No."

"If you had, you would understand. None of us wish to relive the humiliation."

He held his cardigan together over his chest, still studying her face. A small, frail man with a deeply lined, pale face, broken by the past.

"Would you know the men you saw in the bar if you saw them again?" she asked.

"My memory is not so good anymore," he said softly.

"The man in the bar with Bika?" she repeated.

Gábor stood, using the arms of his chair to help him. He walked slowly to the window, his hands in the pockets of his baggy cardigan.

"Do you remember a man called Krestin?" she asked.

He stayed at the window, his head down as if he was trying to see something on the pavement.

She joined him at the window and showed him the small black-and-white, head and shoulders photograph of a man staring at the camera — a passport photo or a mugshot. Géza had given it to her, together with the photo of the possible Titian.

"I don't think so," he said, barely glancing at the picture. "I can't see him in the Vorkuta uniforms. It's been almost fifty years since we came home."

"I could send you another photo," she said. "You have a computer?"

"Never saw the need," he said. "I suppose all the kids use them these days. But I don't teach anymore."

"Did Géza talk to you about a big painting his family owned? Religious. Christ entering Jerusalem. He says it was by Titian."

"No. Why?"

"He wants to buy it back."

Gábor's smile widened. "Good luck with that."

"Could we meet again?" she asked.

"I am not very busy," he said.

"Géza sends his best wishes," she said.

"He could have come himself. He could afford to fly first class. There's nothing to be afraid of now, I think." But he hesitated over the last sentence.

"When did you see him last?"

"He was here in the late '70s, when we had a spell of goulash Communism."

Géza had failed to mention that to her.

"Even in Vorkuta, Géza talked about getting out of the country. He said he couldn't live here anymore after what happened. But I stayed. There was a girl I wanted to see again. She was what kept me alive. The thought of her long brown hair. Her smile. I needed to know that she had waited for me."

"Is that her in the photos?" she asked.

He nodded. "She died last year. I visit her every Sunday."

She waited a few moments in case he decided to say something else. But he seemed comfortable saying nothing. A man at the end of his life, she thought. Nothing left to wish for, nothing left to prove.

Géza Márton was different.

 It was a small building close to the old synagogue, in an area that had once been part of the ghetto. Some of the houses had been converted into apartment buildings. One of the developers who had sprung up like weeds after '89 had laid claim to much of the land around here, but he had not yet succeeded in evicting the tenants from this building.

There were no names on the board, only apartment numbers, but Attila had no problem identifying the man Helena had met. The old pre-democracy police files were still useful, when needed. Gábor Nagy, eighty-four years old. He lived alone, a retired school teacher. He had spent three years in Vorkuta, one of the Soviet labour camps. He was lucky to be alive. He got in trouble again in 1956, joining a group of students he had taught — or so the indictment said. He was tried and jailed for ten years but got out after only five. He couldn't return to teaching, so he had moved to Eger and worked in the state winery. He had been married. His wife had taught engineering at the university, but she gave up her job when they moved to Eger. Two daughters who both left the country in November 1956. After 1989, they visited every Christmas. His wife died in 2014 and he came back to Budapest.

"Is this some sort of Jewish thing?" Attila asked Tóth.

"What do you mean, Jewish thing?"

"I mean is this woman, Marsh, is she of interest because she is after some Second World War Nazi or a homegrown Arrow Cross man? Something he stole from the Jews? Is that whom we are protecting?"

Tóth sighed theatrically before he answered.

"I've already told you this has nothing to do with Jews. We took care of them years ago. That 2011 conference dealt with all their remaining claims."

"What about the Herzog lawsuit?"

"Never heard of it."

"A bunch of paintings in several museums that used to belong to a guy called Herzog. They were confiscated by the Nazis, shipped to Germany with all their loot. Now Herzog is suing the government."

Tóth rolled his eyes with frustration. "He is damned lucky his stuff wasn't reclassified as Soviet loot. If it were hanging in the Kremlin, he'd have no chance of ever seeing it again. But I told you, this woman is not here about Nazi loot. It's nothing to do with Herzog or whoever else. And I am not sharing any more information with you unless it helps you find her and get her out of the country. We want no fuss."

"The man she met on Dob Street seems to be Jewish," Attila said.

Tóth shrugged. "There are still a lot of Jews about."

"Any idea what the connection is between her and Nagy?" Attila asked. "She wouldn't go to see him if there is no connection. Right?"

Tóth paced the room, then dropped back into his chair (the one that used to be Attila's chair), his balls slapping on the wood as he sat down, legs wide apart. On full display. "Look, Fehér," he said, trying for a more considerate tone, "what we have here is a foreign national on some sort of private mission invading the home of someone who was once close to the prime minister and to the former prime minister. Meanwhile, the Ukrainians are claiming that she may be a threat to their peace of mind. We don't need to know why. We need to encourage her to leave the country. Encourage her hard, if that's what it takes. That's where you come in."

"The former prime minister?" Attila raised his eyebrows in exaggerated astonishment. "Which one? The young Commie or the dictator?"

"That's on a need-to-know," Tóth said, not quite succeeding in hiding his grin under the ridiculous moustache. There had been a time when had Attila used those words in this office both of them would have laughed openly. "You are wasting time. The Ukrainians didn't sound very patient, and I gave them my word that we were using one of our best. That's you. But tomorrow, it may have to be someone else."

"You could arrest her."

"No. We can't."

Attila sighed. There was no sense pushing Tóth once he had dug his heels in. He tried another tack.

"The lawyer she met at the Gerbeaud is known for selling antiques. And art." Attila had been assigned to watch him once before. Nothing came of the investigation, because everyone had been paid a share of the profits. They had been handsome profits, with several zeros at the end, and the antique credenza was, for sure, happier where it landed than in the storage space of the old Buda building where its former owners used to hide stuff before the Soviets came.

Tóth nodded.

"So, she is after something valuable," Attila prompted.

"Could be."

"And the thing is in the former comrade's house, where it's been safe and sound for many years, but someone now wants it. And the thing stays unguarded when the former comrade is out for an evening. Why?"

"You were on the job, so it wasn't supposed to be unguarded."

"And you are absolutely sure this is not about recovering Jewish stuff from the Second World War."

"I told you those fucking cases were settled long ago," Tóth shouted. "Dammit. You know that. Not our job."

"Do you know who she's been talking to on her cell?"

"No. She is very careful. She uses only disposable phones."

"What about those handy little listening devices the state police installed in the guest rooms?" Attila had helped remove a number of them from hotel washrooms and overhead lights in '90, but there would have been thousands more all over the city. The Communists displayed an almost insatiable curiosity about everyone, including tourists.

"No. The touristy '56-ers had them all removed from the hotels."

"Even in the toilet bowls?"

"Especially the toilet bowls."

"Well, as you said, the lawyer is only interested in buying and selling stuff. He tells us something now and then just for business insurance. I expect he could tell us more."

Tóth threw a navy blue business card on the desk between them. "Don't damage the golden goose," he said and answered his cell phone, signalling the end of the meeting.

The silver type on the card read, "Dr. Ferenc Kis, Counsel and Specialist in European paintings and antiquities." Hungarian on one side, English on the other. No address, just a phone number for downtown Pest. It had been a few years since Attila's last visit.

In the hall outside Tóth's office, Attila called Ferenc Kis and politely asked the secretary for an appointment in an hour. After a short pause and a disbelieving gust of breath, the secretary told him that Dr. Kis was busy and asked the reason for this appointment. She sounded like the sort of self-important, management-school type Attila specialized in irritating, so he got rolling with his least polite voice, accent tending to the lower prairies near the Serbian border, descending to the offensively familiar, and advised her that his business was strictly between Mr. (he refused to call anyone with a law degree "doctor") Kis, and that if Mr. Kis valued his ass, he would be in his office in exactly forty-five minutes, which is how long it would take Attila to get to — where was it again?

She gave him some dead air, then an address at the high end of Váci Street, and hung up. He used that tone of voice to persuade petty bureaucrats of some impending doom breaching their comfortable horizons. Members of local organized crime gangs often spoke that way. Grand bureaucrats usually had their own enforcers, so scum threats rarely worked with them.

Although traffic congestion had made driving in the city almost impossible, he was at the entrance to Váci Street in less than fifteen minutes. He parked illegally in front of the old Vigadó Palace, where his grandmother, when she was a debutante, used to dance through the autumn nights. The petty nobility would come up to Budapest for "the season," expecting their daughters to be hooked up before Christmas. Very civilized before the First War, if you were in the right economic class or had inherited a reasonable title. Attila was glad his great grandpa just had an added surname, a Hungarian form of the German "von," otherwise his grandfather would have ended up in some godforsaken dump of a village for enemies of the state during the Rakosi years, and his father may never have been conceived.

Attila's father died in 1970 when Attila was only ten, but he still remembered the rough skin on his hands, his swollen fingers, the bristly hair on his chin when he kissed Attila goodnight.

The private offices of Dr. Ferenc Kis were on the second floor of a building with street-level windows that displayed the bucolic art of the late nineteenth century — hay wagons, sturdy white horses, overdressed wranglers, the usual kitsch tourists loved. Attila didn't bother with the doorbell. He held the door for a man who was carrying parcels and struggling with his keys. Then he slipped in after him.

The door to Kis's office faced the courtyard. He had fancied it up with mosaic glass and fake white pillars on either side of the wide wooden door. Attila opened it with just a push of his elbow and walked up the short flight of stairs into a room reserved for clients who had time to read American magazines while waiting. Attila didn't. He marched into the inner office, where Kis and his stick-thin secretary were enjoying a mid-afternoon coffee.

Attila announced his name. "I called in advance," he told Kis, nodding at the formally dressed woman daintily holding her coffee cup in the air. "I am following up on your meeting with the American agent yesterday."

"American agent?" Kis seemed genuinely surprised. "Whose agent? You don't mean like CIA, or whatever?"

Attila tried to look very serious.

"Who said she is an American agent? She is not even American," Kis protested. "And what do you mean 'following up'?"

Kis was shorter than he had seemed at the Gerbeaud, but he compensated for his lack of height by styling his hair in a high wave. It didn't work. He had rimless glasses over a tight mouth and a narrow forehead that struggled to be seen under the big hair. He wore a blue-striped shirt with a matching blue-and-white square peeking out of the breast pocket of his navy blazer. Did ordinary mortals still wear this sort of garb?

"We have had prior dealings with her, and we are keen to avoid the problems she brought with her the last time," Attila said. It was not a good lie, but he hoped it would do the job. People nowadays seemed more concerned about being seen with American agents than Russian FSB guys, although the latter were scarier. This government was paranoid about Americans. Russians, not so much.

"What kind of problems?" Kis asked, his left eyebrow lifting ever so slightly in a futile effort to indicate he was not seriously interested.

"The kind you would want to avoid is my guess," Attila said. "Involving a bit of violence with guns and an unexplained death. Lots of mess for the police."

Kis leaned back in his chair and regarded Attila with curiosity. "I don't think so."

"Which part?"

Kis shrugged. "I have a good relationship with the police. As you know."

Attila nodded. "But not with the Ukrainians."

He sat down in one of the gilt-armed chairs across from Kis. Its silk-embroidered seat groaned. Clearly, it was a chair made for a much smaller man.

"The who?"

"Ukrainians," Attila repeated, still nodding.

"I don't know any Ukrainians."

"So you say."

They sat for a while, letting the information simmer between them, then Kis said, "And I am not interested in dealing with them."

"They may not care what interests you," Attila said, making it up as he went. "They believe they have a prior claim on the property you're peddling."

Kis dabbed his face with the back of his hand, then took a cigarette from a silver case. The secretary lit it with her own silver lighter. How quaint, Attila thought, how old black-and-white Hollywood, how pre-war.

"That's impossible," Kis said. "The Canadian couple registered with me thirty years ago . . ."

Now we are getting somewhere, Attila thought. "Ms. Marsh's clients," he said, nodding, as if he had known all along.

"Márton. He called as soon as one could do that sort of thing. He sent photographs. Okay, so they are black and white, but you don't have to be much of an expert to recognize this painting. He paid the retainer and renewed every year, so I could keep an eye out. The painting means a lot to this guy. He doesn't even care if he has to pay a bit more than the market price."

"And you found it for him," Attila prompted.

"It's what I do," Kis said. "This man up in Buda asked me to look at a Renoir he wanted to sell. Nothing special, just a small unfinished thing in a big frame, but I got him top price, and he didn't even have to bother with the usual papers. The buyer lives right here in the city. He owns a bunch of companies. Some buildings, a shopping mall, a TV station, couple of radio licences. Well connected," he jerked his head in the direction of the parliament buildings.

"And he wanted to sell the other painting, as well?"

"No. I asked him when I saw it. I told him it could fetch at least forty million, and that got him interested."

"Forints?"

"Dollars."

Attila whistled.

"No one I know deals in forints," Kis said. "They are weak and stupid and keep going down."

"So you called these Canadians?"

Kis looked uncomfortable.

"After making sure of the market?" Attila prompted.

"I had to make sure it was what it seemed to be." Kis was not admitting anything.

"And?"

"My original judgement was correct," Kis said. "It usually is," he added with a supercilious smile.

"Then this woman arrived." Attila was beginning to piece it together. Tóth could have saved him a lot of time had he filled in the blanks earlier.

"She represents Géza Márton."

"And anyone else?"

Kis seemed aghast. "That's not done in this business."

Attila shrugged. "No. More like the CIA."

"The CIA? Are you kidding?" Kis said, but he seemed hesitant. "Why? She is an art expert. She is known in the business."

"Your phones are bugged," Attila said, although he had no more reason to assume they were than to suggest that Helena Marsh had a connection with the CIA. Sometimes it was useful to be inventive.

Kis said he couldn't imagine why anyone would want to bug his phones, but he seemed concerned.

"With a guy like you, it's normal," Attila said. Hell, if the Americans could bug the Israelis, who have exemplary security of their own, why not record the arcane deal-making that went on in this office?

Kis kept his mouth shut.

At least he had succeeded in making him uncomfortable, Attila thought. He wanted to know more, but he'd leave it for the next time. It would be unwise to let on that he knew less than Kis.

"So," Attila said, "you expect her to leave soon as she has the painting she came for. Right?"

"It's not that simple," Kis said. "There is a ton of paper-work. You can't just buy a painting like that in Hungary and expect to wrap it up and leave with it just like that."

"How long will it take?"

"It depends," Kis said meaningfully, implying that there were more middlemen and bureaucrats to pay off. Attila knew that, for a painting worth forty million dollars, the line of out-stretched hands could reach from here to Vienna.

"I will be meeting with her handlers," Attila said, as omi-nously as he could manage, when he opened the door. Let Kis ponder what he meant by that. He, himself, had no idea what he meant, but "handlers" was a word the local press used when they talked about spies reporting to the U.S. Embassy.

Attila stood outside the building for a minute. It was Wednesday. A warm, sunny day, fluffy clouds in a clear sky, the Danube rippling along its banks, a few old men fishing. It would have been pleasant to sit on the embankment for a while and enjoy the day. But it was Wednesday, and on Wednesdays he had to visit his mother on Naphegy.

Her room looked undisturbed.

Helena closed the curtains, undressed, pulled on her bathing suit, and slipped her arms into the large hotel terry bathrobe (obviously made for a much bigger person). She slid her thin-bladed knife into one pocket, rearranged the wig, the pillows, the shoes, and took the cage elevator down to the baths. The bathrobe and slippers identified her as a guest to the old woman who operated the elevator as part of the hotel's effort to seem friendly to guests. She walked under the baths' mosaic-inlaid arches, past the massage areas, to the "champagne" swimming pool in the atrium. The room was luminous in the late afternoon gloom, with flickering sconce lights mirrored and fracturing on the green tile walls and light from the art nouveau glass roof dancing on the pale green water, the bubbles barely reaching the surface before they popped.

There were two children at the shallow end, their mother sitting on the steps, supervising their splashing. A man wearing a Gellért Baths' plastic bathing cap was swimming a vigorous crawl along the side near the showers. Two men in similar caps sat on the edge on the same side, dangling their feet in the pool. One of them was drinking from a cardboard cup, the other was smoking something, cupping his hand to hide the cigarette. They both glanced up as she entered but didn't interrupt their conversation.

There was no attendant.

She lowered herself slowly into the pool, shuddering when the cool water reached her hips. She swam with measured breast strokes, keeping her head well out of the water and staying close to the side farthest from the men. She didn't slow when she reached the shallow end where the kids were playing, just turned and swam back the way she had come, her leg muscles stretching with each kick. It felt good. The long flight, the drive, the jog up the Buda hill, her anxiety about the painting, and the lack of adequate time to study it had taken their toll. She was out of practice, and maybe out of patience, with this sort of venture. She wasn't going to be able to take the painting out of the country legally, even if she paid its worth and even if she was re-patriating it to its original owner. There were too many laws around taking art out of the country. So she was forced once again to utilize her father's noxious legacy.

The big clockface showed 5 p.m. when the man she had been expecting came to the side of the pool, executed a perfect shallow dive (despite the "No Diving" sign), and began to swim to the far end, now abandoned by the children, whom she'd overheard agitating to go to the outdoor wave pool.

Miroslav stopped in the middle, trod water, and smiled at her. He was about her height, narrow-shouldered, and the sinews on his neck stood out, as did his Adam's apple. He had a wide forehead, sparse hair under the transparent shower cap, and long earlobes. The hotel's compulsory shower caps flattered no one but were particularly unkind for men with prominent ears.

"How are you enjoying Budapest?" he asked, his voice cracking and his Slavic accent a bit less obvious than the last time she had met him.

"Pleasant enough," she said. "You?"

"I prefer warmer weather," he said.

She swam closer and waited, also treading water.

"We could go to the café?" he said. "They make good espresso here. Just as you like it."

"Here is fine."

"You know you can't leave with it, don't you?" he said. He had very bad breath. "This is not Bratislava."

"Obviously."

She had first met him in Bratislava. She had been trying to recover a prized Raphael taken by a city official as payment for allowing a family to depart for France in the 1960s. In 1993, the family wanted the painting back. The former official had become a senior functionary in Robert Fico's quasi-democratic government and showed great reluctance to hand it over.

"And there is no reason we should both chase the same prize again, now, is there?" he added. He had been trying to buy the Raphael from the functionary at about the same time

Helena was hoping to retrieve it for the family. They were both agents for others, but she had felt righteous about her cause. A dangerous sentiment when you need a clear head.

She had lost. The family had to pay a ransom for the painting, and Helena had cancelled her own fee.

"You were satisfied with our deal the last time. Fair. Fast. Safe. Why change horses now?"

"Not entirely," she said.

"Vladimir sends his regards."

Vladimir Azarov was one of the less violent Ukrainian oligarchs. Sensibly, he had shown little interest in politics until the demonstrations started in 2013, and then he took no sides except to suggest to the new president and to the press that violence was not a solution to the country's east–west divide. During the Yanukovych years, he had kept his nose clean and the price of gas constant, and he had not tried to liberate anyone from jail.

"Fifty thousand dollars to walk away and no questions asked," he said. "We don't know what your take-home is on this deal, but I assume your clients are one-timers, not like us. Fifty thousand is good money."

"Or vice versa?"

He chuckled. "Vladimir doesn't need the money. And you can't hope for a better deal," he said. "It's easier to keep old clients happy than to find new ones every time. It's all about mutual trust. With trust, business is easier, more predictable."

Not to mention that it was easier not to go through his middlemen, she thought. The last time she had dealt with Azarov directly, he had commissioned her to buy him a Renoir from a secretive collector in Croatia.

"Is he still collecting Renoirs?"

He looked down his flat nose at her and sniffed. "Renoir? Not this time."

"A pity," she said. Then she told him she needed to finish her lengths. "Exercise is good for the mind."

"You need to watch your health," he said. "Things happen."

He emerged from the pool near the entrance to the four other pools, wrapped himself in his bathrobe, crossed his arms in front of his belly, and smiled at her.

She swam back and forth, now stretched out in a full American crawl, barely turning her face for a short breath every third stroke. Her body cut through the water, softly, like a knife. Miroslav waited while she swam her fifty lengths. "Not bad," he said. "Working out a lot, are you?"

Then he watched her climb out at the other end of the pool and whistled appreciatively. "Nice ass," he said. His voice echoed in the shimmering green dome. "Still," he added, "who knows how long that will last. You need to think about the future, my lady."

She wrapped a white towel over her head and waved at him as she left, her Gellért slippers slapping on the mosaic tiles. She considered Miroslav to be one of Vladimir Azarov's least objectionable men. She had never known him to be overtly violent, at least not with her, although, as with men of his profession, there was always a first time.

"You still enjoy music?" he asked her retreating back. "Vladimir likes opera."

She turned to look at him.

"Especially Puccini," he said.

The man standing at her door rattled the change in his pockets, pretending to look for the key, which, of course, he didn't have. He was playing for time, waiting for her to disappear into one of the other rooms or to pass him. She did neither.

Obviously, he didn't know what she looked like, or he had a different mental picture of the woman he saw coming down the corridor, absently rummaging in her pocket.

He wore an ill-fitting brown suit, a blue-and-white striped shirt, black lace-ups. His hair was cut short, and he looked almost bald. Mid-thirties. About 230 pounds. He was watching her with a lopsided grin that revealed a gold tooth, maybe two gold teeth. He stopped jangling his loose change and faced her, still uncertain but beginning to think about her size, shape, height. Helena could read it in his face. She kept going toward him till she was close enough to reach him with an outstretched arm. Then she stopped, took a deep breath, planted her feet wider, and waited. Perhaps he would turn away. Perhaps . . .

Still grinning, he reached under his jacket and pulled out a handgun with a silencer. She waited for a moment, in case he wanted to ask her something. He didn't. The gun was almost at her chest-level. She kicked him in the gut with the side of her right foot, in the back of his knees with her left, then hit his temple with her fist as he fell. He rolled onto his back, an expert roll, showing no reaction to the pain, and raised the gun with both hands. He was not nearly quick enough. She ducked. The bullet whizzed by her neck and lodged in the wall. She hit him hard across the nose with her heel and again in the gut. She spun, kicked the gun out of the way and smacked him in the neck under the chin with her other foot. He grabbed her ankle and twisted, his hands slippery with the blood from his nose.

She yanked her leg up and out of his reach, her fingers already closing on the hilt of her knife. She dropped to her knees and slid the point in just under his ear. He stopped thrashing for a second then tried to grab the knife, but his fingers slid off it. He reached to where he must have thought his gun was, but he was wrong. She slid the knife in farther. He lay very still, his breathing shallow. Then he stopped breathing. His tongue lolled out of his mouth, as if he was licking his lips.

"What the hell?" she whispered, pulling out the knife. "Why would you do that? Why? I didn't want to kill you. I didn't. Damned stupid kid." She was still panting from the exertion. Fear, her father had said, was a great motivator. If you're scared enough, you'll have more strength than you imagined possible. You would be more focused. Damned dumb kid.

She yanked off the slippers and pressed them against the knife wound to slow the blood leakage. She wound her towel tightly around his neck and draped his right arm over her shoulder, pulled him upright, and dragged him to the chintz chair at the end of the corridor, close to the elevators. He fell into its plush gold pillows, his chin on his chest.

He seemed younger now than before. Dark, thin skin under his eyes. Bruised knuckles on his right hand. Uneven teeth. The gold incisors, probably extracted and replaced for effect. She quickly rifled through his suit. Five hundred Euros in his breast pocket. No ID. Car keys. A single, large door key. The gun was a Glock 21, a model Swiss & Wesson had stopped selling a couple years ago.

She crossed his arms, wrists over his testicles, legs out in front. Balanced. She wiped the gun with the damp end of her robe and shoved it, barrel down, into his belt. "Sorry," she whispered, as she took four hundred from his stack of euros and the door key. "You needn't have died. Stupid waste. Whatever they paid you, it wasn't worth it."

Whoever had sent him had not told him about her reputation, which she had worked hard to acquire to avoid such a situation. Or he was just too cocky, too determined, to give up.

Using her airplane handy-wipes, she cleaned up the blood she had been unable to staunch as best she could. But it would show if anyone was really looking. No one came along the corridor. It was a few weeks before the tourist season, so there were not many people booked into the rooms at the rear of the hotel, and it was close to lunchtime. As long as no one discovered him or the blood in the next ten minutes, she would be fine.

As she opened the door to her room, a man and a woman emerged from the elevator, talking in Croatian. They said hello in English to the motionless young man in the armchair. Coincidence? Or did they know him? They kept walking and talking. They hadn't noticed he was dead.

She threw her stuff into the holdall, changed into the black pants, running shoes, sweater, hoodie, and paid her bill with one of her American Express cards via the hotel's TV channel. On the way to the elevator she had another look at the man in the armchair. Such a bloody waste.

What she needed to know was who had sent him and why. Azarov knew she was here, but he wouldn't have booked a seat for her at the opera if he wanted her dead. Had Kis alerted other collectors? If so, how many of them would want to have her killed? Kis had mentioned there could be some Russian interest in the painting, but she had thought that he was inventing the extra competition to raise the stakes, and the price. Even if there were interested Russians, would Kis have let a Russian know she was here?

She checked with her office for messages, but there were only two relevant ones: no threats, no warnings, no explanation for the attack. Her secretary, Louise, sounded bored. She liked to be busy, and there was never enough to do when Helena was away. One message was from János Krestin suggesting they meet for a meal in a Budapest restaurant. The other was from James at Christie's. Would she look at an 1872 Corot? The owner claimed to have inherited it, but authenticity was hard to establish with Corot.

Why would James choose her for this? Had he found out something about her father?

Simon had been fond of Corots. Jean-Baptiste, he had told her, was so careless about his work, so happy to have his paintings copied by his students, so obliging, or greedy, he even signed them all. What, then, was the harm in continuing his practice? There was such confusion over which ones were really painted by Corot that few buyers bothered to check authenticity.

She left by the front door, declined the doorman's offer of one of the hotel taxis. Long after the doorman had lost interest in her, she boarded a tram at the stop in front of the Gellért and rode it across the river to Pest.

This time, the sturdy policeman (if her guess was correct about him) was not waiting outside.

His mother, it seemed to Attila, had never been a happy woman. Given the post-war privations, the lack of choice in grocery stores, the lineups for pretty much everything — milk, fruit, shoes, even fabric for her dresses — unhappiness was one of the few things that remained easy to come by. When she could no longer afford a dressmaker, she had learned to sew her own clothes. Her first efforts hadn't been successful, but by the mid '60s, she could make most patterns, no matter how complicated, and she offered her services to richer women. Most of them were wives of Party members. Attila would sit at his mother's feet with a pin cushion, pressing in pins one by one as she passed them down while feeding the fabric through her sewing machine. It was an old German model, black with metal curlicues and a worn-out foot pedal that sometimes bucked under her foot and, at other times, resisted all pressure.

She would recite poems to keep him amused while she sewed. He was a small boy, eager to play with his friends in the street, resentful that he had to stay inside, not much interested in poetry or stories. When her clients came to try on their dresses, he was allowed to go out at last and, even in winter, he preferred to stay outside.

He'd told his mother he wanted to be a peasant. "I want to work with chickens and pigs."

"Seems to me you have fulfilled your ambition," she told him when he signed up for the police force.

In 1990, she had moved from her old apartment to a more spacious one on Naphegy, but the new lodgings failed to make her happy. But, since her recent acquisition of a boyfriend, she had begun to take better care of her looks, wearing more makeup, dying her hair a rusty red, and buying clothes in the new shopping mall. Her unannounced visits to Attila's apartment had become less frequent, and she had stopped making him indigestible casseroles.

"A surprise," she said, when he opened the door with his key. "Not much crime in the city today?"

She was sitting on the balcony with a long drink, a grim expression on her face, talking on the phone, while sweeping her hair back with her free hand. Even during the dreadful 1960s, when she was making clothes for Communist Party ladies, she would go to the hair salon a couple of times a month — always before his father had a day off from his job at the Csepel factory. He would come home smelling of oil and grease from handling tractors on the production line, and every time she would pretend to be surprised — but not pleasantly — at his arrival. Whether it was intentional or not, they never managed to make Attila a brother or a sister. He had had no misgivings at the time, but now that his mother was older and indulging her whims with boyfriends, it would be helpful to consult with a sibling.

At eighty-four, she was still a good-looking woman. She wanted the company of men and liquor, and the single life, all of which had been denied her by the post-war economy and the disillusioning presence of Attila's father. But now that he was dead, even getting what she wanted had failed to make her happy. She used her dead husband to underscore her unhappiness. He had somehow taken on the mantle of "provider," a role he'd never managed while he was alive. His loss, which she considered hers alone, opened up a whole field of recrimination, where Attila's failures flourished undisturbed by his paltry contributions to her well-being. In her view, he had never earned enough money and persisted in disappointing her even after he left the police force.

He placed the bottle of Olasz Riesling (her favourite wine) in the fridge. She asked whether he would like a glass of vodka, since that was what she was drinking.

He poured himself a finger, and without much interest, she asked about the girls, his ex, the charming woman down the hall from his apartment ("She'd be good for you, likes cooking, likes dogs, even likes you"), and whether he was looking for a steady job. Something more reliable than this. When she said "this," she spread her hands palms up to indicate she considered his current occupation to be worth nothing.

They were working on their refills when the new boyfriend arrived with a "mind if I join you," and lit a cigarette that he said, apologetically, was only his third of the day. He had given up smoking in his forties but took it up again now that he was seventy-eight. That made him a few years younger than his mother, but he had a definite stoop and walked with a cane. She didn't.

"You may as well. Not much chance of an early grave," Attila's mother remarked, with her customary good humour.

 After leaving his mother's, Attila went to the Historical Archives of Hungary's State Security at 7 Eötvös Street, close to the Franz Liszt Music Academy and south of the former headquarters of both the Arrow Cross and State Security, now retooled as the House of Terror museum. The building was painted a dull, nondescript beige, perhaps, Attila thought, so it would not stand out from its surroundings. He registered his name with the guard, filled out the requisite forms, and walked down the long courtyard and into wide hallway to the far end, where a third storey had been added.

During the first confusing weeks of the 1989 regime change, the government had retrieved purloined filing cabinets from the laid-off security men and built the extra floor to house them. Every time he came here now, Attila remembered the new Internal Affairs Minister asking parliament what he was supposed to do with the two thousand people employed to spy on their fellow Hungarians. Should he drag them into the cellars for interrogation? Threaten them into co-operating? The new regime could hardly revenge the dead here on these marble steps. What could they confess to that wasn't already known? Petty secrets? Best let them go and get on with their lives in the brand-new democracy. Plus, he was not a vengeful man.

Attila opened the door to the waiting room. He knew Magda Lévay well and she was still in charge of the archives. He also knew her personal assistant and the two other lower-level assistants who could, or could choose not to, grant you entrance. They may have been suspicious of his relationship with their boss, but there was nothing they could do about it. Magda was well-connected and didn't mind using her connections when she felt threatened.

The assistants would be observing him through the small two-way mirror at one end of the waiting room. He walked slowly to a narrow chair next to the table and squeezed himself between its arms. Difficult to seem comfortable.

One of the assistants came in. "Same files as before, Dr. Fehér?"

The "doctor" was a mark of excessive, old-world respect that could sometimes get you a table at a pricey restaurant or help you obtain State Security files. "No," he said leaning toward her, wanting it to look as if they were about to share a secret.

"You are not looking for dead men, then?"

She was an attractive woman, about forty-five, but, judging from her high-necked dress, pulled-back hair, and the way she shielded her body with her hands, she lacked confidence in her looks. Magda Lévay, on the other hand, did not lack confidence in her appearance. Some time ago, when he felt a lot younger and was still smarting from the ex's departure, he had invited her to dinner at the Kedves and for some Zack Golden Pear back at his apartment. She had been an enthusiastic lover, treating sex as if it were part of her pilates routine.

"I am not sure. He would be in his eighties if he were alive." He remembered her name from his last visit, but he had no idea whether she was married and didn't want to risk offending her by saying either Mrs. or Ms.

"Not the same file, then," she said.

"Not today. His name is Márton. He lives abroad now. Probably a '56-er."

"And your interest in this man?" she asked, a bit archly. Attila was accustomed to women with little power and no self-confidence loving moments like this.

"It's a police matter," Attila whispered. She would enjoy thinking this was something confidential. "We need to know, for sure, that he survived, that it's the same man we have been tracking. We need to know what he did while he lived here, why — other than it was '56 — he left, and what happened to him after he left."

She nodded and left him alone to contemplate the posters celebrating the government's decision to turn all tobacco shops into state enterprises and hand out new licences to their new owners. The former owners could, of course, apply for licence renewals, but they had no chance unless they had connections at the highest levels of the gothic palace. There was nothing unusual about the government's decision to control tobacco sales, his ex had said. Some other countries did that sort of thing with liquor. Here, that might have caused riots in the streets. But tobacco, not likely. And for the new concessionaires, it's what people here had grown to expect: privilege and punishment.

Attila noticed that the prime minister's face had been airbrushed in the official portrait hanging among the posters. He was getting old, like everyone else in the country. The young didn't like it here anymore. It was easier to find jobs in Germany or the Netherlands.

The assistant came back with a thick file and a few audiocassettes. "He didn't seem to interest them as much as the last one you checked," she said, her voice apologetic. "One audio is him and his girlfriend planning a trip they were not allowed to take. It was 1953. The rest . . . well, you can use the far table, if you like."

Géza Márton had been sixteen when the Russian army replaced the Germans in Budapest and took him off the street, on the Buda side, for a little work — that's what they called it — in the Soviet Union. He was there for almost three years. No. 442 Vorkuta Gulag.

That would be the connection with Gábor Nagy, Attila thought. Four years in a labour camp is a long time. It would have marked both men for life.

Márton hadn't made it out in the first wave in 1947. He may have been put on a train at the end of '48. There was no list of the men who had been sent there or of those who were allowed to go home. And no mention of Nagy anywhere.

Márton had gone back to his family's house, or what was left of it, on Sashegy, but the whole lot of them, his parents and his sister, were moved in December 1948 to make room for a government television installation. There was a report from one of the neighbours (unnamed) about the Mártons arguing at home, the mother wanting to know whether they could stay in the same area and the father saying they were better off somewhere cheaper. He said they didn't want to stick out, draw attention to themselves.

Next, they lived in an apartment near the opera house. Not a bad neighbourhood, although not as pretty as Sashegy. Márton senior had been an engineer. Railways and roads. Not important enough for the post-war Communists to hold a grudge against him. Géza's older brother had been killed at the Don River bend in 1942. He had been a simple foot soldier in the Second Hungarian Army when it was annihilated by the Soviets. That and Géza's years in Vorkuta had marked their father as a potential enemy of the state, a man worth watching.

There was a notation in the file to the effect that Károly Márton, Géza's great-grandfather had been wealthy but the next generation had squandered the fortune. There was nothing left except the house on Sashegy by the time Géza's father, also named Károly, was born.

There were reports from a neighbour in the apartment building that the Mártons listened to Radio Free Europe — a black mark against them, but not enough to get Márton senior fired from the State Roads and Railways Department. A lot of people listened to Radio Free Europe, and Géza's father seemed to have been good at building bridges. Another hand-written note said he had purchased cheese and cherries on the black market from a farmer who had not yet joined the co-op in the Bakony area. That must have been before the co-ops took over the orchards and the farms, leaving the cherries to rot and downgrading the cheese to state-approved bland.

After his return from Vorkuta, Géza had finished high

school in evening classes where some of the sons of the former nobility eked out meagre marks. He was not admitted to university, although his father tried to pull some strings with the ministry. Another black mark against him. Having been a Soviet prisoner was bad enough, but having a father with no strings to pull who thought he could influence people in office was worse.

In 1951, he met a woman called Gertrude Lakatos, eighteen, the daughter of farmers from Czechoslovakia, the part that used to be in Hungary. There were some grainy photos of them walking along the Danube, holding hands. After the war, the new coalition government had confiscated her parents' farm, and the family moved to Budapest. They lived on Rökk Szilárd Street. The father worked on a farm near Pécs. He came home for weekends only. There was reference to separate files on him and on the daughter, but this one noted only that he had been observed secreting corn, beets, potatoes, and apples in a sack and taking it home to his family.

Géza spent time at the Lakatoses' apartment. But there was no report on what they talked about or whether they listened to any forbidden radio stations.

In these years, Géza worked as a plumbing apprentice in a state enterprise that took care of toilets in Pest. There was a long report on his attempt to organize a group of draft resisters. A couple of them were arrested, and Géza went into the army. His superior officer recorded, with an astonishing number of grammatical errors, that Géza was a lazy soldier and had earned two demerits, one for smoking in his bunk, the other for being found with a girl (not named) in the potato field. There was a photograph of Géza in uniform: a thin face with large staring eyes, jug ears (although their size may have been exaggerated by the close haircut and the dumb-looking cap centred on his head). He had thin lips and dark lines down the sides of his mouth.

There was another photo of Géza in civvies with Gertrude wearing a wide-skirted floral dress cinched in by a wide belt, puffy white sleeves, knee-socks, ballet slippers, and a ribbon in her pleated hair. She had an oval face with finely drawn eyebrows and a pert little mouth. She looked shy or frightened.

The recording of a conversation between Gertrude Lakatos and Géza Márton was made in January 1956. He was suggesting a trip to Trieste; she didn't want to go and doubted they could get a permit, even if they were on a honeymoon.

Attila's cell phone had buzzed as soon as he arrived at the Archive. It buzzed again now, and he turned it off. He was tired of Tóth.

The report on Géza stated he was in the Killian Army Barracks in Budapest when the revolution began in 1956. There was no mention of his whereabouts when the army joined the rebels, but his father was arrested in 1957 for activities promoting civil disobedience and for taking part in the attack on the Communist Party's headquarters in Budapest. The photographs taken at the scene were horrific, especially the one of a group of seven young men with their hands up in surrender and a second one, taken a moment later, of their bodies falling, riddled with bullets. One of them was already on the ground, lying face up, soaked in blood, eyes still open.

There were no photographs of either Géza or Károly Márton at the scene, although there were a lot of pictures of others, including a woman helping to string someone from a lamppost and people in white coats, carrying stretchers, running toward Köztársaság Square. There were several more bodies lying under the trees at the edge of the square. Attila had seen most of these photographs before.

Géza Márton had crossed the border into Austria in late December 1956.

Károly Márton was tried and condemned to death in March 1957. His sentence was commuted to life in 1959. He served only two more years in jail. In September 1961, he was allowed to return to his home but not to his job. He ended up working on a pig farm near Debrecen. His wife joined him. There was no further mention of their listening to Radio Free Europe or Voice of America.

The only report filed on the Mártons' activities at the farm was written in pencil. It stated that Márton Sr. was a good worker and Mrs. Márton helped in the kitchen. The person who supplied the report, identified only by the number 507, said he or she had attempted to involve them in discussions of the Soviet army unit in the Debrecen barracks and of local youths taking part in the '56 "Counterrevolution," the official word for the Revolution.

The Mártons had made no comment on either topic.

The most interesting part of the file for Attila was the notes showing that surveillance of Géza Márton continued after he settled in Canada. They detailed his rejection of the State Police's request that he report on his fellow refugees. There was a handwritten notation on the margin of the request for continued surveillance stating that this man is an enemy of the state. A woman, identified as M379, had told Géza Márton that things could go very badly for his father if he continued to refuse. There were a lot of recorded conversations with M379. She made sure he knew of his father's incarceration at Recsk, one of the nastiest forced-labour camps for convicts.

Géza was kept under close observation for a year to determine whether he was sending anti-government letters home. He wasn't.

There was a note about his investment in 300 acres of land north of Toronto in 1965, more notes about his land development scheme for housing in a place called Vaughan, and, later, his building two shopping malls, a two-level underground parking garage, four old-age homes, and an extension of Toronto's York University. In all this time, he showed a complete lack of interest in joining the post-'56 community, or taking part in events at the Hungarian House in Toronto. Twice a year he sent packages of food and clothing to his parents and sister. The packages were opened and nothing but food and clothing was ever found in them. In the late 1970s, he started sending money transfers.

He married a Croatian girl named Klara in a civil ceremony in Vaughan in 1968. There was a photograph of the two of them, both looking thin and gawky, she in a long dress with a somewhat ravaged fox stole, he in a sagging suit with a white flower pinned to his top right pocket. In 1975, he joined the boards of the Art Gallery of Ontario and the Bank of Nova Scotia.

Géza visited Budapest in 1977. He claimed that he was interested in building a hotel on the Pest side of the Danube. He took his mother and sister to dine at the Alabárdos. He put flowers on his father's grave in Kerepesi Cemetery.

The last entry was from 1987, when Géza was celebrated by both the Toronto Chamber of Commerce and the Vaughan Chamber of Commerce. The brochure advertising the event claimed that he had received an honorary doctorate from York University and that his two children — a boy and a girl — were both York graduates.

Attila turned on his cell phone but ignored its persistent buzzing.

The assistant had been standing quietly by the window, watching Attila but not interrupting while he read through the file. He'd pretended not to notice until he had finished. Then he said, "We are also searching for other men from number 442 Gulag. Vorkuta. Mining."

She returned with a slim white file and waited while he opened it.

"Not much here," she said. "The location and the camp was emptied by 1951. Is there anyone in particular?"

"I want to know who was in Vorkuta with Márton."

In the file, he found a note from the Ministry of Internal Affairs declaring that the contents had been removed or destroyed before the material was handed over to the Archives.

"Please," Attila asked, "could you bring me the file on János Krestin."

When she hesitated, he added that he thought Mrs. Lévay would have no objections. Attila wondered whether the assistant knew that he and Magda Lévay had been lovers — for a night only, but still. This time she was gone for about half an hour, returning empty-handed but with a new attitude. She was defiantly self-important, her head held high, although her arms were still crossed over her breasts.

"We have no file on Dr. Krestin," she said.

Attila wondered when Krestin had acquired his degree and whether universities now ran courses in bribery and corruption. If so, Krestin would certainly have earned his doctorate. For the assistant's benefit, he nodded and smiled, hoping she would report that he had known all along and was just testing the system.

"Any chance you could find the file on Gertrude Lakatos? Or the Lakatos family? They were from Slovakia," Attila asked.

This time the assistant didn't feel she needed to check with anyone. "There is no such file, Dr. Fehér," she said.

"But you didn't look," Attila said.

"I don't have to. There was a request for that file earlier today and we didn't have it then, so we do not have it now."

"Who requested it?"

"Sorry, we can't divulge that information," she said, not sounding particularly sorry.

Back outside, in the courtyard, Attila finally checked his phone. There were ten increasingly furious messages from Tóth, the last one, barely coherent, about a dead body at the Gellért.

"What the fuck?" was Tóth's opening line when Attila called.

Attila said nothing.

"A man was found in a chair near the elevator, and he has been sitting there for at least two hours," Tóth shouted.

"Dead," Attila added.

"Why the fuck do you think I called you? If he was resting after a long night —"

"How?"

"Knife in the neck."

"Professional job?"

"How the fuck would I know that?" Tóth spluttered. "You haven't seen the son-of-a-whore —"

"Anyone we know?"

"Maybe one of your friends. His face was battered a while back, nose broken, but not today. I don't know him."

"What floor?

"The third. Where that fucking woman's room was. The one you haven't been able to keep track of. Right?"

"Any ID on him?"

"None. A hundred euros. Two hundred forints and change. Car keys."

"You found the car?"

"Son-of-a-whore parked right in front of the Gellért. They had the car towed."

"I guess he didn't expect to stay long," Attila said. "Registration?"

"Car was stolen last night. The owners were having dinner in that fancy place near Hösök Square. Guy reported the car missing at ten forty-five last night."

"The Gündel?"

"Yes. Never been there. Can't afford it on my salary," Tóth said.

What about the bit you take on the side? Attila thought. "They have parking attendants," he said. "Why didn't he use them?"

"How the fuck should I know?" Tóth yelled.

"The coroner has the body?"

"He is here."

"Anything unusual about it?"

"He's had some teeth replaced with gold," Tóth said. "Does that tell you anything?"

"Russian," Attila suggested. "Or Albanian? Maybe Ukrainian?"

"Not Ukrainian," Tóth said.

"Oh?"

"Get your ass over here."

"There is always a chance he is Bulgarian. Or a Turk." Attila hung up before Tóth became seriously unhinged.

He called the Gellért's front desk and was informed that Ms. Marsh had checked out.

He sat in his car for a while, thinking about the strands tying these people together and Helena Marsh's interest in Old Master painters.

He googled her name and got several hits from sites in the USA and UK but nothing from Hungary. She was born in Vienna, went to university in Montreal, studied art history. She later trained in art restoration at Montreal's Musée des Beaux Arts and at Christie's in London. She had been awarded research grants by the Social Science Research Council of Canada and the Ministry of Culture, Monuments, and Fine Arts Office of Venice. She had worked as a restorer at the Galleria dell'Accademia in Venice, and there were colour photos of a few paintings her team had restored, both before and after, including several of the Giotto frescoes in the Scrovegni Chapel, some of the frescoes in the Church of San Salvador, a niche in the twelfth-century church I Gesuiti, and one of Titian's Gonzaga portraits. She had curated a 1998 Titian retrospective at the Alte Pinakothek in Vienna. Her biography also listed twenty articles she had written about various artists, including Titian, Raphael, and Giorgione. She had worked for the Commission for Looted Art in Europe, had been consulted on the identification of paintings taken by Goering for his personal collection, and had spent 1994 at the Hermitage in St. Petersburg, authenticating its collections of Titian and Raphael. She had been a speaker at several conferences on the restitution of Holocaust-era artworks. She had been called as a witness in the case of *Laurent v. the New Gallery* in Vienna for the recovery of two paintings by Egon Schiele.

Kis was right. The woman was well-known in the business. She had a ton of credentials. What Attila couldn't figure was why a bunch of Ukrainians would be so eager to have her leave the country that they were happy to pay Tóth the kind of bribe the Hungarian police demanded for such services.

Helena checked in to the Tulip Hotel as Marianne Lewis at 2 p.m. She left her Marianne Lewis passport with the manager, telling her she was going shopping for those "wonderful Hungarian sausages and zsemle" they sold at the Great Market Hall. She didn't go there, but bought a canary-yellow dress at Pixie on Váci Street, the dress shop recommended by the manager. When she reclaimed the passport, she asked for a wake-up call at 4 p.m., explaining that she needed to sleep off the long flight from New York via Munich. To make sure the manager would remember her, Helena pulled the yellow dress out of its package and held it in front of herself. "My first Hungarian purchase," she said in her best imitation of a New York accent.

The manager remarked that Marianne ("If I may call you that? Americans all use first names only, don't they?") showed no signs of fatigue. The manager, an overly made-up woman with hennaed hair, said that she too was exhausted and needed a long rest. She hoped to have a long-overdue holiday in Chicago, where her brother was in the building trade. She seemed disappointed that Marianne didn't know him.

In her room, Helena took off the Marianne Lewis wig, changed into her black outfit, and put on the makeup but not the blond wig she'd worn earlier. By now, staff at the Gellért would have found the dead man, and whoever had hired him would know more about her than was good for her health. If the police were looking for her, they would be watching for a blonde. The sooner she could get her hands on the painting and take it out of the country, the better.

She slipped out of the hotel while the manager was chatting with another guest and headed for the Kis gallery a short distance away. She stopped for a quick espresso at the Anna Café and watched the street for a couple of minutes in case that policeman came by to ask Kis about her. It was only a few steps from the Anna to Kis's. She pressed the bell, was buzzed in, and entered to the pleasant accompaniment of a tinkly bell.

"You have an appointment?" asked the small man sitting behind the large mahogany desk. At least that was what Marianne thought he had said. She spoke only a few words of Hungarian, so she was just guessing.

"I have an appointment," she said in English, "with Mr. Kis."

"Mr. Kis," said the little man in reasonable English, "is tied up at the moment, but perhaps I could make you an appointment for another time. May I ask what this is concerning?"

"Tell him it's Ms. Marsh."

When the man hesitated, she sat on the edge of his desk, picked up his white phone, and offered it to him. "Now."

He seemed more surprised than offended. He backed up as far as his chair allowed and glared at her, but then he took the phone and rang upstairs.

"You may wait here," he said, indicating a round-backed armchair. Instead of sitting down, she wandered about the gallery, glancing at the paintings without really looking at them. They were not worth a second look.

Kis came in, his hand outstretched, blue jacket buttoned, glasses perched over his teased hair, cravat and smile in place. He stopped a few steps into the room. "What . . . ?"

Helena said she didn't have much time, so they could dispense with the niceties. "The merchandise is acceptable," she told him.

"You . . . ?" Kis said, his hand had dropped to his side and the smile had turned into something much less friendly but still uncertain. "And you are?"

"Marsh. Helena Marsh."

"You look different today." He was looking at her closely. "Your hair . . ."

"I had it cut, Mr. Kis. And I don't have time to chat with you now. We need to make the exchange. The funds have been transferred to me. All we need to do now is for you to hand over the item and I will release the money."

"I am not sure that can be done in a day," he said, looking at her even more closely. "There are some formalities."

"Exactly as we agreed," she said. "No formalities. I will take the item and transfer it as and when I determine. Not your problem."

"I don't think you understand," Kis was regaining his composure. "There are complications."

"Not my concern," she said flatly.

"I disagree. It is your concern. Or your client's concern, assuming that you are authorized to make the purchase." Kis pursed his lips.

Helena told him to phone Géza Márton in Toronto. Kis waved his assistant out of the gallery.

It was about midnight in Toronto, but Kis called anyway. People buying Titians were not fussy about time. He described the new Helena — none too flatteringly — and told Márton he didn't trust her with the merchandise. He listened for a few moments then hung up.

"Don't you want to see it at least?" he asked.

"I have seen it," she said.

"Dr. Krestin has made arrangements. We could go to the house tonight, if you like."

"I just told you, I have seen it," she said. "I will take delivery at 2 p.m. tomorrow in front of the Café Ruszwurm up in the old town. Take it out of the frame and wrap it in oilcloth. I will have a van."

"That is not possible," he said. "A painting like that cannot be taken out of its frame. It could be damaged. No one who understands paintings of such value would even suggest —"

"It is not the original frame," she said. "It's a good imitation, but it's not the real thing."

"I am not responsible for the frame," he said. "But no serious collector would want the canvas removed." He sighed in obvious frustration. "It is simply impossible."

She stepped closer to him. "And why would that be?"

"There are, as I said before, complications." He was gazing at the door down to the street.

She was now so close to Kis, she could smell his acrid red-wine breath. He must have enjoyed a fine lunch today. He backed up, but she again stepped into his personal space. "As a rule," she said, "I do not believe in complications."

"There is another party interested in the painting," he said at last.

"Mr. Kis, in the world we inhabit, our word is our bond."

"I don't think you understand," he suggested. "Another bidder . . ."

Vladimir. She knew this territory well.

"It's not what you think," he said. "I had nothing to do with it. It's Dr. Krestin. He has told people he has a painting he wants to sell. For the right price."

"And that is not the price you quoted me?"

"Not exactly." Kis's forehead was shining with sweat.

"It wasn't my idea," he said. "But now there are other offers, and Géza Márton's is no longer enough. We have been offered more."

She was tempted to grab Kis by the lapels and push him through the window, but she didn't want to attract more police attention. She needed to meet János Krestin. "How much more?"

"Twenty-five million," Kis said.

With a great effort of will, Helena smiled.

 On his way to the Gellért Hotel, Attila stopped by the swish Danube embankment apartment his friend Tibor Szelley shared with his mother and two cats that were possibly even older than his mother. Tibor and Attila had gone to the same school on Ráday Street, close to the old National Theatre. It had been demolished in 1964 to make room for the new theatre building. Both boys had been repeatedly singled out for detentions and unpleasant letters home about fighting in the corridors. But Tibor was fortunate to have a grandfather who had been a bus conductor, while Attila's had inherited the signet ring of his modestly noble ancestors. His grandfather's pre-war occupation as small factory owner counted against him, despite the fact that the

factory turned out fine boots for the army. Once the factory was taken over by the state and a new manager with impeccable Party credentials was installed, the quality of boots plummeted, the factory closed, and everyone had to find a new job. In the people's republics, a person could not be unemployed. Attila's grandfather found work as a wrangler on a sheep farm. He was not particularly good at it, but no one else was either, since the real wranglers had been relocated to the factories.

Attila's father had found a job in a leather-goods factory as a machinist. He thought he knew a bit about leather-cutting machinery, but being the son of the owner hadn't taught him anything. The machine mangled two of his fingers. After that, all he could get was assembly-line work at the Csepel car factory.

Tibor's father had become a Party member with a modicum of power over his own and his son's lives. After Tibor was admitted to Eötvös Loránd University, his father used his influence in Party circles to ensure Attila a place at the police academy. Attila considered writing Tibor's essays for him to be a small price to pay for the privilege. After Attila graduated, he joined the Metropolitan Police at its thirteenth district location.

Tibor had retired a couple of years ago on his state pension, supplemented by his bank pension and some odds and ends he had collected while nominally serving the public. The apartment had been Tibor's for some years. Even in the 1990s, when the pendulum was supposed to swing in the direction of those who had nothing, there was never any question that he would surrender it (or his state pension). Without the slightest difficulty, he had made the smooth transition from government apparatchik to senior management of a new bank. Capitalism favoured those with a facility in English and the ability to appear unperturbed by a profusion of numbers.

When Tibor opened the front door, both cats wound around Attila's legs, their tails held high. They recognized his smell.

Tibor looked at his Rolex and said it was not yet Friday — the day they usually met for Scotch and chess in the Király Baths — but Attila was more than welcome to share the fine Scotch in the apartment. Tibor was wearing a casually expensive cashmere sweater and soft woollen pants. Obviously, he was enjoying his days away from the formalities of banking.

"I can't stay, Tibor," Attila said. "I am on my way to a murder investigation, and Tóth's in charge."

Tibor's face fell. "Tóth."

"I need to find out about a guy you may have known back in the day. Name of Krestin."

"János?"

"Yes. He was in one of the ministries, I think. I haven't had time to check, but I remember he used to be in the papers, making announcements."

"He was in Justice," Tibor said. He lit a scented Turkish cigarette and tilted his head back as he inhaled. His mother didn't like him to smoke in the apartment, but it was permitted on the landing. "Why are you interested in him? Surely, he didn't kill anyone. Personally, I mean."

"What do you mean, personally?"

"It's not that he is not capable of killing someone, but he wouldn't do it himself."

"He was made a judge after '56," Attila said.

"Not quite that. He never had the education to be a judge. Having the right connections was not enough for the law, not even back then. But he worked for one of the judges. State Security. An officer in the security forces. He was decorated for resisting the revolutionaries when they attacked a jail outside

Budapest. Hero of the Socialist Republic. Then he worked at Party headquarters. He helped identify some of the rebels in Köztársaság Square and send them to be executed. He was an adviser to the justice ministry at some of the trials, a witness at a few others. He was promoted to security supervisor when they obtained confessions before the trials, so everything could go off without a hitch. But personal violence, I don't think so."

"How did he identify anyone in the Köztársaság Square attack if he was resisting the revolutionaries at a jail somewhere else? And where was that?"

"In Hatvan. But back then, Attila, we paid scant attention to such details. A man like Krestin could say he saw something and no one would challenge him. Who knows, perhaps they showed him photos. There were photographers on the scene when the Party building was emptied. Even someone from *LIFE* magazine. As for those trials, guilt was a foregone conclusion."

"What happened to him after the Wall fell?"

"He did well."

"How well?"

"He spoke four languages, including English and Russian. Knowing Russian didn't seem that useful in the early '90s, but we were so wrong about that! God knows, somebody had to negotiate with the Russians. Krestin was the perfect person for the job. We may not like them, but we do like their gas. Both the Socialists and the dictator's guys used him."

"Then he bought the Lipótváros football team."

Tibor nodded.

"With what funds?"

"An American movie-mogul's and his own money," Tibor said.

"Name of?"

"Tihanyi. You can look him up. Makes mindless trash but he's always had government backing, some outside investors, and TV sales."

"Bribes?"

"I wouldn't know," Tibor said. "And don't want to know."

"So how did Krestin get to be an art collector?"

Tibor rubbed his thumb against two fingers. "Too much money — and vanity. He used to display his stuff at cocktail parties he threw, although he wasn't much of a drinker and, as far as I know, he wasn't much of a connoisseur, either. He always had single malts and French Champagne on offer. There were some Impressionists on the walls and, I think, even a Raphael. He thought art made him look intellectual. Plus, it may have been a smart investment. Art was easy and cheap to buy here in the '50s and '60s. Nobody had anything after the war and even less after the state nationalized businesses, so people were selling their valuables. You can't eat sculptures. Or paintings."

"Did you ever see a painting by an Italian called Titian?"

"There was one in Krestin's living room, but I assumed it was just a copy."

"What does he do now?"

"Not much. As far as I know, he travels a lot, playing golf in Ireland, Scotland, and Bermuda. He complains about the quality of golf in Hungary. He also enjoys going to concerts and operas. He's listed as a patron of the National Opera. Also the National Theatre. Come to think of it, I haven't seen him recently. There were rumours that he had a few financial problems. He sold the football team. But there was a time I was on his invitation list. His wife was a charming hostess."

"Didn't anybody sue him for something? Like giving false evidence. Or taking part in interrogations."

"When we let all the security guys go in '89, tons of files were destroyed. Later, no one had access to the remaining files while we squabbled over who should have access and why. Now we have access, but I don't think anyone cares anymore."

Attila was aware that the government had instituted complicated rules that allowed the immediate family and a few privileged academics access to each person's file. Even then, access could be denied if the minister deemed it detrimental to the national interest.

"Didn't anyone who got out of jail in the amnesty go after Krestin?"

Tibor seemed amused. "Too long ago. Haven't you noticed?" He grinned, showing his still neat rows of state-straightened teeth. Attila had already lost a few of his. "You know, Attila, I believe we should let sleeping cats lie."

"And think of the future, not worry about the past, as our former PM, the Commie, used to say. I still couldn't get Krestin's file at the Historical Archives."

"I will talk to Mrs. Lévay, if you like."

"Thanks, but I think I have that covered."

"Ah, the redoubtable Magda. Many have tried and many have failed. She must like you."

"Not enough to let me see Krestin's file."

"Sure you don't want to come in? Mother would be pleased to open a new bottle of J&B."

"Next time, for sure. Tóth's waiting."

"You need a new employer."

Attila thanked him and continued on to the Gellért on

foot. It was hard to find parking spots in the city, so he was not going to risk losing the one he had just to save himself a fifteen-minute walk along the river.

He counted seven police cars at the entrance of the hotel and two more up the side street near the baths. The meat wagon was right in front where the guests would normally be coming and going, but weren't, Attila presumed, because the police had barred everyone from entering or leaving the hotel. That accounted for the agitated desk manager and two guys in black suits and striped ties who were outside talking to a senior officer in hushed but anxious tones. Near them was a man he recognized, Dr. Bayer, the chief medical examiner.

Attila slapped him on the back and asked how he'd been since they last met, at a murder site in the Belváros district.

"Can't complain," Bayer said. He stood aside while the scene of crime guys in white coveralls brought out the body and began to slide it into the wagon. "Anyone you know?" he asked as he unzipped the plastic body bag from over the man's face. The dead man's jaw had dropped to reveal a blue tongue and his upper teeth. He wore a thin gold chain around his neck; a small gold cross lay tangled in his curly brown chest hair.

"I don't think so," Attila said. "How many gold teeth?"

"Two gold incisors plus a couple of back molars with diamond inserts. Or cut glass. I'll tell you more after the autopsy. Some scarring on his forehead, knuckles, and side of his jaw. Broken nose. He's been hit before, and he did some hitting of his own. I'll know once I take a good look at him."

"What killed him?"

"Looks like a stab to the neck. Whoever did it knew exactly where to stick the knife, a long thin blade of some sort, sharpened on both edges. Could be a German-made switchblade. It penetrated the muscle and sliced the nerve and the artery. A centimetre to the left or the right, our guy would still be alive." He hesitated for a moment, then he asked the obvious: "Not exactly your case, though?"

"Tóth's."

"You're the hired help?"

"Something like that," Attila said.

"There was a small Glock in his belt, maybe his own prints on the handle. We'll scope his fingers. It looks like whoever killed him was a professional. They haven't left us much to work with."

Bayer zipped up the body bag and told the waiting attendants they could load the corpse into the wagon. Then he nodded at Attila and made his way to his car.

A couple of minutes later, Tóth appeared, his shoulders up, face grim, his sunglasses perched on his shaved head. When the hell had he shaved his head? Attila wondered. And why? It made his neck seem thicker and his ears pendulous. The wife wouldn't have let him, so that's why he had taken her photo off what used to be Attila's desk. She must have left him. Smart woman.

"Good of you to show up," Tóth shouted. Attila thought wearily that Tóth was always shouting these days.

"I was following the woman you hired me to follow. She checked out of the hotel."

"What can you tell me that I don't already know?"

"She is still in the country," Attila said without conviction. He assumed that Helena Marsh wouldn't leave until she got what she came for, and Kis seemed to think she hadn't succeeded yet.

"Why? Why is she still here?" Tóth demanded. "She could

have left right after she murdered this man, and she would be someone else's problem. But no, she stays to admire your incompetence."

"Why do you think she is the one who did it? She is an art expert, not a professional killer. Plus she is a small woman, can't weigh more than fifty kilos, and this guy is a beefy hundred with beat-up hands. He'd know how to defend himself from a small art expert."

"He was found dead on the floor where her room is. There is a bullet hole in the wall across from her door, and she has vanished."

"Do you know what kind of gun fired the bullet?"

"Not yet, but our guys are analyzing it."

"Could it have been his own Glock?"

Tóth didn't deem that worth a comment. Attila knew that Tóth didn't like that Dr. Bayer had been talking to him, but there wasn't much he could do about it.

"What do we know about the dead man?" Attila asked.

"You tell me, since you are so bloody smart."

"He is probably Bulgarian," Attila said. "Old enough to have caused some damage already. When you check his car for prints, I bet they will match someone you have in the system. Meanwhile, you'll find his mug shot on the Interpol server in your office, the one that the Brits and the French share. Not a star, just a regular grunt. Piecework, but profitable piecework, so there will be others looking for him."

"Profitable?"

"Those teeth must have cost a bundle."

"Bulgarian?"

Attila nodded. He didn't mention that diamonds in the teeth were a Bulgarian fad, although some Croats had also started using them. The newish president of Bulgaria, a former bodyguard, had diamonds in his teeth, although few people had seen them and lived to tell the tale.

"And the woman? Does she have a record somewhere?" Attila asked.

"For killing people? It's not her specialty," Tóth said as he steered Attila away from the other police and across the driveway. "Which is not to say she doesn't."

"Kill people?" Attila asked, still incredulous. He was thinking of the slim blonde swinging past him on the Szabadság Bridge, her small handbag, her white cardigan, her long legs.

"So far, she has never been convicted," Tóth said. "No proof. She is very, very clever, they say."

"Who says?" Attila asked.

"My sources."

"Please don't tell me you're talking with the Ukrainians again."

"None of your damned business, Fehér," Tóth said, but this time he hadn't raised his voice. The Ukrainians might be his secret, Attila surmised, not shared with his colleagues.

"I had a talk with your friend Kis," Attila said. "Charming. Honest as the day is short. He says Marsh is working for a couple in Canada. They want her to bring back a painting. But you knew that already, didn't you?"

Tóth was looking at the bridgehead. He scratched his bald head and said nothing.

"It would have saved me some time if you had told me," Attila said. "Does this guy Márton she works for have a claim on the painting that she went to see at Comrade Krestin's house? Does anyone else have a claim?"

"Krestin's the only person who has proof he bought it. He

has all the papers and, before you ask, yes, they do check out. The Ukrainian just wants to buy it. Fair and square. He likes it, and he can afford to buy it. That's all I know," Tóth said.

"Not quite. You haven't explained why they want her out of the country so badly that you hired me. It would make my job much easier if I knew all the details. Just ordinary police work, rather than chasing my tail in the dark."

"You have no idea what you're dealing with here, Fehér." Tóth had started to raise his voice again. "And if you don't want the job, say so, now! There are other guys who'd salivate at the chance to work for me. You're not the only fish in the fish market." No one used that old saying much anymore, so Attila was fairly sure Tóth was reverting to childhood in his anxiety. But why? What was he scared of?

"I'll try to find her," Attila said and walked away. He was still thinking about the fish when he rescued his car from an eager parking-ticket guy who had already called to have it towed for overstaying its welcome at the meter near Tibor's apartment. Sometimes he found it useful to flash his expired police ID. Street cops wouldn't think of checking the dates. This was one of those times, and, for emphasis, he added that there had been a murder up at the Gellért, and this was the closest he could park.

He drove to the underground lot near the Great Market Hall, picked up an expensive salami sandwich, and ate it as he walked along Váci Street to the Kis gallery. Salami was not what he yearned for but, since they had no soft cheese pastries, it would keep him breathing for the time being.

Kis was in the gallery, extolling the virtues of a small brown-and-beige painting to an expensively dressed woman. (American, was Attila's guess.) He spoke appallingly accented English that had to be an affectation. A man who deals with foreigners all the time might think it was charming. Or disarming. Perhaps both.

"Excuse me for interrupting," Attila said to the woman, then turned to Kis and went on in Hungarian. "You should know that we now have a murder connected with this business. My guess is the Ukrainians had something to do with it, although it could be one of the other guys you have been making nice with. Could we go to your office now?"

Kis whispered his apologies to the client and handed her

over to the assistant hovering by his side. "Mr. Fontos will be able to tell you more about the artist," he said. "His work is already in the Neue Pinakothek. I'll be back in a minute."

Attila wondered how the diminutive assistant managed to get a name that meant "important," but he didn't ask. The painting Kis had left him to sell reminded him of Gustav's protest leavings on the carpet, a ploy he used only when Attila stayed away overnight.

Once in the gallery's inner sanctum, he told Kis that a body had been found in the Gellért on the floor where Ms. Marsh had been staying before she checked out, in a bit of a hurry, it seemed, as she had paid for two more days in advance.

"Has she come by to see you in the past six hours?" he asked. Kis stared at Attila.

"To ask about the painting," Attila added helpfully.

Perhaps Kis was not used to the rough stuff, although if he was in the antiques trade and if he sold Old Masters, he must have been concerned about his clients and their ability to hire muscle when needed. Not many regular guys could afford to pay millions for pretty, old things to hang on their walls. And if that weren't bad enough, the government took a dim view of exporting art. Kis would have to grease more than one greedy palm.

"She is eager to conclude the deal," Kis said finally. He took out his white handkerchief and wiped his hands.

"And . . ." Attila prompted.

"I told her the Mártons would have to match another offer now. It's not my doing, you understand, officer, it's Dr. Krestin. He wants more money, and he knows — we both know — that he can get it."

"From?"

Kis shook his head. "I am not at liberty to divulge that information. I am merely the agent. It is not my property, and I don't determine the price. My client does. And Dr. Krestin has decided he can get a better offer from someone other than the Mártons."

"This other offer, was it a Ukrainian gentleman?"

Kis shook his head. "As I told you the last time, I have not dealt directly with any Ukrainians. Yet."

Attila knew the man was lying. He had been a policeman long enough to recognize the fixed, direct stare, lips closed tight in a stiff smile, and why he'd positioned his coffee cup in the dead centre of the desk like a barrier between them.

Attila wondered who would hire a Bulgarian thug. "Perhaps the other person is from Turkey?"

Kis shook his head. "Not Turkey."

"Russia." Attila moved his not inconsiderable body closer to Kis and flexed his shoulders to seem threatening.

"I don't think you understand," Kis said. "There are several bidders. It's how this business works. When you have something valuable, you want to get the best price, and Dr. Krestin is not a fool." He rolled his chair back, putting a few more inches between himself and Attila.

"How valuable?" Attila asked.

"Well, that depends on how much someone is willing to pay, officer," Kis relaxed into dealer talk. "For a Titian, these days, you would be looking at more than eighty million dollars. And this is a large Titian. They don't come on the market very often. The last time I remember, it was the Hermitage off-loading a piece Catherine the Great had bought in 1779, from Robert Walpole's grandson, the profligate George. The new curator at the Hermitage thought it might not even be a Titian, but it fetched fifty million anyway."

"Titian," Attila said. He had only seen his paintings in books. Eighty million seemed like a hell of a lot for a piece of old art, but if that's what it was worth, he could see why it could be a reason for killing someone. What kind of money would a person need to have if they could spend that much for something to hang on a wall? Hiring a guy like the dead man in the Gellért would be chump change.

All that money could be reason enough for Tóth's desire to clear the field of bidders, so his preferred candidate — the Ukrainian, of course — would have an easier time buying the painting. Helena Marsh was an expert on Titian. What would Tóth's take be if Attila managed to persuade the woman to leave now?

"How much do you think?" Attila asked to keep Kis going. He figured the temptation to show off would overwhelm whatever reluctance the man had to share what he knew.

"This one was done in Titian's studio," Kis said, his tone sliding into his comfort zone. "He may have had help from one or more of his students. A lot of Titians are not a hundred per cent Titian. But they are executed to his design, his choice of colours, even when the colours were mixed by the students. He would have painted all the major figures. He used to have five or six canvases on the go at the same time. He may have done a bit of each painting here and there and left the grunt work — filling in the sky or the earth tones — to his assistants."

"Is it signed?" Attila asked, although, of course, he had no idea whether Old Masters bothered to sign their paintings. The two prints he had bought after the ex removed the watercolours were both signed and numbered. The vendor at the Budapest Art Show had assured him they were more valuable when they were signed and numbered. "The one Krestin is selling? Is it done, for sure, by Titian himself?"

"Yes, yes," Kis said. "And now, I must see to my client."

"You are expecting to see Ms. Marsh again, then," Attila said.

"Only if the Mártons want to pay what the painting is worth."

"Otherwise, you will sell it to a Russian," Attila prodded. "Or to the Ukrainian."

"As it happens, there are interested parties in all parts of the world. In Norway, in Italy, and the United States, of course. It's not up to me," Kis said, buttoning his jacket and making sure his handkerchief was neatly peaked in the breast pocket. "As I said, there are several bidders."

"I suppose there would be no problem taking the painting out of the country," Attila said.

Kis lowered his gaze to Attila's midriff. "Normally, there would be a problem, since this is a work of great value, but my part in the transaction is over once a deal is struck. I am not the vendor. The deal is with Dr. Krestin. The buyer may wish to keep it in Hungary. If he decides to take it elsewhere, he would, of course, need to get the proper paperwork."

"Of course."

When Marianne Lewis left the Tulip at 6 p.m. for a night cruise on the Danube, she was wearing the new yellow dress, high heels, and the white cardigan. ("So becoming, Marianne," the manager offered.) She was carrying a small bag with a few warmer things, she explained, in case it was cool on the river. She took a cab to Szabadság Square, pretended to be interested in the grand building that used to house the Hungarian National Television and, before that, the Stock Exchange. She read the brass plaque on the side of the building twice while checking whether she had been followed. She saw only two American tourists trying to locate the U.S. Embassy, the white colossus on the far side of the square, guarded by several uniformed policemen and a few U.S. marines.

She walked back along Nádor Street to the Four Seasons Hotel Gresham Palace and flashed a smile at the doorman as she entered quickly, pretending to be busy on her cell phone. She sat in the lobby and waited to see if anyone was following. She knew that if you looked like a tourist, it was safe to sit around in a good hotel in a foreign city, as long as it was not in the Middle East.

It was a quiet evening at the Gresham. Light music wafted from the bar. A few people were checking in or out. A half hour later, she went to the ladies' room, where she changed out of the yellow dress into the track pants and a grey sweater, took off the black wig, gelled her hair into soft peaks, and added a bit of eye makeup and lip gloss. In the lobby, a big man in a blue tracksuit, pretending to read the newspaper, was sitting across from the front desk, where he had a good view of everyone coming in or leaving. He looked at her for a moment, returned to his paper, then looked at her again. She wondered whether she had seen him before, whether he was one of Azarov's men.

She sat down in an armchair a bit to his left, where she could observe him, and ordered a café crème. She was polite to the waiter, but not too polite, and friendly but not too friendly to the concièrge when she asked about reservations for the Budapest Dance Theatre, then for a cab. She wanted to leave the general impression she was a guest in the hotel but not so as to draw undue attention to herself.

Using one of her disposable cell phones, she called James at Christie's. Why would they ask her to identify a Corot when he was well past her own era of interest?

"Because it's in Saint-Denis," he said. "Close to where you live. And you had to have studied Corot, even if he was not of great interest."

"I never cared for Corot," she said. "What is it?" Could James have found out about Simon? If so, when? Very few people knew. Who could have told him?

"A Farnese Gardens, and it's a late work, judging from the photograph they sent me. Or he didn't even paint it."

Corot had done at least twenty of those, she thought, and there were always copies floating around. Some of those may even be his own. Most of the Corots Simon had sold were fakes but, as he told her, this had not decreased their resale value. Besides, since they were fakes, they were unlikely to ever appear on the Art Loss Register.

"I'll do it in a couple of days," she said. Christie's paid well and unusually quickly. Her only concern was whether James had decided to use her for this because he knew, or suspected, something.

She asked the driver to take a scenic route along the river and up through the Buda side streets. When she emerged from the taxi at the Budget rental in Óbuda, she was fairly sure no one had followed her. She had learned the evasive techniques from Simon, but back then she thought they were playing a game. It was a couple of years before he told her the truth.

The small grey Fiat was waiting two streets west of the Budget lot, where she had left it when she arrived. She had paid in Vienna for the whole week and had arranged to drop it off at their office in Dunakeszi, a short drive upriver. She applied a bit more lipstick and a touch more gel to her hair, drove the car to the Budget lot, and dropped the car keys into the car-return kiosk's safety box, then she walked to the small railway station nearby. There was no ticket booth here and no lounge. It was just a short stop where the Budapest–Bratislava run took on food and drink.

The conductor stamped her Eurorail Pass and told her that it was good for only another two days. She should maybe purchase a new one.

She smiled at him, nodded, but didn't say anything. She didn't want to be remembered.

At the Slovak border, the Hungarian crew was replaced by a Slovak crew who stamped the ticket again.

She got off at Dunajská Streda.

Knowing little about Dunajská Streda, she had suggested the Roman Catholic church as a rendezvous. If there was one thing you could be sure of in a small town that had belonged to six countries in three decades, it was its people's devotion to religion, and this part of central Europe was Catholic. The church was easy to find by its tall white tower. Heavy black door. It was cool inside, a white cross over the altar, a statue of the Virgin, translucent glass windows, wooden confessional, a couple of vases with flowers. A man was praying in the back pew.

She waited near the white baptismal font until he approached. Tall, lean, and slightly hunched, wearing jeans and a loose black jacket, he was about thirty years old and singularly plain.

"Have you been waiting long?" she asked in English.

"Not long," he said, his voice barely above a whisper. He looked down at his worn brown sandals. Then they stood quietly surveying the transept as if there were something there to see.

When he unbuttoned his jacket, her right forefinger curled around the SwissMini, but she didn't take it out of her pocket. She could pull it out, aim, and fire it in under five seconds, another of Simon's legacies. He was moving slowly, breathing through his open mouth. Since he had been kneeling only a few pews away, it couldn't have been from exertion. More likely, he was nervous. A stale, unwashed smell hit her as he opened his jacket. Under it, his shirt was grimy and frayed around the collar. Lying flat under his right arm and across his belly, there was a loud orange-and-yellow painting: striped hay, round yellow sun, a patch of dark sky.

"My mother wants to sell it," he said.

The woman she had spoken with was Gertrude, Géza Márton's girlfriend from his youth. She had a strong Hungarian accent over a reasonable, old-fashioned French, the kind they had once taught in Catholic schools in central Europe: traditional, strict grammar but not much conversation. Helena had suggested they speak in German, but she wouldn't abandon French.

"She said you would know what it's worth," he said.

"I don't do Impressionists," Helena said.

"We need the money."

"I am sorry."

"My mother said you want to meet her. And we thought . . ."

Buying this poor van Gogh imitation could be the price of a visit with Gertrude. Helena said she would think about it. When he didn't move, she said she knew other people who might want the painting, and that bit of encouragement worked. She wondered what Géza had told them. He'd objected to Helena's insistence that there had to be confirmation that the painting was his and had needed some persuading to make the call, but she noted that he already had the number. He would have had to explain why she was coming all the way to Dunajská Streda, why it was important that she should meet Gertrude. He had said he had never talked with Gertrude about the painting in Budapest.

"I'll show you the way," the young man said and walked stiffly up the aisle to the side door. When he opened it and offered to let her go through first, she declined. She did not like anyone behind her and this man seemed deceptively strong. It was an old habit that had saved her life before.

They walked along a narrow street, then through a square behind the church.

The house was small, but it overlooked the churchyard, pretty this time of year with sour-cherry trees heavy with bloom. "The gravestones are all Hungarian," he told her. "Some of them were knocked over when Fico was in power. He always hated Hungarians." Helena knew that Fico had been the Slovak prime minister for a few years in the 2000s and that he was an ultra-nationalist with an abiding hatred of Hungarians and tearful nostalgia for the time Hitler had granted Slovakia independence under Father Tiso, a Catholic priest with not much holiness and a fondness for fascists.

"My grandmother is in one of those graves," he said. "She died in Budapest, but she wanted to be buried here. It was not easy to make the arrangements. We were both socialist republics by then, but suspicions didn't die with Soviet rule. My grandfather survived for a little while. He missed the fertile earth here. Mother told me he never could settle for the scrub in Eastern Hungary."

"They moved here after the war?"

He nodded. "I think they had no choice."

"And you? Are you Slovak or Hungarian?"

"I was born in Budapest," he said. "I've learned the language here, but not much else."

Gertrude was brewing tea in the tiny kitchen. She wiped her hands on her full gingham skirt and, although she seemed nervous and uncertain, she offered her hand for a friendly shake. "Was the train late?" she asked in French. She must have kept the skirt in a trunk for special occasions. It smelled of lavender and was in pre-war country style.

Helena shook her head. "Mais nous n'avons pas beaucoup de temps," she said, "je suis presque en retard pour le rendez-vous avec votre ami."

"If you mean my former husband, he is not my friend," Gertrude said. "I haven't seen him in twenty-five years, and our relationship has not — how do you say? — remained close."

She was in her mid-eighties, but Helena could see she had once been an attractive woman. She had soft white hair with flecks of brown, brushed to one side and flipped at the ends. Her face was lightly lined under the eyes and around the mouth, which gave her a sad, thoughtful expression, as if she were trying to recall something upsetting. The only signs of age were the skin pouch under her chin and the deep wrinkles around her neck that she had tried to cover by pulling her collar up. She had blue eyes, the same shade as her blue blouse, and a high forehead she had emphasized by pinning her hair back from her face.

She led the way into a small living room that looked onto the churchyard. "Sit here," she said, pointing to a pink chair with warped cushions facing the window. When they were both settled, Gertrude said, "You have come a long way to ask me about someone I hardly know now, and I am not sure I ever really knew."

Her son brought in a pretty floral tea service on a tray and then left. The cups hadn't seen much use — the thin gold bands around their rims were largely undamaged.

Her hands were steady when she poured the tea.

"Géza said you married János in 1957. You left him in 1981.

That's twenty-four years, a long time," Helena said. "You must have known him reasonably well. In 1970, he was in the justice ministry, wasn't he? He must have been quite special to have achieved such a high position. Géza said he was a man with little education."

"Not much formal education, but he read a great deal. He read in Russian and English and French. Hungarian, of course. Russian was easy, we were all taught the basics in school, but he really had to work for the rest. I was his French tutor. That's how I met him. My mother had taught me French. She had gone to a convent school. He learned quickly. He was interested in reading French writers in the original: Victor Hugo, Rabelais, Stendhal, Francois Villon. Did you know that Villon was a big success in Hungary? Translated by György Faludy. János was interested in how much Faludy had changed the poems from the original."

"Faludy?"

"A great Hungarian poet. János was also interested how Faludy came to translate those particular poems. He told me that Faludy was not to be trusted, either as a translator or as someone serving the cause."

"The cause?"

"Socialism. Communism. Whatever. Faludy was, I think, still in jail at the time. János suspected most Hungarians offered lip service to such politics but they were not engaged by the ideas."

"Why did you leave him?"

Gertrude gazed at the low table between them for a few minutes before she answered. "He changed with the times. I didn't. I prefer a simple life. János knew what was going to happen, long before they reburied Imre Nagy with all the pomp and circumstance fitting for a former prime minister. You know he was killed after '56."

"And you came here. Why?"

"Why here? It's safer. János is a powerful man. I wanted to move my son out of his way, so he could be whatever he wanted to be. And my mother is buried over there." She turned to face the churchyard.

"Did he ever talk about Géza Márton?"

"Maybe a couple of times. I was glad Géza had left in '56. It was safer for him to be elsewhere."

"Did he talk about Géza's father's trial?"

"Not to me," Gertrude said. "I told him I had been to Géza's home and met his parents. Géza's father was not in the Party. He didn't believe in it. He was the one who convinced Géza to leave in '56."

"But you knew János helped convict Géza's father?"

Gertrude picked up her cup but put it down quickly. Her hand was shaking. "Not really. I knew he was involved in the trials, but I thought it was just about what he'd seen in front of Party headquarters. János was lucky he wasn't inside that day and lucky no one recognized him where he was. Everybody knew about the killings. The ÁVO men coming out of the building with their hands up, shot all the same, then strung up by their feet and left to hang upside down from the trees. It was in all the papers. Even in America. But whether Géza's father was there, I don't know."

"He wasn't. But that didn't matter. János claimed that he was there, and he was believed. Perhaps there was some unfinished business between János and Géza?"

Gertrude giggled, a bit girlishly, but it suited her face, and her sad expression lightened. "You mean because I had walked out with Géza? I doubt János would have cared, even had he known." Helena liked the old-fashioned expression "walking out," though it didn't really work in French.

"He would have known everything about Géza," Helena said. "There were files. State security collected information on everyone — you know that — and they were particularly interested in anyone who had been in a Soviet labour camp. When did you meet him?"

"A couple of years after he came home," Gertrude said. "He was still emaciated, starved for human contact as much as food. We met on the street near the opera house, where we both lived. He helped me with a bag of coal. I thought he was too weak to carry it, but he insisted. Later, he would sometimes visit and hover in our kitchen while I cooked. He said he wanted to smell the dinner. It's how we became . . ."

"Friends?"

"We were more than friends," Gertrude said quietly, as if her son were still in the room. "But he was still so . . . damaged."

"Did he ever mention anyone he knew in Vorkuta?"

"I don't think so. But he didn't like talking about his time there. He had suffered too much. He wanted a new start in life. How is he now?"

"He's fine. We tend to get over things more easily when we are older, don't you think?"

"Some of us brood," Gertrude said, lightly. "I think he brooded too much. He couldn't forget, no matter how hard he tried. He was never happy to be living in Hungary under the Communists. He didn't say anything, but it was obvious. He must have decided to leave after the Revolution. He didn't tell me. He sent me a postcard later, from Salzburg, saying goodbye and wishing me a long, happy life."

"He waited for you until December, more than a month after the Russians came in."

Gertrude nodded. "He may have thought I would go with him," she said with a shrug. "But I couldn't leave my parents. They were already old in middle age. They'd had a hard life."

"Have you heard from him since then?"

"Not for years. It had been such a long time since I last heard his voice, but I recognized it when he called."

"When?"

"When did he call? A few weeks ago. He wanted to know about János at the end of the war. Whether he had been sent to a Soviet labour camp. Such an odd question. Especially as I didn't meet János until '57."

"Did you know?"

"What?'

"What happened to János in '45."

Gertrude shook her head. "He never talked much about the war. Only about the liberation and the Soviet army handing out food to the kids who emerged from the cellars after the siege. I thought his father had been in the Communist Party before the war. The police picked his father up in '43 or '44 and handed him over to the Germans. János never saw him again. He later got some kind of medal in recognition of his father's bravery. He wore it sometimes — it had a five-pointed star, I remember that. He always marched in the May 1 parades, even after we didn't have to. When barely anyone else went out to celebrate International Workers' Day."

"When was Jenci born?"

"In 1978. And no one marched as enthusiastically as János did, holding baby Jenci in the crook of his arm. He was so little." She smiled. "János took him up to the top of Gellért Hill where the Soviet memorial stood and told him about the liberation, as if Jenci could understand. I think those two statues have been moved."

"To the Communist statues park, in the 1990s."

"I guess we were no longer grateful for being liberated."

"Did János ever mention the Soviet labour camps?"

Gertrude seemed to be thinking. "I am almost sure he didn't. That was a forbidden subject then. No one talked about the *maljenki roboters*. Not even people who had been there. Géza barely mentioned it, although he was there for more than three years. Once, we were walking along the river, and I asked him. We knew enough not to talk about it inside. Our homes were bugged, and there were informers everywhere — people we knew who sold other people's secrets for personal gain."

"And János?"

"He was a ranking officer in the service of the state. He wouldn't have acknowledged they existed except to re-educate enemies of the regime. Fascists. People like Faludy, Rajk. Or to punish spies serving the capitalist conspiracy."

"Do you think it's possible János was in one of the camps himself?"

Gertrude shook her head. "I can't imagine that. He was such a true believer. Why would they have picked him up?"

"The soldiers were not particularly choosy whom they picked up. They didn't question them about their politics. János, like Géza, could have just been in the wrong place."

"But, unlike Géza, János believed all the Soviet propaganda. He was not cynical like Géza was. He didn't complain about lack of freedom. Had he been in a Soviet camp, he would have had doubts."

"Would you have known if he had doubts?" Helena asked.

"I think I would have known, if anyone did."

"But you're not sure . . ."

Gertrude gazed out the window for a moment before she replied. "Can you ever be sure of anything about another person? Why do you ask?"

Helena shrugged. "It's important for Géza."

"Now? Why now?"

Helena was not going to tell Gertrude the whole story, but she had to give her something or she would not help them. "There is something of Géza's that János has and Géza wants it back."

"What is it?"

"It's a big painting of Christ entering Jerusalem," Helena said.

"János has an eye for paintings," Gertrude said. "Even works by foreign artists. Some were religious, although he doesn't believe in religion. There were even a few he liked that the regime would not have found socialist enough. Abstracts. My mother had pictures of Jesus and Mary in our apartment. János said they made him feel uncomfortable. Too much religion, he said. We didn't even have a church wedding."

"But you do remember a large painting of Christ on a donkey with a bunch of people waving and cheering . . ."

"There was one painting of Christ. I didn't much like it. It was too dark."

"Had you ever seen it before?"

"I don't think so."

"Maybe at Géza's?"

"I didn't go to his place."

"And you have no idea when he got it?"

Gertrude shook her head.

"Did he use a dealer to buy his art?"

"I don't think so. But back then, he invited a lot of people to our place. Some of his friends from work, some he had known for many years. One of them may have been a dealer." She stirred more sugar into her cup. The tea must have been cold by then.

"Among János's friends, do you remember anyone they called Bika?"

Gertrude shook her head again. Did she do it too quickly? "But sometimes I would go to my room and he would meet with his friends alone."

"Are you quite sure?"

Gertrude looked down at her lap. "Bika?" she asked.

"Yes. Bull, in Hungarian."

"I don't think so," she said. Helena didn't believe her.

"Did you ever invite your own friends?" Simple curiosity, but Helena couldn't resist.

Gertrude seemed to think about that for a while, as if it were a question that had never occurred to her before. Then she decided not to answer. Instead, she said, "Géza said you were an art expert."

"Yes. It's what I do." Which was part of the truth. "Géza grew up with this painting. It has sentimental value. He wants it back before he dies."

"Has he been ill?"

"No, but he is old."

"Why would he even want such a painting? Has he become Catholic?"

"He has a collection."

"Géza has an art collection?"

"A few pieces. But this particular one has sentimental value."

"You want me to talk to János?"

"I don't think it would help," Helena said.

Gertrude gathered the cups and went to the kitchen. Her son appeared and placed the fake van Gogh on the table. He had stuck it in a brown frame but that didn't improve its appearance.

"Perhaps Géza would like this one, as well," Gertrude said when she came in, "if he has the money to buy art."

"I told your son I would see what I can do," Helena said.

"Please take another look at it. I want to send Jenci back to school. I think he would do well in Canada. He was a good student and he speaks English already." She took a deep breath. "We need the money, you see."

"How much?" Helena asked.

"Could you manage ten thousand euro?"

Not wanting her decision to seem too quick, Helena looked at the painting for a few minutes before she nodded. "We'll have the money transferred to your bank." Géza would surely send the money, and if he refused, she would send it herself.

When his mother went into the bedroom, Jenci took the painting out of the frame, rolled it up, and tied it with a ribbon. Helena told him to keep it until she came back to collect it. She couldn't risk taking it on a train, she said. They might ask to see its papers. They both knew they didn't bother with that sort of stuff now that both Slovakia and Hungary were in the European Union, but he let it go. Their interest was in getting the money, not in selling a painting.

"Have you ever met Géza Márton?" Helena asked him.

"Yes, of course," he said with an uncertain smile.

"Here?"

"Not only here."

"Where else?" Helena asked, but Gertrude came in just then, and Jenci stayed quiet.

Twenty minutes later, Helena was in an almost-new dark-blue Fiat Sport. She had rented it, paying cash, using her Austrian licence for identification in the name of Maria Steinbrunner. The photo was of a woman with black hair cut in a fringe, dark under the eyes, rimless glasses. It was not one of Helena's favourites, nor had Ms. Steinbrunner been.

She called Géza before crossing the border back into Hungary. He wanted to know what Gertrude had said about the Titian, but he was even more interested in how Gertrude was and what she had said about Krestin. Were they still in touch? When she described the painting Gertrude had offered to sell, Géza laughed so hard he dropped the phone — at least that was what Helena assumed from the crash and scramble at Géza's end of the conversation.

"We'll give her the money," he said when he had recovered. "I'll have it transferred in the morning."

Interesting, she thought, he must already have her account information.

It's easy for someone to disappear in a big city, people do, but that someone like Helena Marsh — obviously foreign, in need of a hotel room, or at least a car, or a bus, or a train ticket, or a flight out of the country — could vanish was ridiculously improbable. The police had checked every hotel and exit point. She was nowhere.

Tóth had left Attila a message on his cell phone, reluctantly confirming that the man found dead in the Gellért was, indeed, a Bulgarian national. Attila could tell just how loath Tóth was to tell him this from his bored voice, his sigh, and the lack of information. If he knew the man was Bulgarian, no doubt he also knew his name and maybe his quasi profession. Tóth would have searched the Interpol site for his mug shot, as Attila had recommended, but that would be too much for him to admit.

Attila was nursing an espresso at his usual table in the Gerbeaud and poring over the day's news without the slightest interest. Another demonstration in Kossuth Square, with protestors demanding more say in the affairs of state — completely pointless. People wanting to change some government policies usually find that the government ignores them. Once when the government decided to tax internet use and were taken aback by the hysterical reaction of internet users. That was the last time the government had backed down on anything, but that single occasion encouraged people to imagine there was still democracy in this country, so they protested. There were photographs of an impressive turnout in front of the bust of Miklós Horthy in Szabadság Square. The flattering bronze had been installed by a Reform Church minister nostalgic for the bad old days when it was easy to pass anti-Jewish laws and there was hope that Admiral Horthy would reattach the lost pieces of the country, whatever the price. Well, the price had turned out to be the lives of half a million Hungarian soldiers on the Eastern Front and the murder of about the same number of Hungarian Jews. Perhaps for the cheering people who gathered around the monument, none of that mattered.

At the next table, two German women were reviewing the day's shopping. Attila had mixed feelings about Germans. He resented their air of untrammelled self-confidence, but there was a time when he had appreciated their predictable response to established authority.

When asked by a policeman, they would hand over their passports, car registration papers, even their birth certificates, without so much as a raised eyebrow. Though they would never get their stolen wallets or cars back, they would spend uncomplaining hours at the Rakoczy Street station filling out forms.

In the old days, the cars, parts missing, were usually found, but the "market economy" had provided a market for stolen cars. Thieves had become more sophisticated. They ran smooth operations that included assembly lines for processing vehicles, erasing all signs of their origins, returning them to the streets and the eager arms of their new owners complete with fake registration, licence plates, new colours, changed interiors, no detail too tiny to overlook.

Attila had stumbled into one of these plants in Csepel, near the former automobile factory, once the pride of the Socialist Republic, now owned by Belgians. Unlike the old factory where his father had worked, the thieves' plant was spotless, computer-run. Of course, the files had been erased and the documents vanished along with the criminals. It was impossible to determine the origins or destinations of the stolen cars. Someone had, obviously, warned them. A citation would be added to his own file.

Someone else had received more tangible rewards.

At a nearby table, two little girls in flowery overalls were spooning ice cream from a glass bowl and dribbling it down their pretty clothes. Their father was sitting way back from the table, one raised knee touching the edge, surveying the square. A divorced man with children for the weekend: Attila knew all about it. He booked his weekends with the kids way ahead of time to forestall the ex's refusal to let them go at short notice. She always had other plans for them, and those plans were usually more interesting — and more expensive — than whatever he had in mind. Most of the time they included her new man (a few of them had become slightly used as time went on, but eventually each one outlived his usefulness). She was still an irritatingly beautiful woman with soft curves, well-muscled haunches, and a soft voice that belied her ability to deliver sharp verbal blows to a man's sense of self-worth.

At least that was the marriage counsellor's quick diagnosis after just one meeting with "both parties." Bea had not been interested in a second session. "This marriage," she had said, "is as dead as last week's fish and smells worse."

Their two daughters seemed to have weathered the breakup better than Attila and the dog had. They were busy with friends and considered their parents mostly irrelevant.

He had a date with them for the weekend. Early afternoon pickup, perhaps some swimming or a movie, a sleepover at his apartment (he had to clean up before he picked them up), maybe a day at a beach near Leányfalu. He had found an eddy close to the bank of the Danube, with gentle waves and shallow water that would be safe even for Gustav.

Gustav, attempting to seem both humble and cute, was curled up close to his feet. From time to time he lifted his head and looked at Attila in silent supplication. He loved sugar cubes, but they made him fart. Attila was about to give in and offer him a second one when Alexander arrived.

The undersecretary for government relations at the Russian Embassy, Alexander was a former KGB man, now a ranking member of its proud successor, the FSG — the same organization that had employed sometimes-president, sometimes-prime minister Vladimir Putin. Alexander loved Budapest. He was first stationed here as a Soviet "adviser" during the Party "disturbances" in the 1980s, and he had made the excruciating effort to learn the language.

The Kremlin had become increasingly concerned about

János Kádár's new brand of Communism that allowed for small private enterprise and cozying up to Western Europe. The Central Committee of the Communist Party, particularly Yuri Andropov, rather than the addled Brezhnev, had ordered the surveillance of those close to Kadar. Andropov had been Soviet ambassador to Hungary during the '56 Revolution and he remained suspicious of Hungarians. One leading historian, whom Alexander had read in English, opined that Andropov had a "Hungarian complex." It had been Andropov who had voted to crush the Prague Spring but he never developed an active Czech complex. Alexander had thought Andropov's antagonism had something to do with the language. Czech, as distinct from Hungarian, was discernibly Slavic.

Alexander, who was only two in 1956, had seen film footage of the Hungarian Revolution and thought the rebels looked rather brave against the tanks. He was delighted with his new posting.

Attila had first met Alexander back when he was a young detective learning about the international drug trade. There wasn't much of it in Hungary, but Alexander was sure it would follow the tourists. Alexander had a surprisingly sunny disposition, a weakness for fine wines, and a penchant for pretty Hungarian women. They had developed a bantering friendship over cases of dry Hungarian sausages, bottles of palinka, and discussions of laundered rubles that showed up in Hungary as dollars or, more recently, as euros invested in real estate developments and open-air restaurants.

Today, he wore one of his trademark light wool jackets over a striped brown T-shirt and Hugo Boss chinos that made the most of his slim figure. He favoured soft blue walking shoes without socks in the summer, had a watch that displayed both

Budapest and Moscow time, and absolutely eschewed all other jewellery. He had once told Attila that heavy gold jewellery tended to distinguish Russian organized crime heavies from other citizens of the failed state he served.

"*Szia*," he greeted Attila and flopped into the chair next to his. "Your usual table, too. All the better to hear you," he said, nodding at the statue of Mihály Vörösmarty. Attila knew that Alexander was sure there were cameras hidden in the marble folds of the great poet's outfit, recording everyone's conversation.

"It's a lot easier these days to hack into computer networks than to stick a recorder into a crevice in a statue," Attila said. "The old technology is outdated, unreliable, and it was mostly removed. Haven't you heard of covert channels of radio waves?"

"Sure, but we don't use that for small fry like you and me. And the Americans use it mostly on the Chinese and the Arabs. Complicated stuff called Quantum," he whispered. "And your government? They don't have Quantum. They can't afford it."

Attila sighed. "How was your trip to Moscow?" he asked.

"More or less the usual. Family grumpy, complaining about the lack of opportunities for the grandkids. My mother is old and hates being a burden on everyone. The government is still bowing at the waist every time the Big Boys pass by, and every petty official is eager to take a bit on the side. Did I say 'a bit'? I meant 'a lot.' Thank God for the gas. The price has dropped, but it keeps us rolling." He lit a black gold-tipped cigarette and grinned for the possible cameras. "Good to be back."

"I didn't think they made those anymore," Attila said about the cigarettes.

"Sobranie. Black Russian, only nine milligrams of tar and it's low in nicotine," Alexander said. "And I like the way they look. How is your mother?"

"Much the same. She has acquired another man. She thought the last two had become tiresome."

"How are Sofi and Anna?"

"Fine, I think. But they are more and more like their mother. Into their weird teens. We never had those teen years. Did you?"

"Not allowed in the people's federation. Back then, we did what we were told. Now we have Pussy Riot and twerking."

Attila ordered a Vilmos brandy, his favourite. "I have been working for Tóth," he said.

"That idiot? Why?"

"Nothing much else on offer these days. At least nothing interesting. I think I am too old to start spying on wives and husbands, and it's boring work."

"You shouldn't have retired just as things started to get intriguing."

Attila shrugged. He had told Alexander at the time that he was not attracted to bribes or influence peddling and so they hadn't exactly given him an option. "I was too old to adapt."

"You're not too old; you're too stubborn. I would have taken the money, stashed it in a numbered bank account, and been enjoying the weather in Jamaica."

"I don't think I would like Jamaica," Attila said. "They don't make good coffee there." The waitress had just placed Alexander's espresso in front of him with a smile that suggested she would be free later in the day, if he was. Alexander thanked her effusively, making sure he touched her hand with his fingertips. Nice.

"So," Alexander said, leaning across the table, "what is all this about paintings?"

"Would you be more comfortable in another café?" Attila asked, wondering whether their closeness would put off the waitress before she delivered the torte.

Alexander shrugged. "Makes no difference, they have cameras everywhere, and you should know. You stuck some of them up."

"So did you," Attila said, "and it was not for the drug squad."

"We had a lot to worry about those days . . ." He lit another cigarette.

"This is not a contest."

"Good thing," Alexander said with a happy smile. "I am tired of winning. The paintings?"

"There seems to be a competition to buy a Titian from a casual collector, and one of your guys may be involved."

Alexander cupped his mouth with the hand holding the cigarette. "How big?" he whispered.

"If you mean the man, big enough to be able to buy a painting worth many millions."

"On the level, or under the table?"

"It would have to be illegal because you can't take Titians out of the country, even if you own them. We consider them national treasures."

"Whatever Titian was, he wasn't one of your national treasures," Alexander said. "Wasn't he a Venetian?"

"No matter. If it's here, it's a national treasure. The last time a couple of Titians were sold in Britain, the National Gallery bought them for a hundred million pounds, and the sellers said they were doing the gallery a favour. They could have got more on the open market. Last year, one was sold at Christie's for seventy-nine million US." Attila had done his homework.

Alexander whistled. "That would buy a lot of champagne!"

"This sort of art rarely comes on the market," Attila said, "so people think it's worth a ton. And this is a big painting."

"We have some in St. Petersburg," Alexander said.

"Stolen from the rich guys who had that sort of art before 1917."

"Ah, the glorious revolution . . ."

"Some of them are marked donated by, but shit, everyone knows how eager all those rich men were to donate to Stalin and Lenin."

"If it's *pod stolom*, there will be a big lineup of buyers."

"And some of them will be Russians."

"Most likely," Alexander said. "If you already have everything you need, why not add some priceless paintings to your giant yacht. Makes for a nice backdrop to deal making in Montenegro, or just resting after a hard day of trying to stay out of the Krasnokamens labour camp. It's hard work but worthwhile — I mean trying to keep your nose out of politics and your face out of our president's way. But it's not nearly as hard work as slaving in a uranium mine."

"I was wondering whether one or more of your super rich has landed here in the past week or so."

"At least one," Alexander said, leaning even closer and cupping his chin in his hand.

"Very pretty buffed nails," Attila said.

"He brought his own security, so nothing to do with the embassy."

"Would he employ Bulgarians for security?"

"Bulgarians? Why?"

"Some people like to hire them for security," Attila said. "And we found a dead one at a four-star hotel."

"ID?"

"None."

"So how do you know he is Bulgarian?"

Attila laughed. "It's what you would have said, had you seen him. Does the one wealthy Russian newly in town use Bulgarian muscle?"

"Only if he has to. We really prefer our own. But this one spends a lot of time in the Adriatic, so he may find Bulgarians handy, closer, and cheaper. He has a ton of money, though, so I ask myself, why bother? The answer is that these guys don't like to waste money. They know the value of a good thing, and the Bulgarians are good." Alexander said. He leaned back and took a bite of the torte that the waitress had just brought. "This guy has bought art before to launder his excess cash."

"Drugs?"

"No. Mostly megaprojects. A pipeline across Ukraine. A sports pavilion at Sochi. Megabuildings on the steppes. Some big deal in Bulgaria with the government and a local oligarch. Buying art makes the extra profits harder to track, especially if you keep the art in one of the airport warehouses in a tax-free zone. Freeports, they call them. There are several in Europe: Findel in Luxemburg. Chiasso, Geneva, Zurich — the Swiss were always smarter than the rest of us. Now even London is getting into the act. Uber-warehouses for the uber-rich who dislike paying taxes. And, as you know, our modern czar has his people watch tax returns. He doesn't like wealth flooding out of the country unless he is a direct beneficiary. We use tax laws to punish the over-greedy and anyone with political ambitions." Alexander took another bite. "Or we have them killed."

"What's his name?"

"Piotr Denisovich Grigoriev. Forty-five years old. He has a

twenty-year-old wife and an eighteen-year-old girlfriend. He also races horses. Owns a Gulfsteam IV, a massive yacht on the Black Sea, close to the czar's summer retreat. They get together for vodka and gossip."

"Where is he staying?" Attila asked.

"The Gresham. He usually takes a floor."

"Would he be so upset by someone knocking off his Bulgarian that he would talk to the Hungarian police?"

Alexander shook his head, then leaned in again to speak directly into Attila's ear. "Easy come, easy go. He wouldn't grieve over a lost Bulgarian. He wouldn't talk to the police. But he would talk to me, and maybe I could talk to you if you leave him alone."

It was early evening when Maria Steinbrunner checked into the Gresham. Helena had made a reservation using Maria's Visa and, although she had requested an atrium room with a view of the Széchenyi Chain Bridge and the castle, she settled for a room with a view of Pest. King-sized bed, of course. She didn't have time to wait for the late-departing guests to vacate the room she had paid for in advance.

She was surprised to note that the plastic key she had taken from the dead man at the Gellért was similar to her own new Four Seasons' key card. Given the man's looks and clothes, she would not have classified him as a typical Four Seasons guest. More likely, his room had been paid for by someone staying at this hotel. His had been the kind of side assignment considered easy, but why would the person who had hired him want her dead? And why was he not warned that Helena was expert at self-defence? The poor sap had even smiled when he saw her approach.

She had been running through variations of the scene at the Gellért. Could she have disarmed but not have killed him? Her split-second decisions were not usually so lethal, but as she got older, she found herself less able to make the right choice when she was threatened. She was afraid of becoming like Simon: quick, efficient, and self-absorbed. He had not been interested in other people unless they furthered his own aims. He had been proud of his own exploits and delighted in easy money. An adventurer who lacked empathy.

Her rented Fiat could be returned by one of the doormen in exchange for a handsome tip. The concièrge had already booked her a taxi to the opera house and provided a map showing the nearby restaurants and cafés, although he had pointed out that the hotel's Kollázs restaurant was one of the best in the city and that its café offered one of the best selections of freshly made cakes.

She washed her hair, frizzed it with her fingers and a bit of gel, then pulled on the black pants, the black top, the linen jacket, the silk scarf, and lastly high heels over her bare feet. No need for a wig tonight.

She took the taxi to the opera house.

Vladimir Azarov was waiting at the long curved bar. He was wearing a tuxedo, which was too much even for the Hungarian National Opera, but it did make him look distinguished. He didn't turn when she reached him, he just handed her a fluted glass of Champagne. "I hope you like *La Bohème*," he said. "If not, we could try *Nabucco* tomorrow night."

"Puccini is fine," she said.

"I wondered whether it might be too light for you, but it should make a pleasant change from your difficult day." He grinned over the rim of his glass. .

He was built like a wrestler: tall with broad shoulders and long, muscular thighs and arms. The material of his elegant outfit stretched over his chest and shoulders. He had wide-spaced black eyes, wide cheekbones, thick greying hair, a healthy tan, and a soft Slavic accent under his breathy English.

"I doubt we'll still be here tomorrow night," she said.

He preceded her to the baroque auditorium. "It's impolite, but I know how much you hate anyone at your back," he said over his shoulder.

Even by central European standards, the opera house was excessive with its vast, sweeping staircase, red plush seats and carpets, golden balcony rails, and its massive bronze chandelier hanging from the centre of a huge ceiling fresco of languorous Greek gods. It was the perfect setting for the son of a miner who had made a fortune under the gaze of the recent czar of Ukraine. And a woman who would kill if the situation demanded it.

"We have seats in the third row," Vladimir said, "so you can see the orchestra. Farther forward and you'd have to crane your neck. The conductor tonight is Pinchas Steinberg. I think you'll like him."

She followed him to their seats. "Have you bought any more Renoirs?" she asked when they were seated.

"None were offered, except an early sketch."

As the overture began, she asked him whether he would be willing to let the Krestin painting go if she offered him another Titian.

"I like this one," he said.

"This one may not be genuine. Besides, there is a prior claim."

"I don't think so. I first learned of this painting when I was a little boy. My father heard about it in the mines."

"Vorkuta," she said. "He was one of the guards."

"Is that a question?"

"No. But he must have been at that mine to hear about the painting. Of course, he could have been one of the prisoners, but you are educated, so he must have had a Party position during the '60s and '70s. Not many Ukrainian Gulag prisoners had Party pins, and their sons didn't study at the London School of Economics."

"You always do your homework," he said, chuckling.

"Do you know what the painting is?"

"Yes, it's of Christ entering Jerusalem."

The people in the seats behind theirs shushed them.

During the intermission, Vladimir bought more Champagne and asked what the other painting was.

"*The Last Judgement.* It's in Romania, in Cluj-Napoca," she said. "It was probably commissioned by Mary of Hungary in the early 1540s. Mary had a more educated taste in art than Philip or her brother, the emperor. She was less demanding, less bent on dictating how Titian should paint. Sadly, a lot of his works for her were lost in the great fire. Less of *The Last Judgement* is painted by his assistants than is the case for several works in the Accademia. Much less than Krestin's painting." She made an effort to look thoughtful. "Frankly, I am not sure *Christ's Entry into Jerusalem* is a genuine Titian," she said. "I suspect it was done by one of his followers. Not even his studio."

"Is that the expert speaking, or the competition?" Vladimir asked.

"Could it be both? I have studied the painting, and you know I am an expert."

"Does the one in Cluj have provenance?"

"Since when is that an issue for you? So many of the Augsburg documents were destroyed in the war. But it's clearer than Krestin's painting. It was taken from a Jewish timber trader in '41 by his assistant, who was not Jewish. He killed the trader."

"Is there a family?"

"All killed. Most by the Nazis during the '40s. A son who escaped was executed during one of the Soviet purges."

"Whose son? The thief's or the trader's?"

"Both families were killed. There are no descendants."

"So how did the new owner get his hands on it?"

"I'll tell you in Cluj."

They returned to their seats for the second act.

"There is a Russian who also wants in."

"Isn't there always?" Vladimir said. "Which painting?"

"He doesn't know about *The Last Judgement*."

There were a limited number of Russians who were interested in acquiring fifteenth- and sixteenth-century art; even fewer who could afford it. Helena had checked with her contact at Ferihegy Airport, and only two private jets had landed this week: one from Kiev, the other from Sochi. Budapest was no longer a magnet for the mega-rich. The Russian airplane belonged to a man she already knew: Piotr Denisovich Grigoriev.

"I would like to see it," Vladimir said. "I'm not promising anything, but I'll look at it and then decide which one I want."

"There's nothing to decide," Helena said. "You cannot have *Christ's Entry*, simple as that."

He laughed. "I suppose you are going to stop me."

"That's right, but I will show you the other painting, the one you can have, the day after tomorrow, if you are available."

"Where? And what time?"

"Around nine in the evening. You know the big church, St. Michael's?"

He nodded. "There is a statue of a Hungarian king on horseback in front of it. One of my companies was involved in Mayor Funar's effort to destroy the statue by excavating for an underground shopping mall."

"That's the one," she said.

After the performance, he handed her into a taxi and said he would see her in Cluj.

"Meanwhile," he said, "take care of yourself."

"Strange," Helena said. "That's precisely what Miroslav suggested. And by the way, did you send a thug to make sure I stayed out of your way?"

"Would I do something like that? Really? Would I?" He did not sound offended by the question.

"Of course you would, but I don't think you did, not this time."

Back at the hotel, the receptionist was apologetic but Mr. Grigoriev was not to be disturbed tonight. He had taken the fifth floor, and the Gresham would not allow anyone to enter that floor without Mr. Grigoriev's express permission. The elevator had been reprogrammed to go from the fourth to the sixth floor without stopping.

When Helena tried the stairs, she was met by a decisive

man with a sparse command of English and a bulge under his arm. She apologized profusely.

It was late at night, she was tired, and she was not ready to take on the Russians.

Krestin had chosen the restaurant on Múzeum Boulevard, a bright, crowded place where the food cost the same as at the Gresham but was served with a lot less fuss.

Helena, wearing the short black wig, the yellow dress, the long grey jacket, high heels, and a white silk scarf she had picked up at the Gresham's boutique, was a few minutes early, so she could observe his entrance. She assumed that the local police and the ex-policeman would be looking for a blonde with long hair. So Maria Steinbrunner was safe.

She took the metro to the Astoria stop. In her experience, policemen on duty rarely took the metro.

She knew this part of the city well. The Bauers had lived

near the Dohány Street Synagogue and survived the Germans and the homegrown fascists by hiding in the supposedly Aryan apartment of a school friend of Agata Bauer, who lived near the Károlyi Palota. Luckily for them, the Soviets had arrived just when the food ran out in the Palota's spacious cellars.

The Bauers had hired Helena in early 1990 to recover their two plundered vellum etchings by Rembrandt. As it turned out, the Rembrandts had not been taken by the Germans or the Soviets, but by the Bauers' friendly neighbours, who would visit them for coffee and cakes before the Third Anti-Jewish Law came into effect.

Andras Bauer had not thought of taking the etchings with them when the authorities demanded they leave their apartment in March 1945. "Suddenly our things seemed rather meaningless," he had explained to Helena. They had packed only what they could carry.

Helena had returned their Rembrandts some months before they both died. The etchings were now with their daughter in New York.

Shortly after she was seated, Krestin approached the front door. He was wearing a well-pressed formal grey suit, white shirt, thin blue-and-grey tie. His sparse white hair gave him a high-forehead look, and he appeared younger than his age. He walked strenuously upright — no old-man's shuffle — head held high, looking dead ahead. At the maître d's stand, he squinted when he saw Helena. He needed his glasses. The head waiter led him directly to where she was sitting.

He stood for a moment, straight-backed, powerful, then he leaned over the table and lifted her hand. His lips almost brushed her fingers as he bent over them and said "*Kezi csókolom*," which she knew meant "I kiss your hand," a greeting that had gone out of fashion long ago. Not even the Germans were doing *kuss die hand,* any longer, let alone a former Party member with a history of nastiness. But, as Gertrude had said, János had changed with the times.

"Would you prefer to converse in English?" he asked as the maître d' pushed the brown-and-cream striped chair in under his ass.

"Nous pouvons parler en français, si vous préférez," she said.

He shook his head. "English," he said. "It's good practice for me. I am glad you could make it to our rendezvous. I was concerned that you would still be on the road and had no way to reach me." He spoke with a definite, front-loaded Hungarian accent, but the words were clear.

"It's a long way," she said, uncertain what he meant.

"From Slovakia," he filled in the blank. "Yes, Gertrude called. We are still in touch. Perhaps she told you. I support her and our boy."

Not very well, she thought. "Of course," she said. "Your son."

"Mater semper certa est, as the Romans put it. And, of course, I support both of them." He laughed. "You must already know a lot about Gertrude. Did she mention that she might even have married Géza, once."

"I am interested only in the painting," she said. While that wasn't strictly true, she had come with only one purpose and it didn't include learning about a love triangle. She was as keen to leave Hungary as the would-be killer's employer was to eliminate her. Her only reason for finding out more about Gertrude, Krestin, and Márton was if their relationship explained why. Géza had been quite dismissive about his early "infatuation," as he called it, with Gertrude, yet he, too, still supported her.

"I know." He glanced at his menu and waved to the waiter.

"If I may make a suggestion, madame, the foie gras four ways is a favourite of mine, and the restaurant is rather famous for its duck à la Russe with gnocchi. We could have a glass of Chablis each, or would you prefer red with the foie gras?"

"The Chablis sounds fine," she said, "and I am okay with the duck."

She studied his easy elegance as he gave the order to the waiter, carefully closed his menu, placed it at the side of the table, and patted it. A meticulous man. Orderly. Fastidious, as was his home, especially his study.

"How did Gertrude seem to you?"

"Well," she said. "But then, I've never met her before, so I don't know how she looked in the past."

"She has had a difficult time since she left me."

"I have also met Mr. Kis," she said, sidestepping further discussion of Gertrude. She would come back to it later.

"Oh yes, the talented Dr. Kis. And how did you find him?" he asked as their wine was poured. Krestin's English was exacting, rather like subtitles on a foreign film.

"Greedy . . . and perhaps a little scared."

Krestin laughed and raised his glass to her: "Should we drink to our good health, then, madame? Yours and mine. And maybe poor Gertrude's. Or to a successful deal, if you like?"

"All that," she said, examining the foie gras that had just arrived. "Kis told me the price had gone up by twenty-five million, overnight."

"It is the nature of a negotiation. You make an offer, we make a counter offer. You saw the merchandise. Although I haven't any idea why you chose to break into my house, rather than wait for my invitation. I could have offered you more time for a close inspection. We could have shared a few stories. Had a little wine. But," — he held up his hands to indicate that the opportunity had passed — "you should know it is worth a great deal in today's market. A great deal. The last time a large Titian was sold, the price was one hundred million dollars. Correction: it was a smaller piece. But you know that, too, don't you?"

"It was not one painting, but several, and there was no question about the provenance. There had been twelve prior owners, all named, the first one as early as 1580. The subsequent ones, all listed and accounted for. A clean bill of health, in other words. Not like your painting."

"You have me there," he said with a chuckle. "But what something is worth is dictated by the market, not by a series of owners who may have made their money in very questionable ways. It's the basic principle of capitalism, and the market for this particular piece tells me that your original offer was too low."

The duck arrived, one breast and one leg, crispy and well browned.

"Perhaps Vladimir Azarov is willing to pay more than the Mártons," she said.

"He is not the only one," Krestin said, before biting into his duck leg. He had picked it up with his fork, rather than by the white paper holder the restaurant supplied. This made it difficult to eat without smearing grease on his cheek, but he managed it. "And the painting has been authenticated by an expert."

"Which expert?" she asked.

"An Italian art expert, since you ask. Someone who appraised it for a museum." He waved his hand as if to indicate the appraisal was a matter of small importance. "There are several bidders."

"Géza Márton has a prior claim."

"That's ridiculous. I don't see how he could. I purchased the painting in good faith. I didn't even know he was desperate to have it until Kis mentioned their arrangement when he came to see my paintings. Even now, if you don't mind, we have only your word for that. I purchased it after his fascist father was arrested. And Géza, himself, made no attempt to procure it after he chose to emigrate."

"His father was hardly a fascist."

"In the judgement of the court, he was certainly a fascist and likely a killer as well. It seems your arrangement with his son does not include him telling you everything."

"And Géza didn't exactly choose to leave," Helena said. "He escaped after the Russians invaded in November '56. It would have been very difficult for him to cross the border on foot with a painting that size. Presumably, you know that."

"Actually, madame, I know very little about Géza Márton." He was starting to eat the gnocchi, spearing each one separately. "But I do know about his dalliance with Gertrude, of course," he said between bites. "She told me he had been heartbroken when she advised him it was over. Her decision was, at the time, a smart one. She had no desire to leave the country with him. He was not such a good find. Women like security. Even after he arrived in Canada, he did not do so well. Presumably he has done better since, otherwise he would hardly be bidding on this painting."

"Most people who came back from Siberia didn't do so well," she said. "But you did."

His fork stopped halfway to his mouth. "What makes you think I was in Siberia?" he asked.

"Vorkuta was in Siberia, wasn't it?"

Krestin sat farther back in his chair with an almost perfect expression of astonishment.

"It's where you first met Géza Márton," Helena said.

He shook his head. "You have been woefully misinformed," he said. "Did Márton tell you I was serving the Soviet cause in the Gulag?"

That was a strange way to define slave labour in the Soviet Union, Helena thought, but it might take another year or two before Krestin abandoned all his Communist terminology.

"Is that what you called it?" Helena asked. "Most people picked up by the Soviet army were not keen to serve the Soviet cause, as you so charmingly put it, Dr. Krestin, although perhaps you were one of the few who enjoyed himself there?"

"I was never imprisoned in the Gulag," Krestin said, emphasizing each word. "Do you think I would have been chosen to work with the justice ministry if I had been a fascist?"

"Oddly enough, yes. From what I have learned, you adapt well. And you are smarter than most Communists."

"Whatever it is you are implying, madame, it is unacceptable," he said. "I was not so involved. Check your sources; they are not to be trusted." His English was deteriorating but he was still quite coherent. "I am a businessman. I am respected in my country. I have never been accused of any wrongdoing. I was decorated by my government in 2008. I have the Order of St. Stephen and the Magyar Becsület Rend — the Hungarian Legion of Honour. You must check before you accuse people of —"

"I would have thought serving in Siberia would be a badge of honour in these post-Soviet days," Helena said.

He took a deep breath and stared at her.

"The painting," she said, "may not be a Titian."

"I don't care. I will sell it for the highest offer. I don't care who takes it. I don't care about what you call provenance; it is not my problem. I have the papers to prove that I purchased it here, in Budapest, for good consideration, given the times. And I don't care to discuss past history with you, or anyone else." He called for the waiter and asked for the bill.

"Dr. Krestin, if you did not buy the item from Géza Márton, I have to assume that you bought it from someone else who was in Vorkuta with him."

"Whether I purchased it from Márton or someone else does not matter," Krestin said. "I own the painting, and I intend to sell it. If that's not sufficient for you, I shall sell it to one of the other bidders."

"Do you know a man with the nickname of Bika?"

For a moment, Krestin was taken aback, but he recovered quickly. "You can assume whatever the hell you want, madame," he said, "but just for your information, I most certainly do not. As for Géza Márton, I consider him a traitor. And as for the painting he wants, I am tired of it. I will sell it at the end of the week." He signed the bill and stood. "I wish you good day, madame." He inclined his head in military fashion and walked out of the restaurant.

A gentler soul than Helena Marsh would have felt embarrassed. She ordered a cup of coffee and asked to see the dessert menu.

Helena got up from her table at 3 p.m., just as all the other diners began to trickle back to their offices. The maître d' didn't charge her for the coffee or the chocolate-covered pear and insisted that the accompanying pear brandy was also on the house. With compliments. "Dr. Krestin is one of our best customers," he said in passable English. "Has been for many years."

"Did you know his first wife?" Helena asked.

"Yes. We don't see her much anymore. She has moved away, but they do still come from time to time. Last time they ordered the venison with pear and dumplings, and she wanted Champagne. French, not Hungarian. She looked like she hadn't been eating much."

"The first Mrs. Krestin was a real lady — quiet, soft-spoken, never complained about the food or the service. The second one is a different story. She is barely civil, even to him. Nothing is good enough for some people."

Helena smiled and nodded as if she had known all along and tipped him generously, not so much that it would lead him to wonder, but enough to keep him talking. "Thirty years is a long time," she said, assuming he would know how long the Krestins had been separated.

"More than that, I think. But we have been here even longer, since 1885."

"Some things don't change," she suggested.

"But the people who eat here . . ."

"In 1885, the nobility and the newish middle class," she prompted. "Then two world wars. The Communists."

"They weren't all bad, you know."

"Dr. Krestin, for example," with as ingratiating a smile as she could manage.

"Even with his Party pin, he was a gentleman. Always polite. I can't say that about all our guests in those days, but he never changed. Not here, anyway."

Helena took the tram to the East Station, then walked to the Kerepesi cemetery. It was shady, with towering chestnut trees and giant stone mausoleums, but she had no trouble finding the elaborate tomb of the actress and opera singer Lujza Blaha and the nearby arcade. It was a tall, pillared structure with sad putti and an even sadder peasant, boots pointing inwards, bearded head bending over his zither, and inside the colonnade reclined the actress and opera singer, her hair in pleasing ringlets, plump cheeked face, breasts tastefully uncovered. She had died in 1926, but people still made the effort to place fresh red roses and pink carnations in strategic spots around her, and a bunch of gold chrysanthemums was wedged in at the crack of a putty's dimpled bottom.

Helena waited on the stone bench in the arcade, reading her *Aeneid*. She found mystery within it every time she read it — it was the perfect companion for her during a journey that required patience. Her father always carried a well-thumbed copy of Joyce's *Ulysses*. He'd hoped that by the time he died he would finally understand what the book was about. He didn't, of course. He lacked the patience. When she was small, he used to try being the patient parent. There was a tone he used when he spoke to her, one of infinite care, and he chose short words, suitable for a child. When he took her to galleries, he made her stand in front of each painting he considered important and asked her to tell him what she liked about it. He called them "teaching moments." She was ten when she told him that he no longer had to use just short words. She realized then that he hadn't understood this himself because he hadn't ever really listened to her.

It was not a long wait.

The woman arrived wearing a long black overcoat, although it was too warm for coats. She was carrying a furled purple umbrella, although there were barely any clouds. She walked with some difficulty, dragging her heels along the gravel. Her shoes were dusty and cracked with wear. Géza had said she would be in her eighties and would carry a purple umbrella.

She had been the assistant curator of Italian art at the National Gallery. She had assembled the information for Géza's father shortly before she was fired in 1950 and took it with her to Hódmezövásárhely, where she had been sent for re-education. Presumably, it was a piece of a larger trove of papers that she had taken as a form of insurance should circumstances get worse than banishment to a provincial town.

Géza had been concerned about the woman's safety. It had puzzled Helena at the time but she now understood. Krestin would not want anyone else to have these papers and whoever else was after the painting might even kill for them.

The woman circled several of the bigger graves and looked up and down the wide walkway before she approached Lujza Blaha's mausoleum, rather tentatively, as if she had just happened upon it. Considering that, according to Géza, she was neither an actor nor a trained spy, she was doing an excellent job of impersonating a tourist. She stopped next to the statue of the reclining actress and took a closer look at her face. As she straightened up, she slipped something under the great lady's stone wrist.

Helena watched her turn the corner near the end of the arcade before she stood up. She didn't want to endanger the old woman by showing herself. If someone questioned her about Helena, she could truthfully claim never to have met or even seen her.

The papers were carefully folded in four. Yellow with age, but still flexible enough that they hadn't cracked, they fitted comfortably into the arm of her cardigan. She didn't look at them until she was back in her room at the Gresham. They did not disappoint.

Christ's Entry into Jerusalem was painted between 1554 and

1556 for Philip II, King of Spain. It was first described by Pietro Aretino in an ingratiating letter to Philip, a copy of which was attached. There was further mention of it in one of Titian's own fawning letters to the king, dated 1556. The originals of these letters were in the archive of the Ambrosiana Library in Milan. The painting was inherited by Philip V; acquired by Philippe, the second Duke of Orléans, in 1708; and so on through various European royals to Lord Gower in 1803. He sold it to the Viennese dealer Gregor Sabransky in 1850. Sabransky sold it to Max Meisel, also in Vienna. Károly Márton purchased the painting from Meisel for a mere 50,000 osztrák-magyar korona. There was no history after 1900, no sales, no exhibitions, but Károly Márton was Géza's great-grandfather, a man with considerable wealth and assets throughout the decrepit empire. He also had land holdings in Austria, Croatia, and Romania. He had been involved in banking for the Habsburgs and very likely helped finance the First World War. All this she had already heard from Géza, but the proof, should she need it, was now in her hands.

As far as Géza knew, Károly had not been an art collector. The Titian was the only valuable painting he owned, and he had bequeathed it to his son, Ferenc.

She had to find out how it had ended up in Krestin's possession. In their first conversation, Géza had suggested that the painting had been stolen by the State Security Police under Krestin's direction. That would not have been unusual after the war and in the early 1950s. But why had Géza waited until now to claim it and why was he willing to pay the punishing price Krestin was demanding?

It was unlikely that Krestin was the Bika whom Gábor

Nagy remembered from Vorkuta. If Krestin was telling the truth and had bought the painting, what pressure could this man have exerted on Géza or his father to hand over the family's one valuable possession?

She knew now that Géza had failed to tell her the whole story. He had not mentioned meeting Gábor, who would have been wearing the yellow star, somewhere in Pest before the siege. And she had not wondered, then, about the truth behind Géza's story. There had been something arresting about the man and his memories. He had told her his story while standing at the back of his house, looking out of those big bay windows at his early April garden, just beginning to flow into spring.

The family had survived a hundred days in the cellar, eating dried meat and rotten potatoes. Had Géza's older brother, Ferenc, not been killed, he would have been the one to go in search of food. As it was, Géza had had no choice. He'd had to volunteer. With some feelings of guilt, he had realized that this was the first time that he had actually missed his brother. As he left that day, his mother was blackening her face with soot and letting his father cut off her long light brown hair to make her look like a boy. Before the war, she had brushed her hair every evening, one hundred strokes so it would keep its lustre. Ironic, she had said, that she had worried about becoming too fat on black-market butter and chocolates and now she was as thin as she had been when she married his father twenty-two years ago.

Once outside, Géza had searched for food, anything at all that he could buy. He offered a man his father's family ring for a chunk of bloody meat he was carrying half-hidden in his jacket, but the man scurried off without a word. Someone near their home said that there was a farmer's wagon on the embankment with black bread for sale, but the wagon was long gone by the time Géza found the place. A man there told him that the Irányi Street bakery near Váci Street was open for business.

Near the Buda end of the wrecked Széchenyi Chain Bridge, there was a rowboat already packed with a dozen people on makeshift seats. The man who owned the boat was charging each passenger a thousand pengős for the crossing. They all had to row. The Danube was choppy, and bits of wood, dead pets, furniture, even human bodies bumped against the boat. He remembered seeing a horse's head float by. A few waves slopped over the sides, soaking his shoes and his loden coat — a present for his seventeenth birthday. Géza was worried about how he would make it back to Buda and his parents. With all the bridges gone and only a few rowboats on the river, he knew he had to start back early and take the chance that another boat would take passengers.

It was a day he remembered as clearly as if it had been yesterday. In fact, clearer than yesterday. His whole life changed in that hour, and the four lost years that followed could never be recovered. He remembered the young soldier. He was not much older than Géza. He had light-blue eyes, and thin lines of sweat and dirt were caked over his forehead and down his cheeks. His uniform stank of sweat and tobacco. He had shouted at Géza in Russian, but Géza hadn't understood. He stopped only when he saw the machine gun pointed at his midriff. He offered the soldier his father's watch. It wasn't enough.

She should have known better than to believe the whole story, and under normal circumstances she would have known better. Géza had been a friend of her father's, and she had learned never to trust Simon's friends or to take anything he told her at face value. He rarely told the whole truth, and sometimes not even the opposite of what he said was true. She was in her late teens before she found out how he had made the money to send her to the elite boarding school in Montreal, and why he had been eager to finance her apprenticeships at the Musée des Beaux Arts and, later, at Christie's.

When she checked out of the Gresham, she was wearing the innocuous black pants, the T-shirt, the black wig, rimless glasses, and a shawl that would have suited the real Maria Steinbrunner, had she believed in dressing her age, which she hadn't. One of Ms. Steinbrunner's foibles had been her penchant for frilly pink tops and skin-tight, leopard-print leggings. Unlike her current reincarnation, she had dyed her hair a pinkish blond with red highlights and had paid for expensive breast implants and facial improvements that guaranteed her a good living long after she should have thought of changing professions. Not that it was her profession that had got Maria killed. It was her utter ignorance of the need for discretion that led to her body being deposited in a vat of acid near a Bratislava building site. She had been a vain, chatty woman, but her papers had proved to be useful in a pinch. Her passport photo had been taken when she was still mostly her natural self.

Helena left a personal note with the concièrge for Mr. Grigoriev. She wrote it on the hotel's stationery, in Russian to make sure he understood and could ponder it while she was travelling.

*You may find it interesting to study the works
of Elmyr de Hory while you are visiting Budapest.
While he was famous for his Picasso forgeries, he
was equally successful with his reproductions of
earlier artists, especially Titian.*

Helena Marsh

She took a hotel limousine to Ferenc Liszt airport, making sure the driver noticed her fine hair and her old-world leather gloves when she paid the bill. She smiled at him and tipped fifteen per cent.

There were people who wanted to know her whereabouts, including the Hungarian police and the brawny man who had been tailing her since she arrived. But they would never recognize her as Maria.

 Alexander called at midnight. Attila had been watching an improbable American movie, with Bruce Willis taking on an entire army of nasties with bad accents and worse haircuts and dispatching them one by one and sometimes in groups. It was wonderful. American exceptionalism at its finest.

"I'll meet you at Diablo, and if it's closed, we can go to the ruin bar near the cathedral," Alexander said. "Try to come alone," he added — unnecessarily.

"Alone?" Attila asked but the phone was dead. It was only then he realized Alexander's name had not come up on his screen, just "unknown."

It took Attila less than fifteen minutes on foot to get to the Diablo wine bar. It was not a bar he enjoyed, and he hadn't been there since he was following an American securities trader with shady habits involving local hookers who sometimes ended up dead. It was a low-lit, wood-panelled room with vintage mirrors, bobbing purple lights, plush side-booths, and a long bar. Alexander was lounging in one of the booths, his legs stretched out, one hand cradling his cigarette package. He wore a dark grey jacket that he hadn't removed although it was hot inside.

"Are you carrying?" Attila asked when he slid into the narrow gap left for the seat facing Alexander. Once again he resolved to lose a few pounds. Less sausage, more steam baths.

Alexander waved to the barman, indicating that he wanted a refill as well as a drink for his guest. "I am supposed to carry at least one regulation sidearm at all times," Alexander said. "Didn't you know?" He sounded officious.

"Do you think you are in danger?"

"Not necessarily," Alexander said, "but it's best to be cautious."

"I take it you talked to your oligarch."

"It's not Piotr Denisovich I have to worry about, it's the other guys."

"Other Russians?"

Alexander looked at the ceiling and drank his vodka, bottoms up, Russian style. "Maybe. But he is the one who told me there are some very heavy types looking at the painting. One of them killed his boy yesterday. No idea who, but he thought it was the Italians."

"Italians. Why?"

"Makes sense, really," Alexander said. "Titian was Italian. They want to reclaim his works. Sort of like the Elgin Marbles.

Imagine if the Greeks could sell the marbles now to the Brits or the Americans, whoever pays more. It would solve their whole banking problem. Come to think of it, the Germans could buy it and cancel the Greek national debt. We would trade them for gas. We don't have our own marbles, no ancient temples worth a ton of tourist dollars. Besides," he grinned at Attila, "they'd look exceptionally pretty on a Sochi estate right now, one that has no marble temple to its ruling god."

"So, the Bulgarian was Grigoriev's?" Attila asked, getting back to a subject that interested him more than Putin's private castle. Wherever it was.

"He didn't say anything about a Bulgarian. He told me someone attacked one of his boys, unprovoked. Murdered him. He thought I should look into it. He said your police were also beginning to ask questions, but he really didn't want to get involved with the local police. It wouldn't do for his image. Plus he thinks your guys are utterly incompetent. Always have been."

"I thought we did an okay job while I was there," Attila said defensively.

"Nothing personal, Attila, just stating the obvious. We're in a city where uniformed neo-Nazis march up and down carrying their old flags and scaring the hell out of law-abiding citizens, and your vigilant police seem not to notice. Not even when you were in the force."

"What the fuck could I do when half of the boys belong to the Jobbik — I assume you are referring to their militant wing? Otherwise, they are a legitimate political party."

"Exactly," Alexander said. "They have another little demonstration going on today over by the Danube, near the shoes of the departed Jews, celebrating that old reprobate, Horthy."

Attila decided to change the subject, in case he found

himself agreeing with Alexander. "So what does Grigoriev expect you to do?"

"Make the whole nasty business go away." Alexander lifted his hand again and pointed at the two empty glasses. "*Spasibo*," he said to the waiter. "You've got to be careful," he said to Attila, "there are Russians everywhere, including our waiter. He got stuck here after you sent us all packing in '90. I pay him a little extra now and then."

"Why?"

"He is in the right place to hear useful stuff, and I need to know whose side he's on."

"In the Diablo?"

Alexander shrugged. "Even here."

"So, you expect me to divert attention from your oligarch to some imaginary Italian guys who may or may not even be here. Why would I want to do that?"

Alexander smiled. "You mean what's in it for you? Simple. You want to know about the woman who wants the Titian for her client. Right? Even if you don't want to know about her, you should."

"The woman?" Attila asked cautiously. "Why?"

"Because she has also come for the painting. Same as Piotr Denisovich, same as the Ukrainian. And the agents for the Italian investors. Did you know that buying art is an excellent way to launder money? The Ukrainian has been here for a week now and may be ahead of the game."

"Which Ukrainian?"

"Vladimir Azarov, one of the guys who helped fund the Maidan revolution, almost as much as the Americans and the Europeans. Why anybody would take Ukraine for a European country is a mystery. All you need is one visit to Kiev, better still, Donetsk, and you'd know they are all Asians, just like us. This one is tall, good-looking, not overweight, and he even has hair. Our guy is suffering from early onset hair loss and too much good food. You've seen him in the papers, right?"

"Often. He offered to build another shopping mall in Miskolc and a massive shipyard in Crimea. His yacht is too big for Mediterranean ports. What about the woman?"

Alexander grinned. "The one who was staying at the Gellért?"

Attila waited, arms crossed over his belly where the table was cutting into him just above his belt. He knew his friend would tell him, no matter what. He was fairly bursting with the desire to show, once more, his prowess as an FSB major worth his considerable value in whatever currency he earned it.

"The Gellért where the Bulgarian was found dead?" Alexander continued.

"Did I tell you where he was killed?"

"You didn't have to. Piotr Denisovich did."

"She isn't the killer," Attila said, although he was no longer quite so sure.

"Who knows? They come in all shapes and sizes, and the Helena Marsh I remember did well with mixed martial arts, excelled at target practice, and was a mistress of disguises. Better yet, she is the only one of that effete lot of art experts who worked in the basement of Christie's when women weren't allowed below stairs. She has written monographs about Raphael and Giorgione, and she's published a slim book about Veronese. She is a Titian expert. She identified stolen Italian paintings in the Göring collection, and she knows dead collectors well enough she could tell from whom the fat murdering bastard stole them. She was one of the experts the Americans used to reclaim Jewish art."

"You can find all this through Google, except for the martial arts."

"She is very good with a gun and quick with a knife."

"How do you know that?" Attila asked. "She a former girlfriend? A lover?"

Alexander didn't rise to the bait. "I met her in St. Petersburg," he said. "We brought her to the Hermitage to look at some art we classified as war booty. She is tough."

"But not a killer," Attila repeated.

"I wouldn't bet my life on that." Alexander grinned.

"And what do you mean by 'disguises'?"

"She can take on a dozen different personalities — old, young, frumpy, dazzling, whatever strikes her fancy. I assume from the look on your face, you saw her young and dazzling. It's very convincing. She used that look to kill one of my superior officers in Vienna when he came on too strong."

"Came on?"

"Pushed her a bit on one of her findings. She doesn't like to be challenged."

"She killed him for disagreeing with her about a painting?"

"Not as simple as that, Attila. She'd been hired by a Viennese couple to locate a drawing they claimed had been theirs before the war. My superior officer had concluded it belonged to the Russian state. She suggested she would reveal the story to the authorities. He offered to shoot her. She cut his throat."

"Was she arrested?" Attila was incredulous.

"Arrested? No." He shrugged. "It isn't how we do things now. The Viennese police are still listing it as an unsolved. Much the same as you will classify the Bulgarian."

Attila looked at his watch, hurriedly finished his drink, and told Alexander he had to run. He was picking up the girls early the next day and he needed his sleep.

"Give them my kisses," Alexander said in faultless Hungarian. "And be careful with that woman. She could eat you for breakfast and not even burp."

"What about your Russian? Do I have to be careful with him, too?"

"It's never a good idea to annoy a tiger. Safer to stay far away," Alexander said, ordering one more vodka. "Besides, as I told you, he is my responsibility. If you bother him, he would no longer talk to me."

"What are you telling me to do then? The dead Bulgarian was his man, right?"

"I am telling you to stay away. Stick with the woman and try to find out about the Italians."

Once he was outside the bar, Attila checked his phone. There was a message from Tóth. The dead man was a small-time crook and occasional for-hire bodyguard from Sofia. Name of Ivan Dalchev. Unfortunately, the Bulgarian Embassy was not interested in transporting the body home to Mrs. Dalchev when the autopsy was complete. The deputy minister of foreign affairs had written a formal letter to the ambassador. It was not the policy of the Hungarian government to transport dead nationals of other countries to their homes. If neither the Bulgarian government nor the widow wished to have Dalchev's body, he would be buried in an unmarked grave outside Budapest city limits. That would be cheaper than shipping him home.

The bullet in the wall across from what had been Helena Marsh's room was from a Glock 21. The same gun Dalchev had on him when they found him.

 Helena had always loved Nice. In defiance of the recent terrorist attack, it has remained an old, charming seaside city with uncomfortable stony beaches packed with thousands of tourists, many of them bare-breasted women and g-stringed men burned to a crimson crisp. She liked the Promenade des Anglais with its garish hotels, daredevil bikers, suicidal rollerbladers, and small panicked children seeking some place safe from them all. Even the carousel on the promenade was deceptive. The painted horses were known to throw their riders, and the operator demanded double the fare if a kid dropped his ice-cream cone in fright.

Helena had no children. It wasn't a matter of convenience, but of not wishing to commit to a man. Art was self-contained.

Men were dependent or unpredictable, and often violent. She had learned the hard way not to rely on them. She had once been tempted to live here with a man who owned a house in La Gaude, a village perched on the hilltop above Cagnes-sur-Mer, with a view of steep mountains from one side of its marble terrace and of the Mediterranean from the other. She had spent a magical spring there, listening to the birds and cicadas and the tree-frogs at night, with a man who had seemed content just to be. She had enjoyed their forays to the markets for fresh fruit, cheeses, mushrooms, and admired his ability to find the perfect cut of beef and a local wine that tasted like Provence. For a while, all parts of her had come together here. She had thought, then, that another life was possible, that she could adjust her dreams to suit someone else's.

He had been a good lover and an entertaining story-teller with wit and a sense of the silliness of daily life. But as spring turned into summer, he had become clingy, insisting on knowing more about her, listening to her phone conversations. When he discovered she had an office in Paris, he decided to rent a floor in a narrow house on Rue Jacob, a two-minute walk away. She left early one morning, leaving him a note apologizing for having misled him. She was not ready for a permanent relationship.

Simon used to tell her that relationships had a habit of going sour. He had shown her old photographs of him and her mother, looking carefree and much in love. Yet he had left her without a backward glance. He was a man with no regrets and no sense of the hurt he cheerfully doled out. Her father's example had taught Helena a hard lesson: trust no one.

She had imagined, when she was seven or eight, that he would take her to exotic places all over the world, that they would travel and see art in all the places Simon had visited: Paris, Rome, Florence, London, Barcelona, Madrid. Or closer to home: Washington, New York, Chicago. He showed her books from every major museum featuring the paintings in their collections and explained why each artist painted differently although they all had in common the knowledge and skill to make art.

Her father had brought her to Paris for the first time when she was ten. He had said Paris was "his city" and a perfect place for a girl her age. They had walked along the Seine, the Pont Neuf to Île de la Cité, lingered at Sainte-Chapelle and the Conciergerie, where, he said, it would have been all right to be a prisoner. Then he showed her the Notre Dame's chimera and gargoyles and told her stories about them, their past sins and present tasks defending the cathedral. He took her inside to see the magnificent rose window.

They had spent the second day at the Louvre. Her father had pointed out which paintings were the best and which were the most overrated. It was there that she had first seen original paintings by Titian, David, Chardin, and Raphael. Every hour, they stopped "to rest her eyes," so she could still appreciate the best. "You can skip the Mona Lisa," he had said. "It is the most overrated painting in the whole collection." Later, he showed her the two Delacroix paintings in Saint-Sulpice, and when she could no longer see the art because she had seen too much, they climbed to the top of the Eiffel Tower to take in the whole vista of Paris. That was the day she decided she wanted to spend the rest of her life looking at art.

Back then, she had assumed that it was his interest in her health and fitness that prompted the expensive lessons with a master of martial arts. When she was walking home from school one day, a man wearing a mask had grabbed her and tried to drag her into the bushes. At first she had fought back like a child, screaming and whimpering, then all those hours of martial-arts training came back to her with an adrenalin rush and she elbowed him in the stomach, turned and whacked him on the nose with the side of her hand, then, as he struggled to hold on, she kicked him in the balls. He fell as she ran, not once looking back.

Years later, Simon told her that he had hired her assailant to test how well she had learned self-defence.

There was something about the quality of the light in Nice that made sense of its artists' work. She admired their ability to reflect sun without shadows, windows of pure white and blue. These were not the artists whose work she had chosen to study, but their sparkling vision struck her every time she saw their paintings.

It was hard not to feel nostalgic about the months she had lived here.

She drove into the underground parking garage of le Palais de Justice, with its narrow, winding entrance and backlit announcements of how many spots there were at each level. She chose the third, less for convenience than because it was almost empty. She didn't want to meet anyone yet. One fact she knew about the Riviera was its irresistible attraction for Russians with money, the kind of people Helena was planning to avoid. She had done business here with Russians assembling art collections — that was how she had met the man she lived with in La Gaude. Most of them would recognize her undisguised self, and she was too weary to deal with the Grigoriev problem. There would be time enough for that when she was back in Budapest.

She emerged from the parking garage onto the pedestrian square in front of the Palais de Justice and made her way to the back of the Negresco, easily the most garish of the local hotels, with its green-and-pink dome and the juggling ceramic clown outside its main entrance. The hotel held enough movie magic to draw visitors who had left their sense of decorum at home. Giorgio Matamoros was one of them.

He seemed perfectly at ease in the Le Relais bar, occupying one of the burnished-wood and leather banquettes near the windows. He wore a beige suit with a light-blue tie and a matching silk square in his breast pocket. It was not a look he would ever have tried in London or Venice, but here, just like the Negresco itself, it fitted in. Helena, wearing a brown-and-gold dress, golden sandals, and an unobtrusive hat, all picked up at the Nice airport, barely rated a glance from the afternoon crowd. The hat kept her face in shadow and hid her short hair.

"Lovely," he said when he spotted her, "and great to see you here."

"You chose the place," she said, leaning down for a peck on the cheek. His face was more lined than she remembered, perhaps accentuated by the tan. His hair had receded, but its light-brown colour suited him. The last time she saw him, he had seemed ready to embrace the grey.

"We could repair to my place, once you've told me what you came for," he said. "I couldn't remember whether you favoured this bar or not, but it's where I usually come in the late afternoons for a little pick-me-up. Marco has never heard of a drink he cannot mix, and I enjoy giving him a challenge. What will you have? And don't make it easy, please." Giorgio spoke with a plummy English accent left over from attending a public school that took education seriously.

"I don't have a lot of time," she told him.

"A Negroni, then? Classic, Florentine, much favoured by the intelligentsia."

Helena nodded to the hovering waiter.

"So, not a lot of time, but enough to come all this way to see me." He flashed her a deceptively self-deprecating smile, looked down at the polished tabletop, then back up at Helena, his head tilted sideways, his small brown eyes focused. "So tell me."

"It's about a painting," she said.

"As usual." He was still smiling but his eyes were not. "I assume it's of some value."

"Yes, some value," she said. "I am buying it for a client and have to get it out of a country that is not keen to part with its Old Masters. They don't have many."

"Since you are here, I assume Italian. Giorgione? Veronese? Tintoretto?"

"Titian."

"Ah." He nodded. "Il maestro. An early work?"

"No. I am sure it's a late work. A lot of finger dabbing. But it is strong. A big canvas of Christ entering Jerusalem." She took out her camera and showed him the detail of the donkey's hoof. The paint was thick, dark, with a dab of yellow and a scratch of white. Next, the flash of blue next to Mary's face. Then Christ's face, a sketch in close-up with ochre highlights, strings of hair on the forehead. One of a dark spot where a tree stump edged a house. "He was painting a series of religious themes between 1570 and 1575. *The Crowning of Thorns* in the Alte Pinakothek was one of them."

"Retouched?"

"Doesn't seem to be. But I have seen it only once and not in ideal circumstances — no direct lighting, no chance to analyze chips. But it seems to be in good condition. If it has been retouched, it was done by someone who knew what she was doing."

"She?"

"The best have always been women."

He lifted his glass to her. "Provenance?" he asked.

"Perhaps. But incomplete."

"There may be a few undiscovered Titians, but none that haven't been referred to in correspondence. Have you seen a reference somewhere in the archives?"

"There is mention of a large biblical painting of this subject in one of Aretino's letters. And Titian wrote about it to Philip II, the same year he offered Philip *The Entombment.* As you know, there is also that letter in the Prado from Nicolò Stoppio to Max Fugger saying that Titian had trouble seeing, that he used his thumb to create some of his figures, and that others were just sketched, perhaps with the handle of his palette knife or brush. He was getting old and using more of his students to finish his work."

"But he kept going."

"He speeded up, as if the approach of his own death made him want immortality more."

"Any mention in Vasari?"

"No, but it was assumed the painting was burned with the others."

"And you think it wasn't."

She nodded. "I think it may be the real thing. Dark background, strong colours in the people, striking blues for the Madonna, Mary Magdalene's flowing green robe, like he painted in the *Pieta*, the movement of bodies —"

"Stolen, then," he said. His eyes were soft, almost unfocused, as if he were taking in the whole room behind her.

"I am not sure. It may have been stolen sometime since the last war, but the new owner says he bought it. Still, he has not shown me his proof of purchase. I represent the man who used to own it. He claims he met the new owner in a Soviet forced-labour mine camp. He says it was stolen in the heyday of Communist Party rule, but he can't prove it, and the guy who now owns the painting may never have been in a Soviet prison camp."

"Are you trying to steal it or buy it?"

"We have offered a fair price."

"So, why do you need me?"

"There are other buyers, and a couple of them seem to be overly determined. Quite aggressive. They have too much money to care how they spend it, and they are not used to failure."

"Is one of them a Ukrainian, by any chance?" Giorgio asked. He smiled but his eyes stayed round and unsmiling.

"Russian."

"I'm surprised your Ukrainian friend isn't bidding." His smile spread as he raised his glass. "Azarov, isn't it?"

"I am not concerned about him."

"You're not. Why?"

"I offered him another Titian. One without complications."

"Where did you find another Titian? There hasn't been a

Titian on the market for a decade and suddenly you come up with two at once. Am I right to assume I wouldn't know this one either?"

"It's in Poland," she lied. "It's been there for decades, in the home of a former collector. Jewish. His whole family was wiped out. The guy who owns it now has no idea what it is."

"Early or late?"

"Looks to be early 1540s," she said. "Last seen about 1800. The Prado tried to buy it but the man who owns it wouldn't sell. He thought the price was too low. He was right. The Prado assumed he was an ignorant Slav. It's a mistake they have often made."

"Does the Jewish owner have descendants?"

"They were wiped out."

"All of them?"

"All of them."

"How convenient," Giorgio said, shaking his head. "I assume you are not trying to have a bidding war among your client, Azarov, and the Accademia?"

"That's right."

"So what do you want from me?"

"I would like you to write me a formal letter, saying that *Christ's Entry into Jerusalem* is most likely a forgery."

"But I haven't seen the painting," Giorgio protested.

"I know. So you can't be sure it is not a forgery."

He rose from the table, slowly. She could tell that despite his lovely suit and brave pocket square, he was feeling his age. That was sad. He had always been such a dandy, and dandies too often grow old without grace.

"What I need is for you to say you have serious doubts about its authenticity."

"And why would I do that?"

"Because you owe me."

"Hmm."

"And because it's a debt that hasn't been wiped clean."

"You wouldn't use it against me?"

She followed him out of the bar and out the front doors of the Negresco. They stopped by the clown sculpture and waited a moment for Giorgio's chauffeur to spring to attention, jump up the two steps to the door, and lead him to the waiting Mercedes.

A few years ago, Giorgio would have leaped down those steps to hand her into the car himself.

"I think you'll like what I have done with the apartment," he said by way of invitation.

It was the top floor of a faded beige building above the pedestrian streets, with a solid wrought-iron gate that swung open slowly when Giorgio entered his entry code. They crossed a marble courtyard and a glass elevator took them up to his apartment. The apartment had tall windows that gave onto the street, blue-and-white mosaic floors, and whitewashed walls designed to display the Picasso in its simple frame, the tall black Giacometti sculpture, and the two Rembrandt drawings. There was a rolltop French writing desk by the windows, a white chaise longue, two spindly Louis XIV chairs, and a white sofa containing a small white dog that was almost invisible among the cushions until it noticed Helena. Then it made a reasonable attempt at a high-pitched bark.

Giorgio quieted it with a slap.

"Well?" he asked. He was standing in the middle of the room, his hands raised in a theatrical gesture worthy of a diva.

"Very fine," Helena said. "Although I prefer the view from the apartment in Venice."

"Too many people," Giorgio said. "Can I get you something?"

"The letter," she told him. "My plane leaves at six."

"Going to?"

She was studying one of the Rembrandt drawings and didn't reply.

"You didn't tell me exactly where *Christ's Entry into Jerusalem* is," Giorgio said.

"No. I didn't."

"So little trust."

She looked at the Picasso sideways to shut out the reflected light from the windows. "People forget what a fine draftsman he was," she said, "under all that bullshit."

They were both quiet for a few minutes, then Giorgio went to the desk.

"This whole thing makes me uneasy," he said.

"I know."

19 The letterhead was that of the Gallerie dell'Accademia of Venice, done in fine script, brown ink on off-white paper. It was exactly what Helena had requested.

To Whom It May Concern:

I have been consulted by Helena Marsh regarding a painting representing Christ entering Jerusalem. While it is indeed a fine example of Renaissance art, it is my opinion, based on fifty years studying the art of Tiziano Vecellio, known as Titian, that it is not the work of that artist. There is no documentation ascertaining its origins despite the

fact that Tiziano Vecellio's work was documented
during his lifetime as one of the premier artists
of his century. Nor has subsequent scholarship
mentioned the existence of such a work. The Titian
Committee, which spent a decade researching all
of Titian's paintings, fails to classify it or even
mention it in its final volumes.

    It is difficult to ascertain without submitting
the painting to laboratory tests who the artist is. It
is possible that it is the work of Tiziano Vecellio's
studio after his demise, but it is more likely that
the painting was executed by one of the minor
Venetian painters who followed him and tried, in
vain, I might add, to fully emulate his style. It is
to be borne in mind that Tiziano Vecellio was not
only the best-known artist of his time, but that
his work was valued more highly than the work
of contemporary artists, thus making imitation a
lucrative endeavour for dealers and artists alike.

Yours truly,
Dottore Giorgio Matamoros, PhD,
Director Emeritus,
Gallerie dell'Accademia,
Venezia, Italia

    She sent copies separately by DHL to Budapest: to Dr. Ferenc Kis on Váci Street, Mr. János Krestin in Buda, and to Mr. Piotr Denisovich Grigoriev, care of the Gresham. She had no idea where Azarov was staying, but sent his copy care of the Ukrainian Embassy in Budapest. They would make finding him a priority. She had read in the *Süddeutsche Zeitung* that he was running his businesses from Montenegro, because Ukraine had become dangerous for oligarchs, except those connected with the president.

Later, she would deliver Géza Márton's copy of the letter, personally. Márton had told her that he wanted the painting even if it cost him more than Krestin's original price. At his age, he had said, money had little meaning. He was not interested in accumulating more, and was even less interested in his financial legacy. He had already given fine endowments to the Toronto Public Library and the Art Gallery of Ontario and had not asked for any public acknowledgement in return. His two children, he said, could fend for themselves. They had each been given a trust fund and every opportunity to make whatever they wished of their lives.

However, the original price of the painting had doubled in only a few days. The one hundred million price tag could be too much even for Márton.

The flight to Cluj-Napoca was pleasantly uneventful. She was not given to anxiety, but the combination of Azarov's interest forcing her to track down the new Titian and her concern that Márton would not be able to buy his painting back, had caused her to order a second vodka.

She took out her *Aeneid* for the last half hour to settle her nerves. She was beginning to think that she had to replace it with something less taxing, but not so easy that she could whip through it quickly. Reading the *Aeneid* was a bit like doing the *Times* crossword puzzle: never too easy, but always diverting. Queen Dido's obsession with Aeneas and the Trojans reminded her of the obsessions of art collectors, especially those who knew nothing about art.

Once the airplane landed, she discarded the yellow dress, the hat, and the slingback shoes in the airport's grimy washroom, where she changed into a black T-shirt, the grey linen jacket, running shoes, rimless glasses, and black pants. She had hidden the Swiss handgun in the massive potted plant in the Four Seasons lobby in Budapest and had left a parcel containing the knife and her extra wigs and passports in the hotel's safe.

Cluj-Napoca was not the kind of place where a woman, even one like Helena Marsh, should wander around without adequate protection. So before she left the airport, she bought a prepaid cell phone and called Marcia, who said she couldn't oblige with a gun, unless a Russian semi-automatic would do the trick, but she did have a very effective Soviet-made army switchblade with a pedigree she would vouch for. The price was not much more than what Helena would have to pay for a normal handgun.

She took a cab to Marcia's "shop" on Iulia Maniu Street, close to the National Theatre. It was on the third floor of a faded-yellow baroque building, in an area where all buildings had to be one of a few designated colours and most owners had chosen yellow.

Marcia opened her door a crack, leaving the triple chain on until she was sure that it was, indeed, Helena. They hadn't spoken in over a year.

"It wouldn't be hard to break down the door," Helena said when she had extricated herself from Marcia's overwhelming hug. The woman had arms like a gymnast's and the body of a weightlifter. She used to work out for a couple of hours every day and, judging by her strength, Helena thought she still did.

"Oh yes, it would," Marcia said. "It's reinforced steel. It used to be in the Securitate's local jail, as were the windows, in case you're wondering. And you've come from where?" She was speaking an odd mixture of Italian and Russian, a language mashup they had used on previous occasions.

The windows had thick bars, painted white, and were bracketed by ferns in tall baskets. The walls were ochre and decorated with multicoloured knitted hangings.

"Your shoes," Marcia warned when Helena entered. "The wood," she added, indicating the parquet floor, which was buffed to a shine.

Helena slipped off her running shoes.

"How have you been?" she asked.

"Much the same. Tea or something stronger?"

"Tea, I think." She followed Marcia into the kitchen. The kettle was already on the stove, the table laid with a teapot, two cups, and a plate of cheese and olives and thickly sliced black bread.

"You are still in the security business," Helena said.

"But the competition is stiffer. Serbs, Croats, Bosnians, Bulgarians, Hungarians, Russians, and Romanians of course. Sometimes they even work together. They may fight on the streets of their own countries, but here, it's all a common cause: make quick money and live like a prince — not what we had in mind in '89. Transylvania led the revolution against the Ceauşescus, you know. We had borne the brunt of the repression by the Securitate. Now the Securitate has its own gangs. Why are we surprised? The most violent members of the old regime are the most violent insiders of our shiny new democracy."

At sixty, Marcia was still a looker, with her long black hair, now streaked with white, gathered in a knot at the nape of her neck. She stood tall in a dark-blue top and soft corduroy pants, her hands flying as she talked. She was as talkative as she had been when Helena first met her in Odessa in 1995. In those days, you could purchase Old Masters from concerned Communist apparatchiks trying to raise enough money for a one-way journey to Canada or the United States. Marcia had been the curator of seventeenth- and eighteenth-century European art at the Muzeul Naţional de Artă in Bucharest, but after the collapse of the old regime, she became a fixer and also offered her services as a bodyguard if one were needed. She had been willing to settle for a percentage of the selling price, no advance payment, and no residuals. Even with the bribes she'd had to pay at the Yugoslav border, Helena made a tidy profit. Helena had hired her as a backstop. They hadn't had another artwork of mutual interest until the Raphael drawing five years ago, but they had stayed in touch.

"But you live better," Helena said.

"I live better because I work outside the system. If I went back to the museum, I'd have wages, pay taxes and bribes, and I wouldn't be able to afford a decent pot of tea. No milk, no sugar?"

Helena shook her head.

"You don't change, do you?"

"Not much. But this time I may need some serious backup," Helena said.

Marcia nodded. "And the switchblade." She produced it in one swift motion from a pouch wedged into her pants at the back. "Did you even notice I was wearing it?" she asked.

"As soon as I came in," Helena said. "You walked stiffly and it poked out above your waistline."

"You didn't say."

"I have to show a painting to someone tonight. It's in the home of a man called Braunschweiger. He is anxious to sell, too anxious to show it around. He is worried he'll be killed for it or the painting will be stolen. Or both. He isn't sure what it's worth but he suspects it's more than enough to live on for the rest of his life."

"A Saxon?" Marica asked with a curl of her lip.

"I never asked."

"The name," Marcia said.

"He showed me a photograph of the painting when I was in London last year. I came to see it during the winter, and I told him I would find a buyer."

"And you have."

"The buyer wants to see it first," Helena said, reaching for the goat cheese.

"Very sensible. I can find out whether Braunschweiger has shown it to anyone else. And whether it's safe to go to his place with the buyer."

"Okay, but I'd rather you met me there," Helena said. "Nine this evening. He lives near the cemetery in a big house overlooking the gardens. If there is a problem, leave me a message on this phone. I'll call you shortly before ten."

Marcia took the money for the knife without counting it, and both women stood up.

"Bring a gun," Helena said at the door. "I don't care what kind, just have one with you." Suddenly, she was hungry. She hadn't eaten, other than the goat cheese and olives, since Nice.

Marcia opened the door slowly and looked in both directions before saying goodbye.

Helena made her way over to the Hotel Opera Plaza, where she dropped her bag, then walked back to the old town.

She bought a spiced sausage in a rye bun with two generous dollops of mustard and a massive dill pickle from a kiosk on one of the cobblestone pedestrian streets and walked on to Unirii Square. The shops were closed and shuttered, but people were spilling out of restaurants and bars, laughing too loudly and shouting at one another as they parted. Some of the men were wearing football uniforms and yelling that Hungarians had small pricks. There must have been a game here in the past couple of days.

The last time she had been here, Unirii Square had been dark. St. Michael's gothic church had loomed over the square like a fortification, and the statue of King Matthias Corvinus on horseback was a dark, menacing hulk in front of the church. The horse, with one hoof raised, as if to step off its pedestal, had seemed part of the seated man, a satyr in mid stride. She had stopped here then, too, and read the inscription on the pedestal: "Hungariae Matthias Rex."

Now the word "Hungariae" was missing.

Helena stood in front of the great Renaissance King, dead for more than five hundred years, and wondered why the mayor hadn't just removed the statue altogether. It would have been so much simpler. Had he been afraid the Hungarians would invade again to restore their king to his pedestal?

She called Marcia, who confirmed that the place seemed safe and the Saxon had not tried to sell the art. They would meet later.

She felt someone come up quickly behind her, and she tensed. She slid her right hand over the handle of the knife, raised her left hand, palm forward, and swirled around. She was facing a man with a hoodie over his head in mid reach for her shoulder bag. He dropped his arm when she pulled the knife, pointed it at his chest, and told him to scram, in Italian.

Whether he understood the words or not, he certainly

understood the gesture and ran off to the accompaniment of soft laughter coming from under one of the king's armoured men.

"Brilliant," Vladimir Azarov said, laughing. "You're still the toughest lady in the Eastern bloc. Good thing I didn't try to surprise you."

"One of yours?" she asked.

"Mine are older and wiser, and they don't frighten so easily." He came closer and offered her a cigarette. "You know Miroslav."

"Your idea of a joke?" she asked.

"A happy coincidence," he said. "Street theatre." He lit the cigarette, cupping the match in his hand.

"Did you come alone?" she asked, looking behind him.

"Should I have brought a bodyguard? This is a dangerous city. It's always been a bit tricky, what with people not having enough food and their nasty state-security police. It's no better now that it's become the backwater of organized crime syndicates. Democracy hasn't been kind to the Romanians. They still don't have enough to eat, and in the old days at least they knew whose hand was in their pockets." He paused and looked around for a moment. "Should we have supper first and then you show me the Titian?"

"We'll see it now," she said. "Then we can decide whether we still feel like eating supper."

She started to hail a taxi, but the driver of a big, shiny Infiniti JX35 parked by the side of the square was already opening its rear door for them. Of course Vladimir would have a car and driver, Helena realized. That's what he was looking around for.

The Braunschweigers were waiting at the entrance to their building. He was a short, stocky man dressed in a blue shirt and brown tweed suit, once favoured by Party bosses, and she was wearing a loose print dress with a bow at the neck. They were both excited and very nervous. They exchanged greetings in Romanian and German, with a few words of Russian. He said he'd learned Russian at school but had forgotten most of it. Vladimir expressed his regret in Russian that neither his German nor his Romanian was up to par. Marcia would be their interpreter.

She was inside, standing at an open window, her back to the room. The apartment smelled of cooked cabbage and cleaning fluids.

The Braunschweigers had moved the painting to the centre of the living room and leaned it up against the couch. They had rigged a lightbulb over it and moved a lamp close so you could see one corner better than the other.

"We store it under the bed," Braunschweiger said in German. "It does no good to display something like this. There have been robberies on this street, and if anyone knew we had something of value . . ."

His wife nodded vigorously and offered everyone a glass of Silva.

Marcia declined. Vladimir drank his in one gulp. Helena sipped hers, while searching the painting for scratches. The driver stood with his back to the door, eying Marcia.

The painting was about four feet long and three feet high. It was difficult for Helena to tell exactly, as the clunky, black, wooden frame was covering at least two inches of its top and bottom. Christ was in a blue-white gown, standing high above the fray of rising and falling figures. White clouds behind him illuminated his head and face. The rising bodies were identifiable saints and prophets, typical of the Renaissance, all lit by Christ's light. None had haloes above their heads. In the lower left, the doomed struggled in murky green-purple darkness, some still reaching up in hope of redemption, others being pulled down by black figures that dissolved into an inky darkness.

The figures were all finely detailed, not painted in the impressionistic rush of *Christ's Entry into Jerusalem*.

"It's earlier than the other," Helena said. "As I told you, probably commissioned by Mary of Hungary. Clear lines, lots of brushwork. It's in the records as missing."

Vladimir was sitting on his haunches next to her. "It looks different," he said.

"Not so different from his work of this decade," Helena said quickly. "It's before he started to use his fingers and the handles of his brushes. You can see how carefully he outlines each figure. But it's hard to tell what the original colours were. It needs a cleaning and maybe a bit of restoration, but it's remarkable that it has retained so much of its original vigour."

"Vigour," Vladimir said. "I don't see that. It's static, staged, and very gloomy."

"What do you expect? It's a Last Judgement."

Vladimir told his man to help him hold the painting up to the tasselled lamp, then pulled the lightbulb down closer and examined every inch of it, while the Braunschweigers hovered anxiously.

"How did you get this painting?" Vladimir asked in Russian then again English.

Braunschweiger raised his shoulders and spread his hands to indicate he was helpless in the face of these languages.

Marcia asked him in Romanian.

"I bought it," he said after much nodding and sighing.

"From?" Marcia asked.

"From a man who said he had taken it from a Jew before he was killed. I don't know whether he was killed by the Germans or the Russians. His whole family was wiped out."

"So, he just took it," Marcia said.

"He was in the Securitate," Braunschweiger explained.

Marcia nodded as she translated for Vladimir.

"He sold it?" Vladimir asked.

"He needed the money to go to Germany. He was well known around here and thought he would be safer there."

"That's why you want to sell?" Vladimir asked. "You were in the Party, I assume."

Braunschweiger wiped his hands on his pants.

His wife poured another round of Silva.

"When I was six, I was already in the Komsomol," Vladimir said. "If you wanted to get anywhere you had to be in the Party, right?"

When Marcia translated, Braunschweiger nodded enthusiastically.

"But it was slim pickings around here, even for the insiders," Helena said in Russian. "That's why he is wearing old clothes and is selling his painting. He does not have an Infiniti and a chauffeur."

Vladimir rose and stood facing the painting. "It's smaller than the other one," he said.

"And it's less expensive," Helena said.

Vladimir didn't ask how much till they were back in the car, heading toward the Orthodox cathedral. He said he had seen a restaurant near there that served food after midnight.

"I will sell it to you for only twenty million," she said once they were inside. "Dollars," she added when she saw him stiffen.

Marcia joined them after they had already ordered their food. She seemed flushed, breathless, as if she had been running. Her hair was hanging looser than it had been, and there was a new bruise on her wrist. The bulge under her arm was still easy to see, but she no longer had a knife tip poking out of her cuff. Helena hadn't been sure whether Marcia had intended to display the knife and the gun openly at the Braunschweigers or if she was just out of practice and had forgotten how to be less obvious. She had guessed the former.

"Seems like a lot," Vladimir said, returning to the subject of the painting. "It strikes me the deal is shady, the owners are shady, and I am not convinced they even own the thing."

"Talking about shady, did you get a letter from the Accademia?" Helena asked.

"You mean the one from your old friend, Giorgio Matamoros? Yes, I did. How much did you have to pay him for it? Or did he write it for old times' sake?"

"If two experts tell you that a painting is not a real Titian, chances are it's not a Titian," she said. "And since you are so concerned about provenance all of a sudden, *Christ's Entry into Jerusalem* does not belong to Krestin. My client has title to the work. The only reason he is willing to pay for it — although it belongs to him — is to avoid having to launch a lawsuit that could last longer than he will. He is over eighty."

They ate something that could have been stew, and Vladimir talked about his yacht in the Adriatic. He had wanted something on which he could land a small plane. Much more convenient when your business interests are so far flung. What with

the way things looked in Kiev, he thought he might even purchase a house in London. Isn't that where most of the Russian
oligarchs lived? And wasn't it the most civilized country?
Didn't it have the best tailors? The British didn't think they
should interfere in your affairs. They liked business. Vladimir
said "biznis," as if it were some form of rare disease.

He said he would buy the painting for sixteen million and
deliver the cash to Helena in a briefcase the next day, unless she
preferred a bank transfer.

She opted for exchanging the painting for the briefcase of
cash at the Opera Plaza Hotel, at 7 a.m. He offered to drive
both women home.

"I don't think that will be possible," Marcia said.

They were standing in front of the restaurant, waiting for
the Infiniti.

Vladimir turned to Marcia, his eyebrows up, "Why not?"
he asked.

"Your driver has, I am sorry to say, met with an unfortunate
accident."

Vladimir nodded. "Serious?" he asked.

"I think he will recover, but you may need another man to
drive you and the painting to the airport," Marcia said.

"Till the morning, then," he said to Helena and turned on
his heel. He didn't speak to Marcia. They could see him talking
on his cell phone when he reached the corner of the street, then
he marched into a hotel bar.

"What happened?" Helena asked.

"Azarov was trying for a shortcut. He sent his man back for
the painting, but I had already taken the Braunschweigers and
their Titian to your hotel. They are on your floor, in an adjoining
room, in case you need to talk to them before you meet Azarov."

"The driver?"

Marcia grinned. "I went back to the Braunschweigers, as I thought Azarov would try something. His man tried to push his way in. Didn't work. I called an ambulance but, you know how these things go in Romania, he may still be there tomorrow morning. Big brute but no balls. They don't make them like they used to."

Attila had not planned to visit the Russian oligarch that morning, but Tóth, who seemed considerably less concerned about the Russians than the Ukrainians, phoned him and insisted that Piotr Denisovich Grigoriev was owed a personal call. Attila had not mentioned his conversations with Alexander, so Tóth couldn't have known that Grigoriev had hired the dead guy in the Gellért, yet he seemed sure the Russian was somehow involved. Perhaps it was the years of too many Russians walking about in Hungary that made him suspicious, who knew? Tóth couldn't have been around for the worst of it. So why? Had he been chatting with Ukrainians again?

Hired men wouldn't ask such questions, and Attila had been reminded often enough by Tóth that he was just a hired hand.

On the way to the Gresham, he stopped by the Ukrainian Embassy. At least that was what he told himself, ignoring the fact that the Ukrainian Embassy was nowhere near either his home or the hotel, unless you take the longest possible route. The embassy was on Istenhegy on the far side of the Danube, not one of Attila's usual haunts. All he knew about it were the first few lines of Miklós Radnóti's poem, "Istenhegyi Kert." Poor Radnóti had been only thirty-five when he was murdered by one of his fascist countrymen.

Attila had been on nearby Rózsadomb a few times, investigating burglaries, but never on Istenhegy. He prided himself on knowing exactly how his city was laid out and being able to find just about any place in it, but he had to consult a map for a road up God Mountain.

The Ukrainian Embassy was a whole lot less palatial than the Russian one, but still an impressive red brick pile for a country whose national debt outstripped the combined debt of most of southern Europe's laggards, including Greece. There were police barricades along the front of the building, an electronic gate where he showed his old police ID, an X-ray machine for his wallet, gun, and loose change. Then he submitted to a pat-down by a sweaty security guard. Once inside, he was told to wait in a room with two doors and worn leather chairs and sofa. There were white rectangles on its yellow walls the size and shape of large pictures. Attila assumed that staff had removed all photographs of Yanukovich, his son, his wife, and other relatives, but had not yet had time to replace them with suitably prominent photos of the confections king, let alone the rest of Poroshenko's government.

A very pretty woman with serious breasts and long blond hair, in a short skirt and high heels, entered through the other door and smiled at Attila. "You are with the police?" she asked in Hungarian, placing equal emphasis on each syllable.

Attila nodded.

"And you are here to enquire about one of our citizens?"

"Yes," Attila answered. "A Mr. Azarov. He has been in Budapest for about a week. He came on his own aircraft."

Azarov's name seemed to have created a frisson of excitement in the young woman's breasts. At least that was what Attila thought, staring at them. It was a reaction he was sure he had not elicited from a young woman, or a woman of any age, in a long time.

"Mr. Vladimir Azarov." She nodded thoughtfully. "He travels a great deal. He is a very important man, with many business interests and many offices everywhere."

"Indeed," Attila said. "But I am only interested in the part of his busy schedule that he has chosen to spend in our city. Could I speak with the ambassador?"

"I am sorry but that is not possible."

"Why?"

"Because the new ambassador extraordinary and plenipotentiary of Ukraine has not yet been appointed and the old ambassador has already left."

It was Attila's turn to nod.

"We cannot help you, here," she added, standing at attention, her pretty shoes pointing outward, her knees locked together.

"You know Mr. Azarov?" Attila asked.

"Yes. He has visited our embassy a number of times."

"And you are?"

"Mrs. Klitchko," she said. "Counsellor, Science and Education Division."

"Perhaps you would like to sit down?" He gestured at the leather couch across from his chair.

She considered it for a moment, then rejected the idea. Perhaps she was concerned that her short skirt would ride up her thighs if she sat, or she didn't like the feel of leather against her bare legs — Attila had ascertained she was not wearing stockings or pantyhose.

"We are concerned that Mr. Azarov may have become involved in some illegal activity while he has been here. Innocently, I am sure, but nonetheless involved in the potential transfer of illegal goods across the border."

"Which border?" Mrs. Klitchko asked.

"Our border, of course. We would not be much concerned if Mr. Azarov decided to transfer an entire shipload of illegal goods from Romania, for example, to Ukraine, as we have no jurisdiction there and, for all I know, no goods are really illegal. Could you tell me when Mr. Azarov was last here?"

"In the embassy? Let me think. No, definitely not recently. But he did inform us that he was passing through Budapest."

"Would that have been in the past few days, perhaps?" Attila asked patiently.

"Yes. He passed through this morning, on his way to Montenegro."

"Montenegro," Attila repeated, as if it had been just the name he had been expecting to hear. "To his yacht," he added.

It was a happy guess. Mrs. Klitchko smiled for the first time, displaying her fine small teeth, and she risked leaning against the side of the leather couch. "It's where he docks it, most of the time," she said with apparent delight. "It is too large for any of the Italian harbours. He can even land a plane on it."

Attila whistled appreciatively.

"He stopped here for only a few hours," she said. "He has very little business in Budapest."

"Except for buying paintings," Attila said.

"I wouldn't know about that, but Mr. Azarov has a famous art collection in Ukraine. He has been acquiring it since Independence, and he even allows visitors to come and see it sometimes. He is a friend of Mr. Poroshenko. Mr. Poroshenko has some artworks of his own."

Poroshenko was not a name to bandy about lightly, at least not in the Ukrainian Embassy. Attila thanked Mrs. Klitchko and asked her to contact him if Mr. Azarov returned to Budapest. He provided his cell number.

The list of suspects who may have hired a Bulgarian to attack Ms. Marsh had been expanded by one, and Attila's suspicion that Tóth had been paid off seemed to take shape in the dazzling form of Vladimir Azarov.

Attila picked up Sofi and Anna at his ex's new apartment on Nap Street, not far as the crow flies, but with the nightmare of morning traffic and roadworks, he was fifteen minutes late. The ex and the girls were already waiting on the street in front of their building's elegant double doors. He was grateful not to have to climb the stairs to their swish new apartment with its views of the Danube and his furniture and curtains. He hated the way she had recovered the sofa in shiny burgundy and Gustav's favourite chair in what looked like yellow brocade.

"You are late," Bea observed when he emerged from the car. "Again." She was wearing yoga pants, a zip-up top, and red-and-white running shoes. Her hair was gathered in a ponytail, and she wore no makeup but managed to look fresh and pretty. Her new body must have required hours of hard work at some gym, he thought maliciously, and maybe even running along the gas-choked embankment. She hadn't bothered with much of that while they were married.

"I am sorry," he said in the hangdog way he used when addressing his ex. "I was held up in an interview on Istenhegy, and the traffic —"

"I know," she interrupted. "Always something. Please have them back by six. We have plans for the evening."

"I thought they were staying overnight. We're going to go to the beach in Leányfalu —"

"Another time," she said. She kissed both girls on the tops of their heads and left at a fast clip to a short chorus of good-byes. She turned when she reached the corner and called back over her shoulder. "Should I assume that you are still on for next weekend?"

"Of course. I'll pick them up on Saturday. They will sleep over at my apartment."

"Right," she said, not bothering to keep the sarcasm out of her voice.

The three of them watched her get into her Fiat sports car and speed off toward Erzsebet Bridge. When she was well out of sight, Anna hugged him and Sofi said, "Good morning,

Apu," and inspected the front of his beat-up, ten-year-old Škoda. "Somebody hit you again?" she asked.

"They don't like Škodas in Budapest anymore. When I bought it, they were all the rage."

"I've never known you to have another car," she said.

They piled into the back seat, which Gustav had scratched and slashed over the years of circling and pummelling the ungiving plastic in a vain effort to make himself comfortable.

"Anything special you would like to do today?" he asked.

"No," they chorused.

"How about the zoo?"

Vehement head-shaking.

"Vidám Park?"

"Hate that place."

"It's for little kids."

At nine and ten, they were hardly big kids, but Attila conceded that he had been taking them there for the rides and candy-floss since they were three and four, so they may, justifiably have concluded that it was for younger kids.

"The castle?"

"We did that last time," Sofi said. Anna didn't say anything, which meant she was beginning to feel sorry for him. "And it's fake."

"Okay," Attila said. "Let's go to the Gresham Palace. You can have ice cream and play hide and seek among the potted plants. It's the most magnificent palace you will ever have seen, and the ice cream will cost me about a day's pay, so I will have to earn it while we are there. One hour, max. Then we can go to the wave pool at the Gellért."

They were already crossing the Széchenyi Chain Bridge,

the Four Seasons Hotel Gresham Palace rising impressively on the other side of the Danube.

A doorman opened the car doors for the girls, which almost made up for Attila being late, another doorman bowed and waved them through the hotel's exquisite carved metal doors and enquired whether he could take care of their luggage. Attila was grateful for the doormen's impeccable manners in not treating his Škoda as the wreck it was.

The girls giggled all the way to the wide chairs in the marble foyer and whooshed into them in a way that perversely reminded Attila of Mrs. Klitchko's reluctance to sit. He dug in his pockets for a fistful of bills and pointed out to them the less-elegant cafe's open door. He said the menu featured all kinds of ice cream and sorbets. They should order what they wanted, and he'd be with them in a moment or two.

They were still giggling and whooshing when he flashed his old police ID and asked the man on the front desk for Mr. Grigoriev's room number.

"I will call his secretary for you," the man said. The name on his badge was Zoltán, and he looked as if he had spent much of the previous few days in the sun. His nose was peeling, his cheeks below his glasses were bright red. "Your name, sir?" he asked.

"Fehér. Budapest Police Department."

Zoltán relayed that into the house phone and asked what his business was with Mr. Grigoriev.

"I will discuss that with Grigoriev, in person." Attila wondered whether there was still some offence on the books about obstructing the police.

"His secretary will be down in a moment," Zoltán said.

Attila slouched over the mahogany desk, hoping to appear

both threatening and overconfident. "Gotta keep that schnoz out of the sun," he said. Zoltán side-shuffled to talk to a more-polite guest.

The secretary turned out to be a bulky man in an ill-fitting suit, his hair short back and sides, a buzz cut on top. Very 1950s, but perhaps back in style in Russia. He had a face like a potato, as if someone had tried to push it out of shape and almost succeeded. "You explain to me your business with Mr. Grigoriev," he said in halting English.

"Unfortunately, no," Attila said, straightening up from the desk. He noted with joy that he was taller if not wider than the secretary. A shoving match was unlikely here, in Budapest's best hotel, but you could never tell with Russians.

They waited, eyeing each other. "He is busy man," the secretary said. Russians were allergic to pronouns. "He is meetings all day. Leaving Budapest tomorrow. No time in schedule for more appointments."

"Well, Mr. Grigoriev can't leave this country until I have spoken with him. So, I shall wait," Attila said. "Meanwhile, you can tell him the body of his Bulgarian employee is safely stored in a freezer compartment at the chief medical examiner's office, and that we are making every effort to return it to Sofia." English was still a tough language for him, but it seemed to be even more difficult for the secretary.

The secretary looked aggressively indifferent.

"His name is Ivan Dalchev," Attila said. "He came to Budapest with Mr. Grigoriev. Perhaps you remember sitting with him on Mr. Grigoriev's plane?"

"No," the secretary said.

"You don't remember him?"

"No."

"I expect Mr. Grigoriev will remember him. And Mr. Grigoriev could be stuck with paying to return the body to Mrs. Dalchev — after all, Ivan was working for him when he was killed."

The secretary stared straight ahead. His putty face registered not the slightest expression. "It must have taken years of training to perfect your look," Attila said. "FSB?"

The man's eyes shifted for a moment, before repeating his earlier statement that Grigoriev would not be available for a meeting. Then he turned and marched into the elevator.

Zoltán couldn't quite suppress a smile.

"*Faszfej*," Attila said. *Dickhead.*

He looked around for the girls and found them at a corner table in the cafe, near the display of desserts. They were eating chocolate ice cream, arranged with blue violets on gold-edged plates. The waiter was lingering nearby, in case "the young ladies had more requests."

Attila asked for the bill and took a deep breath before examining it.

Alexander's call came as he was stacking his remaining forints on the silver tray.

"*Lófasz a seggedbe*," Alexander said.

"Good afternoon, Alex," Attila said.

"*Lófasz a seggedbe*," Alexander repeated. Roughly, that meant that he wished a horse would screw Attila in the ass, a physical impossibility at the best of times, but especially so in the Gresham, where randy stallions were not welcome. That was what Attila told Alexander, but then he congratulated him on learning yet another Hungarian curse. Alexander had always been a keen student of colourful swearing and had offered to teach Attila a cornucopia of similar expressions in Russian.

"Why did you go and bother Piotr Denisovich after I told you he would speak only with me and I would keep you informed? Now he thinks I am incompetent. I couldn't even stave off a fake police inquiry. You passed yourself off as a policeman. Dumb bastard. How long do you think it took him to find out you're not?"

"You're done?" Attila inquired.

"What the *lófasz* were you thinking?"

"Doing my job. It's what I was hired to do, and I don't recognize that your guy has some sort of diplomatic immunity. Nor that he can get away with murder."

"We can't be having this conversation," Alexander said.

"Right."

"I will meet you tonight. Same time and place as last night. Okay?"

"What was that about a horse, Dad?" Anna asked.

The exchange of *The Last Judgement* for a briefcase full of dollars was relatively simple. Vladimir seemed surly at first, but ended up laughing that his FSB-graduate driver had been so easily taken down by a sixty-year-old Romanian woman, all without a shot being fired. The driver had been transferred to a private clinic, where a surgeon could reattach the dangling fingers of his right hand. Vladimir said it had been thoughtful of Marcia to call the ambulance. Helena's fee was a low ten per cent, and she left Marcia with the balance in the briefcase to work out her own deal with the Braunschweigers.

They would think they owed her their lives.

Helena had planned to phone Kis from Debrecen, but the

Romanian phone she'd bought became unusable long before it was due to expire. She had to rent another car, and she was concerned about the Steinbrunner passport and credit cards. Now that both countries were in the European Union, she had thought it would be easy. It wasn't. The Hungarian border guard spent too long looking at the passport and back up at her. He called over a colleague, they talked in Hungarian, then he asked her what business she had in Hungary.

She had said tourism, but they seemed genuinely puzzled by the smallness of her bag. She said her suitcase had been stolen in Cluj, which made both men giggle. Apparently, suitcase theft was a regular occurence in Cluj. Then they'd let her through.

She decided it would be safer to wait till she reached Budapest before she called Kis. As soon as she got there, she dropped the car at the airport, changed her hair in the women's washroom, and took a limousine to the Gresham. She checked in as Marianne Lewis and assured the clerk on the front desk that her suitcases would follow, and that, in the meanwhile, she would shop for a new outfit at the boutiques along Váci Street. Yes, she had been here before and knew the city.

She was on her way to the staircase (yes, she preferred to walk) when she saw the sturdy ex-policeman, now perhaps a private detective, with two young girls, leaving through the revolving door. Broad shouldered, tall for a Hungarian, with cropped sandy hair, turning grey. The girls were determined to go around several times, and the elegant doorman was looking on, as elegant doormen usually do, with a mix of indulgence and disapproval. The former policeman was trying to arrest the spinning door without stepping into it and seemed to be begging the kids to stop. She admired his self-control. Most fathers would have just yelled. He finally grabbed them by one arm each and propelled them down the driveway, pursued by the doorman, who must have had the car keys and was, doubtless, waiting for his tip.

She spent a couple of minutes looking at the *Budapest News*, and when she was sure no one was watching, she retrieved her gun from the potted plant.

Helena used the first of the four new disposable phones she had bought at the airport, no sense alerting them to her presence in the hotel. This time, Grigoriev's secretary was sure he would wish to speak with her. In fact, he had been expecting her call since yesterday.

She switched from English to Russian the moment he took the phone:

"*Zdrastvuyte, gospodin,* Grigoriev. I assume you have received the letter from Mr. Matamoros."

"*Da.* I have."

"I assume Dr. Krestin's price will be adjusted accordingly."

"If the painting is a fake, I no longer want it," Grigoriev said. "But you were wrong about De Hory."

"I knew it was not a Titian. Just a matter of finding out who did it and when."

"Why did you take the trouble to warn me, madame?" Except for the "madame," he spoke only Russian. When did this antique form of address make its way into eastern Europe? Krestin had also called her madame, and in his mouth the word had taken on an unsavoury connotation. With Grigoriev it merely seemed like affectation.

"Why shouldn't I?" Helena asked.

"Our history back when you worked at the Hermitage . . ."

"Ah yes, Mr. Grigoriev, you were not interested in my findings then. But that's ancient history. I am still in the art-validation business, and you are still a collector. Perhaps our paths will cross again. I wouldn't want you to hold a low opinion of me."

After a cheerful chuckle, Grigoriev said, "Are you staying at the Gellért Hotel?"

Helena laughed. "Not after I met your messenger."

"My messenger?"

She hung up.

She decided to see Kis in person. A walk to the gallery would do her good. With Grigoriev and Azarov out of the picture, there was no reason for Kis to hesitate.

Because there was always a chance that her call to Grigoriev would have been traced, even one made on a disposable phone, she took the phone apart as she walked, dropping the battery and the back piece into a drain at Vigado Square, and the screen and the SIM card into a garbage bin near the entrance of the Hyatt.

Seeing Kis meant she had to make some minor adjustments to her appearance, and in the washroom off the Hyatt's lobby, she changed into the linen jacket, but she didn't bother with the full makeup. She just applied a touch of eyeshadow and the red lipstick she had worn the first time she met him. She thought they were close enough to a deal now that her appearance would not spoil her plan.

The gallery was quiet, and there was no sign of Kis's assistant. A couple of new paintings were on easels in the windows, and a rough wooden statue of a Madonna stood near the desk at the back. It was made to look like it had been rescued from a nineteenth-century church, but whoever did the work should have aged a few details, like the newly distressed wood on the sides and the fresh paint around her eyes.

Kis was talking with a woman wearing a pair of red Blahniks, skinny leather pants, a loose white silk T-shirt, a red cut-away jacket, and a long silk scarf. The whole outfit looked like she had ordered it from a Prada catalogue. Her face was meticulously made up.

"You could ship it to me in London," she said in a husky voice. She spoke French with an overlay of American.

"I do not think that will be possible," Kis said in French.

"Why is that, monsieur?" She ran her fingers through her short, stylishly cut hair, or tried to, but it had been lacquered and didn't budge. There was something about that movement with her hand (red nails) that seemed familiar to Helena, but the ensemble and the face didn't match the memory.

Kis noticed her and tried to excuse himself, but the woman didn't want her conversation interrupted and followed him. "You were in France," Kis said to Helena in English. "In Nice, I believe. We didn't expect you back so soon."

"I would like to pick up the painting tomorrow," Helena said.

"The price? As we agreed?" Kis whispered.

The woman was still at his elbow, now looking at Helena with overt annoyance. "You are interrupting," she said. "Dr. Kis and I will be finished our business in a little while. You can wait."

"*Je regrette*, madame, but that is not possible," Helena said. "My business with Dr. Kis precedes yours by several days and will be concluded today."

"The painting —" Kis began.

"Yes. My clients will transfer the amount you suggested earlier —"

"How much earlier?"

"— less a reasonable discount. I suggest only forty per cent, since not being sure of the artist is disappointing. I think that is a fair price. Better than fair, under the circumstances."

"This is intolerable," the woman said. There was something familiar about the voice, too. "We have not finished our business. Dr. Kis, I will give you an hour — no more than two hours — to let me know whether my offer is acceptable."

"But we will see each other later tonight," Kis said with an ingratiating smile that the woman didn't reciprocate. "At eight. My wife has gone to such trouble for the occasion . . ."

"I'll be there," she said, and with that she flounced out of the gallery.

Sylvie Hoffman. Helena hadn't set eyes on her for more than twenty years. The last time, she had long lank hair that she wore loose and she had favoured black jeans, cotton shirts, and no makeup. During the intervening years, she had done something quite drastic to her face: the high cheekbones, the pouty lips, the aquiline nose. She had a diploma in art history from the Ecole du Louvre. Specialized in European art. She, too, had worked at Christie's, in sales promotion. She had thought she was better than that and, as her present appearance professed, she had been right.

"Given Mr. Matamoros's judgement of the painting," Helena continued, "the price must be discounted. The other buyers have vanished. Since two art experts have now alerted you to the fact that you are peddling a fake, I assume you will be happy with forty per cent off the original price."

Kis managed to look both uncomfortable and defiant, a feat Helena found impressive. "Two?" he asked.

"You already had my opinion, but chose to ignore it. As did your client. Now, I assume you will be pleased that Márton is still interested, when others are not."

"There may be a complication," Kis said. "Dr. Krestin . . ."

Yet again, a complication. "Yes?"

"I have been unable to talk with him. He is not answering his phone, and he does not seem to be at home. I went to visit him this morning, and no one came to the door."

"Was he planning a trip?"

"No, no. We were to meet today to finalize the sale."

"Did you talk with his wife?"

"His wife?" Either he didn't know Krestin had a wife or his enquiries hadn't been very thorough. "His office said Dr. Krestin had not come in today. They were expecting him, and his secretary said she would put him on the phone the moment he arrived. That was at noon." Kis examined his watch, glanced at the big oval clock on his gallery's back wall, then shrugged to make sure Helena noted his utter helplessness in face of these unforeseen problems.

They both looked at the door and watched the big, stocky man enter, his collar undone, his tie askew, his suit rumpled.

"Mr. Fehér," Kis said with a small bow. "This must be my lucky day."

The ex-cop seemed a whole lot more tired than before. The kids. She liked him better this way. For some reason, she had always liked men who paid scant attention to their appearance. She smiled at him as he came toward them.

"Fehér," he said as he took her hand for an over-the-top handshake.

"Hello," she said, ignoring local protocol by not mentioning her name.

"Miss Marsh," he said a bit uncertainly, in English. "I have been trying to find you."

"Why?" Helena asked, eyebrows up, all ingenuous.

"There are some questions I need to ask you," Attila said.

"Oh?"

"A man in your hotel, on your floor actually. He was murdered."

"How very unfortunate."

"You are no longer at the Gellért."

"No."

If Attila was surprised to meet her like this, he didn't show it. During the past couple of days, he had assumed that she had given up on the painting and left. Tóth had even remarked on her absence and there were a few moments when he had seemed pleased with Attila's work.

Close up, she was a little harder than that first time at the Gerbeaud, or crossing the Liberty Bridge, her cotton skirt fanning out around her slim legs. There was a thin line running up from the bridge of her nose, and fine lines framing her mouth, her eyes were green with just a touch of blue, soft light-brown eyebrows. He thought she looked lovely, even when her smile was mocking.

"Perhaps you saw the man on your floor at the Gellért," Attila said. "He was short and wide and had some gold teeth."

Helena shook her head.

"You are welcome to have this conversation here, if you like," Kis said, "but I am very, very busy today and simply can't stay." He repeated the same in Hungarian for Attila's benefit, turned his back, and started for the door to the courtyard.

Attila said, "I think you may want to stay, Mr. Kis. This concerns you as much as it concerns Ms. Marsh. In fact, now

I think about it, perhaps more. I will show you both the photographs." He took them out of his breast pocket and spread them on a low table.

They were creased copies of the photos of the dead Ivan Dalchev that Dr. Bayer had given him. One was of the body, as they had found it, slumped forward in the chair. There was some blood on his chin and down the front of his shirt. His face filled the next picture: hair slicked down, jug ears, his eyes wide open, and his jaw slack with some teeth showing between the darkened lips. Another photo, a side view of his head and shoulders on a slab, showed a thin, deep cut and some smeared blood in the area just under his ear. He had not bled much, Bayer had told Attila, testifying to the skill of his assailant. A close-up of his open mouth showed more blood and the gold teeth.

"Mr. Dalchev," Attila said, turning to face the two of them.

He had always thought it interesting to observe how different people reacted to the sight of the dead.

Kis backed up a step and spread his hands in front of his belly as if to defend himself. "I have never seen him before," he said.

Helena leaned in for a closer look. She examined the photos one by one. "No," she said, "he does not seem familiar. He is certainly no beauty. On the other hand, people look different when they're dead, don't they?"

"You've seen a lot of dead bodies, then?" Attila asked.

"Relatives, mostly," Helena said, lightly. "And I am quite sure he is no relation. As far as I know there are no Hungarians in my family."

Of all the odd reactions to seeing a dead body, this, Attila thought, would have to be one of the strangest.

Helena was enjoying his scrutiny and was now fairly sure there was nothing that could connect her to the killing. She had been very careful not to leave fingerprints. Nor did she think of it as murder, it was an act of self-defence. One of the two of them was going to die that day, and she preferred it not to be herself.

"What did you say his name was?" she asked.

"Ivan Dalchev. Perhaps you saw him in the restaurant, or in the lobby, or in one of the pools. I gather you went for a swim the day you checked out of the Gellért. That was, coincidentally, the same day Mr. Dalchev was killed."

She shook her head. "I never went to the restaurant. I didn't like the menu. The pool . . ." she paused to give the impression of thinking this over, then she said, "Yes, I did go for a swim. It's good exercise. I didn't see Mr. Dalchev, though."

"You talked with someone there."

"I may have," she said. "I don't remember. Those pools are always full, and Hungarians are so friendly, it's hard to avoid a discussion."

Attila was impressed. She was looking right into his eyes (with her own most astonishing green eyes!) and he was certain she was lying. That sort of behaviour took some practice. "He was not Hungarian."

"Wasn't he?"

Attila turned his attention to Kis, who had backed away from the photographs. "Dalchev, as you may know, Mr. Kis, worked for one of your Titian buyers. A Mr. Grigoriev from St. Petersburg, via London. You may have met him with Mr. Grigoriev?"

Kis shook his head. "I didn't," he said in Hungarian. "I didn't even meet Grigoriev. I talked with his secretary, a man called Abramovitz. He said he was empowered to negotiate on behalf of his boss."

"Big guy, pockmarked face?"

"Yes, that's him."

"I guess you were lucky," Attila said, in English. "There was no reason for Grigoriev to send you Dalchev. Although I admit he doesn't look much like any secretary I have ever met, he professes to be Grigoriev's secretary. Wouldn't you agree, Ms. Marsh?"

"Mr. Grigoriev?" Helena asked. "Should I know him?"

Attila laughed appreciatively. She was good. Exceptionally good. "Indeed, you should, Ms. Marsh. You are both here about the same painting. The Titian."

"It is not, as it happens, a Titian," she said.

"It isn't?"

"I am, as I expect you know by now, an expert on Renaissance art. I have had serious doubts about that painting from the first, and now I have consulted a valued colleague from Venice's Gallerie dell'Accademia, and his opinion is the same as mine. This painting was executed by a minor artist after Titian's death."

Helena was deliberately using stilted, precise English. She wanted the policeman to categorize her as an academic and unlikely to cause the death of some hired thug. She was still puzzled about his presence at the Gerbeaud the first time she met Kis. Why would he have thought her worth following?

"You don't look much like your photograph," he said.

"And you don't look much like a policeman," she lied. He looked very much like a policeman, although he acted less formally and certainly less threateningly than some others she had met.

"Now, if you don't mind," Kis said, "I am going to call Dr. Krestin again. We have arranged to meet today, and he has not yet arrived. He is very punctual as a rule. I have been representing him in these matters, and he needs to be kept informed."

"I think that would be pointless," Attila said in Hungarian.

Helena raised her eyebrows, not an easy task, "You were saying?" she asked.

"I was about to explain to Mr. Kis here that János Krestin would not be turning up for his appointment today, or any other day for that matter. Mr. Krestin died sometime earlier today. We are not yet certain of the exact time but our medical examiner will be able to determine when."

"*Jessus*," Kis said in Hungarian.

"How?" Helena asked.

Kis had exhibited genuine shock, though some people can even fake that. Attila would advise Tóth not to remove him from the list of suspects. As for Helena, she seemed neither shocked nor surprised, merely sombre.

"He was murdered," Attila said. "Garroted, if you must know. It's an unusual way to kill a man, especially here. It's a more popular method in countries to the east of us, wouldn't you say, Ms. Marsh? You did, of course, meet him last week. At a restaurant on Múzeum, right?"

"Yes," Helena said. "Very fine food. We were trying to close our deal for the painting."

"I don't understand," Attila said.

"Just because the painting is not a Titian does not mean that it has no value," she said. "By the way, is the painting still there?"

Attila thought that, for the first time, her veneer had cracked. She had sounded almost anxious.

"Where were you last night?" he asked. "And earlier today?"

"Out of town," she said. "There is an old saying about those who lie down with dogs arising infested with fleas, and János Krestin knew a lot of nasty dogs. Do you have any suspects?"

"Other than you two?" Attila asked.

"Can you really picture me garroting anyone?" Helena asked. "I imagine it would take a great deal of strength to do that, assuming the victim is opposed to the proceedings, and I do not think that János Krestin — although I didn't know him well — was the willing-victim type. Do you?"

Attila thought her tone much too light for the subject.

"Was there a sign of struggle?" she asked.

"Well, Ms. Marsh, while I appreciate your interest in Dr. Krestin's death, I am not obliged to give you details. You could go down to police headquarters in the thirteenth district. Big glass building. You can't miss it. Ask for Captain Tóth. This is his case."

Helena nodded. "And the painting?" she asked again.

"The painting's still there."

"That should rule out me and Dr. Kis," she said. "We are only interested in the painting and it is still on the wall in Dr. Krestin's home. I assume you are looking into other options. Have you come across a man called Bika, for example?"

"Why do you ask?"

"He was in Vorkuta with Krestin. They may have had a disagreement."

"Vorkuta?" Kis asked.

"In Siberia somewhere," Helena said.

"While we are considering all new information, I suggest you do not leave the country," Attila said. "Captain Tóth will certainly wish to talk with you. Where, exactly, are you staying this time?"

"The Gresham," Helena said. "And if you are not a member of the police force, under what authority are you following me?"

Attila ignored her question. "That goes for you, too, Kis. Do not leave the country till our inquiries are done. Understood?"

Kis found the strength to nod.

After the ex-policeman left the gallery, Helena turned to Kis.

"You still have authorization to sell Krestin's painting, don't you?"

Kis nodded.

"In writing?"

"Yes."

"In that case, Mr. Kis, let us conclude this deal, no matter the unfortunate circumstances. I will take care of transporting the painting to my client."

Once he was outside the gallery, Attila phoned Tóth and reported that he had found Helena Marsh. As far as the original job was concerned, he could no longer encourage her to leave the country as she might be wanted for questioning. That, he told Tóth, meant that his task was over. He could requisition his cheque, and he would go home and tend to his family. Right?

Tóth's response was remarkably calm. "I assume you know where she is."

"She is staying at the Gresham," Attila said. "The art business must be thriving. I couldn't afford a coffee in that place, at least not on what you are paying me." He was still hurting over the cost of the girls' ice creams.

Tóth asked whether Attila would like to stay on the case. Same daily fee as before. It was summer, the Budapest police force was short-handed, and this was going to make the papers, given who Krestin was.

"I thought the party had the news media under control," Attila said. "The czar sends word and they all buckle, isn't that how it usually is?"

"Usually, but not now. Krestin was known to the offshore media, and if the locals don't cover it, they will be asking why. The minister of communications came down from the castle this morning to tell us the news would be released. He also said the PM expects there to be an arrest within the week."

"Do you have any leads?" Attila asked.

"Not yet, but forensics is on it. At the least, we'll discover when he was topped. We've got four detectives questioning everyone he knew — or everyone we know he knew. You could handle the others."

"The others?"

"This painting he was selling. How many bidders were there, and were any of them unhappy with his choice of buyer?"

"From what I recall of your concern at the start, you were in favour of the Ukrainians."

Tóth was quiet for a few moments, then he asked, "Do you think so?"

"You were adamant that they wanted this woman out of the country. That was the main reason you hired me. Remember?"

Another short silence.

"Was it?" Tóth asked. "By the way, did you manage to establish where that woman was when the Bulgarian was killed?"

"She says she didn't even see Dalchev, never mind kill him. But you need to know where she went and why she left the hotel that afternoon, if she was not planning to leave the city. Why bother changing hotels?"

"Go and talk to her, Fehér. This damned place is a zoo today. I will call you when we know more."

"I visited the Ukrainian Embassy. I thought you would want to be informed, given your fondness for Ukrainians."

"Why?" Tóth asked.

"I've no idea why you are fond of Ukrainians, but it may have something to do with forints. Or hryvnia, if their currency has survived another day."

"I asked why you went there." Tóth's voice had resumed its customary cadence of barely controlled fury.

"Because one of their nationals landed here around the same time as Helena Marsh. He was gone for a day, then he returned — on his own plane, of course — and he may have been here overnight. The embassy was less than cooperative, but I did manage to extract from the voluptuous Mrs. Klitchko that Vladimir Azarov is an art collector."

"Good for him," Tóth said. "As far as I know, there is no law against collecting art. Did you say voluptuous?"

"Exceedingly."

Attila glanced through the gallery window. Helena and Kis were still standing where he had left them. They were both looking out the window but neither seemed to be paying him any attention.

Géza Márton was not particularly surprised to hear that János Krestin had been killed. There were dozens of people who would gladly have murdered the man and felt no remorse, he thought. The news made him feel light on his feet, as if he had been carrying Krestin on his back since 1945. Just knowing that Krestin was thriving had deprived him of sleep. Tonight would be his first peaceful night since before Vorkuta, and he told his wife, Klara, that he was going to bed early to make the most of it.

"I suppose Nagy couldn't have done it?" he had asked Helena when she called with the good news. "You said he is frail, didn't you? But that son of a bitch broke his fingers. He must have wanted to get even, didn't he?"

"He is no longer interested in getting even. And even if he still longs for revenge, he is too old to exact it. And I am pretty sure it was not Krestin who broke his fingers, but a man called Bika."

"Bika. He had the other prisoners beat me. But it was Krestin who ordered Bika to break Gábor's fingers." Géza took a deep breath. "I don't want to talk about him. Nagy told you Krestin used to be in state security, didn't he? In the ÁVO? Those guys were as bad as the Nazis. They may have killed fewer people, but I think they enjoyed it more. I told you that Krestin had my father jailed, had him condemned to death. For no reason at all. He accused my father of shooting ÁVO men during the '56 Revolution."

"Perhaps he had your father jailed because of your relationship with Gertrude?"

Géza was quiet for a while, then he said, "I really doubt that. I don't think Gertrude met him till after my father's trial. Late '57. I was long gone by then."

"Did you talk with Gertrude after you left?"

"Back in '57? She would have been in trouble if she heard from me. Even if she didn't reply, she would still have paid a price. My letters would have been opened, and if I'd still been trying to persuade her to come west, she would have been under suspicion. I was sure her phone was tapped. You must understand, it was a police state. People simply disappeared if the state chose to have them vanish. No formal charges, no trials, just *whoosh*." He took some shallow breaths before he resumed. "I sent her a postcard from Salzburg with a picture of some baroque towers. They were a great tourist attraction even then, but they're much prettier now. Klara and I visited Austria a couple of years ago. Back then, I was in the refugee camp outside town, so I never saw any baroque towers. The Austrians were kind enough, but they didn't want us contaminating their town. Mozart's birthplace, did you know?"

"There was something she said that made me think Krestin was jealous of you."

There was another long silence before Géza said, "She could have come with me when I left. I asked her to come. She chose not to. But, like I said, he didn't even know her then. Once I found out she'd married him, I never gave her another thought. Of all the people she could have chosen . . . How did he die?"

"He was garroted," Helena said. "That would take a great deal more strength than Mr. Nagy has. Even you would find it difficult." She didn't believe him when he said he hadn't given Gertrude another thought. Or that they'd never seen each other again. He had visited Budapest in 1977. He had been to Slovakia. Jenci had said he had met Géza more than once, although he didn't want his mother to know.

"You didn't do it, did you?"

Helena laughed. "I am reasonably good, but not that fond of killing, and I had no reason to want him dead. And he denied he was in Vorkuta. How can you be sure he was the man you sold the painting to . . ."

"I didn't sell it, not in the usual sense," Géza said. "Any one of us would have sold our souls for a crust of bread. A few of us did sell our souls. And what did a painting matter to me when I was dying of hunger? You have to believe me that he was in Vorkuta."

"You said he was in the state security police after Vorkuta. That he forced you to sell."

"Did I? Have you any idea how humiliating it is to talk

about being an inmate in a camp? Can you imagine the cold, the lice, the misery, and, above all, the hunger? None of us can bear to think about what we became in those years. How utterly devoid of pride, humanity . . ."

"All along, didn't you wonder whether you had the right man? How could you be sure? Even after I sent you the photograph. Did he look anything like the person you remembered?"

"People change," Géza said. "I have changed a lot since then. The picture you sent me of Gábor Nagy doesn't look much like the Nagy I spent four years of my life with either. Back then, I knew every pore on his body, every rag he wore, every bit of potato peel he ate. I cleaned up his shit when he got dysentery. I slept next to him in the barracks. In the winter, we held each other to keep warm. But now, I wouldn't know him if we passed each other on the street. He was never a big guy, but he was strong, not the ancient troll in your photograph. I saw him only once after we came home, in '55 or '56, before the Revolution. He was still the same then. But I never met Krestin again after I came back from the Gulag. Did you ask Gertrude about him and Vorkuta?"

"I did. He never talked to her about being there or in any other Soviet labour camp. Why have you never asked her? Haven't you ever wondered?"

"No. I had no reason to wonder. I knew he was a guard. What did she say about the Titian?" he asked.

"She remembered seeing the painting in their apartment and then their house. He kept it in the library, she said, but I doubt there was ever enough wall space in that library. She thought it was an odd picture for him to have at all, since he wasn't religious. He had a Communist's disdain for religion."

"We've been over all that," he said impatiently. "I hope you are satisfied with its provenance, and why I would like you to buy it for me. You have read the documents. You know my family has owned it for more than a hundred years. The money will be transferred to your German account. You can draw on it when the deal is done. Now, you must come to Toronto. We have a lot to talk about, and there are some things best discussed in person. The telephone is not suitable for all subjects. How soon can you get here?"

"About the painting," she said, "I think I may be able to bring it out of the country when the police are done investigating Krestin's murder. I told you it has been de-attributed, so the state cannot now claim it is a national treasure. The paperwork shouldn't take longer than a week. I may need a second payment to draw on, but I doubt it will be more than a few thousand to grease palms. The minister or his deputy will try to shake us down, but he will be reasonable now that we are no longer talking about a Titian."

She told him she would come for only a day, while the painting was being examined by local authenticators and while the police tried to determine who had killed Krestin. She also told him that she doubted anyone would be charged because whoever was behind the murder was likely to be a foreign national, and the locals were more inclined to go for a friendly shakedown than the bother of an extradition, years of delays, and perhaps a long trial.

Since it had been such a productive day, Helena decided to dine in the Gresham Restaurant. She asked for the table in the far corner with a clear view of the entrance, sat with her back to the wall, and ordered a champagne cocktail. The value of the painting had declined substantially with the acceptance of its certification as an imitative work by a talented follower. The bureaucratic wrangling had been reduced, and she no longer had to devise a way to take it out of the country hidden in the roof of a car or, worse, pinned under an antique table cleared for export. She would never have folded it or rolled it into a tube, as so many art-robbers did. She loved Titian, and she was delighted that a painting long believed lost had surfaced. She felt no guilt about Matamoros and none about her role in denigrating a masterpiece. It happened all the time — in both directions. Appraisers had lost their reputations on declaring that a painting was a genuine Old Master, then classifying it as a "school of," then returning it to its former standing. Géza Márton had told her that he would leave it in his will to the Art Gallery of Ontario, at once an act of generosity and a lucrative tax dodge.

Helena believed that great works of art should be accessible to the public. Her paper on private collections had been one of the reasons *The Polish Rider* was still debated among art experts. The argument over whether it was by Rembrandt or Drost may have reduced its resale value (should the Frick ever decide to sell it) but visitors flocked to see it anyway. The debate had added a touch of mystery to its glamour.

Fortunately, Géza had made no mention about donating the rest of his collection. Had he said that was his plan, she would have known, for sure, that he was using it to blackmail her.

Although Fehér had watched her closely when he showed the photographs of the dead Bulgarian (she had thought he was Ukrainian or Russian), he did not appear to suspect her of murdering either the Bulgarian or Krestin. She thought he actually liked her. He may even have been flirting a little, but it was hard to tell with Hungarians. All the men had that somewhat louche attitude toward women.

As for Krestin's death, she considered it an excellent addition to the ever-improving package of events. Kis would now have no reason to delay the sale to Márton.

Her only nagging concern was who had killed Krestin and why. The obvious culprits were Grigoriev and Azarov, who had been bidding on the painting and may have felt he had cheated them on hearing the news that it was a fake. She would rather it wasn't Vladimir, not because she had any illusions about his willingness to have someone killed, but because his being responsible for this particular killing would suggest that he was not pleased with the alternative Titian he had bought in Cluj.

She hadn't been surprised by his driver's attempt to take the painting without payment. One of the advantages of a lifetime spent among tigers is that you are not disappointed when they act like tigers. Azarov was a tiger, no matter how well turned-out he was. Always had been. Or, perhaps since he was Ukrainian, a bear.

Could there be another bidder? Someone who had not seen the Matamoros letter or, if they had, didn't care?

In an effort to rest her mind, she took out the *Aeneid* and prepared to dive headlong into the aftermath of the Trojan wars.

She had just ordered a bottle of Montrachet when she remembered Sylvie Hoffman. What in the world was she doing here?

She remembered hearing that Sylvie had managed to land a fat contract with a hedge-fund guy in New York about twenty years ago, advising him on art purchases. The man was old, had no ideas about art, no experience, and no time to learn. Chances were he would be dead long before he understood the difference between a Tintoretto and a Titian. But, for some mysterious reason, he had convinced himself that he needed paintings and sculptures to confirm that he had made it. It was not an unusual story and one that Sylvie had been happy to tell her friends. She had also been pleased to show the mammoth diamond ring he had given her on the occasion of their engagement. Never having been a friend of Sylvie's, Helena had heard all this second- or third-hand.

On an impulse, while the waiter opened the bottle and poured a splash of wine for tasting, she called Giorgio.

"You are at the Negresco for your afternoon libation," she said.

"How pleasant to hear your dulcet tones," Giorgio said. "Although I hope I don't owe you another favour. This one was painful enough."

"Just a question. Have you seen much of Sylvie Hoffman lately?" She nodded at the waiter and he poured the wine into the crystal glass and left.

"Sylvie, that lovely creature from New York? I do see her from time to time. She has an unlimited travel budget and an overwhelming desire to prove her worth," he said. "She consults me now and then. Why?"

"She has shown up in Budapest."

"Right. Now you are ready to tell me the painting in question is in Budapest. The scent of great art for sale must have wafted across the Atlantic."

"What did you tell her?" she demanded.

"My dear Helena, you are overly suspicious. It does your health and appearance no good. Sylvie, on the other hand, has managed to improve her looks during the past decades — while yours fade, my dear, as do mine. In my case, it is the fault of this excellent barman. What is your excuse?"

"When did you last see her?"

"I am not sure. The days pass so slowly on the French Riviera. The sun shines, the tourists come and go, the few good restaurants still cater to locals and don't advertise in the hotel magazines. One day is much like another, really. And the lovely Sylvie has been here several times. She likes the climate. And, despite random terror attacks, she prefers the Promenade des

Anglais to the docks at Montenegro, where her man keeps his boat."

He is talking too much, Helena thought. Way too much. It meant that he had something to hide. The first time she had caught him out in a lie, he talked so much about every-thing other than the bribe he had taken to authenticate a Raphael, that she'd had to slap him across the face to stop. He had written a brilliant essay about the painting's similarity to *The Sistine Madonna*: the style, the colours, Raphael's tendency to exaggerate certain features, but Helena had suspected the painting was a fake. Not a bad fake, but a fake. However, it was not until she met the owner that she learned Giorgio had taken twenty thousand dollars for the authentication. She could have had him fired by the Accademia. She didn't. Giorgio had run up a huge gambling debt and was more afraid of losing his life than of losing his job.

Over the phone, a slap was not an option.

"How much did she pay you?" she asked.

"I don't understand." He was breathing heavily.

"Was it in the region of twenty thousand dollars?"

"Oh dear, Helena, how could you insinuate that I would —"

"We already know that you would, the question is what did you tell her?"

There was a spluttering sound, a crash, and a man's voice, not Giorgio's, said, "He has dropped the phone. He is very ill." And this new person hung up the phone.

Giorgio was never seriously ill, but occasionally, when he was caught out, he was at a loss for words. She imagined the man who had hung up on her was the Negroni-making barman. All part of the service.

She finished her roast venison loin, dabbed up the cream

sauce with a piece of bread, and ordered the vanilla ice with berries. By then she had almost finished the Montrachet. A moment's serious thought convinced her not to order a glass of Vilmos, although she knew it would be delicious. Everything else had been.

She took the elevator up to her room and called Louise in the office. Louise still called herself a secretary. She had no interest in being known as Helena's assistant. Except for the few paintings she liked in the Louvre, she knew little about art. "A man called this afternoon," she said. "I was to get an urgent message to you. The man you were interested in showed up at his door. The one they used to call 'bull,' spelled B-i-k-a. He said you would know."

"Was he frightened?"

"How the hell would I know?"

It took a long time for Gábor Nagy to answer his phone, and when he did, he sounded even fainter than he had when Helena met him.

"He visited me last night," Nagy said. "He was standing outside for about an hour, then he came upstairs. He must have had a way to open doors."

"Have you called the police?" Helena asked.

"No point. They wouldn't do anything unless I can pay them, and I can't."

"What did he want?"

"For me to forget about Vorkuta. As if I ever could."

"He threatened you?"

"I don't care about his threats. But you have to be more careful now. He knows about you."

"I'll come over later tonight," Helena said.

"There's no point. There is nothing you can do for me. Just

take care of yourself." He disconnected, and Helena took apart the phone she had been using.

Marianne Lewis had checked out of the Tulip Hotel after complaints by the manageress that she spent too little time in Budapest. Now, when Helena contemplated what to wear for the party, she decided that, because Marianne Lewis had also almost outlived her usefulness, she would give her a last outing.

By the time she had changed her clothes, it was 8 p.m. and fair to assume that Kis would be at home, awaiting his party guests. Just to be on the safe side, she stopped by his office. The metal protector bars were up, the door to the courtyard locked but ridiculously easy to open, his office empty. Obviously, anyone wishing to steal valuable art knew better than to break into this gallery. The surprising part was why Krestin had picked Kis to sell the Titian. Géza Márton's annual payments to Kis to find his painting was less surprising since Géza paid similar retainers to five other gallery owners in the city and one in Bratislava. Géza didn't like to take chances.

Ferenc Kis lived in the Castle district — an easy walk even in bad weather — on Fö, the first street off Deák Ferenc Square, parallel with the Danube. It had started to rain and was darker than she had expected, but not so dark that she missed the policeman loitering under one of the great chestnut trees in Roosevelt Square. She thought it might be Fehér, but this man seemed slimmer, about the size of Simon. On the other hand, he could have shrunk in the rain ... The Montrachet must have affected her mind, she thought, grinning into her hood.

She crossed the Széchenyi Chain Bridge. The rain was keeping the tourists away and she encountered only a wet Hungarian flag decorating one of the stone lions, a desultory figure in a black tent begging near the middle, and a few gulls shivering along the rail. She tossed the phone she'd disassembled into the Danube.

The man, whoever he was, hadn't followed her.

Kis's apartment was a couple of blocks along Fö in a swanky building, freshly painted in the soft oranges of the Castle district. There were acacia trees in front of the rust-coloured entrance, a white canvas canopy above, and glass down the sides of the door that gave onto a marble lobby. Helena was surprised to find the door unlocked. According to the board, F. and G. Kis lived on the fifth and top floor. A cheerful woman chirped, "Hello," when Helena rang the bell, and buzzed her upstairs without asking for a name. The woman was already waiting at the apartment's open door when Helena arrived. She had taken the stairs.

Mrs. Kis was a small, chubby woman with blond ringlets, a round face with crimson lips and serious eye-liner, wearing a clinging rose-pink dress cut off above her dimpled knees. She had a soft handshake that slipped out of Helena's grasp the moment after it had slipped in. "Gabi," she said with a show of teeth and upper gums. She took Helena's wet jacket and hung it up near the door. "Gabi Kis. You are a little early but it's okay. Feri is getting dressed in the back room, and the others are not yet here, but you are welcome. Please come in." She spoke English well with a hint of a New York accent in the vowels.

Helena followed her into a spacious living room with tall picture windows offering a view along the Danube. Having nothing else to say, Helena remarked on how majestic the river looked, even in the rain, as she stood a quarter turned toward the view.

There was a long white sofa with soft cushions, a multi-coloured Turkish rug, and a dozen paintings of the kind the

Kis gallery displayed — peasants in fields, shepherds in shaggy costumes smoking long-stemmed pipes, sunsets on the Great Plain. There was one drawing that merited a second glance — nineteenth century, a man in dark clothes with a white shirt at a wooden table with green glasses and a bottle of wine. Could be Munkácsy, or a fine imitation.

Gabi offered her wine — red or white — and some baked hors d'oeuvres on a silver tray, then joined her at the window. "I wish it would stop raining," Gabi said. "It's hard to find parking around here, and it's worse in the rain. People don't like to walk anymore."

Helena smiled and nodded. Her feet were soaked, as was the rest of her. The wine — she'd chosen red — was execrable, cloyingly sweet, with the aroma of a stagnant pool. She placed the glass on an antique sidetable. Either the Kises were economizing, or they planned to poison their guests this evening. Helena didn't expect to be more than a few minutes here and didn't want to spoil the lingering taste of her Montrachet with plonk. She hadn't expected a welcome party, so she must have been mistaken for someone else, but she was ready to enjoy the situation.

A couple arrived with a bottle of wine they described in detail — Eger, second harvest — and introduced themselves to Helena as Dr. and Mrs. Kálmán. They were proud that they had walked from their apartment on Hunyadi János Street. "It's murderous to try to park around here," Mrs. Kálmán said in English. "But we were so looking forward to meeting you. Gabi has told us all about your interesting life."

Gabi introduced Helena as Ms. Hoffman. They all shook hands, then Helena said, "My name, actually, is Helena Marsh. It was very sweet of you to invite me to your gathering."

Gabi stood with her arms at her side, her mouth slightly open, her head swivelling from Helena to the new guests and back. The Kálmáns merely remarked on the fact that Helena spoke excellent English, as did their hostess, who had studied at Bard College in New York State. They, themselves, had studied in London.

Two more guests came just as Gabi started to ask what Helena was doing there, and as those introductions played out, Ferenc Kis appeared. He was freshly shaved, looking trim in a striped dark-blue suit and a white shirt. He practically ran to shake hands with the newest arrival, a man he told Gabi ran the New National Gallery. Kis kissed the woman's hand and her cheek, bubbling with enthusiasm, and insisted on serving them Champagne. "The best for the best," he said in English.

When he saw Helena, he stopped smiling.

"Alas," Helena said, "I can't stay long. I have another appointment tonight. So sorry, Gabi. Perhaps next time we can have a longer chat." Then she turned to Kis. "I assume you have not shown Ms. Hoffman the letter from Matamoros."

"This is a private party," Kis said. "Not the right time to discuss such matters."

"Quite right, Ferenc, but if you should mention that painting to Sylvie, you will have to tell her the truth."

The noise in the room died down as everyone started to listen, everyone except Gabi, who was ushering another guest in, shaking out her wet raincoat, stacking her umbrella with the others in the entrance, and insisting she decide what she wanted to drink. When Sylvie Hoffman saw Helena, she clattered closer, her Blahniks denting the parquet floor, then lifted her face for a Continental air kiss and a stiff smile.

"I thought I recognized you at the gallery," she said. "Helena Marsh, whatever are you doing in this part of the world? And what have you done with your hair?"

"How about coffee in the morning?" Helena said. "We can talk about the Budapest art scene. Where are you staying?"

"The Hilton, of course." Sylvie waved her glass in the direction of Castle Hill.

"Are you staying long?"

"Only a few days, I hope. Nothing but business."

Helena returned to the Gresham a few minutes after 10 p.m. She went into the Ladies Room off the lobby to take off her wig and shake out the jacket and the umbrella. She didn't remove all her makeup, thinking the lights were soft in the lobby at this time of night and no one was likely to look at her closely as she passed through to the elevators. Had she taken the stairs, someone might have wondered, and the doors at her floor might also have been locked. Good hotels don't like having strangers wandering around, bothering the guests.

As she rounded the last bushy palm, she saw the man in the tracksuit. He was lounging in a different leather chair from the one he had slumped in the last time she saw him, and now he made no pretense of reading a newspaper. He stood when he saw her and said, "*Zdrastvuyte, ghevoshka*" — hello, little girl. "You have had a busy day," he added, still in Russian.

"What do you want?" she asked, also in Russian.

He smiled. His two front teeth were missing. Someone's fist must have connected with his mouth at least once. "Piotr Denisovich Grigoriev would like to meet you."

Helena had learned early in her martial arts training never to be intimidated. Another early lesson taught her that being large was no advantage. The bigger they are, the harder they fall, and all that. The Albanian instructor her father had hired had never met a man he could not fell in less than one minute, and he was shorter than Helena and weighed about the same. Helena had studied with him for seven years and learned that practice and split-second decisions were the key ingredients of success. You had to know every move so well, no thought was necessary, only instinct. But she had been too busy the past few days to find time to train. Other than her run up to Krestin's house and marching along sidewalks, she had not been able to exercise. The man who faced her now looked as if he hadn't ever missed a day in the gym.

On the other hand, this was the Gresham lobby and not even a Russian oligarch would want someone in his entourage to attack another guest in full view of the front desk and the concièrge.

"Please come with me to Mr. Grigoriev's suite," the man said.

"After you," she said. Her whole body tensed then relaxed as she balanced on the balls of her feet, her arms tight at her side, her hands flat in their strike position.

When he reached out to usher her into the waiting elevator,

she hit his hand with just enough force to make him drop it. It was comforting to know that, had she decided to do so, she could have broken it.

"You can stand at the back, if you wish," he growled, holding his hand and wincing. "He told me you may not wish to come with me."

"You go in first," she said. A young couple, dressed for a formal occasion swept past them into the elevator. They were smirking at Helena and the tracksuit, as if they had witnessed a lovers' spat. "It's been a long day," Helena said, smiling at them. Tracksuit entered the elevator and stood with his legs apart, his hands in front of his genitals.

He got off at the fourth floor and held the elevator door for her, as a polite man would do, although Helena didn't like his arm at her side as she exited. And she didn't much like the burly man with the pockmarked face who stood next to the elevator, or the man with the buzz cut and crumpled brown suit who said he was Mr. Grigoriev's secretary and that Mr. Grigoriev was waiting inside.

When the secretary tried to follow her in, Tracksuit grabbed his arm. "Ms. Marsh," he said in Russian, "hates anyone behind her." He attempted another toothless smile.

How the hell did he know she was Helena, let alone that she didn't like anyone at her back? It was definitely time to find another alter ego. She would have to stop in Bratislava before this trip was over. The best document thief and forger in Europe, perhaps in the world, lived there, on Michalská Street.

The room was softly lit by a standing lamp near the entrance. A woman in a long dark dress with a loose open back was playing a Chopin nocturne on a grand piano by the window.

Grigoriev was sitting on a brocade-covered sofa, ignoring the view of the lit-up Széchenyi Chain Bridge and the Buda Castle beyond. But as Helena entered, he looked at her and then out the window, holding his hands palm up in a theatrical gesture that said, look, isn't that lovely, and he smiled. "Such a fantastic city, so much like something out of the nineteenth century, don't you think," he said. "It's easy to be fooled by its charms. Not so easy to keep in mind that it was once a Nazi stronghold, that here they shoved Jews into boxcars or dumped them into that picturesque river. No better than the Ukrainians."

Or the Russians, she thought. She didn't move from the entrance.

"Please," he said, "sit."

She didn't.

"A glass of wine, perhaps?"

She stayed where she was.

"The last time we spoke, you said there may be another time we would do business," he said in Russian, "and this could be that time. The Titian —"

"Is a fake," she said. "Unlike Mr. Dalchev, who was the real thing."

Grigoriev laughed. "You have kept your sense of humour after all these years." He got up from the sofa and walked over to the silver drinks trolley. He had less hair on top now, but although he was trying to seem friendly his black button eyes still looked calculating. He was shorter than she remembered, or he had gained some weight and his proportions had changed. Still the overlong arms, the hairy hands, the flashy white shirt with the high custom collar, the long double cuffs, the striped suit with overly wide shoulders, the slightly pointed shoes — crocodile, as before? The years he had spent in the vicinity of the Savile Row's bespoke tailors so beloved by his compatriots had not changed his style.

"I have promised Olga a new painting for her suite of rooms. She had her heart set on the Titian — she is quite religious you know — but I think I could placate her with something else. Another painting." He poured himself a couple of inches of vodka and filled up the crystal glass with crushed ice from the bucket. "Stoli Elit," he said. "They bring it in for people who know what the real thing is — vodka that shouldn't be adulterated with cheap mixes, but drunk pristine as it was intended. Sure you won't change your mind?"

Helena shook her head. She walked over to a straight-backed chair near the piano and sat down, Marcia's switchblade digging into her vertebrae, her feet planted firmly in case she needed to spring up quickly.

"How did your man identify me?" she asked.

"How? Or when? I've had you followed since the day you arrived. These childish disguises? Come now, Helena, they are period pieces. From a different period of your life, don't you think? Seriously?"

"In Nice?" she asked.

"And in Cluj."

Vladimir said he had hired the driver through an agency. He had denied knowledge of the driver's attempt to take the painting without pay. Had he been telling the truth?

"You have other paintings for sale," Grigoriev said. "They may not be as impressive as this one, but Olga would prefer the genuine article to a forgery, if it is a forgery. I have my doubts about your friend from the Accademia, and I suspect his motives. But at this price, I am not going to chance it. I have always preferred to play it safe."

"I didn't say it was a forgery. It is a fake. An imitation of Titian's style."

"Is there a difference? In St. Petersburg you were talking about fakes and authenticity and provenance. Frankly, I don't care which. But if this Titian is not the real thing, I am not going to fork over eighty million."

Helena shrugged. "What do you want from me?" she asked.

"I could settle for a Degas, or a Matisse, maybe a Renoir, something with a bit of colour, and I would prefer it not to have an overtly religious subject. I am reluctant to go home without a gift from this trip." He gazed at the pianist's naked back and smiled again.

"She would not have liked the Titian, then," she said.

"Perhaps not, but she would have liked its value. You know about women. The ones with refined tastes."

"You know I don't do the Impressionists," she said.

Olga would be his fourth wife. Helena remembered seeing her in *Vanity Fair* only a few years ago. She was blond and willowy, much like his previous three wives. The first one, naturally, was the stolid Russian who had lived with Grigoriev in the years when he made his first million, the one who gave birth to all the little Grigorievs, at least one of whom had been at the Hermitage negotiating the purchase of Old Masters when Helena was there. She had noted after the first year that at least a hundred works in the museum were fakes or forgeries. The fact that so many of them had been acquired from scions of the old Russian nobility was no guarantee of their provenance. Back then, Grigoriev could get excited about a Giorgione and a Raphael, but even then, he had admitted to a particular fondness for Impressionists. Bearing in mind Grigoriev's inability to tell the difference between a work of genius and a forgery, she was sure she could find him a suitable painting to take home.

Elmyr de Hory had painted some very fine Picassos, a few excellent Degases, and some Matisses so like Matisse's own that perhaps the master (or his mistress) might have thought he had done them himself. Chances were that Grigoriev wouldn't check. He would imagine that Helena had been sufficiently cowed she wouldn't play a trick on him. And it would be lovely to present him with a de Hory, after her warning about de Hory's work. Then there was that perfectly awful fake that Gertrude had wanted to sell.

She was still smarting from their confrontation in St. Petersberg, and now there was the matter of Dalchev and Grigoriev's penchant for having her followed.

She would make that trip to Bratislava sooner than expected.

At 6:40 p.m., Attila was waiting at the front doors of the Historical Archives. Arriving a half hour early was a pointed way of letting a woman know that her presence in your evening was important. Especially when you had asked her for a favour that could have, in more stringent times, meant her dismissal. Original files, even when requested by relatives, must never leave the building. He still wasn't sure how exactly he had managed to persuade Mrs. Lévay to go against her own strict instructions to staff, never mind her instinct for survival, but he had succeeded.

She appeared a sensible ten minutes past the hour. She was wearing black high-heeled shoes and a simple black dress that managed to cling to her body as she walked, and she was carrying a red purse. The notion of matching shoes and handbags seemed to have entirely bypassed Magda Lévay. That was one of several things Attila liked about her.

Attila leaped from the car with an agility that defied his girth and age, swept Magda up in his arms, and kissed her on both cheeks. "How wonderful to see you," he shouted. There were always cameras and sound equipment outside the Archives. Wild enthusiasm would distract any observers from the suspicion that they needed to pay attention.

Magda, taken aback at first, responded happily. "I hadn't wanted to mention it, Attila, but you have been notable by your absence since . . . well, since the last time we spent an evening with Gustav." She checked the back seat of the car. "Hello, Gustav. Glad you could join us."

Attila handed her into the front seat and dashed around to the driver's side. With the door still open (and the windows down), he said, "Why don't we have a drink on the InterContinental's terrace, then we can take Gustav for a walk along the Embankment? He'll have a little frolic, then" — he put up the car window and lowered his voice — "we can go for dinner at Kisbuda Gyöngye. It's just off Bécsi Street, in the third district, but it's worth the drive. The food is excellent, and you'll like the setting." Of course, he had no idea whether she would like the setting, but it was the best restaurant he could think of where they might be unobserved.

"With Gustav?" she asked somewhat archly.

"Not exactly. The new owner is crazy about dachshunds, and she will take him to the garden in the back."

They drove across the bridge in silence. Attila wasn't sure how or when to ask whether she had brought the file. He didn't want her to think that the file was the only reason he had asked her to dinner. On the other hand, he had to see the file, and the sooner the better. He was quite certain that the past held the key to the identities of the killer or killers. In Hungary, the present was so deeply rooted in the past, it was not even the past. Unless you were born after 1980, in which case you had probably left the country to enjoy the benefits of being a free citizen of Europe.

He was afraid that Magda's silence reflected her disappointment that he had not followed up on their last evening together. He had still been hurting over the loss of his marriage and his apartment had been little better than a student flat. His shirts had been distributed throughout the apartment, Gustav had used the tatty couch as his personal domain, the bed was unmade, the kitchen sink full of dishes, and several days of newspapers, movie tickets, amusement park brochures, milk cartons, sausage wrappers, and a police-issue Ruger handgun were strewn over the kitchen table. He had been embarrassed that the chaos of his private life was so painfully revealed.

It was not until they arrived at the InterContinental that he broke the silence with, "I am so glad you came." He handed his car keys to the doorman, as if he were in the habit of having other people park his car.

"I was wondering," Magda said, "why it took you so long to ask."

"I wasn't sure you would be willing to try again."

Once they were seated on the terrace café, he ordered a bottle of Olasz riesling with a bottle of soda and ice. He wanted to show her he remembered she liked this wine. At first, they talked lightly, about the vast numbers of tourists, the difficulty of finding cafés and restaurants not overrun by visiting Germans and Americans, the recent influx of Scandinavians, the noisy tour boats on the Danube, the drop in the forint's value, Gustav's avid interest in every passerby, the astonishing variety of new acts of parliament, the debate over compensation for those forced to move to the country in the early 1950s — pretty much everything other than whether she had brought the file.

It wasn't until Attila let Gustav off his leash for a run alongside the river that Magda asked whether he was investigating János Krestin's murder. He said he was working for the police, for Tóth, but not for Tóth alone, because Krestin's case had been taken over by Homicide.

"You don't like Tóth much?" she asked.

Attila shrugged. "He's not bad. No imagination, which makes him ideal for the job, but he is on the take. Nothing major, but he likes to keep his hand in the till. If you want to get away with a major crime in this city, there are always policemen you can bribe. I am of the old school. Tóth is more modern."

"When you were in the Archives last time, you wanted to know about Gertrude Lakatos?" Magda asked.

"Yes. She was once Géza Márton's girlfriend, and I was curious about Márton. I still am."

"She was more than that. In 1957, after Márton left, she became Mrs. Krestin."

"She did?" Now he knew why he hadn't been able to get the Gertrude Lakatos file from Magda's assistant.

"She left him in 1981 and moved to Slovakia. Little place called Dunajská Streda — Dunaszerdahely in an earlier life. That's where her family had come from. They are all buried in the cemetery there with the other Hungarians. There were a few reports about her in the Czechoslovak state police files by agents of the ŠtB. Nothing major. While she lived here, she went north every year to tend to her family's graves, on All Saints Day."

"Children?"

"One son. He makes his living as a house painter, and he took a few art courses. He never finished high school."

"What were the reports about?"

"Whether she took part in political gatherings. She didn't. At least not before 1989. The ŠtB was dispersed in '89. There were no more reports after that."

"Has anyone else asked to see her file in the archives?"

"A woman called Marianne Lewis. An American. She claimed she was a relative of Mrs. Krestin, but when my office called Krestin, he denied his wife had American relatives. So we didn't let her in. She came the same day as you."

Marianne Lewis? Who the hell was Marianne Lewis? And how did she fit into the Márton-Marsh-Krestin picture?

Attila didn't ask her about the Krestin file till she slipped it into his hand at the end of their drive along Bécsi Street. The file was a lot thinner than Géza Márton's, but that was not surprising. Krestin had been a stalwart Party member, while Márton was suspected of harbouring ill feelings toward the state.

He read it sitting in the car under an old chestnut tree near the Kisbuda Gyöngye restaurant, while Magda took Gustav for a stroll along the herbaceous border, where other dogs had left messages for Gustav's enjoyment.

The notes started in 1948 when Krestin was twenty-five years old. He had professed he was a member of the Communist Party of Hungary, a group, the first report said, with its own ideas about the future of the country. There was a single line about his having met Comrade Rákosi when both of them were arrested in 1943. Rákosi served a year in prison, but Krestin did not. That was interesting. In 1944, the government imprisoned card-carrying Communists, even suspected Communists, for as long as possible, or as long as it stayed in power. Perhaps it had other uses for Krestin? In 1948, Rákosi, who had become prime minister and first secretary of the Communist Party's Central Committee, must have become suspicious of Krestin for some reason and ordered the surveillance. There was no explanation in the file.

The notes recorded Krestin's meetings with other members of his Communist cell. They met once a week in the old Emke Café, where they drank beer and talked. They had made no attempt to disguise their discussions. The notes had few details — the noise, the note said, was deafening — but what there was read like a bunch of young people debating the fabulous future they were promised under Soviet rule. There was a list of names, with the nicknames they called one another. They had voted on a list of essentials: no more hunger, the ascendency of the working class, voluntary membership in the armed struggle to bring Communist ideas to other countries where workers were still living in the nineteenth century.

One of the nicknames was Bika, the name Helena Marsh had mentioned when he told her that Krestin had been killed. There was a small handwritten note here: "Gulag #442." Alongside that note: "János Krestin was a model prisoner." So, perhaps he, too, had been in Vorkuta.

Krestin had read a great deal of foreign literature: Camus, Sartre, Stendhal, de Maupassant. One member of the surveillance team read several passages from one of the books Krestin had talked about by a man called "Dikens." The writer was unsure of the spelling, but it was certainly a foreign work and, he thought, possibly subversive.

The next surveillance notes were written by a woman with the initials J.S. who had been inside Krestin's apartment in Újpest and wrote about his morning routines of drinking coffee, exercising, and reading the newspaper. He had seemed particularly interested in the trial of László Rajk, one of the original organizers of the Party and the founder of the state security police. She said she thought he was not actively involved with Rajk, who was later accused of being a Titoist spy. This was in the days when being an admirer of Yugoslavia's Tito was a crime, although he had been designated a friend in earlier times. Krestin had told several of his friends, many of whom were already working for the state police, that he supported re-education for people like Rajk. The person who had received this particular report had written on the margin: "Not!" Rajk, as Attila knew, had already been slated for execution by then.

He was amazed to learn that the people who had commissioned these reports worked in the same building and for the same organization as Krestin. How could this surveillance have remained hidden from a man of Krestin's standing in the hierarchy? Had one of the seventeen departments of the ÁVO had special powers that extended to spying on their own?

While in bed with Krestin, J.S. had initiated conversations about Rakosi, then boss of the Communist Party in Hungary; his sidekick Ernö Gerö; Stalin; and even Soviet First Deputy Premier Vyacheslav Molotov. (It must have been a marvelously satisfying experience for both of them, Attila thought and tried to imagine what sexual situation would most readily lend itself to such a dialogue.) Krestin had been fervent in his boundless admiration for all of them. As per instructions, she had installed a number of listening devices in his rooms and assured her handler that no conversations occurred other than those recorded.

There was a neatly typed memorandum dated February 11, 1953, from Krestin to László Péter, recommending continued surveillance of Géza Márton. Péter, Attila knew, had been the feared and despised head of ÁVO, the state security police in Hungary; he was arrested a few months later, tried at a court martial in 1954, and condemned to life in prison. Like his boss, the unlamented Gerö, Péter was charged with being part of the Soviet-invented Jewish conspiracy to control elite positions within the Soviet bureaucracy.

The name Bika popped up again as one of a group of friends who had visited Krestin at home.

Krestin's report on what he had observed during the 1956 Revolution was in the file, together with his sworn testimony that he had been a witness to the attack on Party headquarters. He had been inside the building in the morning, went out for something to eat, and found the crowd had grown much larger while he was away. Instead of entering the building, he had gone home for a camera. It was a German-made Leica, already four years old, a gift from Ernö Gerö, the comrade who had earned his stripes in the NKVD, forerunner of the KGB. (Why would Gerö have given Krestin a camera? He was not known for his generosity even toward those who followed all his orders.) Krestin had taken photos of some of the people in the square. He claimed that he told anyone asking why that he worked for *LIFE* magazine. The photographs were fuzzy, some had been scratched, some folded and bits were missing from five of them. Clearly, someone had decided to eliminate a few faces.

A signed affidavit testified that Krestin had seen Károly

Márton carrying a rifle at the scene and witnessed his aiming it at one of the officers who had escaped from the building.

A new observer wrote that Krestin met Gertrude Lakatos in January 1957 in a bar called Kedves, close to ÁVO headquarters on Andrássy Avenue. She had offered to teach him French. He had accepted. There was a report on his courtship of her, because she was already a person of interest. Her former liaison with Géza Márton had triggered an investigation. The Krestin file cross-referenced a file under her name. There was a note there about her family's move from Slovakia to Hungary and Krestin's first meeting with her parents. The person who wrote the report must have been close to Gertrude, as he (she?) knew that Krestin had been invited to dine with her parents and that the meeting had been frosty. Krestin had not been interested in listening to the elder Lakatos's views on collective farming and his critique of the latest five-year plan. The next time this person reported contact between the parents and Krestin was at the wedding, a civil ceremony.

Krestin had remained friendly with his group of Communists as they aged. One of them died, the others, including Bika, kept meeting Krestin for drinks and dinners.

There was no mention anywhere of a relationship between Géza Márton and János Krestin. No mention that they had ever known each other. If, as Helena Marsh had said, the Titian or quasi-Titian that Krestin had decided to sell had once belonged to Márton, there was no suggestion in the file of how Krestin had acquired it.

There were several reports from Toronto and one from Vaughan, dating from Márton's arrival in Canada in early 1957. The fact that these were in Krestin's file suggested that he had initiated the surveillance, but there was no signature and no names attached to the reports.

Krestin, who had been close to the various governments that followed the collapse of Soviet rule, could easily have accessed these files and just as easily removed anything he thought incriminating. The existence of the file was evidence that Krestin himself had been under suspicion.

Márton had plenty of motives for Krestin's murder: the imprisonment of his father, the loss of Gertrude's affections, or just the fact that Krestin had been a faithful ÁVO officer in the service of a murderous state. Heck, thought Attila, that alone should have been enough to have the bugger killed.

Magda came back to the car with a very cheerful Gustav, and the three of them entered Kisbuda Gyöngye exactly on time for their 8 p.m. reservation. The maître d' looked stunned by this unaccustomed punctuality. Their table was not yet ready, but the owner was delighted to see them ("Such a long time, Attila.") and squired Gustav into the garden.

The restaurant was exactly as he had remembered: low lights, red tablecloths under white ones, gold-edged white plates, tall crystal glasses, deep armchairs, four to a table. The maître d' showed them to the corner table, with just two armchairs, far from the kitchen, and served them glasses of Champagne to start.

"Lovely place," Magda said. She seemed to relax now that the file was safely back in her purse. "Did you find what you were looking for?"

"I am not sure yet. János Krestin was not the most likable guy, but we still need to find out who killed him. Did you read his file?"

"Of course, as soon as I heard that he had been murdered.

He was an old-style Commie, not someone you would have wanted to cross in the good old days. It's interesting how fast he managed to become part of the new capitalist system. He had become useful as a negotiator for gas prices. He spoke good English, French, serviceable Russian. Bought a football team, a couple of apartment houses, a shopping mall. Invested in the movie business. A seamless transition with a great deal of unexplained cash. Friends in high places. A few boards. Connections with all political parties."

"You can buy political connections everywhere. The only questions are how much and to what end," Attila said. "Even Americans use money to buy votes. It's not as obvious as here, but everybody knows."

"You were also interested in his wives?"

"Wives?"

"He had two. Too few for a Hungarian, don't you think? Are you planning to remarry?"

The thought hadn't crossed his mind. He gulped down his water and pretended he hadn't heard the question. He told her what he had gleaned about Gertrude. "I assume his second wife is still alive?"

"Yes. She's much younger than him."

"Children?"

"Just the one with his first wife."

"I wonder whether your great video system managed to get a shot of the woman who had asked to see her file."

"Ms. Lewis? Of course," Magda said triumphantly, and she produced a fuzzy but unmistakable picture of Helena Marsh.

"That's Marianne Lewis?"

"Yes. She showed us an American passport when we asked. We don't let just anyone walk into the Archives, you know."

Alexander had told him that Helena was a master of disguises. She could be anything she wanted. Young, old, pretty, frumpy. And she could be dangerous. This woman had killed a man in Russia. Could she have killed two men in Budapest?

The Russian in St. Petersburg had had his throat cut.

He couldn't shake the image of her walking across the Szabadság Bridge, her skirt swishing around her long, tanned legs, her smile. Then he remembered her clinical concentration when he showed her the photos of the dead Ivan Dalchev. She had shown no shock, no disgust, just that little smile, different from the one on the bridge but still a smile.

He let Magda order the wine, because he was sure she would be frugal. The last time they had met, she told him she had never had Champagne before. Not even Hungarian sparkling wine. He was optimistic she would select something less expensive than what he, in thanks for her bringing him the file, would have felt obliged to order. She studied the list with the attention she would have given a new acquisition for the Archives, or so he thought. In the end, she decided on a half litre of the house red and one of the white. Luckily Kisbuda Gyöngye had chosen its house wines with care.

After they ordered, she talked about the sixty boxes of state police files that had been found in a warehouse in Szúcs and, although she wouldn't mention names, she said they were all on highly placed people whose pasts had been successfully buried until now. Attila presumed the contents would be revealed selectively, depending on whose lives would be hurt and how much those lives were worth.

She thought there might be more information in these files about Krestin and his connections during and after the war.

He did not tell her that he had been hired to follow Helena

Marsh, but he did say that he was interested in the No.442 Gulag file. Everywhere he turned, the camp's name came up. He was becoming convinced that the answers to this case lay there.

"I may be able to help you with that file," she said after her second glass of wine. "I will be in charge of cataloguing them, and my staff will enter them into the records."

He took her hand across the table and held it, gently.

"All the original Gulag files have been transferred to the vaults," she said.

He kissed her palm.

"But I have access to the vaults."

He poured more wine and gazed into her eyes.

"Perhaps—" she said, as his phone buzzed. He ignored it, but it buzzed again almost immediately.

"Helena Marsh," a woman's voice said. "I have something for you. It's about the man they called Bika. Can we meet in half an hour?"

He should have said no, but he didn't. Instead, he gave Magda a sorrowful look and said, "I have to work tonight, after all."

She withdrew her hand.

"Could we do this again next week?" he asked.

Magda didn't reply. Nor did she say anything on the drive across the Danube to her building off Erzsébet Királyné Street. Had Attila been more courageous, he would have ventured a joke or a cheerful remark about the exigencies of after-hours work, but she had turned into a statue. It was only when he drew up in front of the entrance that he dared a gentle "Goodnight then," and climbed out of the car to open her door only to discover that she had already left without so much as a curt farewell.

"I will call you on Monday," he said feebly to her back.

She shrugged without turning and walked into the building without a backward glance. A lost opportunity, he thought, regretfully. But, then, Helena Marsh was waiting for him in the lobby of her hotel. He found even the idea of her exciting and, yes, maybe dangerous. He had assumed that he was long past the age of finding danger an aphrodisiac, but with Helena it was the whole package: attractive, confident, muscular in a feminine way, foreign. That little smile of hers had somehow quickened his pulse. He squared his shoulders and made a valiant effort to rein in his belly.

Even dressed in training pants and a T-shirt, she seemed too attractive for an art expert. But, then, Attila's idea of an art expert was a weedy egghead with a tuft of hair and the facial expression of a giraffe — somewhat like Kis, in fact. She greeted him with the same smile that had got his attention in the gallery. As if she were thinking over a joke or knew something funny she had chosen not to reveal. Yet.

"I thought I would go for a run up and down Gellért Hill and along the Danube," she said. "Since you won't let me leave the city, I may as well get to know it better."

"What is so urgent you had to see me tonight?" he asked as gruffly as he could manage.

"You remember the old man in the apartment building near the synagogue?" she asked.

He stared at her.

"You followed me to Dob Street and waited outside the building where the old man lives."

"I may have . . ."

"Gábor Nagy," she said. "I assume you worked that out."

There was no point in dissembling. "I may have."

"He contacted me today. He says he is afraid. Someone has threatened him."

"What does that have to do with János Krestin? Or with the dead Bulgarian?"

"The man who threatened him is called Gyula Németh. When they were all in Vorkuta, he went by the name of Bika, most likely because he looked like a bull."

"Who all?"

"Nagy, Márton, Németh, and Krestin. Gyula Németh is the man I mentioned to you before, but I didn't know his real name then. Now I do. And I know that he told Gábor Nagy he could find himself being thrown down into his courtyard to sniff the remnants of his potted plants if he talked about Vorkuta to anyone. And one more thing, this guy Németh was in your ÁVO with Krestin."

"It's not my ÁVO," Attila said. "And who told you that?"

"Nagy. It's amazing how his memory returned when he needed it. When I talked with him before, he was all for burying the past and letting the future take care of itself. That's why he didn't tell me Németh's name then. Very philosophical. Now, it turns out, he remembers."

"And why would this man want to kill Krestin?"

"Perhaps they shared a secret he didn't want revealed. Maybe Krestin owed him and didn't pay up. I don't know, but judging by what Nagy told me, Németh was the muscle in that camp. And now that Krestin is dead, Nagy felt free to tell me that Krestin was in charge of a group of prisoners. He was a kapo, and Bika was his enforcer."

"You made me come all the way here to tell me this?"

"Not entirely," she said. "I think Nagy needs protection. If this Bika knows enough to threaten him, he could be thinking of killing him, and you and your friends in the police may be tired of finding dead bodies. The first two may have been unpredictable, but for this one, you have had fair warning."

Alexander was smoking his second Sobranie and enjoying a glass of whisky and crushed ice when Attila arrived at the Diablo. The Russian waiter was hovering over the table, talking in a low voice. Being Russian, he managed to keep his face almost expressionless, but his hands were moving as if he were weighing something. Attila hoped it was nothing that concerned him. Perhaps sins against the ruling czar.

When he saw Attila, Alexander leaned back in his seat, blew a smoke ring, and said, "Hello *faszfej*," then lifted his finger over his glass and pointed at Attila to indicate to the waiter that Attila wanted the same drink. Attila ignored being greeted as a dickhead and wedged himself into the seat across the table. Alexander wasted no time in asking Attila why he had thought it important to take a run at Grigoriev, and, since he had decided to ignore Alexander's very clear instructions, exactly what he thought he had accomplished.

"Not much except to make them think that they are not immune here, that having billions does not justify killing someone or refusing to co-operate with the police when the dead man was one of your employees."

Alexander finished his drink. "You knew he hadn't killed the guy."

"Personally? Of course not. But that so-called secretary of his could have done it."

The waiter arrived with Attila's drink, and Alexander ordered two more.

"I tried to tell you where to look for the killer."

"Italians? There are none here, as far as we can tell."

"Tihanyi?"

"Don't be silly. And he is not Italian."

"Never overlook an Italian connection when there's money involved. But what about the woman?"

"I met her today." More than once, he thought. He decided not to mention Nagy. He had already called Tóth and asked him to send a plainclothes guy to watch the building.

"And?"

"And nothing. I don't believe she did it."

"Of course not," Alexander said with an exaggerated seriousness that may have passed for sarcasm in Russia. "And it wasn't her who did in Krestin either, right?"

Attila was surprised. The police hadn't released any information on how Krestin died. Given his age, he could have died of a heart attack in his bed. The only local newspaper that could still publish uncensored news had merely mentioned that he had died, and it ran a glowing obituary: owner of the Lipótváros football team (no mention of the missing funds), philanthropist, opera buff, art collector, and so on.

"You know already?" he said after the waiter brought their drinks.

Alexander laughed. "I knew before you, I expect. Piotr Denisovich was concerned that a man who tried to sell him a fake Titian should have been killed. And, despite your idiotic meddling, he called me."

"To say?"

"To ask that I look into the matter. He doesn't want any mud sticking to his name."

"Other than the mud we already know about."

Alexander finished his whisky in one gulp and lit another Sobranie. "Attila, you know too little and, at the same time, too much. You have attracted Piotr Denisovich's attention by showing up, asking dumbass questions, and pretending to be a policeman. I can try to save your hide, but it's a waste of effort if you continue to mix in his business. He is a dangerous man, but one who is careful how he acts. For example, if he were to have you drowned in the Danube, there would be no one, other than me, who'd want to know who did it and why. Tóth may even be relieved to have you off his back."

Attila thought of the girls and concluded they were too young to launch an investigation into his sudden death. Tibor had always been a let-sleeping-dogs-lie kind of guy. Tibor's mother wouldn't miss Attila. Despite her tempting invitations to drink J&B and try her delicious homemade desserts, he rarely visited her. That was also the case with Attila's own mother, and besides, she had begun a late-life affair with a spry octogenarian who disapproved of Attila's current profession. There was his cousin in Temesvár (now, for some complicated reasons, Timisoara) who was too busy trying to foment the separatist Hungarian movement in Transylvania to take time over Attila. Magda was pissed off with him and with reason. The ex would miss the monthly payments but not him.

"Furthermore, you should know that Piotr Denisovich did not have Krestin killed. He is not a stupid man. When this whole thing about the fake Titian hits the international press, he does not want to be in the limelight. For one thing, he wouldn't want it known that he can't tell a real Titian from a fake or that he hadn't hired his own expert. It would make him look cheap or unprofessional. But he does know some stuff about Krestin, as do I, that may help bring this sorry mess to a happy end."

"More than there is in the National Archive?"

"Your Archive is shit on the old ÁVO men. Your minister, Barross, let them take whatever they wanted before he decided to have the leftover files stored. The Stasi kept much better records. In Germany, there are some useful files. Here, not so much."

Attila grudgingly told him what he had found in the file. He was still annoyed with Alexander, but a good way to pull him back onside was to share information. He needed to find out what Alexander knew.

"I hear you checked on the Ukrainian," Alexander said. "Good move. Those guys were in the thick of things under the Nazis, and you would want to find out how Azarov knew about the painting."

"Did you have me followed?"

Alexander shook his head. "Not I, old friend, not I, but you have made sure there are others interested in your movements."

"As far as I can tell," Attila said, "everybody knew about the painting. Kis, or Krestin, or both of them, broadcast the sale to collectors and would-be collectors wherever they live."

"This particular Ukrainian had a father interned in the same mining camp where Márton and Krestin were."

"Krestin?"

"They were all there."

"What mine?"

"Number 442 Gulag. One of our great socialist re-education schemes. After we won the war that you guys lost. We picked up some of your losers — not many, considering — and transferred them to the Gulag."

"Re-education!"

"*Maljekij robot*. Slave labour. Call it what you will, it really doesn't matter. Vladimir Azarov's father was in the same mine as Krestin. Vorkuta."

"Why?"

"Why Azarov? One of his neighbours ratted him out as a Nazi sympathizer. There were a lot of those in Ukraine, didn't you know that?"

"And was he?"

"It turned out he wasn't, but what with a war to win and Comrade Stalin issuing orders from the Kremlin, who had time to check?"

"He was a prisoner?"

"Not exactly. He managed to get himself promoted to guard."

"And Krestin?"

"He was a good Communist, and our fathers and grand-fathers were smart to have placed a few of them among the prisoners so they would know what they talked about. There were also some unfortunate whispers about his activities in '44 that he escaped by disappearing into the camps."

"What kind of whispers?"

"The kind that could have had him hanged after the war."

"And was there talk about a big Titian painting?"

Alexander lit another cigarette, although his last one was still smouldering in the ashtray. "Perhaps," he said.

"Was it Márton's?"

"That's what I heard, and if you stop bothering my Russian, I'll tell you more about your Hungarians and that Uke. Is that a deal?"

Attila nodded.

"Word of honour?"

"*Becs szo*, but don't use that expression, please. You're dating yourself."

Alexander laughed. "*Touché.* The longer I spend in the service of the state, the more dated I feel." He was slowly reverting to the usual Alexander: cheerful, friendly, a smartass but with an edge that denoted his FSB connection. "There was talk in the camp of a Titian that Géza Márton had back home. He offered to sell it."

"Sell it? To whom?"

"To anyone who had food to trade."

 Helena found an afternoon flight to Paris. The night before, she had checked into the Gresham in her own name — in case Attila Fehér or a real policeman came looking for her — and this morning she checked out Marianne Lewis. She packed all the essentials for her trip, including the wigs, the gun, the passports, and left all her toiletries and enough clothes for the maid to ascertain that Ms. Marsh was still in residence. Steinbrunner would not need a change of clothes or a passport to go to Slovakia. And, as she had been dead for some years, she was not on anyone's list of suspects.

She ordered a taxi for 7 a.m. They crossed the Széchenyi Chain Bridge and ascended the switchback road to the Hilton at breakneck speed. Other than a couple of other taxis, there was no traffic. No sign of any car following them. Then again, she hadn't noticed Grigoriev's men (or women) tracking her, so they must blend into the environment. Either that, or she had become sloppy.

Her mother had warned her never to confuse comfort with security, as Simon had done with disastrous results. Besides, Annelise argued, Helena was now cutting her own trail. Since he hadn't lived with them or ever acknowledged that Helena was his daughter, she didn't have to carry the burden of guilt for her father's actions. Yet Helena remembered the times Annelise had screamed at him and the days she spent in tears every time he left. Her mother had never learned to cut her own trail, never even tried to walk away from him. It was always Simon who left.

They whizzed past the Matthias Church, the early vendors were unwrapping their wares, and stopped in front of the Hilton's grand entrance. She waved off the eager porter and carried her own small bag into the lobby. Despite its unusual surrounding and being built into a castle wall, it was a standard Hilton lobby. Even the house phone was where Hilton always puts its house phones. She asked the operator for Ms. Hoffman.

Sylvie sounded as if she had just been woken up. Muffled, snotty, hoarse. Perhaps the party had gone on too long or she had indulged too much. Helena hoped she had been drowning her sorrows, rather than celebrating prematurely.

"Hullo, Sylvie," she trilled with exaggerated good cheer. "So happy to catch you in. I'm in the restaurant, should I order you coffee? Juice? A continental? Or would you prefer something more substantial? Eggs?"

Sylvie groaned.

"There is a very tempting buffet with fresh eggs and bacon, Benedict, if you feel like hollandaise or —"

"For God's sake, who are you?" Sylvie mumbled.

"Helena Marsh, of course."

"Dear God. What are you . . . why?"

"How silly," Helena chided, in her over-the-top voice. "We agreed to meet, and here I am. Or would you prefer that I come to your room and we order in? Goodness, Sylvie, you sound a bit under the weather."

"No," Sylvie said, suddenly finding her voice. "You said sometime. Today is not good, really. I have a meeting at ten."

"Perfect," Helena pounced. "That gives us two hours. Sadly, I have only one hour, this morning. So much to tell you. So little time. In the Icon, then?"

"Okay," Sylvie said feebly.

Helena took a table by the window overlooking the Fisherman's Bastion and sat with her back to the wall as she always did.

She made a production of looking at her watch, and when the maître d' came to offer his help, she asked to be connected with Ms. Hoffman in Room 550. The maître d' checked his computer and informed her that she had made a mistake. Ms. Hoffman was not in 550, she was in the Turquoise Suite on the third floor. He would immediately connect her. Helena smiled and said she thought she should maybe just wait a little longer. Her friend had enjoyed herself too much the night before. When the maître d' was no longer watching, she took the elevator to the third floor and waited outside Sylvie's door.

"Oh," Sylvie exclaimed when she saw Helena. "You are here."

She looked considerably less imperious than the day before at the gallery and a great deal less charming than at the party held in her honour. There were dark circles under her eyes, and her shirt was misbuttoned. She was wearing loose grey pants and loafers.

"I thought you might need a little help finding the Icon. We have a table with a lovely view."

"The what?" Sylvie croaked.

"The restaurant is called the Icon." Helena said. She took a paper handkerchief from her bag and suggested that Sylvie dab off the mascara that had collected overnight under her eyes. Then she steered her to the elevator. She still had her by the elbow when they arrived at their table. Helena signalled the waiter for coffee and thrust the menu into Sylvie's hand. "This won't take long," she said. "I want to give you some advice about Kis and the painting. You know, I assume, about the murder?"

The local papers and newscasts had been full of Krestin's death, but Sylvie Hoffman couldn't understand Hungarian. The English-language *Budapest News* hadn't caught up with the story yet. Krestin wasn't a news item in the U.S. media online. Helena presumed that Kis hadn't told her, as he wouldn't have wanted to scare her off.

Sylvie stared at her. So, no, she hadn't known.

Helena was also the first to tell her that Giorgio had played her for a sucker, and that the Titian was a fake. She showed her Giorgio's letter.

When Helena finished, Sylvie hadn't even touched her coffee. She kept looking out the window at the restored fortification, her eyes fixed on the spires. She claimed to have a colossal headache.

"What were you drinking?" Helena asked in the most sympathetic voice she could conjure.

"Wine," Sylvie muttered, dabbing her damp forehead with her napkin. "And something called palinka. Kis said it was the national drink." She had begun to take deep breaths while Helena was talking. Then she stood up.

"I need to think about this," she said and rushed into the lobby.

She needed to throw up, of course. Helena hoped she'd make it to a toilet. Next, Sylvie would call the hedge-fund king for instructions. It was unlikely a man with such an ego would intentionally buy a fake. He had bought a couple of Simon specials back in the day, but experts had certified them. To prove their worth, Simon had sold one to a dealer in Berlin, a Corot landscape with fauns. Hundreds of similar paintings were produced in the late nineteenth and early twentieth centuries, and John Myatt had made a few excellent imitations in the early 1980s.

Simon had been a steadfast supporter of the market in Corot and Cellini fakes. It was difficult to overestimate the gullibility of avid collectors, he had told her, and fakes were, generally, easier to steal than the real thing — unless, of course, they were already masquerading as the real thing, preening on museum walls and protected by elaborate alarm systems.

Myatt's genius for creating acknowledged fakes had been rewarded with a sale that had netted his dealer about sixty thousand dollars. It had been a small step from there to forging "original" works by Matisse, Giacometti, Chagall, and others. Simon had met Myatt a few times before Myatt was convicted of wholesale fraud. He was convinced that Myatt's forgeries would one day be so highly valued that the saps who had bought them would stop complaining. He had been prescient. There was going to be an exhibition of Myatt's works in Prague this summer and next year there would be another, in New York. Myatts had become a valued commodity.

That Simon ended up with a fine collection of Myatts was merely good fortune. He had been able to wait until the furor died down and then slowly trickled the paintings out into the eager art marketplace. Unlike John Drew, who was arrested, charged, and imprisoned, Simon was not caught and discovered. Helena thought there were still hundreds of forgeries in what he had called "safe houses" — watertight metal boxes in which he had hidden the paintings underground. During the last ten years or so of his life, Simon had commissioned high-end forgeries only from Chinese workshops. A few of these had come to light before his death. Most of them had not.

Helena was no longer sure when she realized that Simon was more than an art connoisseur. That he was an expert across several centuries was rare, but not unique. That he was secretive and never flaunted his expertise was more unusual, but Simon had convinced her that his clients were allergic to publicity and that they refused to show off their collections in case of theft or simple envy. They did not want the art world to speculate about how they had acquired their wealth and what they liked to hang on their walls.

That Simon never acknowledged his daughter in public was painful, but since her parents had never married, his vanishing acts were merely irksome. She had never expected him to stay.

Helena was confident Sylvie would be out of her way before she returned from Toronto.

She finished the eggs Benedict and a couple of croissants. They were good and crumbly, but no competition to those at the corner café on Rue Jacob.

She hired a taxi to take her to Bratislava. Two hours on the highway and only $250. She needed the rest.

The second Mrs. Krestin was waiting in Tóth's office while Attila was being given the third degree by the security guard. Although Tóth had left instructions that Attila was expected, the overweight policewoman had subjected him to the usual lengthy search and myriad questions.

Tóth had explained that it would be less stressful for the new widow to be far away from the scene of her husband's death, a place currently cordoned off by the police. The forensics team, he said, had already dusted for prints, examined the gardens for footprints, and photographed every one of them. They had also photographed every room and every object in Krestin's study and, after the medical examiner finished his preliminary examination, had drawn the position of his body on the carpet and bagged it.

Uniformed officers had gone house to house asking residents whether they had seen anyone enter or leave the day before. Tóth had sent another team of detectives to Krestin's office to question his staff. It seemed that during the past couple of years he had reduced the size of his staff and there were now only two people working directly for him. One was an appointments secretary, the other an accountant in charge of Krestin's investments. He no longer ran any companies, had resigned from his boards, and had told most of his staff they would no longer be needed. He did that on his eighty-fifth birthday, during the office party in his honour.

The appointments secretary was sitting on the bench where Tóth usually kept Attila waiting.

Since the homicide team was so busy, Tóth had decided to talk to Vera Krestin himself. He seemed pleased with this new role, leaning back in his chair, arms crossed, almost preening. He'd already told Attila to remain quiet unless asked to speak by Tóth himself. Attila assumed he owed the honour of Tóth's summons to there being too many police officers covering the crime scene and traipsing around Rózsadomb, asking questions. Tóth needed someone to listen and take notes.

Vera Krestin must have been at least thirty years younger than her husband, although she had made the effort to look older, more suited to the role she played. She was wearing a conservative dark-blue suit with a thin belt, a white blouse, and pearls. She had gathered her hair in a thick bun, which made her high cheekbones more prominent. She had slightly slanted grey eyes that would have been attractive had she made the effort to make them so. She wore no makeup at all, and the bare bulb hanging from the ceiling made her look almost ghostly. Her voice matched her appearance: soft and husky, but not tearful. She seemed remote, as if her mind were on something else, not on the questions Tóth was asking about her husband. Attila wondered whether she had taken a large dose of tranquilizers.

Vera Krestin had found the body. She had called emergency around 3 p.m. and told the operator that there had been a terrible accident.

"When was the last time you saw your husband?" Tóth asked in his kindest tone.

"You mean before then?" Vera Krestin asked.

"Yes, before." Since he had died between noon and 3 p.m., according to the medical examiner's initial assessment, that was a good question, Attila thought. Good but acerbic, rather than merely stupid. Attila knew acerbic. He had heard enough of it from his mother.

"When I took him his lunch at noon. He liked me to be punctual and lunch was always at noon. An omelet yesterday. Havarti and ham, tomatoes on the side. Toast."

"He was alone?"

"He liked to eat his lunch alone. He was working."

"What, in particular, was he working on?" Tóth asked.

"I don't know. János never shared that sort of information with me. He had a lot of business interests, here and abroad. He had his computer on and his diary out."

"Diary?" Tóth asked.

"His leather-bound diary, or notepad. He kept notes of his conversations."

The forensics boys had taken the computer but they hadn't mentioned a diary or a notepad. Tóth lumbered to the door and yelled at someone about the notepad. Whatever the answer was, it made Tóth sufficiently angry that he forgot his formerly tender tone when he asked Vera Krestin if she was sure there was a diary on her husband's desk.

"Of course," she said. "He always had one."

"Where did he keep it? On his desk? Next to his phone?"

"On his desk, except when he went out."

"It isn't there now. Did he put it in a drawer? In the safe?"

She didn't respond. She was twisting her ring around her finger and looking at her hands. "I never saw him put it in the safe, but he may have," she said.

Tóth changed tack. "Did he have any visitors yesterday?"

"None that I saw," she whispered, her eyes cast down.

"Were you home most of the afternoon?" Tóth had begun to sound like someone talking to a small child.

"No. I went out to the hairdresser shortly after I took in his lunch, and I had a pedicure right after. In the same place. I stopped for coffee on the way home. Do you need to know where?" She crossed her shapely knees and stared at Tóth, as if she expected him to demand the name of her hairdresser. Attila would have done that, but Tóth didn't. He was still bent on not offending her.

Attila thought she didn't look like a woman with a fresh hairdo. The ex used to have hers done every week, and he knew she had something going when she started to experiment with different styles and colours.

"Was he expecting anyone?" Tóth asked.

"If he was he didn't tell me."

"Did he usually tell you if he was expecting visitors?"

"No."

"Mrs. Krestin, did your husband have any enemies?" Tóth ventured.

She raised her head and looked directly at him. "Enemies? Why would he have enemies?"

"Everybody has enemies," Attila said. And he could not resist adding, "Even Captain Tóth has enemies."

Tóth frowned. "In his work," he resumed, "there may have been someone he had angered. Perhaps an associate or a former business partner?"

Vera Krestin didn't reply.

"He used to have a partner in the movie business," Attila said. "A man called Tihanyi. He was American? Or Italian? And their partnership didn't work out."

"Italian, I think," Vera Krestin said. "A '56-er. He was not very friendly."

"How wasn't he friendly?"

"He didn't speak to me. He was only interested in the business and he stopped coming when the money ran out."

"And the partnership ended when?" Tóth regained his command of the situation.

She shrugged. "As I said, János didn't discuss business with me, but that man stopped coming to the house."

"When?"

"Not sure. About a year ago."

"Your husband had some dealings with Gazprom when he negotiated our price for gas. He told the newspapers that they were not happy with the deal he made. Have they called him recently?"

"Not as far as I know. He had his own phone."

"Mrs. Krestin, did he perhaps discuss the sale of the large painting in your home? The painting of Jesus on a donkey?"

"He didn't sell it," she said matter-of-factly. "He had planned to sell it, but he didn't. Your people saw it is still there."

"Are you going to sell it?" Attila asked.

Tóth stared at Attila in disbelief. How could he be so crude?

"Yes, of course," Vera Krestin said.

Tóth thanked her for her co-operation and asked whether there was someone, a relative perhaps, they could arrange to be with her during this difficult time.

"I would rather be alone," she said. So Greta Garbo, Attila thought. Perhaps, she, too, was a fan of late-night Hollywood fare.

Tóth stood, helped her up from her chair, and escorted her to the door.

"Mrs. Krestin," Attila called after her as she walked down the corridor, "do you know why your husband wanted to sell that painting?"

"He was eighty-seven years old. It was time to think about getting rid of things," she said over her shoulder.

"Was he short of money, perhaps?"

She said nothing.

"It's not difficult to check, Mrs. Krestin. There is no shame in being short of funds, you know."

"I will be settling all his accounts," she said in a clear voice.

"Are you the sole beneficiary of his will?"

She didn't stop to reply.

Attila followed her along the aisle between vacant chairs usually filled by police bodies. "When you phoned the emergency line, you said there had been an accident, yet you had seen your husband's body with a wire around his neck, a lot of blood running down the front of his shirt, a pool of blood under his head, and you told the operator he was not breathing. He was obviously dead. Why did you say it was an accident?"

She stopped and turned around.

"You used to be a nurse," Attila said.

"I am out of practice. And since you asked, no, I am not the sole beneficiary," she said, and she left.

Attila waited. He had seen enough liars during his long career in the force to know that Vera Krestin was not telling the truth. The question was why. And perhaps when. She did not seem stupid. She would certainly have known of Krestin's dealing with the filmmaker and something about his dealings with Russians. But had she lied when she said she did not know of anyone visiting him yesterday?

When Attila returned, Tóth was gazing at the spot where his wife's picture used to be and picking his teeth with the nail on his little finger.

After a while, Tóth noticed him. "I don't know what to make of that woman," he said. "And talking about women, where was your Ms. Marsh yesterday afternoon?"

"She says she was out of town for the day. She checked into the Gresham here last night. It's easy to check."

"Then do it," Tóth said. "Make sure she is still in the Gresham. And while you are checking stuff, make sure Vera Krestin doesn't leave home again today. I have a couple of young cops there, but they are too green to deal with Mrs. Krestin."

"I suppose it would be too optimistic to assume that one of the many video cameras was actually on yesterday?" Attila asked.

"Dr. Krestin didn't like to have his house under observation."

"Of course, not," Attila said. "And Tihanyi, the ex-movie mogul, do you know what kind of stuff he was working on with Krestin?"

"Tihanyi? He used to produce made-for-TV true crime

while he was in Hollywood. He did the same stuff here with East European settings. Then he started a vampire series. She is right, he is a '56-er. I haven't seen anything of his for a while. Do you think he may be involved?"

"Not really," Attila said, "but I could find out about him, if you like. He was Krestin's business associate, and she doesn't like him."

"How do you know she doesn't like him?"

"Body language," Attila said. "I watched her face when you asked about him. But why did she say he was Italian?"

"Maybe there is another film guy he dealt with. Another investor. Isn't our current film czar an American?"

"You mean Szilvas? He did live in the US for a while, but I would hardly call him American."

"You've got Krestin's phone records?" Attila asked.

Tóth cleared his throat and spat into his wastebasket. "You think I am an idiot?"

Attila was spared from responding by a young uniform who came in and handed Tóth a MacBook.

"Krestin's?" Attila asked.

"Good," Tóth said and waved Attila out of the office. All along the corridor, Attila could hear him yelling into his phone about Krestin's diary.

He drove to the Office of the Medical Examiner, parked in his old spot, the one reserved for the police, and asked at the front desk to see Dr. Bayer. He was instantly recognized, fitted into a white coat and mask, and left to shuffle along to the autopsy room. Bayer was working on a man's chest with a saw. He looked up, but his goggles and mask hid his welcoming smile.

"Plus ça change," he said, "plus ç'est la même chose, only the methods differ. I am almost done with your friend here.

He was in fairly good shape for a man of his age. Close to ninety, I'd say. Look at the brachioradialis and his flexors carpi, even his pectoralis look better than mine will when the time comes. Possibly better than mine do now. Not so sure about his abdominals, but they're not bad. How have you been, Attila?"

"Better than the guy on your table," Attila said. "I'm still not sure I like being a private dick, but the hours are better."

"The kids?"

"Good, I think. I am taking them for the weekend. I was going to drive to Leányfalu, but the weather has not been great."

Bayer showed Attila Krestin's palms. "Defensive cuts. He was trying to stop his assailant. He must have got both of his hands under the wire. His index finger and middle finger are almost cut through, as is his throat. Under normal circumstances — if garroting someone is ever normal — it takes a lot of strength to sever a neck all the way to the spine, and this man fought. But not so much strength was needed in this case because the killer used a short stick, or a pen, something to help wind the wire tighter. Here," he lifted the dead man's head and pointed to the back of his neck, "you can see the pressure marks all the way up into his hair. It would still have taken some effort, but the guy didn't have to be that much stronger than the victim. I'm old-fashioned, that's why I said guy. It could easily have been a woman, but she'd be a strong one. And she'd be standing over the victim. You can see the wire ran up behind his ears. To force him down in the chair as he struggled, she'd have to have some serious muscle. Does the room show signs of a struggle?"

Attila said he didn't think so. Tóth had told him very little about the investigation, but he would certainly have mentioned if the place was a mess.

"If there are not a lot of broken things around, he must have known his killer well enough to let him get behind him and stay still while the killer readied himself. The killer can't have been walking around with the wire in his hands. He must have pulled it out when the victim's back was turned. That's an odd one, too, the use of a wire. We don't see much of that here. It's more of an Italian thing. I was at a forensics conference in Naples last year, and they were talking a lot about people being damned near decapitated with wire and the kinds of wire they use. In Sicily, they use very fine double-knit steel. Here, in Hungary, if you're going to asphyxiate somebody, you use old-fashioned rope. Not even our high-end criminals go in for wire."

Italians, again, Attila thought. Maybe Alexander wasn't kidding.

"What time do you think he died?"

"Between noon and three in the afternoon is still as exact as I can be. Closer to two, maybe. He was still digesting his lunch: omelet, tomato, bread. A bit of wine. Not a bad way to go, don't you agree? Pleasant food, fast exit, not much pain. I'll think about that for my own exit."

Attila thanked him and suggested that Bayer could, maybe, not mention their talk to Tóth. The captain was protective of his forensics turf and wouldn't like to see Attila tread on it.

He stopped for a beer at a bistro on Vas Street and googled László Tihanyi, film producer. The man was born in 1938 in Budakeszi, just west of Budapest, and immigrated to Italy in 1956. He worked in Hollywood in the 1970s and was now living in Rome. He had made most of his movies for television — a mystery series set in different cities, a series of risqué love stories with graphic sex — but also a couple of big-screen, science-fiction movies with characters living on Pluto. In 2001, Tihanyi was appointed executive director of the Hungarian Film and Television Fund, but the job lasted only as long as the government of the day. The company he had formed with Krestin got a five-line mention. Their joint venture had produced romantic comedies for export, all supported by the fund. In early 2011, they were in production on a new vampire series for TV. No titles were mentioned, and Attila couldn't find any further mention of the series. They had stopped making movies in Hungary at the end of 2011, when Szilvási was appointed to head up the fund.

Although Wikipedia was too polite to say so, Attila assumed Szilvási didn't like either man. He may have thought a former Commie like Krestin was not trustworthy. More likely, he disliked Tihanyi, or he believed, as the press had pointed out, that it was a conflict of interest to award government money to a company you half owned. Without a tap into government funds, the partnership would not have been lucrative.

Besides, few movies were made here now. There were a lot of out-of-work actors in Budapest, just like in every other big city, waiting tables and driving cabs.

Attila called Tibor, the man most likely to know more about Tihanyi and Krestin. But he didn't have much more to offer. He remembered that Szilvási had had a ton of nasty things to say about both Tihanyi and Krestin, but none as bad as comments made by the members of the Lipótváros football team and its trainer. Several of them had been quoted in the press suggesting that Krestin had siphoned money that should have been invested in renewing the team.

"A while back," Tibor said, "Krestin asked whether I would like to invest in a new venture he had launched with Tihanyi.

Very hush-hush, but easy, secure, low risk, and big returns, or so he said. He showed me some numbers and a kind of prospectus. There were a few outside investors."

"Do you remember who they were?"

"There was a numbered company registered in Canada, but I wasn't interested."

"Any idea what business it was?"

"Only an idea. Selling Romanian guns and ammo to the Ukrainians."

"Seriously? What made him think the Ukrainian government would buy Romanian arms from a Hungarian in the movie business?"

"I didn't listen long enough to find out."

"You know Krestin has been killed?" Attila asked.

"Hardly surprising," Tibor said. "He was one of the least likeable citizens I have ever met."

"You knew him well, personally?"

"Socially. But not well," Tibor said. "And I have not seen him recently. There have been some rumours about his money running out."

"Do you think he had made enemies in the security service?"

"Krestin? Perhaps. He was a real-life Commie of the old school. He never missed an opportunity to rat out a friend. What am I saying? Krestin had no friends. He had fellow travellers in state security, but it was not an outfit where anyone made friends. He was one of their senior guys, but not so senior he didn't enjoy breaking legs. Friends? No."

"Someone had ordered a surveillance of him. Was he suspected of something?"

"I wouldn't know."

"Would you have heard about it?"

"I may have. A lot of the ÁVO guys had served in the Arrow Cross in the forties. But why would anyone care now? Are you still on for chess and J&B next Friday?"

"Wouldn't miss it." He had a regular date with Tibor in the Király Bath. Chess, Scotch, and long soaks with stories.

No sooner had he hung up than Tóth called to tell him to pay a visit to the first Mrs. Krestin in Slovakia. There had been four calls from her the morning Krestin was killed and seven calls during the days before. Krestin had called the number himself twice, once the morning of his murder, but no one answered. One of Tóth's best was going to keep an eye on the second Mrs. Krestin, and he could check on Ms. Marsh when he returned.

Attila walked Gustav around the block, fed him some salami and cheese leftovers, and asked his neighbour to let him into the courtyard if Attila wasn't back by 10 p.m. The neighbour was a cheerful middle-aged woman with a passion for dachshunds and a fondness for Attila that he had tried but failed to reciprocate. Gustav, on the other hand, was besotted with her and didn't mind showing it.

He picked up the girls at three. He had hoped to pick them up earlier, but they were not ready, or ready but the ex wasn't ready for them to leave. She probably enjoyed the sight of him sitting in his car, impatiently drumming his fingers on the steering wheel. It would have reminded her of the years she had spent waiting for him for supper, hanging around with the kids outside the Margit Island Baths, or the cinema, or wherever he had told her he would join her, for sure, at a certain time. It was the job, he had said, by way of excuse, but Bea soon stopped accepting that.

They came with their small suitcases, towels, and multi-coloured purses. "Mommy has given us a bit of spending money, in case you have none," Sofi said. "And towels," Anna added. "She is sure all your towels are very dirty."

"Lucky, then, that we are not going swimming today," he said, pretending to be petulant. "Instead, we are going on an adventure."

They brightened immediately. They loved his little adventures, and swimming was no longer fun. They had gone to the baths too often and were tired of Attila's history lessons while contending with old people in loose bathing suits at the Király (imagine: built in the mid sixteenth century, during the Turkish occupation), more old people playing chess while soaking in the Lukács (monastic period, built in the twelfth century for monks), and the old people at the Széchenyi in City Park who kept insisting that they had to be quiet. Only the Gellért encouraged kids to behave like kids. As for the Leányfalu, the girls were worried about driftwood and frogs.

"We are going to Dunaszerdahely," he said.

"Where?"

"Slovakia."

After reassuring them that Slovakia was not the name for yet another historic spa, he took off for the M1 at top speed, knowing that his driving exhausted the girls' patience after a half hour or so. They played spotting Hungarian flags, then spotting Slovak flags once they were past Komárom, then Slovak names that could easily be translated into their original Hungarian, such as Dunajská Streda (Dunaszerdahely), and others that couldn't. He had planned to play spotting stray dogs, but the Slovaks must have cleared them out, or else dogs didn't like this part of the country. The journey took less than an hour.

The problem of what to do with the girls was solved by the sign for Cirkus Humberto near the city hall. He drove to the big red-and-white tent outside the town, just a five-minute drive away. The sign had mentioned horses, goats, a rotating moon-rider, three lions, and an elephant. Bea would undoubtedly protest that they were too young to be left alone, but Attila had great faith in the natural wariness of his daughters. The ticket seller, a clown, said that the show had already started, but there was still an hour to go. Attila bought two tickets for seats in the "galerie," ushered them into the tent, and arranged to meet them outside in an hour.

He had no difficulty finding Gertrude Krestin's house by the old cemetery.

She looked as if she had recently suffered a loss. Her eyes were downcast, her hair lank, and her mouth tight, but she had pencilled in her eyebrows. She did not resemble the young woman in the old photographs the police had of her. It wasn't just that she was older, which she quite obviously was, but there was a sagging sadness about her clothes and her demeanour that seemed habitual.

"Sorry to bother you so soon after Mr. Krestin's death," Attila began softly. "We have only a few questions to ask you." On the phone, Attila hadn't mentioned that he was no longer a policeman, and now she hadn't asked for his identification.

She ushered him into the living room. It was small and cluttered with worn furniture, including a pink sofa that looked as ancient and saggy as his own. She settled Attila into the sofa, herself into an armchair, and poured tea.

"You left János Krestin in 1979?" Attila said.

"In '81."

"But you stayed in touch."

"Not especially. He had other . . . interests."

"Other women?"

"Including other women. He married Vera soon after we divorced."

"But he sent you money?"

"From time to time. Not very much. As you see, we live modestly. We can't afford a better home, and I couldn't afford a better education for Jenci. That's the one thing I regret. I couldn't give Jenci the chance he needs."

"Jenci?"

"My son. He should be home soon."

"Does he spend much time with his father?"

Gertrude looked down at her hands. "He was just a baby when we left," she said, "but he has had to visit his father from time to time."

"So they have met since?"

"Of course," she said, "but János does not come here, and we don't have the money for Jenci to travel to Budapest very often."

"But he does go there to see Mr. Krestin?"

"Yes."

"They are not close?"

"How could they be close? We live here. He lives there. Their only steady contact was over the money he owed us."

Attila let that settle for a minute while he looked out the window at the cemetery. "Mrs. Krestin, did your husband know people who had been in the Gulag?" he asked.

"Why would he?"

"Because, I am sure, he was also there."

Gertrude went to the kitchen. "It's strange you should ask that question, too," she said when she returned with a kettle of hot water to freshen the tea. "The woman who came a few days ago also asked me, and I told her the same thing. János never mentioned the Gulag."

278

"What woman?"

"Her name was Helena Marsh. She was some kind of art expert, and she was working for Géza Márton. It was Géza who called me and asked that I see her."

Of course. Helena Marsh again. "What else did Ms. Marsh talk about?"

"A painting. Why? Do you think János's death is connected with her? With a painting he bought? Or with the Gulag?"

"It's a possibility," Attila said, "that he bought a painting from a fellow prisoner. When was the last time you saw János?"

"At least ten years ago. No. More like fifteen."

"But you've talked to him?"

"Yes. After the Marsh woman was here, I called him about the money. It hadn't arrived. He asked me what she had wanted."

"And Géza Márton? When did you see him last?"

Her hand holding the kettle stopped over the teapot, and hot water splashed onto the Formica table. She set the kettle down and looked at Attila intently, as if she had just registered his presence.

"Why do you ask?"

"I've read the state police files, and Géza Márton may have had reason to have your former husband killed. He may even have believed he had more than a reason, that he had justification. János Krestin had ordered his surveillance, testified against his father in a phony trial, had him jailed, and stolen his girlfriend."

"He didn't steal the girlfriend," Gertrude said in a loud voice.

Attila noted that she didn't dispute the other charges.

"Perhaps not, but you had been Géza's girl and then you married János."

"I didn't meet János till late '57. Wasn't that in the files you read? A year after Géza left. It was pure coincidence."

"He hired you to teach him French," Attila said.

"There is nothing wrong with that. I gave private lessons for a living. János wanted to learn languages so he'd be ready when the new era came. French and English. He already spoke Russian. He knew what it took to adapt."

"He seems to have adapted very well, indeed," Attila said, "but he must have made a lot of enemies along the way. You knew most of them. Géza Márton, László Tihanyi, a man they called Bika . . ."

"Gyula Németh," she said. "And he didn't hate János. It was me he disliked. Gyula idolized János. They had known each other for many years."

"Perhaps since Vorkuta," Attila suggested.

"János never mentioned that."

"Any idea where Mr. Németh is now?"

"He may still live in Bratislava. I don't know."

"In Bratislava? When did you see him last?"

She thought a long time about that. Then she said, "I think I saw him last year. He lived in Bratislava then. But he used to travel to Budapest to see János. He sometimes brought me something from János."

"An allowance? Is that why you called Mr. Krestin last week?"

"Last week?"

"Monday morning. There were several calls from this number."

She went to the kitchen, then called up the stairs. "Jenci?"

He would have to be in his mid-thirties, Attila thought, given when Gertrude had left her husband. He still lived at home. He still went by Jenci, the diminutive of Jenö. Was there something wrong with him?

When Jenci didn't respond, his mother said, "He is still not home. Some days he comes in late. He does odd jobs for other Hungarians. Slovaks would never hire him. It's tough for Jenci here, living in this little town. And he is such a bright boy . . ."

He met Jenci as he was leaving. A tall, young-ish man with sticky brown hair, big ears, thin lips, a furrowed forehead, and long arms extending well beyond the sleeves of his loose sweatshirt. He was wearing threadbare pants with baggy knees and grimy running shoes. He smelled of stale sweat and some kind of industrial cleaner.

Attila was reluctant to shake his hand but he had no option. Damp palms but a firm handshake. He stared at Attila but seemed to be in a hurry to get inside the house. If Attila had questions, he said, he would be in later, but right now, he needed a bath.

Attila had no trouble agreeing with that.

It was not until after he had gathered the kids at the circus tent that Attila realized Gertrude had not answered his question about Géza Márton. On the way home, when not playing spot the foreign licence plate, he was thinking about the secretive Helena and why she had travelled to Dunajská Streda to meet Gertrude Lakatos Krestin.

When he got home, there was a message from Tóth, telling him that whoever had entered Krestin's study on the afternoon of his murder had wiped all the fingerprints in the study, even those belonging to Vera and Krestin himself. The footprints in the garden all belonged to the gardener. The neighbours had not seen any strangers enter the house or leave it. No one had observed an unfamiliar car on the street. Krestin had set up an appointment with his lawyer for the day after he was killed. Krestin's secretary cancelled the meeting.

"Did he say what the meeting was about?"

"The lawyer thought it was about his will."

Attila cleared off the newspapers and books from the old sofa, collected the dog from the neighbour, and gratefully accepted her offer of a pot of veal paprikash and a dish of layered potatoes with eggs and sour cream. She said she knew the girls were staying for the night, and she was sure he had not had time to cook. Attila assured her that she was a marvel of clairvoyance and a mistress of culinary arts, but failed to invite her into the apartment. Such invitations, he thought, could lead to a relationship, and he was not interested.

While Sofi and Anna watched a show demonstrating that Britain had talent (if not good taste), he called the Gresham and left a long message for Helena Marsh. He went to sleep early. Next day, he would have to drive back to Bratislava.

Helena got out of the cab at the south entrance to Hviezdoslavovo Square in Bratislava, waited for the driver to turn tail and race back toward the border (Hungarian taxis were not welcome in Slovakia), bought a coffee at a café kitty corner to the renovated National Theatre, then strolled along the pedestrian walkway, stopping now and then to look at the metal sculptures of people sitting on the benches or rising out of the pavement. It's what any tourist would do, and it allowed her to check if anyone was following or watching her. For Michal's sake, as well as her own, she couldn't risk being followed to his shop.

Michal had been her chief source of identity papers and disguises for more than ten years. Her father had introduced them some twenty-five years ago, when they were on vacation together, travelling throughout Eastern Europe. They had come to Bratislava from London. Simon said he had some business here and had left her for a couple of hours with a bit of local money. She had walked the pockmarked streets and listened to the rustle of Slavic voices. Back then, Bratislava still looked like it was only just recovering from the war. There was a lot of rubble everywhere but also a lot of construction, thanks to the new money pouring in from Western Europe. The Hilton had just opened in place of an old hotel on Hviezdoslavovo Square, behind the eponymous Slovak poet whose thoughtful statue still dominated the square.

On his return, Simon said he wanted her to meet a man named Michal. "You don't need him right now," he had said, "but you may need him sometime, and an introduction by me still counts."

The idea that she may one day need anyone her father knew seemed weird, but back then, she hadn't known that recovering lost works of art would become part of her profession or that such work would expose her to the fury of those loath to give up what they had.

Her natural reaction to anyone introduced by her father — there had been few such people — had been sullen resistance. She had grown accustomed to his long, unexplained absences and to her mother's unhappiness. She no longer cared that he claimed she was possibly not even his daughter and had learned to ignore his interest in her art studies. But she had begun to suspect that whatever he did for a living was likely not legal. When he took her to galleries and museums to show her fakes and forgeries, she had thought he was merely contributing to her education. "You may be hired to identify fakes," he told her, "and no course you take will help you as much as I can."

She did not like him much anymore, but she listened.

She was suspicious when he was cheerful and expansive and liked him even less when he was quiet and conspiratorial. On this occasion he had chosen to be quiet. He took her arm and walked her along Ventúrska Street, then back to Michalská, stopping in front of a couple of boutiques and pointing at sweaters he had no interest in buying. Window shopping, he explained, was a good way to check whether you were being followed.

Now, she was doing what he had done. She picked a wide window displaying designer dresses because, with her face close to the glass, she could see not only the reflection of the other side of the street but also down both ends. For a moment she thought she recognized the shape of a man studying a placard near the entrance to the university, but he hurried inside before she could take a good look at him. She waited but he did not come out again.

Michal's workshop was upstairs from his small posters-only gallery on Ventúrska, where it had been on her visit with her father, except that back then there was no gallery, just a long dark entranceway.

The two men she had previously met through her father (he had introduced her to both of them as a student, not his daughter) were preening, overconfident, and entirely self-involved. She had expected Michal to be like them. He wasn't. In the years since, he had been invariably helpful and interested in her latest escapades. He rarely complained about the urgency of the work or about how much she paid. He had not increased his prices since 1990, and his papers were still as professionally prepared as ever.

A small man with birdlike features, he seemed delighted to see Helena. He was already printing the passports and driver's licences when he ushered her into his sanctuary. His door was always triple locked, and he had assured her long ago that he kept no records of their transactions. The only records were in his head. He had a remarkable memory for names and numbers; he never forgot an email address and placed all communications in a file labelled "junk," which he claimed he could discard without leaving a trace. He had told Helena once that there might be a few people in the world who could access what he had deleted, but he had yet to meet one.

In addition to his other talents, Michal was a computer wizard.

He gave her a tentative hug and urged her to sit in one of his two "good" chairs.

"So," he said in passable English, "Maria has outlived her usefulness. And you are concerned about Ms. Lewis. I had thought they would last a few more years." He shook his head. "I don't know how anyone could have identified you inside Maria's improbable figure, but shit happens."

"I didn't care for her, anyway," Helena said. "She was a silly woman when she was alive, and I was concerned that some of her clients would seek her out. I wish she hadn't had such fondness for pink frills and leopard-print leggings."

"She had a lot of clients," Michal said, "but no one went to her funeral."

That was Michal's way of telling Helena that Maria's clients may have been unaware that she had died, thus making her identity eminently suitable for Helena's purposes. So long as she didn't vary the disguise too much, anyone who had known Maria would overlook the change in appearance. When Michal had given Helena the Maria papers and appropriate clothes, he had said, with a grin, "It is possible for a woman to grow out of her persona but not to depart completely from what she was when she was alive."

"I think you'll like Eva more," Michal now said. "She was about your shape and age. She worked in the history museum, the acquisitions section, middle management. A serious woman, and a conservative dresser. Brown hair, glasses. You still have Maria's pair?"

"Yes."

"Good. They will do." Michal pulled out a bag with a light-brown wig, a dark-brown pant suit, a blue sweater, and a raincoat. He handed her an Austrian passport, health card, driver's licence, and a Viennese library card, as well as American Express and Visa cards, all in the name of Eva Bergman. "Her accounts are paid up to date," he said, "but she should still be spending, to keep everything above board. She was a woman of conventional tastes. She bought excellent value. She paid her bills promptly, and I have kept up all those habits after her demise."

"Demise . . . how?" Helena asked.

Michal shook his head. "She died unremarkably," he said. "She was let go by the museum and went for a long swim off the pier in Bremen."

Although the clothes were a bit loose, the wig fit perfectly.

"Eva will need new shoes," Michal said. "There is a store five blocks from here. You have cell phones, I presume, in case you run into trouble. I will be here."

She paid him in American dollars.

"Next time, let's retire Marianne Lewis," she said.

"By the way," he asked as he unlocked the door, "do you still speak German with an Austrian accent?"

"Yes. Did she have family?"

"Would I give you a woman with family?"

Helena waited in the gallery for a while, scanning the faces and attitudes of people walking by, then took her time looking at unframed posters. She chose one, paid, and left, carrying a coloured woodcut of old Presburg in a cardboard tube that also held a long-bladed knife, courtesy of Michal. She strolled over to a fashionable shoe store at the end of Ventúrska, where she bought a pair of almost-sensible maroon pumps, then settled at one of the wrought-iron tables outside Tempus Fugit, on Sedlárska. She ordered a glass of wine to celebrate her new alias and kept watching passers-by.

This was the restaurant her father had chosen for dinner the evening after he bought himself a new set of papers from Michal. He said he liked the restaurant because it was not over-decorated. You could still see its fifteenth-century walls.

Simon was not much older then than Helena was now. He still prided himself on being fit, and on his extraordinary ability to fool almost everyone he met. It kept him youthful. As Helena knew now, he had been running an exceptionally successful business selling fakes and forgeries to buyers too eager to demand all the papers proving provenance. That day, he had made what he proudly called "a killing." She didn't know it then, but the painting he sold that day was the genuine article. Dark, gloomy, but real. The man who had wanted it so ferociously had been willing to pay even more than the exorbitant amount Simon had initially quoted. It would complete his collection of late nineteenth-century portraits, Simon had explained. Poland's National Museum in Warsaw was still working out the details of how to guard valuable paintings, so stealing the small Aleksander Gierymski had been easy. In the days before video cameras, a man could hide his identity simply by donning a hat or glasses, but Simon was a perfectionist. He didn't take a chance on someone remembering his lingering near the Gierymski portrait or leaving the museum with a bulky package under his arm. Hence the visit to Michal.

Helena had resisted her father's offer to look at the portrait. "I will take your word for it," she told him when he said the picture was of his client's great grandfather, one of the *szlachta*, the nobility practically eliminated by the Nazis.

"He couldn't afford to buy it, but he can afford your price," she had said.

Simon had laughed. The painting had, obviously, not been for sale — at least not after the war.

He had tried to put a good face on his business when he told her about it. By then, she had a degree in art history and was working at Christie's. "It's better that you know as little as possible," he said. "But one day, you may want to do this yourself. It's a way to keep warm and well fed and to give your kids a good education." He had been proud of being able to send her to a private school and a good university. Now she knew that he had viewed her education and her apprenticeship at Christie's as an investment.

Her mother never explained where the money had come from, and she had prepared for Simon's visits with the excitement of a young girl, putting on a new dress, applying makeup, spraying a bit of Chanel No. 5 behind her ears. Helena was still furious with them both: him for deceiving her all those years and her for going along with the deception. Was it only the money that mattered to her mother? The big house on Roxborough Drive, where the wealthy lived, the expensive cars she bought, including the latest, a Mercedes convertible? Or had she really loved him? And loved him enough to acknowledge that she had an illegitimate daughter at a time when and in a neighbourhood where people still frowned on that sort of thing.

She had not once turned her head to look at Simon while he told her about the Gierymski portrait, which now she regretted, because he had lived for only another month, and they would never have another conversation.

Even now, thinking about her father gave her a toothache.

Her wine was warm by the time she lifted it to her lips. She knew she'd been silly to sit here, not watching the street, but that's what thinking about him did to her. "You must always be aware of your surroundings," he had told her. "Always scan faces. Watch how people move. Do they turn after they pass you? Do they give you a second look?"

She picked up the copy of *SME Bratislava* she had taken from the restaurant's stack of newspapers, but she was looking beyond its open pages at the people walking along Sedlárska, angry at herself for becoming careless. The new wig and the glasses had given her a false sense of security.

She first saw him stop at the corner of Sedlárska and Hlavné Square, looking up at street numbers and down at a map in his hand. He seemed slimmer in his black windbreaker, but still thick-necked and bulky in the shoulders. His sunglasses were balanced on his short-cropped sandy hair. Attila from Budapest. What the hell was he doing in Bratislava?

She hid her face behind the newspaper but kept watching. There was a movement in the doorway of the facing building, a large dark shape. At first she could not make out whether it was male or female, but there was no doubt once he poked his big moonface out and the sun hit the visor of the cap he was wearing. Big chin under the cap, mouth a straight line. He stepped onto the street, huge, leaning forward, like a boxer flexing for a fight. He was not looking at Helena, but at Attila Fehér. There was a barely perceptible movement as he drew something from the front of his bunched-up jacket while Fehér was still looking at his map. Helena put down the newspaper and reached for the cardboard tube.

Fehér turned slowly toward the big man. It was impossible for Helena to see the big man's face from this distance, but he seemed to square his shoulders and bring his arms forward. Then he marched, almost ran, toward Fehér. They met at the corner, facing each other, the bigger man's gun rising up toward Fehér's midriff. Helena threw her new knife at his back with enough force to stop him but not enough to kill him. Given her seated position, she thought it was a pretty good throw.

Everything stopped. The noise in the street suddenly hushed, then started up louder and sharper than it had been before. Everyone froze as Fehér kicked the gun out of the big man's hand and stepped on his arm for good measure. A woman screamed and pulled her child close.

No one was looking at Helena.

She left some euros beside her wine glass, picked up the papers and her handbag, and left for the taxi rank outside the Carlton Hotel. She had a plane to catch.

Attila had been vaguely aware of the man bearing down on him, but had not recognized the imminent danger. He had spent a few hours on the internet looking for Gyula Németh, G. Németh, and a variety of other Némeths. It was amazing how many Némeths there were in this small country, particularly as the name meant German in Hungarian, and neither Germans nor Hungarians were held in high regard in this part of the world. As he could not afford to hire help, he had no option but to phone every one of them until a G & M Németh in Bratislava — specialists in karate, lessons at reasonable prices — agreed that at least one of them was called Gyula and that he knew a Mr. Krestin in Budapest.

Had Attila left it at that, he would never have seen the formidable bulk of Gyula Németh hurtling toward him along Sedlárska Street while he was checking street numbers for the karate studio.

Instinct took over. Attila fended off Németh's upraised arm, kicked the gun out of the way as he dropped to his knees, then twisted his arms behind his back, ready to handcuff him. Except, of course, he had no cuffs with him, so he waited with the shocked crowd for a policeman to arrive. All the time, Németh was screaming that he was the victim here.

The two young Slovak policemen who showed up had little interest in Attila's explanation of his quest to identify who had killed someone in Budapest, but they did agree that this was likely some crazy Hungarian case, since both the victim and Attila were Hungarians, and so was Attila's boss, the man he called on his cell phone when the Slovak police attempted to arrest him.

"Does anybody here speak Slovak?" Attila heard Tóth shouting at the other end of the phone. "Anyone?"

It would have been insanity to admit to any such thing in Budapest, as it was equally risky to admit to understanding Hungarian if you wished to keep your police job in Bratislava, but everyone agreed to speak enough English that Attila was not charged with an offence, not even after a knife — a long blade with a polished wooden handle — was found embedded in the unfortunate Németh's upper thigh. One of the policemen suggested he needed medical attention. No one seemed to know how the knife got there, although some bystanders were sure it could not have been Attila's.

The policemen confiscated the gun and the knife after the laborious work of dislodging the latter from Németh's bleeding thigh. "Evidence," one of them said, admiring the knife's sharp point against his thumb. He asked Attila to stop by the central Bratislava police station the next day before he went on his way back to where he had come from. Attila had only the faintest idea what Németh had said to them in Slovak, but they seemed to have no further interest in the big man or in his reason for attacking Attila, other than in helping him to stand up.

Attila used his shirt to staunch the blood spurting out of Németh's wound but he didn't take off the man's pants, so the blood soaked both the shirt and the pant leg and ran in thin rivulets into his blue Nikes.

The ambulance took them both to Hospital Ružinov, neither the closest, nor the newest, of Bratislava's medical centres, but the one named on Németh's medical ID card. Attila travelled in the front with the driver, who assured him that "his friend" would be fixed up very quickly. The ambulance service was not free and not covered by Németh's policy, according to the driver, but it was by no means the most expensive service in the city, and there would be a small discount if Attila paid cash.

As Németh's card was for the geriatric wing of this old city hospital, it was safe to assume the doctors there would have very few knife-wounds to deal with. The unusualness of this case alone was likely to guarantee immediate attention.

They had been in the waiting room for maybe fifteen minutes before Attila decided to sit next to Németh and try to find out whether the man had been in Budapest the day Krestin was killed. His "Bika" nickname made sense. The man looked like someone who could inflict serious damage on an opponent. His broad forehead was set in deep frown lines, and there were scars along his wide jaw and down from the corner of one eye. Its eyelid drooped.

He refused to look up at Attila but he did answer the question. "I was there to see János," he drawled in deep south-country Hungarian, the sort of accent Attila used when he was bent on irritating someone with class pretensions.

"The day before yesterday?" Attila said.

"He is my oldest friend."

"What time did you visit?"

"What's it to you?"

When one of the emergency doctors took Németh into a curtained-off area, Attila followed. He watched as the doctor stitched and bandaged the knife wound. Attila couldn't under-stand a word of their conversation but he was pretty sure Németh was accusing him of the attack, but, as he had brought the man into the hospital and had given him his own shirt, the doctor seemed prepared to offer Attila the benefit of the doubt. It's possible that Németh had a nasty reputation at the hospital. Or the doctor was just eager to leave the small, stuffy area. In any event, he left.

"Why were you trying to kill me?" Attila said.

"I thought you were going after me," Németh protested. "You called. You asked whether I knew János Krestin. You told me he was dead. You didn't explain what you wanted from me. It's your own damned fault. You could have said you were with the Hungarian police. I've never had any trouble with them. Ever. And János, he was friends with the police chief. And the prime minister. All the prime ministers. He knew everybody." Németh was examining the bandage on his leg. The blood had oozed through it and was trickling down his leg again. When the nurse came back with the release papers, his blood had soaked through the sheets on the narrow slab of a bed and began to pool under its wheels.

She didn't bother with the doctor this time. She just changed the bandage, gave him a spare wad of gauze, a packet of pills, some tape, and written instructions.

"I gotta keep my leg up," Németh said after glancing at the instructions. "My lucky day today! My friend dies. Some chick knifes my leg, and you turn out to be a policeman."

"Chick?"

"I saw her sitting outside the restaurant before I saw you."

"A woman?"

Németh didn't bother to answer that. "She was working with you."

A woman? What kind of woman would have done that? And why?

"She wasn't working with me," Attila said. "I didn't even see her. What did she look like?"

"Thin, brown hair, glasses, blue raincoat."

Attila shook his head. "I have no idea who she is. Maybe something to do with Krestin . . ."

"More like someone who killed him."

"Someone like you, for example?"

"I would never have hurt János," Németh said. "I loved him. Like I said, he was my oldest friend."

"Since Vorkuta?"

"Since Vorkuta."

"Where you were known as Bika?"

"What difference does that make now? It's more than sixty years ago. Who even remembers those camps?"

Attila nodded. Not many did. Most were now dead. "But people still remember the state security men. That's only twenty-some years ago. Guys in the ÁVO and AVH, like you and Krestin. He'd be remembered for that."

"There were a lot of us in the service," Németh said. "There was only one man I know of who was killed for it. And you guys never figured it out. You put it down to a simple robbery gone wrong." He snorted with derision, sounding like his nickname.

"Who would want to kill Krestin?"

"Some guy jealous of his success. A couple of days ago he had a call from this little guy who was in Vorkuta with us," Németh said. "Guy was nursing nasty memories."

"What did he want?"

"He didn't say, but János hadn't liked his tone. He thought the guy could have been looking for a bribe."

"So you threatened him."

"Not threatened. I just told him to stop harassing János. He was one of János's men in the camp. Not too willing at first, but he came around when he saw what was in it for him."

"And that was?"

"More food. It's what we all wanted. Enough to stay alive."

"You mean Gábor Nagy?"

"That little squirrel . . ."

"And what did he do for Janos?"

"Whatever it took to stay alive."

He looked out the grimy window, as if the answer was somewhere out there. "You've seen the photos," he said.

"Like you said, sixty years ago," Attila said. "So what could Nagy have on János that he thought would be worth a bribe?"

"A lot of bad stuff in those camps."

"Like being a kapo?"

Bika shrugged.

"Or something before the war? He was Arrow Cross, wasn't he?" Attila was taking a stab in the dark, relying on the bit of information in Krestin's file that had him emerge from jail, while other members of the Communist Party languished for years behind bars.

"As if that matters now he is dead."

They made their way out of the hospital, Bika leaning hard on Attila, almost pushing him over. The man must have weighed more than a hundred kilos. "And then there is that bastard," Németh said.

"What bastard?" Attila asked.

"The son of a bitch his mother bore before she left János."

"Bastard? You mean Jenci is not Krestin's son?"

"I tried to tell János that the kid was a bastard, but he wouldn't go along with me. He thought his little lady was not interested in other men." Németh's laugh was like a bark, loud and angry. "Last month I got the proof!"

"Last month? How?"

"I took the little bastard out for a drink. Got his DNA."

Attila left another message for Helena at the Gresham. "If you happen to be talking with your client in Canada, please try to find out about a numbered company that made an investment in a big deal of Krestin's that went sour."

Once she'd cleared immigration at Charles de Gaulle airport, Helena took the train to Gare du Nord, transferred to the métro, and came up to bright, crisp sunshine at Odéon. She could have got off at a station closer to her office on Cherche-Midi, but she loved walking in Paris.

Her father's favourite arrondissement had been the sixth. He told her he always stayed on the Left Bank and never failed to make pilgrimages to Saint-Germain-des-Pré and to Les Deux Magots. Although the service there had declined over the years, it was good to sit in the café once frequented by Simone de Beauvoir, Pablo Picasso, and James Joyce. Now, Les Deux Magots reminded Helena only of her father; she avoided it. Even on sunny mornings, when the smell of coffee wafted by her, she crossed to the other side of the street.

She stopped for an espresso on Rue du Four, bought flowers for Louise from the vendor at Saint-Sulpice, discarded her cell phone in the garbage bin meant for junk and dog turds, and picked up a couple of new phones with SIM cards at Bon Marché.

Paris was now her city. Simon, the fake art trader, the occasional thief, the man suspected of both the Gardner and the Stockholm museum heists (he had not done either of them, but he was guilty of others), still sought by Interpol and profiled (quite inaccurately) in "Art Theft," had been dead for more than five years. There had been no announcements, no obituaries, not even Interpol had noted Simon's death. The doctor who had signed the death certificate asserted that he had died of natural causes, despite the bullet wounds in his back. The doctor, "an old family friend," according to her mother, had called Annelise to report that Simon was dead. He had also arranged for the pick-up and cremation of his body. That is how Helena learned that Simon had been living not far from the house on Roxborough where she grew up.

Annelise, who had predicted Simon's demise and even guessed who would pay to have him killed, did not arrange for a funeral. "If there was a funeral, or even a private service, you couldn't be there. Any connection with him at this stage in your career would destroy your credibility," Annelise had told her daughter.

Afterward, they had argued over who would fly to Paris with the ashes. Neither of them was keen to follow Simon's final instructions to scatter them on the Seine.

"His presence in the city will spoil it for me," Helena said.

"Well, he won't exactly be present," Annelise said. "You dump him into the Seine, and God knows where the ashes will drift. I, on the other hand, will have to live here with all of this so-called art until I have disposed of it, one by one, so as not to arouse suspicion."

In the end, her mother stayed in Toronto and Helena flew to Paris. She quickly found out that Simon had not tarnished the city for her at all.

Annelise sold what was left of Simon's paintings as good fakes or skillful forgeries. She had no desire for, as she put it, "a criminal inheritance."

"You chose him, I didn't," Helena said.

Annelise agreed that that was so, but Simon had been young and gorgeous then. Long hair, tanned skin, lovely slender fingers. He had earned his degree, he was a painter, a water colourist, an enthusiastic traveller, a guide to all the best museums in Europe. His excessive admiration for the early Impressionists was the only sign of what he would later become.

"Besides," Annelise said, "we have both benefitted from turning a blind eye."

There was some truth in that, although Annelise had benefitted more and would continue to enjoy the house in Toronto and the airy New York apartment on the Upper East Side, as well as the pleasure of travelling first class, the welcome she had come to expect in both cities' best restaurants, and invitations to gala fundraisers. Helena, on the other hand, had rejected all the comforts her father had offered. Still, she knew that without his loot, she could not have had the privileged education and training she now relied upon. Could not have become a Titian expert or have curated the much-admired 1998 Titian retrospective at Vienna's Alte Pinakothek. Nor would she have been as aware of the fakes and forgeries that had invaded galleries and museums worldwide. Being Simon's daughter offered her a unique view of how easy it was to fool everyone.

Her father may have been serving his own purposes when he made sure she had the right credentials in the art world, but once she discovered what had funded her education, she stopped taking his money. The question she asked herself sometimes was whether she had severed her relations with Simon as soon as she realized what he did or had she waited until she was ready to make it on her own. When her mother insisted she continue the self-defence classes and learn to fire a handgun, was that training only for her stint in Moscow? Or was her mother already thinking about where the career she had chosen might lead?

She now knew how dangerous it could be to obtain certain paintings for galleries and wealthy collectors. Her work for the Commission for Looted Art in Europe had offered fine tests of her martial-arts training. She had been followed and attacked in Vienna right after the 2013 profiles of the Commission's work appeared in *Harper's* and *Tagesspiegel*. Even in Paris, she was always checking whether someone was following her and always careful when entering a building, even a café.

Louise was delighted with the bouquet. She was a plain woman in her fifties and, judging from her reaction, she rarely received flowers. Helena knew that in her previous job at the Orangerie she had rarely been praised for her work. Today was the fifth anniversary of her working for Helena, and she deserved both the praise and the flowers. She was efficient, always unruffled, usually pleasant to callers, and never late for work.

Louise had the map of the arrondissement of Saint-Denis spread out on Helena's architect's desk. She had marked the route Helena should take to where the Corot was awaiting her judgement, but at the last moment, she decided to go along on the journey. It's a perilous part of the city, she said, easy to get lost and even easier to be robbed at knifepoint.

Helena grinned at the idea of this rather prim woman discouraging a robber or a pickpocket, but Louise hadn't been out of the office for the past two weeks and deserved a break.

As for the Corot, it was so close to the genuine article that Helena thought it could pass at the next auction and make the house a tidy sum, but wisdom prevailed. She would not risk either her own reputation or Christie's on a well-executed fake.

What she would do, instead, was buy it for the newest Mrs. Grigoriev, if he didn't like Gertrude's garish painting, after Helena had taken possession of the Titian.

She called Attila on the way to the airport and listened to his tale about Bratislava and Bika.

"Your client, Márton," Attila asked, "has he ever mentioned that Gertrude's son may not be Krestin's?"

"No. But I am sure he has travelled to Hungary and Slovakia more often than he told me. And it doesn't take much to make a child."

"Was he there in 1977?"

"He and his wife visited Budapest then."

"Any idea what time of year?"

"Since he lit candles and put flowers on his father's grave, I would guess around All Saints, November 1 or 2."

"Jenci was born in July 1978."

Neither of them mentioned the extraordinary talent of the woman who had thrown a knife into Bika's thigh.

Since Helena Marsh had to stay ensconced at the Four Seasons in Budapest, the woman who flew to Toronto was Eva Bergman. She had already walked the length of the aircraft cabin several times to identify her tail, but none of the other passengers paid her much attention. The only person who aroused her suspicion was an elderly man who seemed to read the same page in his Lee Child book for most of an hour. No one needed that long to read a page of Lee Child.

It was a long, boring flight, and most passengers slept, or appeared to sleep (even the Lee Child reader). She read her brand-new copy of Homer's *Iliad*, the 2010 Ian Johnston translation. It made a nice change from the *Aeneid*, which she had left in her holdall in her Budapest hotel room.

After the airplane landed, she managed to lose the elderly man on the long walk to the immigration area.

Once she was through customs, she went straight to a washroom and divested herself of Eva's scratchy wig, pocketed the glasses, changed out of the brown suit into her pant suit. She passed through immigration with her own passport and identified herself as Helena Marsh to the uniformed driver holding her name aloft. In under an hour, the limousine reached the Mártons' Rosedale mansion, and Helena walked up the path and the steps to the white-pillared front porch.

The Mártons' house was about ten winding blocks from where Helena had grown up. In Rosedale, all the streets wound around, as if the neighbourhood was still the village it had once been. The tall Japanese-holly hedge was sprouting new shoots, and rhododendrons were glowing pink in their stone vases on either side of the pillared entrance. The grass had been close-cut. She took a long, deep breath of the garden scents before she knocked. Such a difference since her first visit. After some hesitation, spring had arrived in Toronto.

The brass knocker made a booming sound outside and set off a bell inside.

A maid, as neat as the garden, opened the door and ushered her into a spacious living room with double chandeliers hanging from the high ceiling and picture windows overlooking the back garden and the valley below.

Klara Márton arrived just seconds later and told her that Géza would be along in a few minutes. She offered her a glass of wine or spirits from the sideboard, and said that, except on very dark days, when he was under the spell of his memories, Géza drank only red wine that he imported personally from France, Spain, and, of course, Hungary. Helena asked for a glass of burgundy, and Klara left to get a bottle.

Helena wandered around the room, looking at the Persian carpets, the flower arrangements, the shelves of books arranged by colour, the photographs, and the paintings, many of which seemed eerily familiar. She found Géza in the next room, sitting in a bay window and looking out at the garden and the busy bird feeders under the trees. Still with his back to her, he said he was glad she could come. A glass goblet of scotch sat on a small paw-foot table by the window, next to a half-empty bottle. Clearly, it was one of his dark days.

He rose and shook her hand. He was taller than Helena, straight-backed, with sparse grey hair. His eyebrows were almost white, faded by the sun of whatever vacation he had recently enjoyed. He gestured her to sit in a matching chair and lowered himself back into his own.

He asked her again about how Krestin had been killed and what she knew about the police investigation.

She didn't mention that she suspected Gábor Nagy may have tried to blackmail Krestin once he realized that Helena knew that Krestin had been in Vorkuta, and that that secret was out, at least. She was sure Nagy was not interested in money. So what would have been the point in his contacting Krestin?

She told him she knew now that Bika was Gyula Németh. And not Krestin.

"He attacked a guy working for the Hungarian police," she said. "I doubt you'll be hearing from Németh for a while." She watched him closely when she talked about Bika. He seemed impatient when she described how he looked, confirming that Géza already knew this and even that Németh lived in Bratislava.

Instead, he wanted to hear more about Gábor Nagy — whether he had seemed to be in need of money, and how he lived.

"He told me you had pretended not to recognize him once in 1944."

"I did him a favour," Géza said. "There were some young men walking with me who would have thrown him into the river."

"Arrow Cross?"

"Could have been, I don't remember."

Géza said he thought it odd that Nagy had denied knowing about the Titian. "Of course, he knew about my painting. We thought we would die there, and I used to talk about it when we were at the edge of that abyss. Gábor was down to less than forty kilos. I was a skeleton. That painting . . . that was real. It kept me alive. Not the religious thing; Vorkuta was hard on God. It was the hope that I would see the painting again. It represented to me our old life: civilization, beds, sofas, antiques, gold frames on pictures. Windows with sunlight.

"Klara has heard so much about that painting, she is looking forward to seeing it here at last. Of course, I never told her the whole story. You've seen the others," he waved his hand, loose-wristed, elegant, dismissive, around the walls. "They are no match for the Titian."

Helena followed his gesture with her eyes. "They are very attractive," she said cautiously.

"Of course. They are some of your father's best, don't you think?"

"My father?"

"Simon Montreuil, of course."

Son-of-a-bitch, she thought.

"I don't know my father. I've never met anyone who claimed to be my father," she said. Could Simon have told Géza? Why would he?

"He was not here much, but he was your father, wasn't he?"

"My mother brought me up alone."

"Annelise," Géza said with a smile. "A beautiful woman. I think all beautiful women should be entitled to their secrets. Wouldn't you agree?"

"You knew my mother?"

"Of course, we knew your mother," he said. "Perhaps you would like to join me for an early dinner today."

"I don't think so."

"We have so much to talk about."

Had Géza not claimed to have been a friend as well as a customer of her father's, she might have chosen a different moment to give him Giorgio's letter certifying the Titian was a fake. He read it over twice, folded it, and slipped it into the breast pocket of his dove-grey jacket. Then he rubbed his palms together as if they had been dirtied by touching it. He said nothing.

She told him that the other bidders had copies of the same letter and would likely withdraw from the auction. The wife, she said, would still want to sell the painting. Krestin, Attila had told her, had left unpaid debts.

"There is a chance," she said, "that Sylvie Hoffman's customer will still bid on the painting, but it will not be a high bid. Some people prefer inexpensive fakes to the real thing. In other words, you could beat his price. It will still be much lower than what you authorized me to spend."

"Do you know her client?"

"I met him once. He has made too much money too fast and has developed a belief in his own infallibility." A tendency he had in common with Géza Márton, she thought.

Géza laughed. "You mentioned Italians?"

"I am not sure they are real. The admirable Mr. Kis may have suggested Italians, in a generic way, to up the ante on the price, but he hasn't mentioned them recently. I did check on Krestin's former partner, a Mr. Tihanyi. Perhaps you know him?"

"I know very little about the movie business. One thing, though: he doesn't sound Italian."

"I am told you made an investment in Krestin's business."

"Now, why would I do that?"

"Maybe because you saw a chance to ruin him?"

Géza examined the bird-feeder for a full minute before he answered. "If I had a chance to ruin the son-of-a-bitch, I would take it. How long was this Tihanyi partners with Krestin?"

"Four or five years."

"Long enough to have seen my painting."

Géza rose from his chair and asked if she would accompany him for a walk through the garden. "The air from the valley will refresh you. I find walking helps me think. Don't you? About Gertrude . . ." He opened a French door and followed her onto a terrace overlooking the forested ravine.

"You didn't tell me that you had visited her after her divorce."

"I don't see how my seeing her is any of your business," he said.

"You also visited her before her divorce," she said. "Perhaps in 1977."

"In 1977? I was there with Klara, my wife. Putting flowers on my parents' graves."

"In Dunajská Streda?"

He stopped suddenly and stared at her. "Why? Did she say something about that?"

"No, she was very discreet, but I presume you went there as well as Budapest. And you've sent her money."

He neither confirmed nor denied.

"This is the garden I had always imagined I'd have," Géza said.

"I know. You told me."

"It reminds me of my childhood." He looked Helena in the eyes. "I imagine it does not remind you of yours. Otherwise you wouldn't have become proficient in martial arts. Or was that just a hobby?"

Helena, who was not used to answering personal questions, gazed into the distance. "Jenci remembers your visits," she said. "I assume you know he is your son?"

"Don't take it the wrong way, my dear," Géza said. "I entrusted you with a very important mission. I would not have done that if I'd had doubts. I assume you checked my bona fides when I proposed to send you to Hungary?"

"I didn't need to. I knew enough about you long before we met. What I cannot understand is why you decided to buy back your painting. Why you went to all that trouble for me to see the provenance, assuming it is the real provenance. Many of those have also been faked. There have been some master provenance fakers, as we both know."

"The documents I had delivered to you at the Kerepesi Cemetery can all be checked elsewhere," he said. "The archives of the Kunsthistorisches Museum will confirm provenance. And restoring works of art to their rightful owners is one of your specialties, isn't it? That's why I picked you for this job."

"Really?" She didn't believe him. He had picked her because

of her father. He had assumed that once she had seen all the fakes on his walls, she would be worried that her own reputation could be tarnished. He had said when she first came here and sampled his fine wines, "Your reputation precedes you." She had taken that, not as a compliment but as a threat.

"Really," he said, his hands thrust into his pants pockets as he surveyed his domain. His suit alone would have cost more than any one of her father's paintings, she thought. He could have afforded a few genuine articles, had he chosen to do so.

"If you sold that painting for a crust of bread, or even several crusts of bread, you could have taken Krestin to court after 1989," she said. "No court would have recognized his right to own something he had obtained for bread in a Soviet labour camp. Surely, in post-Communist Hungary, you would have won the suit. Or you could have taken him to court in another country. You could have had your painting back years ago, and for less than what you will likely have to pay now."

He didn't respond.

"Yet you chose not to," she said. "And you paid Kis, and maybe some others, an annual retainer to find a painting you knew was in Krestin's possession. Why?"

"I thought he no longer had it. Once the Communists bailed out, I assumed he would have sold the painting. As for the courts, you know remarkably little about how Eastern Europe works. The notion that laws are there to protect citizens is Western. The idea of an independent judiciary is Western. Krestin had nothing to fear from me while he curried favour with both the post-Communists and their opponents. From time to time, he had to make sure he greased a palm, or invited someone to sample his largess. The trial, assuming that my suit against him ever reached a courtroom, would have been endlessly postponed, and both of us would have died before the judgement."

"As it is, only one of you is dead," Helena said, sipping her lukewarm wine. "And I assume if you were going to buy the painting, you could have offered to buy it years ago. Why didn't you?"

"Perhaps I didn't have enough money . . ."

"Or you, too, have something to hide."

He spread his palms in a gesture of perfect openness.

"And before you get around to asking, no, I really don't care whether it is a fake," Géza said, facing her. "You have to understand that. If you do not, you haven't been listening."

He turned abruptly and left her alone on the terrace.

Klara, who must have been waiting somewhere in the garden, appeared by Helena's elbow, with a silver tray of long-stemmed glasses and the open bottle of burgundy. She put it down on the stone railing.

"It's been very hard for Géza these past few weeks," she said. "He has managed to keep those memories at bay most of his life. It's easier to do that in a new country; easier when he was busy. His work, you know, used to be very demanding. But he has mostly retired. Now, he can afford to think about the past."

She took one of the glasses, poured herself a generous amount of wine, and drank it in large gulps, as if it were water and she had been thirsty for a long time. "Since he found out that his family's painting did survive, he has spent more time living in the past than in the present. Some days he imagines he sees the slope of Sas Hill, the black poplars, the lindens, the yews, and in the distance the spires of Saint Michael's. Today was one of those days."

There was one more question Helena had wanted to ask Géza and now asked Klara instead. "Did you go along on Géza's trips to Hungary?"

"Oh no," Klara said. "He usually went for All Saints, to put candles on his parents' graves. It's something he always wanted to do alone."

"And when he went to Bratislava?"

A big, open smile. Would she have known about Gertrude?

"He was visiting relatives, and I don't speak Hungarian. We have two wonderful children, Ms. Marsh. They have always wanted to go to Hungary, but Géza didn't want to take them."

"Did you ever meet Gertrude?"

"Oh no," Klara said again, pursing her lips to emphasize the "o."

"And Jenci?"

Klara poured herself another glass of wine and suggested they go into the house. It looked like rain.

Attila had always been fond of Tibor's mother. During the days when he lacked the funds for a good meal, Mrs. Szelley used to serve him thick slices of fresh chewy bread with butter and salami, one or two short sticks of Csabai sausage, and a piece of strudel or cake. Learning that he had just returned from Slovakia, she dished up her famous Dobos torte with the élan of a master pastry chef, a smile in place for his groans of appreciation.

Attila didn't disappoint her, although he had promised the girls that he would start reducing his belly. He was confident that an hour or two in the baths would do the trick; he didn't have to be churlish about dessert. Nor did he have to decline

Mrs. Szelley's offer of a generous splash of J&B. Tibor lingered by his elbow, drinking but not eating. "I saw myself in shorts yesterday," he explained, much to Attila's annoyance.

The Király Bath was an easy walk from the Szelleys' apartment, but Tibor drove anyway. The car smelled of scented cigarettes and aftershave. "What is the point of having a flashy car," he said, "if you don't get to show it off?" At the bath, a valet parked the car for them in a guaranteed secure place.

Once they were settled in the Turkish thermal pool, Attila told him about the woman who had saved his life in Bratislava, about his conviction that Németh could not have wanted his old friend dead, and about Jenci not being Krestin's son.

"That would explain why they separated. Though for a while he seemed to be fond of the boy." Tibor said. "But he was frugal with support payments to his ex. She used to send the boy down to Budapest every few months to beg for cash. And Krestin would keep him waiting for hours, paying him no heed, so I've been told."

"What did Vera make of that?" Attila asked.

"No idea. She is a hard woman to read. But one of my friends who was a frequent guest at the Krestins said she actually liked the boy."

"That's another thing," Attila said. "Everyone talks about him as a boy. The guy is thirty-six, not much younger than Vera. Did you ever see them together?"

"You're kidding, right?" Tibor ducked underwater for a moment, then raised his head and shoulders out of the water. "It's too damned hot in here today. We'll have a beer when you finish grilling me about the Krestins. This time it's your treat."

"Why wouldn't they get it on?" Attila persisted. "He is not

a bad looking guy in a weedy, undernourished sort of way, and she is pretty in an icy sort of way. It's not like Krestin was likely much of a sex fiend, not at his age."

"Because he wasn't her type."

"How would you know?"

"I know."

"So who is her type?"

"Someone more like me, buddy," Tibor was squinting up at the spots of daylight shining through the dome. "In fact, much more like me."

Attila started to laugh. "You're kidding, right?"

"No. I am not kidding," Tibor said. "I never kid about women." But he was laughing and flapping about in the water like a carp in mating season. "But I didn't kill him, in case you're wondering. Ask my mother. She and I were drinking J&B on the balcony with a couple of her bridge-playing friends until suppertime, when I left to dine at the Gellért."

"Whew!" Attila said. When he recovered, he asked whether Tibor was still fucking the widow.

"None of your business," Tibor said. "Besides, since you seem interested, I was not the only one. And no, she sure as hell didn't kill that asshole. She enjoyed his money while it lasted and all the perks that went with it."

After downing a beer in the outdoor bar, where Tibor could finally smoke, and a short stroll with Gustav, Attila checked in with Tóth to see if there were any new developments.

Tóth seemed almost sad. He complained about pressure from upstairs to make an arrest, no new evidence, the uncooperative widow, and a persistent pain in his gut.

Vera Krestin's alibis had all checked out, the diary was still missing. Krestin had phoned Németh in Bratislava in the morning, but there was no evidence that Németh had visited Krestin the day of the murder. He had also talked either with Gertrude or his son four times during the day. They had phoned him, not the other way around. He had also called Kis. The Russian and the Ukrainian were both gone the afternoon Krestin died, and Tihanyi was in Rome. Krestin had owed a lot of money to Tihanyi and to the bank. "I would be grateful if you could identify the person who almost killed Németh," he suggested, rather than ordered — a whole new phase of their relationship.

Then Attila called Helena at the Gresham and left her a message, saying, "It would be good to know whether you like the coffee in Bratislava." He left his cell number.

A mistress of many disguises, Alexander had said. And a deft hand with a knife. She may have saved his life in Bratislava and, even if she did kill the Bulgarian, it was probably in self-defence. No one cared about that man anyway, except maybe his mother.

When she arrived back in Budapest as Eva Bergman, Helena didn't bother to try a quick change in the back of the limousine. She was too tired and too anxious to conclude the deal, get the painting delivered to Géza so she could collect her fee, then return to Paris to make an offer for the not-Corot, and take a long rest. She was beginning to think that perhaps her future should have fewer surprises, and that there could be some place that didn't require her to resort to self-defence. There had to be another way to live. There had to be a way to stop paying for Simon's sins. Maybe, just maybe, there could even be someone who could share her life.

At 7 a.m., the Gresham was quiet, with just a couple of

guests in the breakfast room, the concièrge reading the morning papers, the smiling young man at the front desk who wished her a good morning. Yes, it could be another fine day in Budapest.

There were messages from Grigoriev (he was back to his apartment in London and waiting to hear from her), Kis (he wanted an urgent word with her since he hadn't been able to reach Mr. Márton directly), and one from Attila about coffee.

She called Attila right after she had a glass of freshly squeezed orange juice. He was still asleep when he answered the phone, his voice gravelly and soft, his breathing heavy. She wondered whether he was a snorer.

"I love Bratislava," she told him. "It's full of old-world charm, and it's sparkling with new-world enthusiasm."

"Mmmm."

"As for the coffee, it's no contest. Budapest coffee is better."

"You were there when Krestin's friend, Bika, attacked me."

"I assumed you would thank me, or whoever it was who saved your life."

"He is too old and uncoordinated to have done me much harm, but I owe you, although you weren't really there. Captain Tóth checked on your whereabouts yesterday, and he was pleased to learn that you hadn't left the city."

"I won't be here long," Helena said. "I will buy the painting tonight. Whoever is looking at it will have confirmed it is a fake. There will be no reason to deem it a national treasure, and it can leave the country."

"You're sure about that?"

"Absolutely. No underqualified Central European art appraiser is likely to second-guess Dottore Giorgio Matamoros of the Gallerie del'Accademia on the authenticity of a Titian."

"Not even you?"

She laughed. "You've been spending time on the internet," she said.

He was out of bed now, pulling on his pants and looking for Gustav's leash, the phone firmly held between his shoulder and chin, until it slipped and fell and he yelled "*Bassza meg.*" He thought she wouldn't understand, but he was wrong. "Do you have time to meet?" he asked somewhat breathlessly when he regained the phone.

"Today?" she asked.

"Today would be good," Attila said. "Or dinner tonight would be good. I thought you wouldn't have —"

"Quite right," she said. "I don't have anything more interesting to do, and, besides, you owe me."

He pulled on his T-shirt and jacket as they settled on lunch. Then it was once around the block with Gustav, a quick call to the ex confirming next weekend with the girls, and a sprint to catch the bus. He wanted to visit Vera Krestin before he was to present himself at the Police Palace at 11 a.m. The prospect of lunch with Helena Marsh was making him feel young again.

There were no policemen around the Krestin house. The camera on the other side of the street was still angled away. The camera above the garage door was still angled uselessly down; it wouldn't record a robber unless he was crawling on hands and knees. The stone fountain in the centre of the lawn had been turned off, and there were signs of digging in the flowerbeds under the bevelled windows. The Mercedes Benz was parked in the driveway.

The lone policewoman in Tóth's department answered the bell almost immediately. She must have been waiting somewhere near the front door. A cheerful, fresh-faced, young recruit, she had no trouble recognizing Attila, although she did have to check with the sergeant whether Attila would be allowed inside. The sergeant had no objection to his visit. Tóth, having made no progress in the investigation, must have wanted to share the blame.

"Mrs. Krestin," the policewoman said, "is in the living room with Mr. Krestin."

"With whom?"

"With Mr. Krestin," she said matter-of-factly, but a tad louder, in case Attila was deaf.

"But Mr. Krestin is dead," Attila said.

The policewoman smiled indulgently. "It's Mr. Jenö Krestin," she said. "I will show you in, if you like."

"Charming," Attila mumbled. "You stay here long enough, you'll qualify as a maid," he added, enjoying his own rudeness, "or a butler."

She ignored the jibe and escorted him along the discreetly lit hallway hung with old photographs, a few gold-framed paintings, and a drawing of a hairy naked man and a fleshy woman cavorting on a bed of pillows. In the bottom-right corner there was Picasso's flamboyant signature. Attila wondered whether Helena had seen this one and, if so, what she thought of it. Would she find it amusing? Would she talk about it being high art? Was she a prude? Would he ever find out?

The living room was three times the size of Attila's entire apartment. Its tall windows threw a soft light over the huge painting that dominated the space. It was overwhelming: the gilded frame, the darkness around the grainy white figures, the grey donkey in the middle, and the glowing purple figure in the centre, a shaft of blue-white light making his head glow. There were drops of red around his neck and red in the faces looking up at him, making them seem sinister, except for the face of the one woman in front of the donkey, her arms full of green fronds. She wore a green robe. Her face was pale pink and white, her eyes stared directly at Attila.

The painting overpowered the colourful Persian carpets and even the furniture arranged around a marble coffee table in the centre of the room. Two people were reclining in velvet armchairs, glass goblets in hand, their faces turned to the painting. One of them was Vera Krestin in a white skirt that rode midway up her tanned thighs — a welcome change from her earlier dowdy attire. The other was Jenci Krestin in a grey three-piece suit.

He looked ten years older than the last time Attila had seen him, and it wasn't just the suit. His shoulders seemed wider, his face less pallid, his eyes were brighter.

"So," Attila said, "this is the famous painting."

Neither Jenci nor Vera confirmed the obvious, nor did they stand to welcome the visitor.

"The police," Vera said coolly, "have not discovered anything new, I presume, or your boss would have called me."

Attila didn't bother explaining the intricacies of his relationship with Tóth, but her tone was annoying enough that he decided to bypass the pleasantries. "On the contrary," he said, "we have discovered a number of interesting facts, which is why I am here."

Jenci raised his eyebrows, making his eyes seem rounder than they were already.

"We have interviewed Mr. Németh, who was in Gulag 442 with your husband and has been in your home a number of times, including once this past week. Oddly enough, he was here the day before your husband was killed."

"He was?" Vera asked. "Then, I assume you have arrested him?"

"No, we have not because he is not the killer. But I thought it interesting that neither you nor the previous Mrs. Krestin saw fit to admit to us that your husband had been in the Gulag, that he was there at the same time as this guy Németh and also Géza Márton, the man wishing to buy this painting. Curious, don't you think?"

"Why?" Jenci asked.

"Why is it curious? Because Mr. Krestin bought this painting from someone who had no wish to sell it but had no choice. In the Gulag, rules of right and wrong didn't apply. Now we have laws of restitution."

Vera Krestin stood, smoothed down her skirt and walked over to a delicate-looking side table, pulled a thin file out of one of its shallow drawers and took it over to Attila.

"I think you will find that this painting was bought after Mr. Márton had already left the country and that the vendor was not him but his father," she said. "The provenance is in order. The papers were certified by the head of European Archives of the National Gallery. And the bill of sale to my husband is confirmed by the Hungarian government."

Attila looked at the top sheet. It was, as she said, confirmation that on September 21, 1961, the government of the Republic of Hungary "condoned" the transfer of one million forints to the account of one Géza Márton, a resident of Toronto, Ontario, Canada. The funds were deposited by Comrade János Krestin, in consideration for the painting allegedly by Italian artist Tiziano Vecellio, purchased by said János Krestin from Károly Márton.

Attila remembered that September 20, 1961, was the date Károly Márton had been released from the notorious Recsk prison. It was in the mid-1960s that Géza Márton bought his first major tract of land in Canada. One million forints, while not a big sum for a real Titian, must have been enough to purchase some fallow farmland north of the city of Toronto. It was the beginning of Géza Márton's becoming a wealthy man.

Both Vera and Jenci were looking at him as he read the documents, she with a little smile, he with utter concentration.

"Interesting," was the best Attila could come up with at the end of his scrutiny. "We will have to ascertain that the papers are in order."

"My husband had them verified in 2000," Vera said, "long after the so-called democratic reforms. But go ahead, you can do it as well. But please leave now. I am rather busy at the moment. I have a funeral to organize, lawyers to meet, debts to settle, and we must deal with the will and conclude the sale of this painting." She was on the verge of pulling a cord near the window when the policewoman reappeared. She must have been standing at the glass double doors, listening.

"The will," Attila said. "You are the beneficiary?"

Vera sighed theatrically. "I already informed you that I am not the sole beneficiary."

"He would have left something for his son?"

She nodded. "Of course."

"You are still selling the painting," Attila said.

"As I said to you and to your boss, that is my intention."

"To settle the debts?"

"I don't see how that could possibly be any of your concern," she said.

He tried to imagine her being charming and sexy but failed.

"Mr. Krestin," he said, "I assume your mother mentioned that we checked your father's telephone records and there were five calls from your number in Dunajská Streda to this house on the morning that Mr. Krestin died. What did you talk to him about?"

"I was arranging another visit to Budapest," Jenci said.

"Yes, I gather you have been coming quite often. Was it to collect your allowance from Mr. Krestin?"

"I had no allowance," Jenci said, his voice cracking. "I came to collect what we were owed. He had financial obligations to my mother. It was in the divorce settlement that he was to pay her each month. Most of the time he forgot."

"He was paying child support?"

Jenci stood up, tensing his shoulders as if he were readying for a fight. He turned to Vera, but she had nothing to say. "I am not a child," he spluttered finally.

"Nor, as I understand it, Mr. Krestin, were you ever his child. Isn't that right?"

There was a sharp intake of breath from the doorway where the policewoman had been waiting for Attila to leave, but Vera remained impassive. "What possible difference could that make now?" she asked with obvious contempt.

Attila tried to imagine her naked and having fun with Tibor. He thought that would help control his desire to deck her.

"Question is, did János Krestin know you were not his son when he prepared his will? Or did he find out on the day he was murdered? Was he planning to make a new will that excluded you?"

Jenci came toward Attila but stopped a couple of metres away. His face was red, his ears crimson. He was breathing deeply. "As Vera says, it makes no difference. My father left very little. He was almost broke. He had too many debts."

Attila looked around the room. All that fine furniture, all the art? Was Vera going to auction it all off now? "But you didn't know that when you came here on Monday," he said, taking a wild guess. "You came to collect for you and your mother, isn't that right? And I assume he was as reluctant as ever to part with his money. In fact, maybe more reluctant if he had just discovered that you were Géza Márton's son."

"Géza Márton's? I barely know the guy."

"Maybe so, but your mother certainly knew him, and she met with him in 1977 and, as a friend of mine pointed out, it doesn't take much to make a child . . ."

"Are you accusing me?" Jenci yelled. "Me? What? Are you drunk? Crazy? Why me?"

"You would have assumed you would inherit half his money when he died, wouldn't you, Mr. Krestin? Unless, of course, someone had just proved to him that you were not his son. I assume you remember Mr. Németh? Old friend of János Krestin's? He took a DNA sample off your glass when he bought you a drink."

Jenci stared at Attila. "He what?"

"That would have changed his mind, wouldn't it, Mr. Krestin?"

Vera laid a hand on Jenci's arm. "We will consult our lawyers," she said. "Jenö has nothing more to say now. And nor, as I have already said, do I."

Attila called Tóth from the walled garden and told him that the prime suspect in the murder of János Krestin was drinking wine with the formidable widow at her Rózsadomb residence. After a long explanation — avoiding any mention of Tibor — Tóth agreed to send a team to the Krestins and question Jenci. "Check the train from Dunajská Streda on the day Krestin was murdered," Attila said. "Jenci doesn't have a car, so he must have taken the train both ways. Someone is bound to remember him."

Vera and Jenci were now standing at the window looking at Attila. She seemed to be talking to Jenci. She still had her hand on his arm, but it no longer seemed like a calming gesture. It was, Attila thought, more affectionate. For the first time since he had clapped eyes on her, she had softened.

"Did you know," Attila asked Tóth, "that Krestin was not Jenö Krestin's father?"

"He wasn't?"

"You should call Krestin's lawyer and ask him whether Krestin was about to change his will when he died."

"How?"

"I think you'll find that young Krestin was no longer going to inherit half his father's estate. That's why the lawyer had an appointment with Krestin on the day after Krestin had died."

"Jenö Krestin?"

"And you could ask the lawyer whether János Krestin was broke."

"I may have heard something to that effect," Tóth said cautiously. "He was selling his paintings, wasn't he?"

"A Titian, worth maybe eighty million dollars, if it's the real thing."

"My sources say that it's not. I mean it's not by this guy Titian. It's a fake."

"Oh yes, the Ukrainians. I take it Mr. Azarov has lost interest in the painting."

Tóth didn't reply.

"If you can bestir yourself to the Krestin residence, you could arrest Jenö Krestin for János Krestin's murder. You could make your day more exciting by discovering a long-running affair between the happy widow and the son."

The bunch of flowers that arrived at the hotel was so enormous the concièrge had to split them among four fat vases, and it took two maids to deliver them. Helena suggested that they place three on the long table by the window, where they blocked her view of the Széchenyi Chain Bridge and the castle beyond, and split the fourth between themselves to take home. The card bore no message, only a name: Vladimir. He must have decided he liked *The Last Judgement*, and perhaps he was admitting that the driver in Cluj had been his man, after all, and thought that flowers would do in lieu of an apology. With Vladimir, you could never be sure.

The call from the Kis Gallery came a few minutes after the flowers. Kis was as polite and accommodating as he had been the first time they had spoken. He said the painting "in question" had been packaged and was ready for her; that ten million dollars was acceptable to Mrs. Krestin, assuming the funds could be wired to Mrs. Krestin's account by the end of the week.

She had planned to enjoy her last day in the city, to take in the views finally, and relax. She bought a new silk blouse at Max Mara and a pair of slim pants at Zara on Váci Street. Then she went to the hotel gym for a workout, had a swim, booked a massage for the afternoon, and dressed for lunch with the robust ex-policeman.

She took the elevator down to the lobby and waited for him near the huge potted plants. He looked utterly uncomfortable entering the marble foyer, his shoes freshly polished, his jacket carefully covering his belly, his blue pants ironed to sharp seams, his hair still damp from the shower. He couldn't stop smiling when he saw her.

Although he had a reservation at the Costes restaurant on Ráday Street, she suggested they order wine and sandwiches in the hotel lobby. On the sort of money he earned, he could not afford Costes, and the lobby was closer to her room — in case the lunch turned out to be more than just a lunch.

1 No one likes to think about suicides. Least of all, the men who run the subways.

On the night of April 8, 1985, at 11:05 p.m., as his train was rounding the bend in the tunnel just before Summerhill, it was the last thing motorman John Hogg wished to think about. On the downtown run Summerhill and Rosedale are the last of the suburban stations and on a week night almost no one gets on. The yellow lights make the platforms seem unreal. He could slow the train, slide into a fast stop, open and close the doors in almost the same movement, and start again as fast, for sport. Something to keep his mind off that other time. As he pulled out of Summerhill, Hogg began to unwrap his chicken sandwich.

When approaching the next stop, Rosedale, late at night, Hogg always had that same nightmare feeling, fear gripping his jaws tight and catching in his throat. His first suicide had been at Rosedale Station. In the heart of chic, residential old-world Toronto, where he sometimes took the kids for a Sunday drive to show them the palatial, Georgian homes.

Then, also, it had been late at night. The girl in front of the train no more than a blur of movement . . .

He had to stop thinking about it.

Most drivers didn't like the late shift, it cut into their family lives, but Hogg had asked for it. And got it. There were a few privileges to be had for twenty-three years on the trains. The kids were grown now, the wife was taking some damn-fool course at Ryerson, and he could get the day to himself. Peaceful. And some nights there were parties. Tonight should be a great one. One of his pals was retiring from the "service" (that's what they called it, like the army), and they were all getting together. No wives. Just the boys. And he'd heard a rumor someone had lined up a couple of strippers — for laughs.

He was running a few minutes behind schedule, the lights were green all the way, so he moved the speed lever to 75 and took another bite of the sandwich. A little dry. He was coming in fast, past that infernal cut-off where the platform starts . . .

He felt it before he saw it. A heavy thump-crunch. A shudder as it smashed into the front. Train slowed by the impact. A shoe hit the window at eye level. Brown. Brown spray splattered the glass. He ducked involuntarily before starting to apply the air-brakes. Somebody screamed. Oh god, no, it can't be. *Not here.*

"For chrissakes, John, stop the fucking car," he heard the guard yell into the microphone.

It was only then that he slammed on the emergency brakes, and pulled the train up, wheels shrieking, halfway down the platform. He jerked open his door.

There were three passengers in the front car. A young man, scrambling from the floor. A young woman, white-faced, holding onto the vertical bar with both hands. She looked at him, eyes wide, her mouth sagging open. Another woman was screaming, hiccupping for breath, her head thrown back. Hogg muttered something at the young woman. *Regulation: calm the passengers so as to prevent panic. They must stay inside the car until the police arrive.*

He reached back into his cubicle and pressed the alarm button, then walked to the first door, withdrew the emergency pass key from his breast pocket and opened it.

"Please, everybody, stay calm. Stay seated. The police will be here in a few minutes," he said to the man who was moving toward him.

He ran to the emergency alarm station at the end of the platform, broke the glass protection strip, pressed the trip lever down to cut rail power. Then he picked up the red phone, and dialed Transit Control. *Dial 555 for suicides.*

"It's a 555 at Rosedale. This is 2454 — Hogg," he added unnecessarily. They would know anyway, as soon as he dialed, where he was and what had happened. They would also notify Police Communications who would direct police officers, ambulance and CIB personnel to the scene.

When Hogg turned, Jake Moore, the guard, was already at the front, bending to look under the train. Hogg jumped down to join him.

"Jeesus, what a lot of blood," he said. One of the two front fenders was bent and twisted out of shape. "That's where he must have hit." Blood splattered all over both fenders, and the lower half of the window. "There he is." Jake was on his hands and knees, pointing down under the belly of the car. There was an arm sticking out over the inside rail. An arm in a raincoat-sleeve, wrist wearing a gold watchstrap. "He's got to be dead," Jake said.

Hogg didn't say anything, he just nodded. No one could have survived that.

"Didn't you have another one here a couple of years back?" Jake asked.

"Yeah. A girl . . . She was just gone fifteen."

"What foul luck. Twice in the same place." Jake crouched down again to get a better look under the train.

"Did you see him jump?" he asked.

"No. I mean, yes, I must have. It all happened so fast."

"I thought you'd never stop the car," Jake said quietly.

Hogg became aware of other people on the platform, a small cluster with their feet at Hogg's shoulder level. Silent. Staring.

"Would all passengers please clear the platform," said the loudspeaker.

"Shit. I had to slow down first, didn't I? People get hurt if you stop too suddenly," Hogg blurted out, angry. "Your first one this, isn't it?"

Jake nodded.

"You'll learn."

They climbed back onto the platform.

"There's been an accident. Everybody please go upstairs," Hogg said.

"Everybody please clear the platform," the loudspeaker tuned in.

The spectators backed away, slowly. They made no move toward the stairs.

"Did you see what happened?" one of them asked.

"I saw him when he came down. Such a nice-looking man."

"Do you suppose he jumped?"

Hogg checked his watch. They were, as ever, efficient, he thought with some pride. The line supervisor was coming along the platform, waving people upstairs. Sensing the authority of the gesture, they began to move. It was 11:18.

Behind the supervisor's gray uniform, Hogg could see four other men in brown — Equipment Department and Track Patrol.

"You're Hogg?" the supervisor asked. "Where did it happen?"

"As I was entering the station. He came at me from the side. There was no way . . . hell, I couldn't even see him."

The supervisor scanned the side of the train for pieces of clothing, or body. Two of the other men were down on the tracks looking under the train. None of them were first-timers on the "jumper squad."

"Under car one. About in line with door one," a Track Patrol man shouted at the approaching police officers.

"Ambulance here yet?"

"On the way."

One of the policemen pulled out the emergency wooden box from the south end of the platform, broke the seal and pulled out the basket stretcher, a rubber sheet, and the chalk for marking the location of the body.

The doctor and two St. John's Ambulance men in white uniforms crawled under the train to determine whether the man was dead. Not that there was any real doubt. Still, one has to follow regulations; it's what makes the job bearable.

"He's dead all right," the doctor said, emerging from under the car. He wiped his hands on his white coat, leaving black and brown smears alongside the pockets. His face was flushed and damp as a policeman helped him up onto the platform.

"OK, everybody off the track. We'll have to move the train to get it out," said the officer in charge. "You the motorman?" he asked Hogg.

Hogg nodded.

In five more minutes they had the body on the stretcher. Most of the body. One arm arrived separately. It had been thrown across the meridian divide toward the Northbound lane.

The back of the head had been smashed. Some soft gray jelly lay beside the face. Blood caked over the forehead, across the neck and down the length of his fur-lined trench coat. The first impact must have broken bones in every part of the man's body, though all you could see was where his chest had caved in. He was covered in dirt, mud and black tar from the undercarriage. Still, he had been a handsome man. Maybe mid-fifties, hair brown to beginning white, face lined by too many smiles, gray-blue eyes staring up at the doctor's hand as he closed the lids, firmly.

Sergeant Levine was jotting in his notebook, policeman's shorthand, while he waited for the CIB photographer. Hogg let him into the first car so he could talk to the passengers. None of them had seen anything, so Levine let them go. The two women were going to take cabs home.

Levine returned to take stock of the man's personal belongings. The doctor, because regulations said he was the one to do it, had removed the blood-soaked wallet and some credit cards from the breast pocket and a cluster of keys, a pair of kid-leather gloves, gold-rimmed reflector-lens sunglasses, some business cards and a checkbook from the other pockets.

As soon as Levine saw that his partner had finished outlining the position of the body, he turned to Hogg who was waiting beside him.

"How did it happen?" he asked, pencil at the ready, not looking up from his notebook.

"I was coming into the station when he jumped. Must have been standing right by the wall. Couldn't really see much. Just a blur. Then his shoe hit the window."

"How fast were you traveling?"

"About 65 and slowing for the station," said Hogg, a little uncertainly, but who would know anyway?

Levine looked up at the line supervisor: "May as well get your show back on the road. I'll talk to the other witnesses upstairs."

"You'd better let Jake Moore take over at the controls," the supervisor said to Hogg.

"We'll have a relief crew waiting at Bloor. You guys take what's left of the night off." Then he jogged to the end of the platform to call Transit Control and ask them to restore traction power.

The two men with the stretcher were already climbing the stairs.

Hogg went into the guard's cubicle. Nobody asked any questions. At 11:31 the train was on its way again. Twenty-one to twenty-two minutes, Hogg thought: they've got it down to a fine art.

Detective Inspector David Parr arrived as the stretcher was leaving. As the officer in charge at Jarvis Street Station on Monday nights he should have been there earlier, but he was in the middle of questioning a particularly hostile assault and battery witness, and gaining momentum, when the call came. The case was coming up for trial within the week, so Parr had decided it wouldn't matter if he was a little late. Not a hell of a lot you can do for a suicide anyway.

Moving past the stretcher, he flicked the white sheet aside, looked briefly into the dead man's face, and continued on with a nod to the ambulance men.

"Bloody mess, eh?" he said to the constable who was bringing up the rear. "You'll notify the coroner?"

"Yes, sir," the constable said. "Sergeant Levine was taking inventory."

Parr waved him on and went to stand beside Levine at the edge of the platform.

"All over?" he asked cheerfully.

"It is now," Levine said, as one of the men in brown overalls scrambled up over the lip of the platform and handed him a highly polished tan leather shoe. Levine turned it over; it had hardly been worn. "Good as new," he said. "Look at that." He pointed to the gold printed label inside the shoe. "A Gucci, yet. Why anyone with a pair of brand new Guccis would want to throw himself at a moving train, I'll never know."

The supervisor came over to tell them he was letting people through at the top again. The two policemen fell in line behind him as he started up the stairs.

"Who was he?" Parr asked.

Levine shrugged. He handed over the plastic bag with the

contents of the pockets, holding it between thumb and fore-finger as if it were some nasty insect.

"Here," he said. "You can have the shoe too. Pick up its mate over at the morgue. He won't need them. Not where he's going."

"Perks go with the job, eh?" Parr smiled as he rummaged through the contents. "Here we are." He pulled a driver's license out of the wallet. "George Harris, sixty years old. Lived at 24 Rose Hill Drive. That's not far from here."

"You'll be going over there tonight?" Levine asked.

"Yes. Soon as this is over."

"Don't you ever do it by phone?"

"Not if I can help it," Parr said quietly. "I sure as hell wouldn't like to be told on the phone. Would you?"

The supervisor interrupted them, opening the door to a small staff room near the Yonge Street exit.

"There were only six people on the platform," he said. "They're all in here."

"Good evening." Parr smiled encouragement as he entered. "We won't want to keep you long. Just a few questions and you can all be on your way again."

Six faces glared at him, silent. In shock, Parr thought. Suicides are damned unsettling.

In the corner, a kid about twenty with short-cropped, greased brown hair, leather jacket, tight blue jeans, scuffed leather boots, not quite punk but thinking about it. He held hands with a girl, same age, long damp hair, pale pinched skin. She huddled close to him, touching his body with hers. She seemed docile and needy. He was defiant. At his age, that was fashionable.

By the window there was a black woman, late fifties, soft felt hat pulled down low over her nose, worn khaki raincoat too narrow and too short, orange Dacron dress. She was holding a white supermarket shopping bag, her arms wrapped around it. She looked scared. Might have weathered some bad times with the law; more likely, she was an illegal.

A man, about thirty-five, sat uncomfortably straight-backed at the narrow table, an ashtray in front of him, his briefcase tucked between his navy-blue lace-ups. He wore a three-piece negotiating-blue suit, tinted rimless glasses, and was smoking his third cigarette. He had an exceptionally thin long neck with a jumpy Adam's apple tucked into his tight white collar.

The other end of the table was occupied by a man in his forties — balding, red-faced — and a pinched, matronly woman, possibly English. Clearly they were not together. They were a study in contrasts. She had half-turned away from him, balancing her outsize monogrammed handbag against the table leg. She wore a black mink coat, casually unbuttoned, her elegant knees composed over each other, foot tapping in anticipation. The man was sweating. He took a crumpled Kleenex from his lumberjack shirt pocket, shook it out, and wiped his forehead.

Levine flicked open his notebook.

"Could we please have your names and addresses. Police procedure, I'm afraid," he said deferentially. "Perhaps you'd like to get the ball rolling." He turned to the executive type, who was closest.

"Joseph Muller, 27 Roseborough," he said, shaking another cigarette out of the package. "Do we get called for an inquest or something?"

"I don't think that will be necessary," Parr said. "Phone number?"

Levine wrote down both the home and business numbers. A stockbroker going home late. Edgy.

"When did you arrive on the platform?" Parr asked.

"Couple of minutes before the train. I wasn't even near him when he jumped . . ."

"Did you see him jump?" Parr asked quickly.

"Well . . . I sort of saw a movement, out of the corner of my eye really. Then there was this awful thud."

"Was he already on the platform when you came down?"

"I don't know, really. I don't remember. I was reading the paper." He waved his rolled-up *Star* at Parr.

Parr thanked him and opened the door to let him out before turning to the others.

The apprentice punk hadn't seen anything. Nor had the girl. It was the thud she remembered. Her lower lip trembled when she spoke. While Parr questioned them the boy was pumping her hand, his eyes steady with hostility.

"Get them out of here," Parr murmured to Levine.

The man in the lumberjack shirt said he was a cab driver named Jenkins, taking a day off. "Teach me to take the gawd-damned train," he grumbled. He had seen Harris march to the edge of the platform, lean out to look up the track when they heard the train coming, then back up as if to get out of the way. But he didn't. He had sort of lurched forward again and fallen in front of it. Somebody screamed.

"Who?" Parr asked, but none of the remaining passengers admitted to screaming, so he went on with the questions.

The black woman, not unexpectedly, had heard nothing and seen nothing. She was so eager to get away Parr could feel her vibrating toward the door. He hoped they wouldn't have to call her or that she had given a false address. He wasn't going to harass her for identification. Rotten luck for her to be in the wrong place at the wrong time.

They had left the gray-haired woman to last. She seemed content sipping her tea, listening with grave interest, like a schoolteacher watching the class take turns at reading. That is what she turned out to be: Mrs. W.A. Hall, a retired school-teacher. The husband must have made the money.

She had seen Harris coming onto the platform. His right hand had been in his trouser pocket. His raincoat was open, loose, the belt swinging as he walked. Such a distinguished-looking man, graying at the temples. Couldn't have been much more than fifty. He had hurried to the end of the platform — the north end.

"To think now what his purpose was!" she said with a sigh. "What a horrible waste. And why would anyone choose such a messy way?"

"Did you actually see him jump?"

"No. I heard him hit, though. Sounded like a ripe pumpkin hitting the pavement. It was the black woman who screamed. She kept screaming afterward too. Very emotional they are, on the islands. Though I daresay they see more violent deaths than we do. She wasn't so far from where I was. I saw she had her mouth open. She'd dropped her bag." She was quite certain the black woman must have seen the man jump.

Parr offered to drive Mrs. Hall home. It was more or less on his way.

She obviously enjoyed the idea of sitting in a police car. Her one regret was that Detective Inspector Parr would not tell her the name of the deceased. He couldn't, before notifying the next-of-kin.

Judith decided it was time for her to draw up a will. Nothing fancy, mind you, no heavy legalese, just the basics, in her own words. At age thirty-eight, a responsible person must have a will. Even if she wasn't consistently responsible. A will is something like a stocktaking.

I, Judith Hayes, being of sound mind (mostly) *and body* (still holding on), *do on this day, April 9, 1985, leave all my clothes to my daughter Anne. My new sling back sandals can be held in trust for her until she is old enough to wear them. She's certainly big enough to wear them. My son, Jimmy, can have the typewriter, and the two of them can wrangle over the couch, the chairs and all the stuff in the kitchen. They can have their own beds. They can split the insurance dough. Their father had better take over the mortgage payments on*

the house. For all I care, he can even move in with them. I don't wish
to have my kids move to Chicago and live with him.

She wondered if she could be quite as specific in a will and whether her instructions would be followed because they were in a will. Could James just declare himself legal guardian, or next-of-kin, or whatever, sell off the house (all the blood-sweat-and-tears to keep it these past seven years) and move the kids to that glass and chrome tower he called home in Chicago? She should probably postpone all thoughts of dying until she had ascertained what her rights would be afterward.

She climbed out of bed and padded down to the kitchen to make herself a cup of coffee. Naturally there was no milk in the fridge. Anne drank about a quart a day, and all those brilliant plans for the kids to keep an up-to-date shopping list on the little blackboard Judith had bought for the purpose had long been abandoned. The idea had been that when you finished something, you wrote it on the board.

No bread either. She didn't care so much about that, but the kids would notice when they got out the jar of peanut butter for their early morning treat. Serve them right.

The black coffee tasted stale, but it would wake her up and might get rid of the pounding in her head. There was a time when she could stay up till 4:00 a.m. drinking, talking and smoking cigarettes. Now, just a few drinks and she had a thumping hang-over. Still, she was entitled to one the day after her thirty-eighth birthday. Fair way on the downhill slope. What gets you is knowing all the things you will never be when you grow up. For example, she would never be a great dramatic actress, or a ballet star, or a famous inventor. She'd never even be rich, damn it. Not even the editor of the lousy *Toronto Star*, let alone *The New Yorker*. Self-pity, Marsha had said . . . on your thirty-eighth birthday you are entitled to indulge in some self-pity. And double martinis on the rocks — hang your diet — and chain-smoking that last package of Rothmans Specials, and staying up until you're ready to drop — alone, or otherwise. She had had a few friends over for a late dinner, but had never quite found the courage to tell them what the occasion was. Allan Goodman had come with two bottles of Asti Spumante, a poor substitute for champagne, and barely enough to go around, but OK for toasting an evening if you weren't having a birthday. And it hadn't been Allan's fault; he didn't know. After they left, she had brought out the cake with all thirty-eight pink candles, all her wishes ready before she blew them out. Then she had finished the entire pitcher of martinis. She vaguely remembered having had a discreet little cry on the expedition up the stairs to her bedroom.

After a thorough search, she located the Alka Seltzer and managed to drink about half a glassful without gagging. The rest of it had stopped fizzing anyway. She took her coffee mug upstairs. In turn, as she passed, she banged on the kids' doors and opened them slightly.

"Time for another fun day at school."

She had got the idea of banging before she opened the door about a year ago when she found Jimmy examining his balls in the mirror. He had been furious at the intrusion. And she had been a little startled herself.

Anne was pulling her jeans on already. Amazing how that kid never had any trouble waking up.

"Hey, Mum," she said over one bony shoulder, "had quite a night last night, didn't you? How is the happy birthday girl this morning?"

"Don't ask," said Judith plaintively. "I doubt if I shall survive the day, let alone the next year."

"Why don't you go back to bed? We'll make our own breakfast."

"Can you get Jimmy out of the sack for me?"

As Judith crawled in between the cooling sheets she heard Anne's familiar hollering at her brother and the equally familiar grumbling reply. Then the phone rang.

"May I speak to Mrs. Hayes?" a polite male voice enquired.

"I think so," said Judith cautiously. "Who shall I say is calling?"

"Detective Inspector Parr, of the Toronto Police Department." A pause. *My god, they're on to me. Parking tickets . . . those parking tickets I haven't paid. They're going to put me in jail.* She was still trying to clear her throat when the polite voice came back on the line.

"Hello. Is this Judith Hayes speaking?"

"Yes. This is she," Judith said firmly and grammatically, remembering to show no weakness in front of the police or they'll suspect you of more than you've committed. An armed robber she had once interviewed in the Kingston pen had given her that piece of advice. Why was it that policemen always made her feel guilty, even now that most of them were younger than she was?

"Mrs. Hayes, I'm afraid I have rather bad news for you," said Parr, in the soft, modulated tone he had developed for such occasions. "Mr. George Harris died late last night. It was a . . . sudden . . . death." He let that sink in, then went on quickly, "I was told by Mrs. Harris that you were with her husband yesterday. I wondered if I might come around and ask you a few questions."

Oh god.

Parr waited a while, then asked: "You did see him yesterday?"

"How did he . . . ?" Judith choked on the last word. She was going to call him today. He had looked so well. Happy, really.

"It happened on the subway," Parr said not very helpfully. "You *did* see him yesterday?"

"Yes, we spent a couple of hours together. Did he have a heart attack? Did you say on the subway?"

"We haven't determined the cause of death yet," Parr interrupted. "May I come over this morning? It will only take a few minutes."

"Well, I had planned to . . ." Oh, what the hell. The day lay about her in ruins already. "Why?"

"It would appear you may have been the last person to talk to Mr. Harris. Routine questions, Mrs. Hayes. It's what we do."

"OK," she said, hesitating.

"Fine. I'll be there in ten minutes."

"Now, wait a minute. I've only just . . ." but the line was already dead. Damn him. Inconsiderate bastard.

She jumped out of bed, yanked her nightgown over her head, threw it back onto the pillow in almost the same movement and grabbed some underwear from the top drawer of her dresser.

"There's no bread," Jimmy said accusingly. He was leaning against the open door wearing torn jeans, a stretched sweater and his best tough-male pose. Cute.

"I have no time for that now, Jimmy. If you want bread, you can write it on the blackboard, or you can get it yourself." She took out a bulky black sweater. Like Jimmy's, it was guaranteed to hide all imperfections. Color appropriate too. What the hell did George have to go and die for anyway?

"Something wrong, Mum?" Jimmy's voice rose a little and

he abandoned the hunched-shoulders-forward segment of the macho stance.

"Somebody I know just died." No tears. Swallow hard.

"Who?"

"George Harris, the publisher. You met him. He was a friend." She pulled on a pair of tailored slacks. They were new, with razor-sharp seams, and made her feel a little less like falling over.

"Hey, Anne," Jimmy yelled. "Can you put the kettle on? Mum would like another cup of coffee."

If Judith had had time, she would have gone over and hugged him. As it was, she just smiled at him in the mirror.

"You should see yourself," Jimmy said helpfully. "Must have had quite a night of it."

"You should see *yourself*," growled Judith. "I still remember when you liked to have your pants in one piece. Takes some asshole in the East End of London to start it, and all you kids think it's cool to have more holes than pants. Cool all right. Specially in the middle of April." Jimmy shuffled his feet for a second. Then he must have decided to let it go. She loved him for it.

Judith examined her face in the bathroom mirror. Even in this dim light it looked dreadful. Dark patches under the eyes, slight sag where the lines were etching themselves further in. She breathed in deeply to make sure her lungs were both still there, then alternated splashing hot water and cold water on her face.

"Jimmy just told me about Mr. Harris dying," Anne said as she deposited a cup of coffee on the cracked toilet lid. "Terrible. He was such a nice man." Anne sat on the rim of the bathtub.

"He wasn't that old, was he?" Jimmy asked.

"Look you two, I'd love to have your company for the rest of the day, but you have school and I have a policeman coming around in about five minutes. So please . . ."

They left, reluctantly.

"Are you going to be all right?" Anne asked from the stairs.

"Yes. I'll be fine, thank you. I mean I'll be OK." Judith coated her face with darker-than-skintone, cover-all, pan-stick make-up. It smoothed over the creases and added a touch of color.

"Not much of a birthday, is it?" Anne yelled.

"Your presents were good. Jimmy, where did you find that chime?"

"Chinatown. I wanted silk slippers but didn't know your size."

"Marsha's coming today, isn't she?"

"I sure hope so."

Judith outlined her eyelids in gray. It was a good color to lift up the green of her eyes, which needed all the help they could get. She picked a smoke-black mascara and pale lipstick.

"Are you kids still down there?" she shouted, feeling a little stronger. She never knew what to say or how to behave, other than busy, when people died — she had never been a good weeper. Must be a fear of losing control — that was Marsha's theory, at any rate. Marsha had endless theories about human behavior, and she had majored in Judith's special fears.

"Mum, I'll get the bread," Jimmy called, "and milk. OK? You can pay me back later."

Fabulous kids.

"Great. Thanks. Listen, tell you what, I'll make you guys a sumptuous dinner if you come home in time. We can all eat together."

Detective Inspector Parr was at the door. Judith grabbed for her hairbrush and whipped it through her long auburn hair. It needed washing, but even so, it was her best feature.

Anne opened the door and she and Jimmy left, making room for Parr to enter.

Detective Parr was not the type. The last time she had talked to a police detective, he had been ex-army, sturdy and square-shouldered. This one was thin and angular, fortyish, tall enough to have to duck at the door. His eyes squinted under heavy eyebrows. He wore a tweed jacket with oversize brown buttons, dark gray pants, a creased white shirt open at the neck and a stained blue-gray tie that had slipped askew.

"Mrs. Hayes?"

"Yes. Detective Inspector Parr, I assume. Come on in," Judith said coolly since he was already progressing toward the living room. He threw his raincoat over the back of a chair and scanned the room quickly. "Must have had a bit of a party here last night," he smiled.

"A birthday party. Sort of. Do sit down."

He chose a straight-backed chair by the dining room table and pushed aside a few of last night's dishes, all business.

"We'll make it as brief as possible." He flicked open his notebook. "I understand you were interviewing Mr. Harris yesterday."

"Yes, I was commissioned by *Saturday Night* magazine to write a profile of George Harris and his publishing house. Yesterday was our second interview."

"You've known him for some time?" Parr said.

"Yes. I worked for him once. Briefly. In the editorial department. Of course, I've seen him since. Parties and that. Lunch sometimes. I liked him—a lot. I think everybody liked him. He was that kind of man." That's another thing about talking to policemen — they make you prattle on like an idiot.

"Yesterday, how did he seem to you?"

"Perfectly normal, I thought. He did complain a bit about his financial problems, but that's par for the course. You can't run a good publishing house in Canada without having financial problems. He seemed very healthy."

"Did you think he was at all depressed?"

"Depressed? No. Why? . . . You're not suggesting he committed suicide . . . ?"

"I'm afraid it's possible he may have," Parr said gravely.

"I don't believe it!" Judith gasped. "He just wouldn't have." She stood up and turned her back to the policeman, swallowed hard, smoothed over her face and her voice. "Would you like a cup of coffee? The kettle just boiled."

"Please. If it's not too much trouble." He was grateful she had gone into the kitchen. There had been more than enough tears already. The wife had had a hysterical screaming fit, then fainted. That was while he was standing at the door. The son was there, visiting, a fortunate coincidence that saved Parr from having to lug the unconscious Mrs. Harris into her house. Besides, he could not have left Mrs. Harris on her own. Harris Jr. had accompanied him to the hospital to identify the body.

Judith came back with a tray.

"How did it happen?" she asked.

"He fell or jumped in front of a subway train at Rosedale. We don't know for sure which."

Judith sighed and took a long sip of hot coffee. He wouldn't have jumped — not George. He was such a fastidious man. Even if he had intended to kill himself, he would have chosen a much more genteel way. Pills, for example.

"And you're sure he didn't seem at all unusual yesterday? What did he talk about?"

"Himself, mostly. And books. He had great hopes that he could pull Fitzgibbon & Harris out of debt by the end of the year. He had a very good list coming up this Fall. He knew he had a big winner. There had been some lean years, but he thought they were now behind him. Of course he knew the company would never get rich, but being out of debt would have meant a lot to him."

"Would mean a lot to anybody," Parr said, mostly to himself. "Harris Jr. gave me the impression that the lean years were very lean indeed. Wasn't he into the bank for a couple of million or more?"

"About two. But George was hanging in. And, as I said, he was optimistic. He seemed sure of himself."

"Would it have been realistic for him to think that one good list — how many books is that?"

"I don't know. Maybe thirty-five . . ."

"Well, could those books alone have got him out of debt?"

"Point is *he* believed it. While he believed it, he had something to fight for, and while he had something to fight for, he would not have given up. Not George."

Parr didn't mind her getting angry. As long as she didn't cry. He sipped his coffee and nodded reassuringly.

"What time did you leave his office?"

"Around 9:30. We were going to continue the interview next week. I was to call him today and set up a time. He thought he would have a drink with Marsha Hillier and me this afternoon."

"Who?"

"Marsha Hillier — a publisher in New York. She's coming because it's my birthday." That's the second time she had brought up the birthday in less than half an hour. Last night she hadn't told her friends, now she insisted on telling the policeman. Perhaps early senility?

"I'm sorry."

Why was *he* sorry? It wasn't his birthday.

"Did you and Harris leave his office together?"

"No. He said he had some work to finish and phone calls to make. He had a lot to do still. He couldn't have been planning to kill himself."

Once Parr had collected his raincoat and she was alone, Judith lit her first cigarette of the day and poured herself a generous Bloody Mary.

"That's for you, George," she said as she took a sip. "You never liked long faces or dreary people and you were a firm believer in Bloody Marys before noon."

She tidied up the kitchen and the living room, then took out the two frozen Quiches Lorraine she had been saving for a special occasion. They would defrost slightly by late afternoon.

It might be wise to invest in a dishwasher, she thought. Kids didn't like washing dishes any more than she did. If only she could get a big enough assignment, she might even prevail on the plumber to come and they'd have two working toilets again. You couldn't revel in such luxuries on $1,500 a month — when the going was good — and two growing kids. That's another thing: at fourteen and sixteen, respectively, shouldn't they stop growing soon? It would make a hell of a difference to the clothes budget. Even if Jimmy enjoyed having his jeans in tatters, he did like them to reach his ankles.

Hard as she tried to fill it with trivia, her mind kept returning to George Harris. What in heaven's name would he have been doing on the subway late at night? What, now that she thought of it, would he be doing on the subway at any time? George drove a car. His office was nowhere near the subway line. He never traveled by subway. Not even in dire straits. Hell, when the company was almost bankrupt, he still took first-class air tickets. Always a man with a sense of style. If he couldn't drive, he'd get a cab. He'd walk, for chrissakes! Worst came to the worst, he'd stay where he was. Let them come to him. Strange how the failure of his business to make money had affected George. The poorer the firm became, the more style he got.

She took out her interview notes which, as usual, were copious. Out of two hours with George Harris, she had recorded over thirty pages of tightly packed shorthand.

She had read through the first twenty when the managing editor of *Saturday Night* called: Had she heard the news, and could she get the story in by the end of the week? Now that George had died, there would be a number of stories. Hers was farthest ahead and they wanted it for the next issue. She said she would try, though she didn't think she could pull it together so quickly, at least not while there was any question of suicide.

The managing editor was quite convinced that they shouldn't probe into the suicide theory. The family wouldn't want that to be a topic of public discussion. They were entitled to *some* privacy.

After she had hung up, Judith finished reading her notes. Just as she remembered, George had been positively ebullient, really enthusiastic about the future. A few years ago he had

had to restrain the publishing list, but those had been hard times in all spheres of business. Now he felt his debts were manageable. He anticipated that the whole industry would benefit from the federal government's new policy paper, and his firm, strong in its history of support for Canadian talent, would undoubtedly benefit the most. He planned to go to the American Booksellers' Association convention this year, for the first time in seven, because he had some important properties to discuss with American publishers. And he had just accepted an invitation to be the luncheon speaker at the annual meeting of the Canadian Authors' Association in Vancouver. He was going to talk about the importance of publicity for the success of a book and had a number of jokes and personal anecdotes already sketched out.

Would a man who was about to kill himself be inventing jokes?